P9-BZO-974

The horse reared with an angry neigh, sprang forward, and beat its wings. Hastie's hat flew off. A bucking leap took them into the air. The world swooped and spun around them.

Hastie, gasping for breath, held on with a fierce elation, knowing that he could not lose, that this was his fated horse, this sky his sky . . .

Magic Tales Anthology Series From Ace Fantasy Books

UNICORNS! edited by Jack Dann and Gardner Dozois
MAGICATS! edited by Jack Dann and Gardner Dozois
FAERY! edited by Terri Windling
BESTIARY! edited by Jack Dann and Gardner Dozois

BESTIARY!

EDITED BY

JACK DANN
AND GARDNER DOZOIS

ACE FANTASY BOOKS
NEW YORK

BESTIARY!

An Ace Fantasy Book / published by arrangement with
the editors

PRINTING HISTORY
Ace Fantasy edition / October 1985

All rights reserved.
Copyright © 1985 by Jack Dann and Gardner Dozois.
Cover art by Carl Lundgren.
This book may not be reproduced in whole or in part,
by mimeograph or any other means, without permission.
For information address: The Berkley Publishing Group,
200 Madison Avenue, New York, New York 10016.

ISBN: 0-441-05506-0

Ace Fantasy Books are published by
The Berkley Publishing Group,
200 Madison Avenue, New York, New York 10016.
PRINTED IN THE UNITED STATES OF AMERICA

Acknowledgment is made for permission to print the following material:

"The Man Who Painted the Dragon Griaule," by Lucius Shepard. Copyright © 1984 by Mercury Press, Inc. First published in *The Magazine of Fantasy and Science Fiction,* December 1984. Reprinted by permission of the author.

"Draco, Draco," by Tanith Lee. Copyright © 1985 by Tanith Lee. First published in *Beyond Lands of Never* (Unicorn). Reprinted by permission of the author.

"The Rule of Names," by Ursula K. Le Guin. Copyright © 1975 by Ursula K. Le Guin. First published in *Fantastic,* April 1964. Reprinted by permission of the author and the author's agent, Virginia Kidd.

"The Black Horn," by Jack Dann. Copyright © 1984 by Mercury Press, Inc. First published in *The Magazine of Fantasy and Science Fiction,* November 1984. Reprinted by permission of the author.

"Walk Like a Mountain," by Manly Wade Wellman. Copyright © 1955 by Fantasy House, Inc. First published in *The Magazine of Fantasy and Science Fiction,* June 1955. Reprinted by permission of the author.

"Treaty in Tartessos," by Karen Anderson. Copyright © 1963 by Mercury Press, Inc. First published in *The Magazine of Fantasy and Science Fiction,* May 1963. Reprinted by permission of the author.

"The Woman Who Loved the Centaur Pholus," by Gene Wolfe. Copyright © 1979 by Davis Publications, Inc. First published in *Isaac Asimov's Science Fiction Magazine,* December 1979. Reprinted by permission of the author and the author's agent, Virginia Kidd.

"The Sleep of Trees," by Jane Yolen. Copyright © 1980 by Jane Yolen. First published in *The Magazine of Fantasy and Science Fiction,* September 1980. Reprinted by permission of the author and the author's agents, Curtis Brown, Ltd.

"The Hardwood Pile," by L. Sprague de Camp. Copyright © 1940 by Street & Smith Publications, Inc.; copyright renewed 1968 by L. Sprague de Camp. First published in *Unknown,* September 1940. Reprinted by permission of the author.

"The Blind Minotaur," by Michael Swanwick. Copyright © 1984 by TSR, Inc. First published in *Amazing,* March 1985. Reprinted by permission of the author and the author's agent, Virginia Kidd.

"Landscape With Sphinxes," by Karen Anderson. Copyright © 1962 by Mercury Press, Inc. First published in *The Magazine of Fantasy and Science Fiction,* November 1962. Reprinted by permission of the author.

"Simpson's Lesser Sphynx," by Esther M. Friesner. Copyright © 1984 by Esther M. Friesner. First published in *Elsewhere III* (Ace). Reprinted by permission of the author.

"God's Hooks," by Howard Waldrop. Copyright © 1982 by Terry Carr. First published in *Universe 12* (Doubleday). Reprinted by permission of the author.

"A Leg Full of Rubies," by Joan Aiken. Copyright © 1974 by Joan Aiken. First published in *A Small Pinch of Weather* (Jonathan Cape, Ltd.). Reprinted by permission of the author, Doubleday & Co., Inc., and Jonathan Cape, Ltd.

"The Valor of Cappen Varra," by Poul Anderson. Copyright © 1957 by King-Size Publications. First published in *Fantastic Universe,* Jan. 1957. Reprinted by permission of the author.

"The Troll," by T. H. White. Copyright © 1978 by T. H. White. First published in *Dark Imaginings* (Delta Books). Reprinted by permission of G.P. Putnam's Sons.

"Return of the Griffins," by A. E. Sandeling. Copyright © 1948 by Hallie Burnett. From *Story* magazine, 1948. Reprinted by permission of Hallie Burnett, Inc.

"The Last of His Breed," by Rob Chilson. Copyright © 1984 by Rob Chilson. First published in *Beyond Lands of Never* (Unicorn). Reprinted by permission of the author.

For Michael Swanwick and Marianne Porter
and Sean

The editors would like to thank the following people for their help and support:

Trina King, Stu Schiff, Michael Swanwick, Susan Casper, Jeanne Dann, Virginia Kidd, Gene Wolfe, Jane Yolen, Hallie Burnett, Janet and Ricky Kagan, Perry Knowlton, Pat Cadigan, Edward and Audrey Ferman, George Scithers, Tom Whitehead and his staff of the Special Collections Department of the Paley Library at Temple University, Patti McLaughlin of the Free Library of Philadelphia, Deborah Williams and her staff of the Binghamton, N.Y., Public Library, Brian Perry and Tawna Lewis of Fat Cat Books (263 Main St., Johnson City, New York 13790), Tom and Mike of Quick Printing in Binghamton, the staff of Sir Speedy Printing on 13th Street in Philadelphia, Beth Fleisher, Sue Stone, and special thanks to our own editors, Ginjer Buchanan and Susan Allison.

CONTENTS

PREFACE

A Bestiary is, quite literally, a "book of beasts." Most of the ones we are familiar with were codified in medieval times, some as late as the Renaissance, but they drew upon a body of traditional animal lore that had been passed along from scholar to scholar for many hundreds of years. Ancient authorities such as Aristotle, Herodotus, Pliny the Elder, Oppian, Gaius Julius Solinus (sometimes referred to as "Pliny's ape"), and Claudius Aelianus were the sources for much of the information in the Bestiaries, supplemented by oral tradition (some of *it* hundreds of years old), Christian allegorical lore, "traveller's tales" (i.e.: lies) by charlatans like Sir John Mandeville or the later Baron Munchausen, and the genuine (if often somewhat muddled) reports of legitimate explorers, especially those who (by Renaissance times) were beginning to penetrate the unknown fastnesses of the New World.

The Bestiaries, particularly the later ones, were not just compilations of marvels, but serious and substantial works of science, the beginnings of modern zoology . . . but because reliable zoologic information was so rare, the compilers of the Bestiaries often had difficulty distinguishing the real from the imagined, so that you will find dragons and crocodiles, manticores and rabbits, beavers and cockatrices, all sharing the same pages—pages where, in the words of M. St. Clare Byrne, "superstition and fact, myth and observation are all inextricably mixed." In his *Historie of Foure-Footed Beasts* (1607), for instance, Edward Topsell devotes 152 pages of text to the horse, much of it closely observed, and then, a bit later on, tells us that dragons hide in ambush for elephants by watering holes, and that when the elephant "putteth downe his trunke they take hold thereof, and instantly in great numbers leap up unto his eare . . . where out they sucke the blood of the Elephant untill he fall downe dead, and so they perish both together." It should also be noted that Topsell makes a careful distinction between the rhinoceros and the unicorn, and then goes on to chide his readers for the "impiety" of not believing in the existence of the magical beast just because there are various one-horned creatures in mundane nature that might superficially resemble it.

This last point is particularly important. Although, as many biologists point out, there are still hundreds of species of insects and plants in the Amazon Basin alone that have never been described or classified by science, in our modern smugness we sometimes seem to feel that we have explored even the remotest corners of the world and know everything there is to be known about the creatures who inhabit it. We congratulate ourselves on the fact that *we* have no difficulty distinguishing the real from the fabulous, that *we* can flip through the pages of a medieval Bestiary and with easy confidence relegate elephants, antelopes, cats, beavers, and bison to one category, and manticores, unicorns, dragons, griffins, and cockatrices to the other. We might even allow ourselves to sneer a little at the credulity of our forebears. And yet, even though we know that they're not "real," the fabulous creatures of legend and mythology have not gone away. They still live in the pages of fantasy literature all over the world, and new generations of readers still encounter them there with the same shock of recognition, the same thrill of wonder and awe as their forefathers. In that sense, we still "believe" in them, just as credulously as our ancestors did. There is something about these creatures which is still potent, and their images still speak to something that lives in the deep places of the spirit. In the words of Jorge Luis Borges, "We are as ignorant of the meaning of the dragon as we are of the meaning of the universe, but there is something in the dragon's image that appeals to the human imagination, and so we find the dragon in quite distinct places and times. It is, so to speak, a necessary monster, not an ephemeral or accidental one . . ."

In this anthology we will examine some of those "necessary monsters," the magical beasts who are still alive and well in the pages of fantasy literature: Creatures from the pre-Dawn world of myth, from before the coming of man. . . . Creatures who walk the neon-lit streets of our own modern world. . . . Creatures civilized and charming. Creatures ravening and monstrous. Creatures who'll make you laugh, creatures who'll freeze the marrow of your bones. Creatures born of fire, creatures of dreadful night, creatures of gentle magic. The fabulous creatures that still stalk through our dreams . . . and our nightmares.

THE DRAGON

Dragons are by far the most potent and widespread of all mythological beasts, and dragons or dragon-like creatures appear in just about every mythology in the world. So omnipresent is the image of the dragon, and so powerful the emotions that it evokes, that Carl Sagan, among others, has suggested that dragons are actually a racial memory of dinosaurs, left over from the days when our remote ancestors were tiny tree-dwelling insectivores who cowered in shivering terror whenever one of the immense flesh-eaters like Tyrannosaurus Rex came crashing through the forest. Whatever the truth of that, it's certainly true that dragons are one of the few mythological creatures that it's almost pointless to bother describing. As Avram Davidson puts it, "Although the wombat is real and the dragon is not, nobody knows what a wombat looks like, and everybody knows what a dragon looks like." There are variations, of course—sometimes the dragon is wingless and rather like a gigantic worm; sometimes like a huge snake; most often like an immense, winged lizard. Sometimes it breathes fire, sometimes not—but, for the most part, the rule holds. With very few exceptions, almost everyone *does* know what the dragon looks like, which is why it is one of the master-symbols of fantasy. (Or perhaps it's the other way around.)

Although the Eastern Dragon (and particularly the Chinese Dragon) is usually depicted as a wise and benevolent creature, a divine being associated with the bringing of the life-giving rains, what we have been describing here primarily fits the Western Dragon . . . and, not surprisingly, it is the Western Dragon, the terrible fire-breathing dragon of folklore and fairy tales, that has been the dominant image of the dragon in Western literature and art. In addition to its well-known fondness for snacking on princesses, the Western Dragon is a covetous beast, and can often be found guarding the immense treasures of gold and jewels that it's ravaged from human realms. Although sometimes portrayed as merely a huge mindless beast, the dragon is just as often depicted as having the gift of speech; in this guise, it is frequently a sorcerer, an active magic-user itself as well as merely being a magical *creature,* and some say that Dragon Magic is the strongest and most ancient magic of all . . .

In the stories that follow, we'll see a dragon so immense that he has literally become part of the landscape, watch a battle between a Hero and a ferocious dragon of the genuine old-fashioned maiden-eating variety, and then, for a change, get to see a little of the *dragon's* side of the story . . .

Lucius Shepard is a hot new writer whose work has appeared in *The Magazine of Fantasy and Science Fiction, Isaac Asimov's Science Fiction Magazine, Universe,* and elsewhere. His acclaimed first novel *Green Eyes* was published as an Ace Special last year. Upcoming is a new novel, called *Foreign Devils.*

Tanith Lee is one of the best known of modern fantasists, and one of the most prolific, with well over a dozen books to her credit. Her most recent book is the collection *The Gorgon and Other Beastly Tales.* She has won two World Fantasy Awards for her short fiction.

Ursula K. Le Guin is a multiple award-winner, and has been widely hailed as one of the major writers of our times. She is the author of such landmark books as *The Left Hand of Darkness, The Dispossessed,* and the reknowned "Earthsea" trilogy, among others. Her most recent book is the novel *Always Coming Home.*

Theme anthologies about dragons include *Dragons of Light* and *Dragons of Darkness*, both edited by Orson Scott Card, and *Dragon Tales*, edited by Isaac Asimov, Martin H. Greenberg, and Charles Waugh.

The Man Who Painted The Dragon Griaule

by

Lucius Shepard

". . . OTHER THAN the Sichi Collection, Cattanay's only surviving works are to be found in the Municipal Gallery at Regensburg, a group of eight oils-on-canvas, most notable among them being *Woman With Oranges*. These paintings constitute his portion of a student exhibition hung some weeks after he had left the city of his birth and traveled south to Teocinte, there to present his proposal to the city fathers; it is unlikely he ever learned of the disposition of his work, and even more unlikely that he was aware of the general critical indifference with which it was received. Perhaps the most interesting of the group to modern scholars, the most indicative as to Cattanay's later preoccupations, is the *Self Portrait*, painted at the age of twenty-eight, a year before his departure.

"The majority of the canvas is a richly varnished black in which the vague shapes of floorboards are presented, barely visible. Two irregular slashes of gold cross the blackness, and within these we can see a section of the artist's thin features and the shoulder panel of his shirt. The perspective given is that we are looking down at the artist, perhaps through a tear in the roof, and that he is looking up at us, squinting into the light, his mouth distorted by a grimace born of intense concentration. On first viewing the painting, I was struck by the atmosphere of tension that radiated from it. It seemed I was spying upon a man imprisoned within a shadow having two golden bars, tormented by the possibilities of light beyond the walls. And though this may be the reaction of the art historian, not the less knowledgeable and therefore more trustworthy response of the gallery-goer, it also seemed that this imprisonment was self-imposed, that he could have easily escaped his confine; but that he had realized a feeling of stricture was an essential fuel to his ambition, and so had chained himself to this arduous and thoroughly unreasonable chore of perception. . . ."

—from *Meric Cattanay:*
The Politics of Conception
by Reade Holland, Ph.D.

1.

In 1853, in a country far to the south, in a world separated from this one by the thinnest margin of possibility, a dragon named Griaule dominated the region of the Carbonales Valley, a fertile area centering upon the town of Teocinte and renowned for its production of silver, mahogany, and indigo. There were other dragons in those days, most dwelling on the rocky islands west of Patagonia—tiny, irascible creatures, the largest of them no bigger than a swallow. But Griaule was one of the great Beasts who had ruled an age. Over the centuries he had grown to stand 750 feet high at the midback, and from the tip of his tail to his nose he was 6,000 feet long. (It should be noted here that the growth of dragons was due not to caloric intake, but to the absorption of energy derived from the passage of time.) Had it not been for a miscast spell, Griaule would have died millennia before. The wizard entrusted with the task of slaying him—knowing his own life would be forfeited as a result of the magical backwash—had experienced a last-second twinge of fear, and, diminished by this ounce of courage, the spell had flown a mortal inch awry. Though the wizard's whereabouts were unknown, Griaule had remained alive. His heart had stopped, his breath stilled, but his mind continued to seethe, to send forth the gloomy vibrations that enslaved all who stayed for long within range of his influence.

This dominance of Griaule's was an elusive thing. The people of the valley attributed their dour character to years of living under his mental shadow, yet there were other regional populations who maintained a harsh face to the world and had no dragon on which to blame the condition; they also attributed their frequent raids against the neighboring states to Griaule's effect, claiming to be a peaceful folk at heart—but again, was this not human nature? Perhaps the most certifiable proof of Griaule's primacy was the fact that despite a standing offer of a fortune in silver to anyone who could kill him, no one had succeeded. Hundreds of plans had been put forward, and all had failed, either through inanition or impracticality. The archives of Teocinte were filled with schematics for enormous steam-powered swords and other such improbable devices, and the architects of these plans had every one stayed too long in the valley and become part of the disgruntled populace. And so they went on with their lives, coming and going, always returning, bound to the valley, until one spring day in 1853, Meric Cattanay arrived and proposed that the dragon be painted.

He was a lanky young man with a shock of black hair and a pinched look to his cheeks; he affected the loose trousers and shirt of a peasant, and waved his arms to make a point. His eyes grew wide when listening, as if his brain were bursting with illumination, and at times he talked incoherently about "the conceptual statement of death by art." And though the city fathers could not be sure, though they allowed for the possibility that he simply had an unfortunate manner, it seemed he was mocking them. All in all, he was not the sort they were inclined to trust. But, because he had come armed with such a wealth of diagrams and charts, they were forced to give him serious consideration.

"I don't believe Griaule will be able to perceive the menace in a process as subtle as art," Meric told them. "We'll proceed as if we were going to illustrate him, grace his side with a work of true vision, and all the while we'll be poisoning him with the paint."

The city fathers voiced their incredulity, and Meric waited impatiently until they quieted. He did not enjoy dealing with these worthies. Seated at their long table, sour-faced, a huge smudge of soot on the wall about their heads like an ugly thought they were sharing, they reminded him of the Wine Merchants Association in Regensburg, the time they had rejected his group portrait.

"Paint can be deadly stuff," he said after their muttering had died down. "Take vert Veronese, for example. It's derived from oxide of chrome and barium. Just a whiff would make you keel over. But we have to go about it seriously, create a real piece of art. If we just slap paint on his side, he might see through us."

The first step in the process, he told them, would be to build a tower of scaffolding, complete with hoists and ladders, that would brace against the supraocular plates above the dragon's eye; this would provide a direct route to a seven-hundred-foot-square loading platform and base station behind the eye. He estimated it would take eighty-one thousand board feet of lumber, and a crew of ninety men should be able to finish construction within five months. Ground crews accompanied by chemists and geologists would search out limestone deposits (useful in priming the scales) and sources of pigments, whether organic or minerals such as azurite and hematite. Other teams would be set to scraping the dragon's side clean of algae, peeled skin, any decayed material, and afterward would laminate the surface with resins.

"It would be easier to bleach him with quicklime," he said. "But that way we lose the discolorations and ridges generated by growth and age, and I think what we'll paint will be defined by those shapes. Anything else would look like a damn tattoo!"

There would be storage vats and mills: edge-runner mills to separate pigments from crude ores, ball mills to powder the pigments, pug mills to mix them with oil. There would be boiling vats and calciners—fifteen-foot-high furnaces used to produce caustic lime for sealant solutions.

"We'll build most of them atop the dragon's head for purposes of access," he said. "On the frontoparital plate." He checked some figures. "By my reckoning, the plate's about 350 feet wide. Does that sound accurate?"

Most of the city fathers were stunned by the prospect, but one managed a nod, and another asked, "How long will it take for him to die?"

"Hard to say," came the answer. "Who knows how much poison he's capable of absorbing. It might just take a few years. But in the worst instance, within forty or fifty years, enough chemicals will have seeped through the scales to have weakened the skeleton, and he'll fall in like an old barn."

"Forty years!" exclaimed someone. "Preposterous!"

"Or fifty." Meric smiled. "That way we'll have time to finish the painting." He turned and walked to the window and stood gazing out at the white stone houses of Teocinte. This was going to be the sticky part, but if he read them right, they would not believe in the plan if it seemed too easy. They needed to feel they were making a sacrifice, that they were nobly bound to a great labor. "If it does take forty or fifty years," he went on, "the project will drain your resources. Timber, animal life, minerals. Everything will be used up by the work. Your lives will be totally changed. But I guarantee you'll be rid of him."

The city fathers broke into an outraged babble.

"Do you really want to kill him?" cried Meric, stalking over to them and planting his fists on the table. "You've been waiting centuries for someone to come along and chop off his head or send him up in a puff of smoke. That's not going to happen! There is no easy solution. But there is a practical one, an elegant one. To use the stuff of the land he dominates to destroy him. It will *not* be easy, but you *will* be rid of him. And that's what you want, isn't it?"

They were silent, exchanging glances, and he saw that they now believed he could do what he proposed and were wondering if the cost was too high.

"I'll need five hundred ounces of silver to hire engineers and artisans," said Meric. "Think it over. I'll take a few days and go see this dragon of yours . . . inspect the scales and so forth. When I return, you can give me your answer."

The city fathers grumbled and scratched their heads, but at last they agreed to put the question before the body politic. They asked for a week in which to decide and appointed Jarcke, who was the mayoress of Hangtown, to guide Meric to Griaule.

The valley extended seventy miles from north to south, and was enclosed by jungled hills whose folded sides and spiny backs gave rise to the idea that beasts were sleeping beneath them. The valley floor was cultivated into fields of bananas and cane and melons, and where it was not cultivated, there were stands of thistle palms and berry thickets and the occasional giant fig brooding sentinel over the rest. Jarcke and Meric tethered their horses a half hour's ride from town and began to ascend a gentle incline that rose into the notch between two hills. Sweaty and short of breath, Meric stopped a third of the way up; but Jarcke kept plodding along, unaware he was no longer following. She was by nature as blunt as her name—a stump beer keg of a woman with a brown, weathered face. Though she appeared to be ten years older than Meric, she was nearly the same age. She wore a gray robe belted at the waist with a leather band that held four throwing knives, and a coil of rope was slung over her shoulder.

"How much further?" called Meric.

She turned and frowned. "You're standin' on his tail. Rest of him's around back of the hill."

A pinprick of chill bloomed in Meric's abdomen, and he stared down at the grass, expecting it to dissolve and reveal a mass of glittering scales.

"Why don't we take the horses?" he asked.

"Horses don't like it up here." She grunted with amusement. "Neither do most people, for that matter." She trudged off.

Another twenty minutes brought them to the other side of the hill high above the valley floor. The land continued to slope upward, but more gently than before. Gnarled, stunted oaks pushed up from thickets of chokecherry, and insects sizzled in the weeds. They might have been walking on a natural shelf several hundred feet across; but ahead of them, where the ground rose abruptly, a number of thick, greenish black columns broke from the earth. Leathery folds hung between them, and these were encrusted with clumps of earth and brocaded with mold. They had the look of a collapsed palisade and the ghosted feel of ancient ruins.

"Them's the wings," said Jarcke. "Mostly they's covered, but you can catch sight of 'em off the edge, and up near Hangtown there's places where you can walk under 'em . . . but I wouldn't advise it."

"I'd like to take a look off the edge," said Meric, unable to tear his eyes away from the wings; though the surfaces of the leaves gleamed in the strong sun, the wings seemed to absorb the light, as if their age and strangeness were proof against reflection.

Jarcke led him to a glade in which tree ferns and oaks crowded together and cast a green gloom, and where the earth sloped sharply downward. She lashed her rope to an oak and tied the other end around Meric's waist. "Give a yank when you want to stop, and another when you want to be hauled up," she said, and began paying out the rope, letting him walk backward against her pull.

Ferns tickled Meric's neck as he pushed through the brush, and the oak leaves pricked his cheeks. Suddenly he emerged into bright sunlight. On looking down, he found his feet were braced against a fold of the dragon's wing, and on looking up, he saw that the wing vanished beneath a mantle of earth and vegetation. He let Jarcke lower him a dozen feet more, yanked, and gazed off northward along the enormous swell of Griaule's side.

The swells were hexagonals thirty feet across and half that distance high; their basic color was a pale greenish gold, but some were whitish, draped with peels of dead skin, and others were overgrown by viridian moss, and the rest were scrolled with patterns of lichen and algae that resembled the characters of a serpentine alphabet. Birds had nested in the cracks, and ferns plumed from the interstices, thousands of them lifting in the breeze. It was a great hanging garden whose scope took Meric's breath away—like looking around the curve of a fossil moon. The sense of all the centuries accreted in the scales made him dizzy, and he found he could not turn his head, but could only stare at the panorama, his soul shriveling with a comprehension of the timelessness and bulk of this creature to which he clung like a fly. He lost perspective on the scene—Griaule's side was bigger than the sky, possessing its own potent gravity, and it seemed completely reasonable that he should be able to walk out along it and suffer no fall. He started to do so, and Jarcke, mistaking the strain on the rope for signal, hauled him up, dragging him across the wing, through the dirt and ferns, and back into the glade. He lay speechless and gasping at her feet.

"Big 'un, ain't he," she said, and grinned.

After Meric had gotten his legs under him, they set off toward Hangtown; but they had not gone a hundred yards, following a trail that wound through the thickets, before Jarcke whipped out a knife and hurled it at a raccoon-sized creature that leaped out in front of them.

"Skizzer," she said, kneeling beside it and pulling the knife from its neck. "Calls 'em that 'cause they hisses when they runs. They eats snakes, but they'll go after children what ain't careful."

Meric dropped down next to her. The skizzer's body was covered with short black fur, but its head was hairless, corpse-pale, the skin wrinkled as if it had been immersed too long in water. Its face was squinty-eyed, flat-nosed, with a disproportionately large jaw that hinged open to expose a nasty set of teeth.

"They's the dragon's critters," said Jarcke. "Used to live in his bunghole." She pressed one of its paws, and claws curved like hooks slid forth. "They'd hang around the lip and drop on other critters what wandered in. And if nothin' wandered in . . . " She pried out the tongue with her knife—its surface was studded with jagged points like the blade of a rasp. "Then they'd lick Griaule clean for their supper.

Back in Teocinte, the dragon had seemed to Meric a simple thing, a big lizard with a tick of life left inside, the residue of a dim sensibility; but he was beginning to suspect that this tick of life was more complex than any he had encountered.

"My gram used to say," Jarcke went on, "that the old dragons could fling themselves up to the sun in a blink and travel back to their own world, and when they come back, they'd bring the skizzers and all the rest with 'em. They was immortal, she said. Only the young ones came here 'cause later on they grew too big to fly on Earth." She made a sour face. "Don't know as I believe it."

"Then you're a fool," said Meric.

Jarcke glanced up at him, her hand twitching toward her belt.

"How can you live here and *not* believe it!" he said,

surprised to hear himself so fervently defending a myth. "God! This . . . " He broke off, noticing the flicker of a smile on her face.

She clucked her tongue, apparently satisfied by something. "Come on," she said. "I want to be at the eye before sunset."

The peaks of Griaule's folded wings, completely overgrown by grass and shrubs and dwarfish trees, formed two spiny hills that cast a shadow over Hangtown and the narrow lake around which it sprawled. Jarcke said the lake was a stream flowing off the hill behind the dragon, and that it drained away through the membranes of his wing and down onto his shoulder. It was beautiful beneath the wing, she told him. Ferns and waterfalls. But it was reckoned an evil place. From a distance the town looked picturesque—rustic cabins, smoking chimneys. As they approached, however, the cabins resolved into dilapidated shanties with missing boards and broken windows; suds and garbage and offal floated in the shallows of the lake. Aside from a few men idling on the stoops, who squinted at Meric and nodded glumly at Jarcke, no one was about. The grass blades stirred in the breeze, spiders scuttled under the shanties, and there was an air of torpor and dissolution.

Jarcke seemed embarrassed by the town. She made no attempt at introductions, stopping only long enough to fetch another coil of rope from one of the shanties, and as they walked between the wings, down through the neck spines—a forest of greenish gold spikes burnished by the lowering sun—she explained how the townsfolk grubbed a livelihood from Griaule. Herbs gathered on his back were valued as medicine and charms, as were the peels of dead skin; the artifacts left by previous Hangtown generations were of some worth to various collectors.

"Then there's scale hunters," she said with disgust. "Henry Sichi from Port Chantay'll pay good money for pieces of scale, and though it's bad luck to do it, some'll have a go at chippin' off the loose 'uns." She walked a few paces in silence. "But there's others who've got better reasons for livin' here."

The frontal spike above Griaule's eyes was whorled at

the base like a narwhal's horn and curved back toward the wings. Jarcke attached the ropes to eyebolts drilled into the spike, tied one about her waist, the other about Meric's; she cautioned him to wait, and rappelled off the side. In a moment she called for him to come down. Once again he grew dizzy as he descended; he glimpsed a clawed foot far below, mossy fangs jutting from an impossibly long jaw; and then he began to spin and bash against the scales. Jarcke gathered him in and helped him sit on the lip of the socket.

"Damn!" she said, stamping her foot.

A three-foot-long section of the adjoining scale shifted slowly away. Peering close, Meric saw that while in texture and hue it was indistinguishable from the scale, there was a hairline division between it and the surface. Jarcke, her face twisted in disgust, continued to harry the thing until it moved out of reach.

"Call 'em flakes," she said when he asked what it was. "Some kind of insect. Got a long tube that they pokes down between the scales and sucks the blood. See there?" She pointed off to where a flock of birds were wheeling close to Griaule's side; a chip of pale gold broke loose and went tumbling down to the valley. "Birds pry 'em off, let 'em bust open, and eats the innards." She hunkered down beside him and after a moment asked, "You really think you can do it?"

"What? You mean kill the dragon?"

She nodded.

"Certainly," he said, and then added, lying, "I've spent years devising the method."

"If all the paint's goin' to be atop his head, how're you goin' to get it to where the paintin's done?"

"That's no problem. We'll pipe it to wherever it's needed."

She nodded again. "You're a clever fellow," she said; and when Meric, pleased, made as if to thank her for the compliment, she cut in and said, "Don't mean nothin' by it. Bein' clever ain't an accomplishment. It's just somethin' you come by, like bein' tall." She turned away, ending the conversation.

Meric was weary of being awestruck, but even so he could not help marveling at the eye. By his estimate it was seventy feet long and fifty feet high, and it was shuttered by an opaque membrane that was unusually clear of algae and lichen, glistening, with vague glints of color visible behind it. As the westering sun reddened and sank between two distant hills, the membrane began to quiver and then split open down the center. With the ponderous slowness of a theater curtain opening, the halves slid apart to reveal the glowing humor. Terrified by the idea that Griaule could see him, Meric sprang to his feet, but Jarcke restrained him.

"Stay still and watch," she said.

He had no choice—the eye was mesmerizing. The pupil was slit and featureless black, but the humor . . . he had never seen such fiery blues and crimsons and golds. What had looked to be vague glints, odd refractions of the sunset, he now realized were photic reactions of some sort. Fairy rings of light developed deep within the eye, expanded into spoked shapes, flooded the humor, and faded—only to be replaced by another and another. He felt the pressure of Griaule's vision, his ancient mind, pouring through him, and as if in response to this pressure, memories bubbled up in his thoughts. Particularly sharp ones. The way a bowlful of brush water had looked after freezing over during a winter's night—a delicate, fractured flower of murky yellow. An archipelago of orange peels that his girl had left strewn across the floor of the studio. Sketching atop Jokenam Hill one sunrise, the snow-capped roofs of Regensburg below pitched at all angles like broken paving stones, and silver shafts of the sun striking down through a leaden overcast. It was as if these things were being drawn forth for his inspection. Then they were washed away by what also seemed a memory, though at the same time it was wholly unfamiliar. Essentially, it was a landscape of light, and he was plunging through it, up and up. Prisms and lattices of iridescent fire bloomed around him, and everything was a roaring fall into brightness, and finally he was clear into its white furnace heart, his own heart swelling with the joy of his strength and dominion.

It was dusk before Meric realized the eye had closed. His mouth hung open, his eyes ached from straining to see, and his tongue was glued to his palate. Jarcke sat motionless, buried in shadow.

"Th . . . " He had to swallow to clear his throat of mucus. "This is the reason you live here, isn't it?"

"Part of the reason," she said. "I can see things comin' way up here. Things to watch out for, things to study on."

She stood and walked to the lip of the socket and spat off the edge; the valley stretched out gray and unreal behind her, the folds of the hills barely visible in the gathering dusk.

"I seen you comin'," she said.

A week later, after much exploration, much talk, they went down into Teocinte. The town was a shambles—shattered windows, slogans painted on the walls, glass and torn banners and spilled food littering the streets—as if there had been both a celebration and a battle. Which there had. The city fathers met with Meric in the town hall and informed him that his plan had been approved. They presented him a chest containing five hundred ounces of silver and said that the entire resources of the community were at his disposal. They offered a wagon and a team to transport him and the chest to Regensburg and asked if any of the preliminary work could be begun during his absence.

Meric hefted one of the silver bars. In its cold gleam he saw the object of his desire—two, perhaps three years of freedom, of doing the work he wanted and not having to accept commissions. But all that had been confused. He glanced at Jarcke; she was staring out the window, leaving it to him. He set the bar back in the chest and shut the lid.

"You'll have to send someone else," he said. And then, as the city fathers looked at each other askance, he laughed and laughed at how easily he had discarded all his dreams and expectations.

". . . It had been eleven years since I had been to the valley, twelve since work had begun on the painting, and I was appalled by the changes that had taken place. Many of the hills were scraped brown and treeless, and there was a general dearth of wildlife. Griaule, of course, was most changed. Scaffolding hung from his back; artisans, suspended by webworks of ropes, crawled over his side; and all the scales to be worked had either been painted or primed. The tower rising to his eye was swarmed by laborers, and at night the calciners and vats atop his head belched flame into the sky, making it seem there was a mill town in the heavens. At his feet was a brawling shantytown populated by prostitutes, workers, gamblers, ne'er-do-wells of every sort, and soldiers: the burdensome cost of the project had encouraged the city fathers of Teocinte to form a regular militia, which regularly plundered the adjoining states and had posted occupation forces to some areas. Herds of frightened animals milled in the slaughtering pens, waiting to be rendered into oils and pigments. Wagons filled with ores and vegetable products rattled in the streets. I myself had brought a cargo of madder roots from which a rose tint would be derived.

"It was not easy to arrange a meeting with Cattanay. While he did none of the actual painting, he was always busy in his office consulting with engineers and artisans, or involved in some other part of the logistical process. When at last I did meet with him, I found he had changed as drastically as Griaule. His hair had gone gray, deep lines scored his features, and his right shoulder had a peculiar bulge at its midpoint—the product of a fall. He was amused by the fact that I wanted to buy the painting, to collect the scales after Griaule's death, and I do not believe he took me at all seriously. But the woman Jarcke, his constant companion, informed him that I was a responsible businessman, that I had already bought the bones, the teeth, even the dirt beneath Griaule's belly (This I eventually sold as having magical properties).

" 'Well,' said Cattanay, 'I suppose someone has to own them.'

"He led me outside, and we stood looking at the painting.

" 'You'll keep them together?' he asked.

"I said, 'Yes.'

" 'If you'll put that in writing,' he said, 'then they're yours.'

"Having expected to haggle long and hard over the price, I was flabbergasted; but I was even more flabbergasted by what he said next.

" 'Do you think it's any good?' he asked.

"Cattanay did not consider the painting to be the work of *his* imagination; he felt he was simply illuminating the shapes that appeared on Griaule's side and was convinced that once the paint was applied, new shapes were produced beneath it, causing him to make constant changes. He saw himself as an artisan more than a creative artist. But to put his question into perspective, people were beginning to flock from all over the world and marvel at the painting. Some claimed they saw intimations of the future in its gleaming surface; others underwent transfiguring experiences; still others—artists themselves—attempted to capture something of the work on canvas, hopeful of establishing reputations merely by being competent copyists of Cattanay's art. The painting was nonrepresentational in character, essentially a wash of pale gold spread across the dragon's side; but buried beneath the laminated surface were a myriad tints of iridescent color that, as the sun passed through the heavens and the light bloomed and faded, solidified into innumerable forms and figures that seemed to flow back and forth. I will not try to categorize these forms, because there was no end to them; they were as varied as the conditions under which they were viewed. But I will say that on the morning I met with Cattanay, I—who was the soul of the practical man, without a visionary bone in my body—felt as though I were being whirled away into the painting, up through geometries of light, latticeworks of rainbow color that built the way the edges of a cloud build, past orbs, spirals, wheels of flame. . . ."

—from *This Business of Griaule*
by Henry Sichi

2.

There had been several women in Meric's life since he arrived in the valley; most had been attracted by his growing fame and his association with the mystery of the dragon, and most had left him for the same reasons, feeling daunted and unappreciated. But Lise was different in two respects. First, because she loved Meric truly and well; and second, because she was married—albeit unhappily—to a man named Pardiel, the foreman of the calciner crew. She did not love him as she did Meric, yet she respected him and felt obliged to consider carefully before ending the relationship. Meric had never known such an introspective soul. She was twelve years younger than he, tall and lovely, with sun-streaked hair and brown eyes that went dark and seemed to turn inward whenever she was pensive. She was in the habit of analyzing everything that affected her, drawing back from her emotions and inspecting them as if they were a clutch of strange insects she had discovered crawling on her skirt. Though her penchant for self-examination kept her from him, Meric viewed it as a kind of baffling virtue. He had the classic malady and could find no fault with her. For almost a year they were as happy as could be expected; they talked long hours and walked together, and on those occasions when Pardiel worked double shifts and was forced to bed down by his furnaces, they spent the nights making love in the cavernous spaces beneath the dragon's wing.

It was still reckoned an evil place. Something far worse than skizzers or flakes was rumored to live there, and the ravages of this creature were blamed for every disappearance, even that of the most malcontented laborer. But Meric did not give credence to the rumors. He half-believed Griaule had chosen him to be his executioner and that the dragon would never let him be harmed; and besides, it was the only place where they could be assured of privacy.

A crude stair led under the wing, handholds and steps hacked from the scales—doubtless the work of scale hunters. It was a treacherous passage, six hundred feet above the valley floor; but Lise and Meric were secured by ropes, and over the months, driven by the urgency of passion, they adapted to it. Their favorite spot lay fifty feet in (Lise would go no farther; she was afraid even if he was not), near a waterfall that trickled over the leathery folds, causing them to glisten with a mineral brilliance. It was eerily beautiful, a haunted gallery. Peels of dead skin hung down from the shadows like torn veils of ectoplasm; ferns sprouted from the vanes, which were thicker than cathedral columns; swallows curved through the black air. Sometimes, lying with her hidden by a tuck of the wing, Meric would think the beating of their hearts was what really animated the place, that the instant they left, the water ceased flowing and the swallows vanished. He had an unshakable faith in the transforming power of their affections, and one morning as they dressed, preparing to return to Hangtown, he asked her to leave with him.

"To another part of the valley?" She laughed sadly. "What good would that do? Pardiel would follow us."

"No," he said. "To another country. Anywhere far from here."

"We can't," she said, kicking at the wing. "Not until Griaule dies. Have you forgotten?"

"We haven't tried."

"Others have."

"But we'd be strong enough. I know it!"

"You're a romantic," she said gloomily, and stared out over the slope of Griaule's back at the valley. Sunrise had washed the hills to crimson, and even the tips of the wings were glowing a dull red.

"Of course I'm a romantic!" He stood, angry. "What the hell's wrong with that?"

She sighed with exasperation. "You wouldn't leave your work," she said. "And if we did leave, what work would you do? Would . . ."

"Why must everything be a problem in advance!" he shouted. "I'll tattoo elephants! I'll paint murals on the chests of giants, I'll illuminate whales! Who else is better qualified?"

She smiled, and his anger evaporated.

"I didn't mean it that way," she said. "I just wondered if you could be satisfied with anything else."

She reached out her hand to be pulled up, and he drew her into an embrace. As he held her, inhaling the scent of vanilla water from her hair, he saw a diminutive figure silhouetted against the backdrop of the valley. It did not seem real—a black homunculus—and even when it began to come forward, growing larger and larger, it looked less a man than a magical keyhole opening in a crimson set hillside. But Meric knew from the man's rolling walk and the hulking set of his shoulders that it was Pardiel; he was carrying a long-handled hook, one of those used by artisans to maneuver along the scales.

Meric tensed, and Lise looked back to see what had alarmed him. "Oh, my God!" she said, moving out of the embrace.

Pardiel stopped a dozen feet away. He said nothing. His face was in shadow, and the hook swung lazily from his hand. Lise took a step toward him, then stepped back and stood in front of Meric as if to shield him. Seeing this, Pardiel let out an inarticulate yell and charged, slashing with the hook. Meric pushed Lise aside and ducked. He caught a brimstone whiff of the calciners as Pardiel rushed past and went sprawling, tripped by some irregularity in the scale. Deathly afraid, knowing he was no match for the foreman, Meric seized Lise's hand and ran deeper under the wing. He hoped Pardiel would be too frightened to follow, leery of the creature that was rumored to live there; but he was not. He came after them at a measured pace, tapping the hook against his leg.

Higher on Griaule's back, the wing was dimpled downward by hundreds of bulges, and this created a maze of small chambers and tunnels so low that they had to crouch to pass along them. The sound of their breathing and the scrape of their feet were amplified by the enclosed spaces and Meric could no longer hear Pardiel. He had never been this deep before. He had thought it would be pitchdark; but the lichen and algae adhering to the wing were luminescent and patterned every surface, even the scales beneath them, with whorls of blue and green fire that shed a sickly radiance. It was as if they were giants crawling through a universe whose starry matter had not yet congealed into galaxies and nebulas. In the wan light, Lise's face—turned back to him now and again—was teary and frantic; and then, as she straightened, passing into still another chamber, she drew in breath with a shriek.

At first Meric thought Pardiel had somehow managed to get ahead of them; but on entering he saw that the cause of her fright was a man propped in a sitting position against the far wall. He looked mummified. Wisps of brittle hair poked up from his scalp, the shapes of his bones were visible through his skin, and his eyes were empty holes. Between his legs was a scatter of dust where his genitals had been. Meric pushed Lise toward the next tunnel, but she resisted and pointed to the man.

"His eyes," she said, horror-struck.

Though the eyes were mostly a negative black, Meric now realized they were shot through by opalescent flickers. He felt compelled to kneel beside the man—it was a sudden, motiveless urge that gripped him, bent him to its will, and released him a second later. As he rested his hand on the scale, he brushed a massive ring that was lying beneath the shrunken fingers. Its stone was black, shot through by flickers identical to those within the eyes, and incised with the letter *S*. He found his gaze was deflected away from both the stone and the eyes, as if they contained charges repellent to the senses. He touched the man's withered arm; the flesh was rock-hard, petrified. But alive. From that brief touch he gained an impression of the man's life, of gazing for centuries at the same patch of unearthly fire, of a mind gone beyond mere madness into a perverse rapture, a meditation upon some foul principle. He snatched back his hand in revulsion.

There was a noise behind them, and Meric jumped up, pushing Lise into the next tunnel. "Go right," he whispered. "We'll circle back toward the stair." But Pardiel was too close to confuse with such tactics, and their flight became a wild chase, scrambling, falling, catching glimpses of Pardiel's smoke-stained face, until finally—as Meric came to a large chamber—he felt the hook bite into his thigh. He went down, clutching at the wound, pulling the hook loose. The next moment Pardiel was atop him; Lise appeared over his shoulder, but he knocked her away and locked his fingers in Meric's hair and smashed his head against the scale. Lise screamed, and white lights fired through Meric's skull. Again his head was smashed down. And again. Dimly, he saw Lise struggling with Pardiel, saw her shoved away, saw the hook raised high and the foreman's mouth distorted by a grimace. Then the grimace vanished. His jaw dropped open and he reached behind him as if to scratch his shoulder blade. A line of dark blood eeled from his mouth and he collapsed, smothering Meric beneath his chest. Meric heard voices. He tried to dislodge the body, and the effects drained the last of his strength. He whirled down through a blackness that seemed as negative and inexhaustible as the petrified man's eyes.

Someone had propped his head on their lap and was bathing his brow with a damp cloth. He assumed it was Lise, but when he asked what had happened, it was Jarcke who answered saying, "Had to kill him." His head throbbed, his leg throbbed even worse, and his eyes would not focus. The peels of dead skin hanging overhead appeared to be writhing. He realized they were out near the edge of the wing.

"Where's Lise?"

"Don't worry," said Jarcke. "You'll see her again." She made it sound like an indictment.

"Where is she?"

"Sent her back to Hangtown. Won't do you two bein' seen hand in hand the same day Pardiel's missin'."

"She wouldn't have left . . . " He blinked, trying to see her face; the lines around her mouth were etched deep and reminded him of the patterns of lichen on the dragon's scale. "What did you do?"

"Convinced her it was best," said Jarcke. "Don't you know she's just foolin' with you?"

"I've got to talk with her." He was full of remorse, and it was unthinkable that Lise should be bearing her grief alone; but when he struggled to rise, pain lanced through his leg.

"You wouldn't get ten feet," she said. "Soon as your head's clear, I'll help you to the stairs."

He closed his eyes, resolving to find Lise the instant he got back to Hangtown—together they would decide what to do. The scale beneath him was cool, and that coolness was transmitted to his skin, his flesh, as if he were merging with it, becoming one of its ridges.

"What was the wizard's name?" he asked after a while,

recalling the petrified man, the ring and its incised letter. "The one who tried to kill Griaule. . . ."

"Don't know as I ever heard it," said Jarcke. "But I reckon it's him back there."

"You saw him?"

"I was chasin' a scale hunter once what stole some rope, and I found him instead. Pretty miserable sort, whoever he is."

Her fingers trailed over his shoulder—a gentle, treasuring touch. He did not understand what it signaled, being too concerned with Lise, with the terrifying potentials of all that had happened; but years later, after things had passed beyond remedy, he cursed himself for not having understood.

At length Jarcke helped him to his feet, and they climbed up to Hangtown, to bitter realizations and regrets, leaving Pardiel to the birds or the weather or worse.

". . . It seems it is considered irreligious for a woman in love to hesitate or examine the situation, to do anything other than blindly follow the impulse of her emotions. I felt the brunt of such an attitude—people judged it my fault for not having acted quickly and decisively one way or another. Perhaps I was overcautious. I do not claim to be free of blame, only innocent of sacrilege. I believe I might have eventually left Pardiel—there was not enough in the relationship to sustain happiness for either of us. But I had good reason for cautious examination. My husband was not an evil man, and there were matters of loyalty between us.

"I could not face Meric after Pardiel's death, and I moved to another part of the valley. He tried to see me on many occasions, but I always refused. Though I was greatly tempted, my guilt was greater. Four years later, after Jarcke died—crushed by a runaway wagon—one of her associates wrote and told me Jarcke had been in love with Meric, that it had been she who had informed Pardiel of the affair, and that she may well have staged the murder. The letter acted somewhat to expiate my guilt, and I weighed the possibility of seeing Meric again. But too much time had passed, and we had both assumed other lives. I decided against it. Six years later, when Griaule's influence had weakened sufficiently to allow emigration, I moved to Port Chantay. I did not hear from Meric for almost twenty years after that, and then one day I received a letter, which I will reproduce in part.

"'. . . My old friend from Regensburg, Louis Dardano, has been living here for the past few years, engaged in writing my biography. The narrative has a breezy feel, like a tale being told in a tavern, which—if you recall my telling you how this all began—is quite appropriate. But on reading it, I am amazed my life has had such a simple shape. One task, one passion. God, Lise! Seventy years old, and I still dream of you. And I still think of what happened that morning under the wing. Strange, that it has taken me all this time to realize it was not Jarcke, not you or I who were culpable, but Griaule. How obvious it seems now. I was leaving, and he needed me to complete the expression on his side, his dream of flying, of escape, to grant him the death of his desire. I am certain you will think I have leaped to this assumption, but I remind you that it has been a leap of forty years' duration. I know Griaule, know his monstrous subtlety. I can see it at work in every action that has taken place in the valley since my arrival. I was a fool not to understand that his powers were at the heart of our sad conclusion.'

"'The army now runs everything here, as no doubt you are aware. It is rumored they are planning a winter campaign against Regensburg. Can you believe it! Their fathers were ignorant, but this generation is brutally stupid. Otherwise, the work goes well and things are as usual with me. My shoulder aches, children stare at me on the street, and it is whispered I am mad . . .'"

—from *Under Griaule's Wing*
by Lise Claverie

3.

Acne-scarred, lean, arrogant, Major Hauk was a very young major with a limp. When Meric had entered, the major had been practicing his signature—it was a thing of elegant loops and flourishes, obviously intended to have a place in posterity. As he strode back and forth during their conversation, he paused frequently to admire himself in the window glass, settling the hang of his red jacket or running his fingers along the crease of his white trousers. It was the new style of uniform, the first Meric had seen at close range, and he noted with amusement the dragons embossed on the epaulets. He wondered if Griaule was capable of such an irony, if his influence was sufficiently discreet to have planted the idea for this comic opera apparel in the brain of some general's wife.

". . . not a question of manpower," the major was saying, "but of . . . " He broke off, and after a moment cleared his throat.

Meric, who had been studying the blotches on the backs of his hands, glanced up; the cane that had been resting against his knee slipped and clattered to the floor.

"A question of *matériel,*" said the major firmly. "The price of antimony, for example . . ."

"Hardly use it anymore," said Meric. "I'm almost done with the mineral reds."

A look of impatience crossed the major's face. "Very well," he said; he stooped to his desk and shuffled through some papers. "Ah! Here's a bill for a shipment of cuttlefish from which you derive . . ." He shuffled more papers.

"Syrian brown," said Meric gruffly. "I'm done with that, too. Golds and violets are all I need anymore. A little blue and rose." He wished the man would stop badgering him; he wanted to be at the eye before sunset.

As the major continued his accounting, Meric's gaze wandered out the window. The shantytown surrounding Griaule had swelled into a city and now sprawled across the hills. Most of the buildings were permanent, wood and stone, and the cant of the roofs, the smoke from the factories around the perimeter, put him in mind of Regensburg. All the natural beauty of the land had been drained into the painting. Blackish gray rain clouds were muscling up from the east, but the afternoon sun shone clear and shed a heavy gold radiance on Griaule's side. It looked as if the sunlight were an extension of the gleaming resins, as if the thickness of the paint were becoming infinite. He let the major's voice recede to a buzz and followed the scatter and dazzle of the images; and then, with a start, he realized the major was sounding him out about stopping the work.

The idea panicked him at first. He tried to interrupt, to raise objections but the major talked through him, and as Meric thought it over, he grew less and less opposed. The painting would never be finished, and he was tired. Perhaps it was time to have done with it, to accept a university post somewhere and enjoy life for a while.

"We've been thinking about a temporary stoppage," said Major Hauk. "Then if the winter campaign goes well . . . " He smiled. "If we're not visited by plague and pestilence, we'll assume things are in hand. Of course we'd like your opinion."

Meric felt a surge of anger toward this smug little monster. "In my opinion, you people are idiots," he said. "You wear Griaule's image on your shoulders, weave him on your flags, and yet you don't have the least comprehension of what that means. You think it's just a useful symbol. . . ."

"Excuse me," said the major stiffly.

"The hell I will!" Meric groped for his cane and heaved up to his feet. "You see yourselves as conquerors. Shapers of destiny. But all your rapes and slaughters are Griaule's expressions. *His* will. You're every bit as much his parasites as the skizzers."

The major sat, picked up a pen, and began to write.

"It astounds me," Meric went on, "that you can live next to a miracle, a source of mystery, and treat him as if he were an oddly shaped rock."

The major kept writing.

"What are you doing?" asked Meric.

"My recommendation," said the major without looking up.

"Which is?"

"That we initiate stoppage at once."

They exchanged hostile stares, and Meric turned to leave; but as he took hold of the doorknob, the major spoke again.

"We owe you so much," he said; he wore an expression of mingled pity and respect that further irritated Meric.

"How many men have you killed, Major?" he asked, opening the door.

"I'm not sure. I was in the artillery. We were never able to be sure."

"Well, I'm sure of my tally," said Meric. "It's taken me forty years to amass it. Fifteen hundred and ninety-three men and women. Poisoned, scaled, broken by falls, savaged by animals. Murdered. Why don't we—you and I—just call it even."

Though it was a sultry afternoon, he felt cold as he walked toward the tower—an internal cold that left him light-headed and weak. He tried to think what he would do. The idea of a university post seemed less appealing away from the major's office; he would soon grow weary of worshipful students and in-depth dissections of his work by jealous academics. A man hailed him as he turned into the market. Meric waved but did not stop, and heard another man say, "*That's* Cattanay?" (That ragged old ruin?)

The colors of the market were too bright, the smells of charcoal cookery too cloying, the crowds too thick, and he made for the side streets, hobbling past one-room stucco houses and tiny stores where they sold cooking oil by the ounce and cut cigars in half if you could not afford a whole one. Garbage, tornados of dust and flies, drunks with bloody mouths. Somebody had tied wires around a pariah dog—a bitch with slack teats; the wires had sliced into her flesh, and she lay panting in an alley mouth, gaunt ribs flecked with pink lather, gazing into nowhere. She, thought Meric, and not Griaule, should be the symbol of their flag.

As he rode the hoist up the side of the tower, he fell into his old habit of jotting down notes for the next day. *What's that cord of wood doing on level five? Slow leak of chrome yellow from pipes on level twelve.* Only when he saw a man dismantling some scaffolding did he recall Major Hauk's recommendation and understand that the order must already have been given. The loss of his work struck home to him then, and he leaned against the railing, his chest constricted and his eyes brimming. He straightened, ashamed of himself. The sun hung in a haze of iron-colored light low above the western hills, looking red and bloated and vile as a vulture's ruff. That polluted sky was his creation as much as was the painting, and it would be good to leave it behind. Once away from the valley, from all the influences of the place, he would be able to consider the future.

A young girl was sitting on the twentieth level just beneath the eye. Years before, the ritual of viewing the eye had grown to cultish proportions; there had been group chanting and praying and discussions of the experience. But these were more practical times, and no doubt the young men and women who had congregated here were now manning administrative desks somewhere in the burgeoning empire. They were the ones about whom Dardano should write; they, and all the eccentric characters who had played roles in this slow pageant. The gypsy woman who had danced every night by the eye, hoping to charm Griaule into killing her faithless lover—she had gone away satisfied. The man who had tried to extract one of the fangs—nobody knew what had become of him. The scale hunters, the artisans. A history of Hangtown would be a volume in itself.

The walk had left Meric weak and breathless; he sat down clumsily beside the girl, who smiled. He could not remember her name, but she came often to the eye. Small and dark, with an inner reserve that reminded him of Lise. He laughed inwardly—most women reminded him of Lise in some way.

"Are you all right?" she asked, her brow wrinkled with concern.

"Oh, yes," he said; he felt a need for conversation to take his mind off things, but he could think of nothing more to say. She was so young! All freshness and gleam and nerves.

"This will be my last time," she said. "At least for a while. I'll miss it." And then, before he could ask why, she added, "I'm getting married tomorrow, and we're moving away."

He offered congratulations and asked her who was the lucky fellow.

"Just a boy." She tossed her hair, as if to dismiss the boy's importance; she gazed up at the shuttered membrane. "What's it like for you when the eye opens?" she asked.

"Like everyone else," he said. "I remember . . . memories of my life. Other lives, too." He did not tell her about Griaule's memory of flight; he had never told anyone except Lise about that.

"All those bits of souls trapped in there," she said, gesturing at the eye. "What do they mean to him? Why does he show them to us?"

"I imagine he has his purposes, but I can't explain them."

"Once I remembered being with you," said the girl, peeking at him shyly through a dark curl. "We were under the wing."

He glanced at her sharply. "Tell me."

"We were . . . together," she said, blushing. "Intimate, you know. I was very afraid of the place, of the sounds and shadows. But I loved you so much, it didn't matter. We made love all night, and I was surprised because I thought that kind of passion was just in stories, something people had invented to make up for how ordinary it really was. And in the morning even that dreadful place had become beautiful, with the wing tips glowing red and the waterfall echoing . . ." She lowered her eyes. "Ever since I had that memory, I've been a little in love with you."

"Lise," he said, feeling helpless before her.

"Was that her name?"

He nodded and put a hand to his brow, trying to pinch back the emotions that flooded him.

"I'm sorry." Her lips grazed his cheek, and just that slight touch seemed to weaken him further. "I wanted to tell you how she felt in case she hadn't told you herself. She was very troubled by something, and I wasn't sure she had."

She shifted away from him, made uncomfortable by the intensity of his reaction, and they sat without speaking. Meric became lost in watching how the sun glazed the scales to reddish gold, how the light was channeled along the ridges in molten streams that paled as the day wound down. He was startled when the girl jumped to her feet and backed toward the hoist.

"He's dead," she said wonderingly.

Meric looked at her, uncomprehending.

"See?" She pointed at the sun, which showed a crimson sliver above the hill. "He's dead," she repeated, and the expression on her face flowed between fear and exultation.

The idea of Griaule's death was too large for Meric's mind to encompass, and he turned to the eye to find a counterproof—no glints of color flickered beneath the membrane. He heard the hoist creak as the girl headed down, but he continued to wait. Perhaps only the dragon's vision had failed. No. It was likely not a coincidence that work had been officially terminated today. Stunned, he sat staring at the lifeless membrane until the sun sank below the hills; then he stood and went over to the hoist. Before he could throw the switch, the cables thrummed—somebody heading up. Of course. The girl would have spread the news, and all the Major Hauks and their underlings would be hurrying to test Griaule's reflexes. He did not want to be here when they arrived, to watch them pose with their trophy like successful fishermen.

It was hard work climbing up to the frontoparietal plate. The ladder swayed, the wind buffeted him, and by the time he clambered onto the plate, he was giddy, his chest full of twinges. He hobbled forward and leaned against the rust-caked side of a boiling vat. Shadowy in the twilight, the great furnaces and vats towered around him, and it seemed this system of fiery devices reeking of cooked flesh and minerals was the actual machinery of Griaule's thought materialized above his skull. Energyless, abandoned. They had been replaced by more efficient equipment down below, and it had been—what was it?—almost five years since they were last used. Cobwebs veiled a pyramid of firewood; the stairs leading to the rims of the vats were crumbling. The plate itself was scarred and coated with sludge.

"Cattanay!"

Someone shouted from below, and the top of the ladder trembled. God, they were coming after him! Bubbling over with congratulations and plans for testimonial dinners, memorial plaques, specially struck medals. They would have him draped in bunting and bronzed and covered with pigeon shit before they were done. All these years he had been among them, both their slave and their master, yet he had never felt at home. Leaning heavily on his cane, he made his way past the frontal spike—blackened by years of oily smoke—and down between the wings to Hangtown. It was a ghost town, now. Weeds overgrowing the collapsed shanties; the lake a stinking pit, drained after some children had drowned in the summer of '91. Where Jarcke's home had stood was a huge pile of animal bones, taking a pale shine from the half-light. Wind keened through the tattered shrubs.

"Meric!" "Cattanay."

The voices drew closer.

Well, there was one place where they would not follow.

The leaves of the thickets were speckled with mold and brittle, flaking away as he brushed them. He hesitated at the top of the scale hunters' stair. He had no rope. Though he had done the climb unaided many times, it had been quite a few years. The gusts of wind, the shouts, the sweep of the valley and the lights scattered across it like diamonds on gray velvet—it all seemed a single inconstant medium. He heard the brush crunch behind him, more voices. To hell with it! Gritting his teeth against a twinge of pain in his shoulder, hooking his cane over his belt, he inched onto the stair and locked his fingers in the handholds. The wind whipped his clothes and threatened to pry him loose and send him pinwheeling off. Once he slipped; once he froze, unable to move backward or forward. But at last he reached the bottom and edged upslope until he found a spot flat enough to stand.

The mystery of the place suddenly bore in upon him, and he was afraid. He half-turned to the stair, thinking he would go back to Hangtown and accept the hurly-burly. But a moment later he realized how foolish a thought that was. Waves of weakness poured through him, his heart hammered, and white dazzles flared in his vision. His chest felt heavy as iron. Rattled, he went a few steps forward, the cane pocking the silence. It was too dark to see more than outlines, but up ahead was the fold of wing where he and Lise had sheltered. He walked toward it, intent on revisiting it; then he remembered the girl beneath the eye and understood that he had already said that good-bye. And it *was* good-bye—that he understood vividly. He kept walking. Blackness looked to be welling from the wing joint, from the entrances to the maze of luminous tunnels where they had stumbled onto the petrified man. Had it really been the old wizard, doomed by magical justice to molder and live on and on? It made sense. At least it accorded with what happened to wizards who slew their dragons.

"Griaule?" he whispered to the darkness, and cocked his head, half-expecting an answer. The sound of his voice pointed up the immensity of the great gallery under the wing, the emptiness, and he recalled how vital a habitat it had once been. Flakes shifting over the surface, skizzers, peculiar insects fuming in the thickets, the glum populace of Hangtown, waterfalls. He had never been able to picture Griaule fully alive—that kind of vitality was beyond the powers of the imagination. Yet he wondered if by some miracle the dragon were alive now, flying up through his golden night to the sun's core. Or had that merely been a dream, a bit of tissue glittering deep in the cold tons of his brain? He laughed. Ask the stars for their first names, and you'd be more likely to receive a reply.

He decided not to walk any farther—it was really no decision. Pain was spreading through his shoulder so intense he imagined it must be glowing inside. Carefully, carefully, he lowered himself and lay propped on an elbow, hanging onto the cane. Good, magical wood. Cut from a hawthorn atop Griaule's haunch. A man had once offered him a small fortune for it. Who would claim it now? Probably old Henry Sichi would snatch it for his museum, stick it in a glass case next to his boots. What a joke! He decided to lie flat on his stomach, resting his chin on an arm—the stony coolness beneath acted to muffle the pain. Amusing, how the range of one's decision dwindled. You decided to paint a dragon, to send hundreds of men searching for malachite and cochineal beetles, to love a woman, to heighten an undertone here and there, and finally to position your body a certain way. He seemed to have reached the end of the process. What next? He tried to regulate his breathing, to ease the pressure on his chest.

Then, as something rustled out near the wing joint, he turned on his side. He thought he detected movement, a gleaming blackness flowing toward him . . . or else it was only the haphazard firing of his nerves playing tricks with his vision. More surprised than afraid, wanting to see, he peered into the darkness and felt his heart beating erratically against the dragon's scale.

". . . It's foolish to draw simple conclusions from complex events, but I suppose there must be both moral and truth to this life, these events. I'll leave that to the gadflies. The historians, the social scientists, the expert apologists for reality. All I know is that he had a fight with his girlfriend over money and walked out. He sent her a letter saying he had gone south and would be back in a few months with more money than she could ever spend. I had no idea what he'd done. The whole thing about Griaule had just been a bunch of us sitting around the Red Bear, drinking up my pay—I'd sold an article—and somebody said, 'Wouldn't it be great if Dardano didn't have to write articles, if we didn't have to paint pictures that color-coordinated with people's furniture or slave at getting the gooey smiles of little nieces and nephews just right?" All sorts of improbable moneymaking schemes were put forward. Robberies, kidnappings. Then the idea of swindling the city fathers of Teocinte came up, and the entire plan was fleshed out in minutes. Scribbled on napkins, scrawled on sketchpads. A group effort. I keep trying to remember if anyone got a glassy look in their eye, if I felt a cold tendril of Griaule's thought stirring my brains. But I can't. It was a half hour's sensation, nothing more. A drunken whimsy, an art-school metaphor. Shortly thereafter, we ran out of money and staggered into the streets. It was snowing—big wet flakes that melted down our collars. God, we were drunk! Laughing, balancing on the icy railing of the University Bridge. Making faces at the bundled-up burghers and their fat ladies who huffed and puffed past, spouting steam and never giving us a glance, and none of us—not even the burghers—knowing that we were living our happy ending in advance. . . ."

—from *The Man Who Painted The Dragon Griaule*
by Louis Dardano

For Jamie and Laura

Draco, Draco

by

Tanith Lee

You'll have heard stories, sometimes, of men who have fought and slain dragons. These are all lies. There's no swordsman living ever killed a dragon, though a few swordsmen dead that tried.

On the other hand, I once travelled in company with a fellow who got the name of 'dragon-slayer'.

A riddle? No. I'll tell you.

I was coming from the North back into the South, to civilisation as you may say, when I saw him, sitting by the roadside. My first feeling was envy, I admit. He was smart and very clean for someone in the wilds, and he had the South all over him, towns and baths and money. He was crazy, too, because there was gold on his wrists and in one ear. But he had a sharp grey sword, an army sword, so maybe he could defend himself. He was also younger than me, and a great deal prettier, but the last isn't too difficult. I wondered what he'd do when he looked up from his daydream and saw me, tough, dark and sour as a twist of old rope, clopping down on him on my swarthy little horse, ugly as sin, that I love like a daughter.

Then he did look up and I discovered.

"Greetings, stranger. Nice day, isn't it?"

He stayed relaxed as he said it, and somehow you knew from that he really could look after himself. It wasn't he thought I was harmless, just that he thought he could handle me if I tried something. Then again, I had my box of stuff alongside. Most people can tell my trade from that, and the aroma of drugs and herbs. My father was with the Romans, in fact he was probably the last Roman of all, one foot on the ship to go home, the rest of him with my mother up against the barnyard wall. She said he was a camp physician and maybe that was so. Some idea of doctoring grew up with me, though nothing great or grand. An itinerant apothecary is welcome almost anywhere, and can even turn bandits civil. It's not a wonderful life, but it's the only one I know.

I gave the young soldier-dandy that it was a nice day. I added he'd possibly like it better if he hadn't lost his horse.

"Yes, a pity about that. You could always sell me yours."

"Not your style."

He looked at her. I could see he agreed. There was also a momentary idea that he might kill me and take her, so I said, "And she's well known as mine. It would get you a bad name. I've friends round about."

He grinned, good-naturedly. His teeth were good, too. What with that, and the hair like barley, and the rest of it—well, he was the kind usually gets what he wants. I was curious as to which army he had hung about with to gain the sword. But since the Eagles flew, there are kingdoms everywhere, chiefs, war-leaders, Roman knights, and every tide brings an invasion up some beach. Under it all, too, you can feel the earth, the actual ground, which had been measured and ruled with fine roads, the land which had been subdued but never tamed, beginning to quicken. Like the shadows that come with the blowing out of a lamp. Ancient things, which are in my blood somewhere, so I recognise them.

But he was like a new coin that hadn't got dirty yet, nor learned much, though you could see your face in its shine, and cut yourself on its edge.

His name was Caiy. Presently we came to an arrangement and he mounted up behind me on Negra. They spoke a smatter of Latin where I was born, and I called her that before I knew her, for her darkness. I couldn't call her for her hideousness, which is her only other visible attribute.

The fact is, I wasn't primed to the country round that

way at all. I'd had word, a day or two prior, that there were Saxons in the area I'd been heading for. And so I switched paths and was soon lost. When I came on Caiy, I'd been pleased with the road, which was Roman, hoping it would go somewhere useful. But, about ten miles after Caiy joined me, the road petered out in a forest. My passenger was lost, too. He was going South, no surprise there, but last night his horse had broken loose and bolted, leaving him stranded. It sounded unlikely, but I wasn't inclined to debate on it. It seemed to me someone might have stolen the horse, and Caiy didn't care to confess.

There was no way round the forest, so we went in and the road died. Being summer, the wolves would be scarce and the bears off in the hills. Nevertheless, the trees had a feel I didn't take to, sombre and still, with the sound of little streams running through like metal chains, and birds that didn't sing but made purrings and clinkings. Negra never baulked or complained—if I'd waited to call her, I could have done it for her courage and warm-heartedness—but she couldn't come to terms with the forest, either.

"It smells," said Caiy, who'd been kind enough not to comment on mine, "as if it's rotting. Or fermenting."

I grunted. Of course it did, it was, the fool. But the smell told you other things. The centuries, for one. Here were the shadows that had come back when Rome blew out her lamp and sailed away, and left us in the dark.

Then Caiy, the idiot, began to sing to show up the birds who wouldn't. A nice voice, clear and bright. I didn't tell him to leave off. The shadows already knew we were there.

When night came down, the black forest closed like a cellar door.

We made a fire and shared my supper. He'd lost his rations with his mare.

"Shouldn't you tether that—your horse," suggested Caiy, trying not to insult her since he could see we were partial to each other. "My mare was tied, but something scared her and she broke the tether and ran. I wonder what it was," he mused, staring in the fire.

About three hours later, we found out.

I was asleep, and dreaming of one of my wives, up in the far North, and she was nagging at me, trying to start a brawl, which she always did for she was taller than me, and liked me to hit her once in a while so she could feel fragile, feminine and mastered. Just as she emptied the beer jar over my head, I heard a sound up in the sky like a storm that was not a storm. And I knew I wasn't dreaming any more.

The sound went over, three or four great claps, and the tops of the forest reeling, and left shuddering. There was a sort of quiver in the air, as if sediment were stirred up in it. There was even an extra smell, dank, yet tingling. When the noise was only a memory, and the bristling hairs began to subside along my body, I opened my eyes.

Negra was flattened to the ground, her own eyes rolling, but she was silent. Caiy was on his feet, gawping up at the tree-tops and the strands of starless sky. Then he glared at me.

"What in the name of the Bull was that?"

I noted vaguely that the oath showed he had Mithraic allegiances, which generally meant Roman. Then I sat up, rubbed my arms and neck to get human, and went to console Negra. Unlike his silly calvary mare she hadn't bolted.

"It can't," he said, "have been a bird. Though I'd have sworn something flew over."

"No, it wasn't a bird."

"But it had wings. Or—no it couldn't have had wings the size of that."

"Yes it could. They don't carry it far, is all."

"Apothecary, stop being so damned provoking. If you know, out with it! Though I don't see how you can know. And don't tell me it's some bloody woods demon I won't believe in."

"Nothing like that," I said. "It's real enough. Natural, in its own way. Not," I amended, "that I ever came across one before, but I've met some who did."

Caiy was going mad, like a child working up to a tantrum.

"Well?"

I suppose he had charmed and irritated me enough I wanted to retaliate, because I just quoted some bastard non-sensical jabber-Latin chant at him:

Bis terribilis—
Bis appellare—

Draco! Draco!

At least, it made him sit down.

"What?" he eventually said.

At my age I should be over such smugness. I said, "It was a dragon."

Caiy laughed. But he had glimpsed it, and knew better than I did that I was right.

Nothing else happened that night. In the morning we started off again and there was a rough track, and then the forest began to thin out. After a while we emerged on the crown of a moor. The land dropped down to a valley, and on the other side there were sunny smoky hills and a long streamered sky. There was something else, too.

Naturally, Caiy said it first; as if everything new always surprised him, as if we hadn't each of us, in some way, been waiting for it, or something like it.

"This place stinks."

"Hn."

"Don't just grunt at me, you blasted quack doctor. It does, doesn't it. Why?"

"Why do you think?"

He brooded, pale gold and citified, behind me. Negra tried to paw the ground, and then made herself desist.

Neither of us brave humans had said any more about what had interrupted sleep in the forest, but when I'd told him no dragon could fly far on its wings, for from all I'd ever heard they were too large and only some freakish lightness in their bones enabled them to get airborne at all, I suppose we had both taken it to heart. Now here were the valley and the hills, and here was this reek lying over everything, strange, foul, alien, comparable to nothing, really. Dragon smell.

I considered. No doubt, the dragon went on an aerial patrol most nights, circling as wide as it could, to see what might be there for it. There were other things I'd learnt. These beasts hunt nocturnally, like cats. At the same time, a dragon is more like a crow in its habits. It will attack and kill, but normally it eats carrion, dead things, or dying and immobilised. It's light, as I said, it has to be to take the skies, but the lack of weight is compensated by the armour, the teeth and talons. Then again, I'd heard of dragons that breathed fire. I've never been quite convinced there. It seems more likely to me such monsters only live in volcanic caves, the mountain itself belching flame and the dragon taking credit for it. Maybe not. But certainly, this dragon was no fire-breather. The ground would have been scorched for miles; I've listened to stories where that happened. There were no marks of fire. Just the insidious pervasive stench that I knew, by the time we'd gone down into the valley, would be so familiar, so soaked into us, we would hardly notice it any more, or the scent of anything else.

I awarded all this information to my passenger. There followed a long verbal delay. I thought he might just be flabbergasted at getting so much chat from me, but then he said, very hushed, "You truly believe all this, don't you?"

I didn't bother with the obvious, just clucked to Negra, trying to make her turn back the way we'd come. But she was unsure and for once uncooperative, and suddenly his strong hand, the nails groomed even now, came down on my arm.

"Wait, Apothecary. If it *is* true—"

"Yes, yes," I said. I sighed. "You want to go and challenge it, and become a hero." He held himself like marble, as if I were speaking of some girl he thought he loved. I didn't see why I should waste experience and wisdom on him, but then. "No man ever killed a dragon. They're plated, all over, even the underbelly. Arrows and spears just bounce off—even a pilum. Swords clang and snap in half. Yes, yes," I reiterated, "you've heard of men who slashed the tongue, or stabbed into an eye. Let me tell you, if they managed to reach that high and actually did it, then they just made the brute angry. Think of the size and shape of a dragon's head, the way the pictures show it. It's one hell of a push from the eye into the brain. And you know, there's one theory the eyelid is armoured, too, and can come down faster than *that.*"

"Apothecary," he said. He sounded dangerous. I just knew what he must look like. Handsome, noble and insane.

"Then I won't keep you," I said. "Get down and go on and the best of luck."

I don't know why I bothered. I should have tipped him

off and ridden for it, though I wasn't sure Negra could manage to react sufficiently fast, she was that edgy. Anyway, I didn't, and sure enough next moment his sword was at the side of my throat, and so sharp it had drawn blood.

"You're the clever one," he said, "the know-all. And you do seem to know more than I do, about this. So you're my guide, and your scruff-bag of a horse, if it even deserves the name, is my transport. Giddy-up, the pair of you."

That was that. I never argue with a drawn sword. The dragon would be lying up by day, digesting and dozing, and by night I could hole up someplace myself. Tomorrow Caiy would be dead and I could leave. And I would, of course, have seen a dragon for myself.

After an hour and a half's steady riding—better once I'd persuaded him to switch from the sword to poking a dagger against my ribs, less tiring for us both—we came around a stand of woods, and there was a village. It was the savage Northern kind, thatch and wattle and turf banks, but big for all that, a good mile of it, not all walled. There were walls this end, however, and men on the gate, peering at us.

Caiy was aggrieved because he was going to have to ride up to them pillion, but he knew better now than to try managing Negra alone. He maybe didn't want to pretend she was his horse in any case.

As we pottered up the pebbled track to the gate, he sprang off and strode forward, arriving before me, and began to speak.

When I got closer I heard him announcing, in his dramatic, beautiful voice,

"—And if it's a fact, I swear by the Victory of the Light that I will meet the thing and kill it."

They were muttering. The dragon smell, even though we were used to it, sodden with it, seemed more acid here. Poor Negra had been voiding herself from sheer terror all up the path. With fortune on her side, there would be somewhere below ground, some cave or dug out place, where they'd be putting their animals out of the dragon's way, and she could shelter with the others.

Obviously, the dragon hadn't always been active in this

region. They'd scarcely have built their village if it had. No, it would have been like the tales. Dragons live for centuries. They can sleep for centuries, too. Unsuspecting, man moves in, begins to till and build and wax prosperous. Then the dormant dragon wakes under the hill. They're like the volcanoes I spoke of, in that. Which is perhaps, more than habitat, why so many of the legends say they breathe fire when they wake.

The interesting thing was, even clouded by the dragon stink, initially, the village didn't seem keen to admit anything.

Caiy, having made up his mind to accept the dragon—and afraid of being wrong—started to rant. The men at the gate were frightened and turning nasty. Leading Negra now, I approached, tapped my chest of potions and said:

"Or, if you don't want your dragon slain, I can cure some of your other troubles. I've got medicines for almost everything. Boils, warts. Ear pains. Tooth pains. Sick eyes. Women's afflictions. I have here—"

"Shut up, you toad-turd," said Caiy.

One of the guards suddenly laughed. The tension sagged.

Ten minutes after, we had been let in the gate and were trudging through the cow-dung and wild flowers—neither of which were to be smelled through the other smell—to the head-man's hall.

It was around two hours after that when we found out why the appearance of a rescuing champion-knight had given them the jitters.

It seemed they had gone back to the ancient way, propitiation, the scape-goat. For three years, they had been making an offering to the dragon, in spring, and at midsummer, when it was likely to be most frisky.

Anyone who knew dragons from a book would tell them this wasn't the way. But they knew their dragon from myth. Every time they made sacrifice, they imagined the thing could understand and appreciate what they'd done for it, and would therefore be more amenable.

In reality, of course, the dragon had never attacked the village. It had thieved cattle of the pasture by night, elderly or sick cows at that, and lambs that were too little and weak to run. It would have taken people, too, but only those who were disabled and alone. I said, a dragon is lazy and prefers carrion, or what's defenceless. Despite being big, they aren't so big they'd go after a whole tribe of men. And though even forty men together undoubtedly couldn't wound a dragon, they could exhaust it, if they kept up a rough-house. Eventually it would keel over and they could brain it. You seldom hear of forty men going off in a band to take a dragon, however. Dragons are still ravelled up with night fears and spiritual mysteries, and latterly with an Eastern superstition of a mighty demon who can assume the form of a dragon which is invincible and—naturally—breathes sheer flame. So, this village, like many another, would put out its sacrifice, one girl tied to a post, and leave her there, and the dragon would have her. Why not? She was helpless, fainting with horror—and young and tender into the bargain. Perfect. You never could convince them that, instead of appeasing the monster, the sacrifice encourages it to stay. Look at it from the dragon's point of view. Not only are there dead sheep and stray cripples to devour, but once in a while a nice juicy damsel on a stick. Dragons don't think like a man, but they do have memories.

When Caiy realized what they were about to do, tonight, as it turned out, he went red then white, exactly as they do in a bardic lay. Not anger, mind you. He didn't comprehend any more than they did. It was merely the awfulness of it.

He stood up and chose a stance, quite unconsciously impressive, and assured us he'd save her. He swore to it in front of us all, the chieftain, his men, me. And he swore it by the Sun, so I knew he meant business.

They were scared, but now also childishly hopeful. It was part of their mythology again. All mythology seems to take this tack somewhere, the dark against the light, the Final Battle. It's rot, but there.

Following a bit of drinking to seal the oath, they cheered up and the chief ordered a feast. Then they took Caiy to see the chosen sacrifice.

Her name was Niemeh, or something along those lines.

She was sitting in a little lamplit cell off the hall. She wasn't fettered, but a warrior stood guard beyond the screen, and there was no window. She had nothing to do except weave flowers together, and she was doing that, making garlands for her death procession in the evening.

When Caiy saw her, his colour drained away again.

He stood and stared at her, while somebody explained he was her champion.

Though he got on my nerves, I didn't blame him so much this time. She was about the most beautiful thing I ever hope to see. Young, obviously, and slim, but with a woman's shape, if you have my meaning, and long hair more fair even than Caiy's, and green eyes like sea pools and a face like one of the white flowers in her hands, and a sweet mouth.

I looked at her as she listened gravely to all they said. I remembered how in the legends it's always the loveliest and the most gentle gets picked for the dragon's dinner. You perceive the sense in the gentle part. A girl with a temper might start a ruckus.

When Caiy had been introduced and once more sworn by the sun to slay the dragon and so on, she thanked him. If things had been different, she would have blushed and trembled, excited by Caiy's attention. But she was past all that. You could see, if you looked, she didn't believe anyone could save her. But though she must have been half dead already of despair and fright, she still made space to be courteous.

Then she glanced over Caiy's head straight at me, and she smiled so I wouldn't feel left out.

"And who is this man?" she asked.

They all looked startled, having forgotten me. Then someone who had warts recalled I'd said I could fix him something for warts, and told her I was the apothecary.

A funny little shiver went through her then.

She was so young and so pretty. If I'd been Caiy I'd have stopped spouting rubbish about the dragon. I'd have found some way to lay out the whole village, and grabbed her, and gone. But that would have been a stupid thing to do too. I've enough of the old blood to know about such matters. She was the sacrifice and she was resigned to it; more, she didn't dream she could be anything else. I've come across rumours, here and there, of girls, men too, chosen to die, who escaped. But the fate stays on them. Hide them securely miles off, across water, beyond tall hills, still they feel the geas weigh like lead upon their souls. They kill themselves in the end, or go mad. And this girl, this Niemeh, you could see it in her. No, I would never have abducted her. It would have been no use. She was convinced she must die, as if she'd seen it written in light on a stone, and maybe she had.

She returned to her garlands, and Caiy, tense as a bowstring, led us back to the hall.

Meat was roasting and more drink came out and more talk came out. You can kill anything as often as you like, that way.

It wasn't a bad feast, as such up-country things go. But all through the shouts and toasts and guzzlings, I kept thinking of her in her cell behind the screen, hearing the clamour and aware of this evening's sunset, and how it would be to die . . . as she would have to. I didn't begin to grasp how she could bear it.

By late afternoon they were mostly sleeping it off, only Caiy had had the sense to go and sweat the drink out with soldiers' exercises in the yard, before a group of sozzled admirers of all sexes.

When someone touched my shoulder, I thought it was warty after his cure, but no. It was the guard from the girl's cell, who said very low, "She says she wants to speak to you. Will you come, now?"

I got up and went with him. I had a spinning minute, wondering if perhaps she didn't believe she must die after all, and would appeal to me to save her. But in my heart of hearts I guessed it wasn't that.

There was another man blocking the entrance, but they let me go in alone, and there Niemeh sat, making garlands yet, under her lamp.

But she looked up at me, and her hands fell like two more white flowers on the flowers in her lap. "I need some medicine, you see," she said. "But I can't pay you. I don't have anything. Although my uncle—"

"No charge," I said hurriedly.

She smiled. "It's for tonight."

"Oh," I said.

"I'm not brave," she said, "but it's worse than just being afraid. I know I shall die. That it's needful. But part of me wants to live so much—my reason tells me one thing but my body won't listen. I'm frightened I shall panic, struggle and scream and weep—I don't want that. It isn't right. I have to consent, or the sacrifice isn't any use. Do you know about that?"

"Oh, yes," I said.

"I thought so. I thought you did. Then . . . can you give me something, a medicine or herb—so I shan't feel anything? I don't mean the pain. That doesn't matter. The gods can't blame me if I cry out then, they wouldn't expect me to be beyond pain. But only to make me not care, not want to live so very much."

"An easy death."

"Yes." She smiled again. She seemed serene and beautiful. "Oh, yes."

I looked at the floor.

"The soldier. Maybe he'll kill it," I said.

She didn't say anything.

When I glanced up, her face wasn't serene any more. It was brimful of terror. Caiy would have been properly insulted.

"Is it you can't give me anything? Don't you have anything? I was sure you did. That you were sent here to me to—to help, so I shouldn't have to go through it all alone—"

"There," I said, "it's all right. I do have something. Just the thing. I keep it for women in labour when the child's slow and hurting them. It works a treat. They go sort of misty and far off, as if they were nearly asleep. It'll dull pain, too. Even—any kind of pain."

"Yes," she whispered, "I should like that." And then she caught my hand and kissed it. "I knew you would," she said, as if I'd promised her the best and loveliest thing in all the earth. Another man, it would have broken him in front of her. But I'm harder than most.

When she let me, I retrieved my hand, nodded reassuringly, and went out. The chieftain was awake and genial enough, so I had a word with him. I told him what the girl had asked. "In the East," I said, "it's the usual thing, give them something to help them through. They call it Nektar, the drink of the gods. She's consented," I said, "but she's very young and scared, delicately-bred too. You can't grudge her this." He acquiesced immediately, as glad as she was, as I'd hoped. It's a grim affair, I should imagine, when the girl shrieks for pity all the way up to the hills. I hadn't thought there'd be any problem. On the other hand, I hadn't wanted to be caught slipping her potions behind anyone's back.

I mixed the drug in the cell where she could watch. She was interested in everything I did, the way the condemned are nearly always interested in every last detail, even how a cobweb hangs.

I made her promise to drink it all, but none of it until they came to bring her out. "It may not last otherwise. You don't want it to wear off before—too early."

"No," she said. "I'll do exactly what you say."

When I was going out again, she said, "If I can ask them for anything for you, the gods, when I meet them . . ."

It was in my mind to say: Ask them to go stick—but I didn't. She was trying to keep intact her trust in recompence, immortality. I said, "just ask them to look after you."

She had such a sweet, sweet mouth. She was made to love and be loved, to have children and sing songs and die when she was old, peacefully, in her sleep.

And there would be others like her. The dragon would be given those, too. Eventually, it wouldn't just be maidens, either. The taboo states it had to be a virgin so as to safeguard any unborn life. Since a virgin can't be with child—there's one religion says different, I forget which—they stipulate virgins. But in the end any youthful woman, who can reasonably be reckoned as not with child, will do. And then they go on to the boys. Which is the most ancient sacrifice there is.

I passed a very young girl in the hall, trotting round with the beer-dipper. She was comely and innocent, and I recollected I'd seen her earlier and asked myself, Are you the next? And who'll be next after you?

Niemeh was the fifth. But, I said, dragons live a long while. And the sacrifices always get to be more frequent. Now it was twice a year. In the first year it had been once. In a couple more years it would happen at every season, with maybe three victims in the summer when the creature was most active.

And in ten more years it would be every month, and they'd have learned to raid other villages to get girls and young men to give it, and there would be a lot of bones about, besides, fellows like Caiy, dragon-slayers dragon slain.

I went after the girl with the beer-dipper and drained it. But drink never did comfort me much.

And presently, it would be time to form the procession and start for the hills.

It was the last gleaming golden hour of day when we set off.

The valley was fertile and sheltered. The westering light caught and flashed in the trees and out of the streams. Already there was a sort of path stamped smooth and kept clear of undergrowth. It would have been a pleasant journey, if they'd been going anywhere else.

There was sunlight warm on the sides of the hills, too. The sky was almost cloudless, transparent. If it hadn't been for the tainted air, you would never have thought anything was wrong. But the track wound up the first slope and around, and up again, and there, about a hundred yards off, was the flank of a bigger hill that went down into shadow at its bottom, and never took the sun. That underside was bare of grass, and eaten out in caves, one cave larger than the rest and very black, with a strange black stillness, as if light and weather and time itself stopped just inside. Looking at that, you'd know at once, even with sun on your face and the whole lucid sky above.

They'd brought her all this way in a Roman litter which somehow had become the property of the village. It had lost its roof and its curtains, just a kind of cradle on poles, but Niemeh had sat in it on their shoulders, motionless, and dumb. I had only stolen one look at her, to be sure, but her face had turned mercifully blank and her eyes were opaque. What I'd given her started its work swiftly. She was beyond us all now. I was only anxious everything else would occur before her condition changed.

Her bearers set the litter down and lifted her out. They'd have to support her, but they would know about that, girls with legs gone to water, even passed out altogether. And I suppose the ones who fought and screamed would be forced to sup strong ale, or else concussed with a blow.

Everyone walked a little more, until we reached a natural palisade of rock. This spot provided concealment, while overlooking the cave and the ground immediately below it. There was a stagnant dark pond caught in the gravel there, but on our side, facing the cave, a patch of clean turf with a post sticking up, about the height of a tall man.

The two warriors supporting Niemeh went on with her towards the post. The rest of us stayed behind the rocks, except for Caiy.

We were all garlanded with flowers. Even I had had to be, and I hadn't made a fuss. What odds? But Caiy wasn't garlanded. He was the one part of the ritual which, though arcanely acceptable, was still profane. And that was why, even though they would let him attack the dragon, they had nevertheless brought the girl to appease it.

There was some kind of shackle at the post. It wouldn't be iron, because anything fey has an allergy to stable metals, even so midnight a thing as a dragon. Bronze, probably. They locked one part around her waist and another round her throat. Only the teeth and claws could get her out of her bonds now, piece by piece.

She sagged forward in the toils. She seemed unconscious at last, and I wanted her to be.

The two men hurried back, up the slope and into the rock cover with the rest of us. Sometimes the tales have the people rush away when they've put out their sacrifice, but usually the people stay, to witness. It's quite safe. The dragon won't go after them with something tasty chained up right under its nose.

Caiy didn't remain beside the post. He moved down towards the edge of the polluted pond. His sword was drawn. He was quite ready. Though the sun couldn't get into the hollow to fire his hair or the metal blade, he cut a grand figure, heroically braced there between the maiden and Death.

At the end, the day spilled swiftly. Suddenly all the shoulders of the hills grew dim, and the sky became the colour of lavender, and then a sort of mauve amber, and the stars broke through.

There was no warning.

I was looking at the pond, where the dragon would come to drink, judging the amount of muck there seemed to be in it. And suddenly there was a reflection in the pond, from above. It wasn't definite, and it was upside down, but even so my heart plummeted through my guts.

There was a feeling behind the rock, the type you get, they tell me, in the battle lines, when the enemy appears. And mixed with this, something of another feeling, more maybe like the inside of some god's house when they call on him, and he seems to come.

I forced myself to look then, at the cave mouth. This, after all, was the evening I would see a real dragon, something to relate to others, as others had related such things to me.

It crept out of the cave, inch by inch, nearly down on its belly, cat-like.

The sky wasn't dark yet, a Northern dusk seems often endless. I could see well, and better and better as the shadow of the cave fell away and the dragon advanced into the paler shadow by the pond.

At first, it seemed unaware of anything but itself and the twilight. It flexed and stretched itself. There was something uncanny, even in such simple movements, something evil. And timeless.

The Romans know an animal they call Elephantus, and I mind an ancient clerk in one of the towns describing this beast to me, fairly accurately, for he'd seen one once. The dragon wasn't as large as elephantus, I should say. Actually not that much higher than a fair-sized cavalry gelding, if rather longer. But it was sinuous, more sinuous than any snake. The way it crept and stretched and flexed, and curled and slewed its head, its skeleton seemed fluid.

There are plenty of mosaics, paintings. It was like that, the way men have shown them from the beginning. Slender, tapering to the elongated head, which is like a horse's, too, and not like, and to the tail, though it didn't have that spade-shaped sting they put on them sometimes, like a scorpion's. There were spines, along the tail and the back-ridge, and the neck and head. The ears were set back, like a dog's. Its legs were short, but that didn't make it seem ungainly. The ghastly fluidity was always there, not grace, but something so like grace it was nearly unbearable.

It looked almost the colour the sky was now, slatey, bluish-grey, like metal but dull; the great overlapping plates of its scales had no burnish. Its eyes were black and you didn't see them, and then they took some light from somewhere, and they flared like two flat coins, cat's eyes, with nothing—no brain, no soul—behind them.

It had been going to drink, but had scented something more interesting than dirty water, which was the girl.

The dragon stood there, static as a rock, staring at her over the pond. Then gradually its two wings, that had been folded back like fans along its sides, opened and spread.

They were huge, those wings, much bigger than the rest of it. You could see how it might be able to fly with them. Unlike the body, there were no scales, only skin, membrane, with ribs of external bone. Bat's wings, near enough. It seemed feasible a sword could go through them, damage them, but that would only maim, and all too likely they were tougher than they seemed.

Then I left off considering. With its wings spread like that, unused—like a crow—it began to sidle around the water, the blind coins of eyes searing on the post and the sacrifice.

Somebody shouted. My innards sprang over. Then I realized it was Caiy. The dragon had nearly missed him, so intent it was on the feast, so he had had to call it.

Bis Terribilis—Bis appellare—Draco! Draco!

I'd never quite understood that antic chant, and the Latin was execrable. But I think it really means to know a dragon exists is bad enough, to call its name and summon it—call twice, twice terrible—is the notion of a maniac.

The dragon wheeled. It—*flowed.* Its elongated horse's-head-which-wasn't was before him, and Caiy's sharp sword slashed up and down and bit against the jaw. It happened, what they say—sparks shot glittering in the air. Then the head split, not from any wound, just the chasm of the mouth. It made a sound at him, not a hissing, a sort of *hroosh.* Its breath would be poisonous, almost as bad as fire. I saw Caiy stagger at it, and then one of the long feet on the short legs went out through the gathering dark. The blow looked slow and harmless. It threw Caiy thirty feet, right across the pond. He fell at the entrance to the cave, and lay quiet. The sword was still in his hand. His grip must have clamped down on it involuntarily. He'd likely bitten his tongue as well, in the same way.

The dragon looked after him, you could see it pondering whether to go across again and dine. But it was more attracted by the other morsel it had smelled first. It knew from its scent this was the softer more digestible flesh. And so it ignored Caiy, leaving him for later, and eddied on towards the post, lowering its head as it came, the light leaving its eyes.

I looked. The night was truly blooming now, but I could see, and the darkness didn't shut my ears; there were sounds, too. You weren't there, and I'm not about to try to make you see and hear what I did. Niemeh didn't cry out. She was senseless by then, I'm sure of it. She didn't feel or know any of what it did to her. Afterwards, when I went down with the others, there wasn't much left. It even carried some of her bones into the cave with it, to chew. Her garland was lying on the ground since the dragon had no interest in garnish. The pale flowers were no longer pale.

She had consented, and she hadn't had to endure it. I've seen things as bad that had been done by men, and for men there's no excuse. And yet, I never hated a man as I hated the dragon, a loathing, deadly, sickening hate.

The moon was rising when it finished. It went again to the pond, and drank deeply. Then it moved up the gravel back towards the cave. It paused beside Caiy, sniffed him, but there was no hurry. Having fed so well, it was sluggish. It stepped into the pitch-black hole of the cave, and drew itself from sight, inch by inch, as it had come out, and was gone.

Presently Caiy pulled himself off the ground, first to his hands and knees, then on to his feet.

We, the watchers, were amazed. We'd thought him dead, his back broken, but he had only been stunned, as he told us afterwards. Not even stunned enough not to have come to, dazed and unable to rise, before the dragon quite finished its feeding. He was closer than any of us. He said it maddened him—as if he hadn't been mad already—

and so, winded and part stupefied as he was, he got up and dragged himself into the dragon's cave after it. And this time he meant to kill it for sure, no matter what it did to him.

Nobody had spoken a word, up on our rocky place, and no one spoke now. We were in a kind of communion, a trance. We leaned forward and gazed at the black gape in the hill where they had both gone.

Maybe a minute later, the noises began. They were quite extraordinary, as if the inside of the hill itself were gurning and snarling. But it was the dragon, of course. Like the stink of it, those sounds it made were untranslatable. I could say it looked this way comparable to an elephantus, or that way to a cat, a horse, a bat. But the cries and roars—no. They were like nothing else I've heard in the world, or been told of. There were, however, other noises, as of some great heap of things disturbed. And stones rattling, rolling.

The villagers began to get excited or hysterical. Nothing like this had happened before. Sacrifice is usually predictable.

They stood, and started to shout, or groan and invoke supernatural protection. And then a silence came from inside the hill, and silence returned to the villagers.

I don't remember how long it went on. It seemed like months.

Then suddenly something moved in the cave mouth.

There were yells of fear. Some of them took to their heels, but came back shortly when they realized the others were rooted to the spot, pointing and exclaiming, not in anguish but awe. That was because it was Caiy, and not the dragon, that had emerged from the hill.

He walked like a man who has been too long without food and water, head bowed, shoulders drooping, legs barely able to hold him up. He floundered through the edges of the pond and the sword trailed from his hand in the water. Then he tottered over the slope and was right before us. He somehow raised his head then, and got out the sentence no one had ever truly reckoned to hear.

"It's—dead," said Caiy, and slumped unconscious in the moonlight.

They used the litter to get him to the village, as Niemeh didn't need it any more.

We hung around the village for nearly ten days. Caiy was his merry self by the third, and since there had been no sign of the dragon, by day or night, a party of them went up to the hills, and, kindling torches at noon, slunk into the cave to be sure.

It was dead all right. The stench alone would have verified that, a different perfume than before, and all congealed there, around the cave. In the valley, even on the second morning, the live dragon smell was almost gone. You could make out goats and hay and meade and unwashed flesh and twenty varieties of flowers.

I myself didn't go in the cave. I went only as far as the post. I understood it was safe, but I just wanted to be there once more, where the few bones that were Niemeh had fallen through the shackles to the earth. And I can't say why, for you can explain nothing to bones.

There was rejoicing and feasting. The whole valley was full of it. Men came from isolated holdings, cots and huts, and a rough looking lot they were. They wanted to glimpse Caiy the dragon-slayer, to touch him for luck and lick the finger. He laughed. He hadn't been badly hurt, and but for bruises was as right as rain, up in the hay-loft half the time with willing girls, who would afterwards boast their brats were sons of the hero. Or else he was blind drunk in the chieftain's hall.

In the end, I collected Negra, fed her apples and told her she was the best horse in the land, which she knows is a lie and not what I say the rest of the time. I had sound directions now, and was planning to ride off quietly and let Caiy go on as he desired, but I was only a quarter of a mile from the village when I heard the splayed tocking of horse's hooves. Up he galloped beside me on a decent enough horse, the queen of the chief's table, no doubt, and grinning, with two beer skins.

I accepted one, and we continued, side by side.

"I take it you're sweet on the delights of my company," I said at last, an hour after, when the forest was in view over the moor.

"What else, Apothecary? Even my insatiable lust to

steal your gorgeous horse has been removed. I now have one of my very own, if not a third as beautiful." Negra cast him a sidelong look as if she would like to bite him. But he paid no attention. We trotted on for another mile or so before he added, "And there's something I want to ask you, too."

I was wary, and waited to find out what came next.

Finally, he said, "You must know a thing or two in your trade about how bodies fit together. That dragon, now. You seemed to know all about dragons."

I grunted. Caiy didn't cavil at the grunt. He began idly to describe how he'd gone into the cave, a tale he had flaunted a mere three hundred times in the chieftain's hall. But I didn't cavil either, I listened carefully.

The cave entry-way was low and vile, and soon it opened into a cavern. There was elf-light, more than enough to see by, and water running here and there along the walls and over the stony floor.

There in the cavern's centre, glowing now like filthy silver, lay the dragon, on a pile of junk such as dragons always accumulate. They're like crows and magpies in that, also, shiny things intrigue them and they take them to their lairs to paw possessively and to lie on. The rumours of hoards must come from this, but usually the collection is worthless, snapped knives, impure glass that had sparkled under the moon, rusting armlets from some victim, and all of it soiled by the devil's droppings, and muddled up with split bones.

When he saw it like this, I'd bet the hero's reckless heart failed him. But he would have done his best, to stab the dragon in the eye, the root of the tongue, the vent under the tail, as it clawed him in bits.

"But you see," Caiy now said to me, "I didn't have to."

This, of course, he hadn't said in the hall. No. He had told the village the normal things, the lucky lunge and the brain pierced, and the death-throes, which we'd all heard plainly enough. If anyone noticed his sword had no blood on it, well, it had trailed in the pond, had it not?

"You see," Caiy went on, "it was lying there comatose one minute, and then it began to writhe about, and to go into a kind of spasm. Something got dislodged off the hoard-pile—a piece of cracked-up armour, I think, gilded

—and knocked me silly again. And when I came round, the dragon was all sprawled about, and dead as yesterday's roast mutton."

"Hn," I said. *"Hn*n."

"The point being," said Caiy, watching the forest and not me, "I must have done something to it with the first blow, outside. Dislocated some bone or other. You told me their bones have no marrow. So to do that might be conceivable. A fortunate stroke. But it took a while for the damage to kill it."

"Hn*n."*

"Because," said Caiy, softly, "you do believe I killed it, don't you?"

"In the legends," I said, "they always do."

"But you said before that in reality, a man can't kill a dragon."

"One did," I said.

"Something I managed outside then. Brittle bones. That first blow to its skull."

"Very likely."

Another silence. Then he said:

"Do you have any gods, Apothecary?"

"Maybe."

"Will you swear me an oath by them, and then call me 'dragon-slayer'? Put it another way. You've been a help. I don't like to turn on my friends. Unless I have to."

His hand was nowhere near that honed sword of his, but the sword was in his eyes and his quiet, oh-so-easy voice. He had his reputation to consider, did Caiy. But I've no reputation at all. So I swore my oath and I called him dragon-slayer, and when our roads parted my hide was intact. He went off to glory somewhere I'd never want to go.

Well, I've seen a dragon, and I do have gods. But I told them, when I swore that oath, I'd almost certainly break it, and my gods are accustomed to me. They don't expect honour and chivalry. And there you are.

Caiy never killed the dragon. It was Niemeh, poor lovely loving gentle Niemeh who killed it. In my line of work, you learn about your simples. Which cure, which bring sleep, which bring the long sleep without awakening. There are some miseries in this blessed world can only end in death, and the quicker death the better. I told you I was a hard man. I couldn't save her, I gave you reasons why. But there were all those others who would have followed her. *Other* Niemehs. Other Caiys, for that matter. I gave her enough in the cup to put out the life of fifty strong men. It didn't pain her, and she didn't show she was dead before she had to be. The dragon devoured her, and with her the drug I'd dosed her with. And so Caiy earned the name of dragon-slayer.

And it wasn't a riddle.

And no, I haven't considered making a profession of it. Once is enough with any twice-terrible thing. Heroes and knights need their impossible challenges. I'm not meant for any bard's romantic song, a look will tell you that. You won't ever find me in the Northern hills calling "Draco! Draco!"

The Rule of Names

by

Ursula K. Le Guin

MR. UNDERHILL CAME out from under his hill, smiling and breathing hard. Each breath shot out of his nostrils as a double puff of steam, snow-white in the morning sunshine. Mr. Underhill looked up at the bright December sky and smiled wider than ever, showing snow-white teeth. Then he went down to the village.

"Morning, Mr. Underhill," said the villagers as he passed them in the narrow street between houses with conical, overhanging roofs like the fat red caps of toadstools. "Morning, morning!" he replied to each. (It was of course bad luck to wish anyone a *good* morning; a simple statement of the time of day was quite enough, in a place so permeated with Influences as Sattins Island, where a careless adjective might change the weather for a week.) All of them spoke to him, some with affection, some with affectionate disdain. He was all the little island had in the way of a wizard, and so deserved respect—but how could you respect a little fat man of fifty who waddled along with his toes turned in, breathing steam and smiling? He was no great shakes as a workman either. His fireworks were fairly elaborate but his elixirs were weak. Warts he charmed off frequently reappeared after three days; tomatoes he enchanted grew no bigger than canteloupes; and those rare times when a strange ship stopped at Sattins Harbor, Mr. Underhill always stayed under his hill—for fear, he explained, of the evil eye. He was, in other words, a wizard the way walleyed Gan was a carpenter: by default. The villagers made do with badly-hung doors and inefficient spells, for this generation, and relieved their annoyance by treating Mr. Underhill quite familiarly, as a mere fellow-villager. They even asked him to dinner. Once he asked some of them to dinner, and served a splendid repast, with silver, crystal, damask, roast goose, sparkling Andrades '639, and plum pudding with hard sauce; but he was so nervous all through the meal that it took the joy out of it, and besides, everybody was hungry again half an hour afterward. He did not like anyone to visit his cave, not even the anteroom, beyond which in fact nobody had ever got. When he saw people approaching the hill he always came trotting out to meet them. "Let's sit out here under the pine trees!" he would say, smiling and waving towards the fir grove, or if it was raining, "Let's go have a drink at the inn, eh?" though everybody knew he drank nothing stronger than well-water.

Some of the village children, teased by that locked cave, poked and pried and made raids while Mr. Underhill was away; but the small door that led into the inner chamber was spell-shut, and it seemed for once to be an effective spell. Once a couple of boys, thinking the wizard was over on the West Shore curing Mrs. Ruuna's sick donkey, brought a crowbar and a hatchet up there, but at the first whack of the hatchet on the door there came a roar of wrath from inside, and a cloud of purple steam. Mr. Underhill had got home early. The boys fled. He did not come out, and the boys came to no harm, though they said you couldn't believe what a huge hooting howling hissing horrible bellow that little fat man could make unless you'd heard it.

His business in town this day was three dozen fresh eggs and a pound of liver; also a stop at Seacaptain Fogeno's cottage to renew the seeing-charm on the old man's eyes (quite useless when applied to a case of detached retina, but Mr. Underhill kept trying), and finally a chat with old Goody Guld, the concertina-maker's widow. Mr. Underhill's friends were mostly old people. He was timid with the strong young men of the village, and the girls were shy of him. "He makes me nervous, he smiles so much," they all said, pouting, twisting silky ringlets round a finger. "Nervous" was a newfangled word, and their mothers all replied grimly, "Nervous my foot, silliness is the word for it. Mr. Underhill is a very respectable wizard!"

After leaving Goody Guld, Mr. Underhill passed by the school, which was being held this day out on the common. Since no one on Sattins Island was literate, there were no books to learn to read from and no desks to carve initials on and no blackboards to erase, and in fact no schoolhouse. On rainy days the children met in the loft of the Communal Barn, and got hay in their pants; on sunny days the schoolteacher, Palani, took them anywhere she felt like. Today, surrounded by thirty interested children under twelve and forty uninterested sheep under five, she was teaching an important item on the curriculum: the Rules of Names. Mr. Underhill, smiling shyly, paused to listen and watch. Palani, a plump, pretty girl of twenty, made a charming picture there in the wintry sunlight, sheep and children around her, a leafless oak above her, and behind her the dunes and sea and clear, pale sky. She spoke earnestly, her face flushed pink by wind and words. "Now you know the Rules of Names already, children. There are two, and they're the same on every island in the world. What's one of them?"

"It ain't polite to ask anybody what his name is," shouted a fat, quick boy, interrupted by a little girl shrieking, "You can't never tell your own name to nobody my ma says!"

"Yes, Suba. Yes, Popi dear, don't screech. That's right. You never ask anybody his name. You never tell your own. Now think about that a minute and then tell me why we call our wizard Mr. Underhill." She smiled across the curly heads and the woolly backs at Mr. Underhill, who beamed, and nervously clutched his sack of eggs.

"'Cause he lives under a hill!" said half the children.

"But is it his truename?"

"No!" said the fat boy, echoed by little Popi shrieking. "No!"

"How do you know it's not?"

"'Cause he came here all alone and so there wasn't anybody knew his truename so they couldn't tell us, and *he* couldn't—"

"Very good, Suba. Popi, don't shout. That's right. Even a wizard can't tell his truename. When you children are through school and go through the Passage, you'll leave your childnames behind and keep only your truenames, which you must never ask for and never give away. Why is that the rule?"

The children were silent. The sheep bleated gently. Mr. Underhill answered the question: "Because the name is the thing," he said in his shy, soft, husky voice, "and the truename is the true thing. To speak the name is to control the thing. Am I right, Schoolmistress?"

She smiled and curtseyed, evidently a little embarrassed by his participation. And he trotted off toward his hill, clutching his eggs to his bosom. Somehow the minute spent watching Palani and the children had made him very hungry. He locked his inner door behind him with a hasty incantation, but there must have been a leak or two in the spell, for soon the bare anteroom of the cave was rich with the smell of frying eggs and sizzling liver.

The wind that day was light and fresh out of the west, and on it at noon a little boat came skimming the bright waves into Sattins Harbor. Even as it rounded the point a sharp-eyed boy spotted it, and knowing, like every child on the island, every sail and spar of the forty boats of the fishing fleet, he ran down the street calling out, "A foreign boat, a foreign boat!" Very seldom was the lonely isle visited by a boat from some equally lonely isle of the East Reach, or an adventurous trader from the Archipelago. By the time the boat was at the pier half the village was there to greet it, and fishermen were following it homewards, and cowherds and clam-diggers and herb-hunters were puffing up and down all the rocky hills, heading towards the harbor.

But Mr. Underhill's door stayed shut.

There was only one man aboard the boat. Old Seacaptain Fogeno, when they told him that, drew down a bristle of white brows over his unseeing eyes. "There's only one kind of man," he said, "that sails the Outer Reach alone. A wizard, or a warlock, or a Mage . . ."

So the villagers were breathless hoping to see for once in their lives a Mage, one of the mighty White Magicians of the rich, towered, crowded inner islands of the Archipelago. They were disappointed, for the voyager was quite young, a handsome black-bearded fellow who hailed them cheerfully from his boat, and leaped ashore like any sailor glad to have made port. He introduced himself at once as a sea-peddlar. But when they told Seacaptain Fogeno that he carried an oaken walking-stick around with him, the old man nodded. "Two wizards in one town," he said. "Bad!" And his mouth snapped shut like an old carp's.

As the stranger could not give them his name, they gave him one right away: Blackbeard. And they gave him plenty of attention. He had a small mixed cargo of cloth and sandals and piswi feathers for trimming cloaks and cheap incense and levity stones and fine herbs and great glass beads from Venway—the usual peddlar's lot. Everyone on Sattins Island came to look, to chat with the voyager, and perhaps to buy something—"Just to remember him by!" cackled Goody Guld, who like all the women and girls of the village was smitten with Blackbeard's bold good looks. All the boys hung round him too, to hear him tell of his voyages to far, strange islands of the Reach or describe the great rich islands of the Archipelago, the Inner Lanes, the roadsteads white with ships, and the golden roofs of Havnor. The men willingly listened to his tales; but some of them wondered why a trader should sail alone, and kept their eyes thoughtfully upon his oaken staff.

But all this time, Mr. Underhill stayed under his hill.

"This is the first island I've ever seen that had no wizard," said Blackbeard one evening to Goody Guld, who had invited him and her nephew and Palani in for a cup of rushwash tea. "What do you do when you get a toothache, or the cow goes dry?"

"Why, we've got Mr. Underhill!" said the old woman.

"For what that's worth," muttered her nephew Birt, and then blushed purple and spilled his tea. Birt was a fisherman, a large, brave, wordless young man. He loved the schoolmistress, but the nearest he had come to telling her of his love was to give baskets of fresh mackerel to her father's cook.

"Oh, you do have a wizard?" Blackbeard asked. "Is he invisible?"

"No, he's just very shy," said Palani. "You've only been

here a week, you know, and we see so few strangers here. . . ." She also blushed a litttle, but did not spill her tea.

Blackbeard smiled at her. "He's a good Sattinsman, then, eh?"

"No," said Goody Guld, "no more than you are. Another cup, nevvy? keep it in the cup this time. No, my dear, he came in a little bit of a boat, four years ago was it? just a day after the end of the shad run, I recall, for they was taking up the nets over in East Creek, and Pondi Cowherd broke his leg that very morning—five years ago it must be. No, four. No, five it is, 'twas the year the garlic didn't sprout. So he sails in on a bit of a sloop loaded full up with great chests and boxes and says to Seacaptain Fogeno, who wasn't blind then, though old enough goodness knows to be blind twice over, 'I hear tell,' he says, 'you've got no wizard nor warlock at all, might you be wanting one?' 'Indeed, if the magic's white!' says the Captain, and before you could say cuttlefish Mr. Underhill had settled down in the cave under the hill and was charming the mange off Goody Beltow's cat. Though the fur grew in grey, and 'twas an orange cat. Queer-looking thing it was after that. It died last winter in the cold spell. Goody Beltow took on so at that cat's death, poor thing, worse than when her man was drowned on the Long Banks, the year of the long herring-runs, when nevvy Birt here was but a babe in petticoats." Here Birt spilled his tea again, and Blackbeard grinned, but Goody Guld proceeded undismayed, and talked on till nightfall.

Next day Blackbeard was down at the pier, seeing after the sprung board in his boat which he seemed to take a long time fixing, and as usual drawing the taciturn Sattinsmen into talk. "Now which of these is your wizard's craft?" he asked. "Or has he got one of those the Mages fold up into a walnut shell when they're not using it?"

"Nay," said a stolid fisherman."She's oop in his cave, under hill."

"He carried the boat he came in up to his cave?"

"Aye. Clear oop. I helped. Heavier as lead she was. Full oop with great boxes, and they full oop with books o' spells, he says. Heavier as lead she was." And the stolid fisherman turned his back, sighing stolidly. Goody Guld's nephew, mending a net nearby, looked up from his work and asked with equal stolidity, "Would ye like to meet Mr. Underhill, maybe?"

Blackbeard returned Birt's look. Clever black eyes met candid blue ones for a long moment; then Blackbeard smiled and said, "Yes. Will you take me up to the hill, Birt?"

"Aye, when I'm done with this," said the fisherman. And when the net was mended, he and the Archipelagan set off up the village street towards the high green hill above it. But as they crossed the common Blackbeard said, "Hold on a while, friend Birt. I have a tale to tell you, before we meet your wizard."

"Tell away," says Birt, sitting down in the shade of a live-oak.

"It's a story that started a hundred years ago, and isn't finished yet—though it soon will be, very soon. . . . In the very heart of the Archipelago, where the islands crowd thick as flies on honey, there's a little isle called Pendor. The sealords of Pendor were mighty men, in the old days of war before the League. Loot and ransom and tribute came pouring into Pendor, and they gathered a great treasure there, long ago. Then from somewhere away out in the West Reach, where dragons breed on the lava isles, came one day a very mighty dragon. Not one of those overgrown lizards most of you Outer Reach folk call dragons, but a big, black, winged, wise, cunning monster, full of strength and subtlety, and like all dragons loving gold and precious stones above all things. He killed the Sealord and his soldiers, and the people of Pendor fled in their ships by night. They all fled away and left the dragon coiled up in Pendor Towers. And there he stayed for a hundred years, dragging his scaly belly over the emeralds and sapphires and coins of gold, coming forth only once in a year or two when he must eat. He'd raid nearby islands for his food. You know what dragons eat?"

Birt nodded and said in a whisper, "Maidens."

"Right," said Blackbeard. "Well, that couldn't be endured forever, nor the thought of him sitting on all that treasure. So after the League grew strong, and the Archipelago wasn't so busy with wars and piracy, it was decided to attack Pendor, drive out the dragon, and get the gold and jewels for the treasury of the League. They're forever wanting money, the League is. So a huge fleet gathered from fifty islands, and seven Mages stood in the prows of the seven strongest ships, and they sailed towards Pendor. . . . They got there. They landed. Nothing stirred. The houses all stood empty, the dishes on the tables full of a hundred years' dust. The bones of the old Sealord and his men lay about in the castle courts and on the stairs. And the Tower rooms reeked of dragon. But there was no dragon. And no treasure, not a diamond the size of a poppyseed, not a single silver bead . . . Knowing that he couldn't stand up to seven Mages, the dragon had skipped out. They tracked him, and found he'd flown to a deserted island up north called Udrath; they followed his trail there, and what did they find? Bones again. His bones—the dragon's. But no treasure. A wizard, some unknown wizard from somewhere, must have met him single-handed, and defeated him—and then made off with the treasure, right under the League's nose!"

The fisherman listened, attentive and expressionless.

"Now that must have been a powerful wizard and a clever one, first to kill a dragon, and second to get off without leaving a trace. The lords and Mages of the Archipelago couldn't track him at all, neither where he'd come from nor where he'd made off to. They were about to give up. That was last spring; I'd been off on a three-year voyage up in the North Reach, and got back about that time. And they asked me to help them find the unknown wizard. That was clever of them. Because I'm not only a wizard myself, as I think some of the oafs here have guessed, but I am also a descendant of the Lords of Pendor. That treasure is mine. It's mine, and knows that it's mine. Those fools of the League couldn't find it, because it's not theirs. It belongs to the House of Pendor, and the great emerald, the star of the hoard, Inalkil the Greenstone, knows its master. Behold!" Blackbeard raised his oaken staff and cried aloud, "Inalkil!" The tip of the staff began to glow green, a fiery green radiance, a dazzling haze the color of April grass, and at the same moment the staff tipped in the wizard's hand, leaning, slanting till it pointed straight at the side of the hill above them.

"It wasn't so bright a glow, far away in Havnor," Blackbeard murmured, "but the staff pointed true. Inalkil answered when I called. The jewel knows its master. And I know the thief, and I shall conquer him. He's a mighty wizard, who could overcome a dragon. But I am mightier. Do you want to know why, oaf? Because I know his name!"

As Blackbeard's tone got more arrogant, Birt had looked duller and duller, blanker and blanker; but at this he gave a twitch, shut his mouth, and stared at the Archipelagan. "How did you . . . learn it?" he asked very slowly.

Blackbeard grinned, and did not answer.

"Black magic?"

"How else?"

Birt looked pale, and said nothing.

"I am the Sealord of Pendor, oaf, and I will have the gold my fathers won, and the jewels my mothers wore, and the Greenstone! For they are mine—Now, you can tell your village boobies the whole story after I have defeated this wizard and gone. Wait here. Or you can come and watch, if you're not afraid. You'll never get the chance again to see a great wizard in all his power." Blackbeard turned, and without a backward glance strode off up the hill towards the entrance to the cave.

Very slowly, Birt followed. A good distance from the cave he stopped, sat down under a hawthorn tree, and watched. The Archipelagan had stopped; a stiff, dark figure alone on the green swell of the hill before the gaping cave-mouth, he stood perfectly still. All at once he swung his staff up over his head, and the emerald radiance shone about him as he shouted, "Thief, thief of the Hoard of Pendor, come forth!"

There was a crash, as of dropped crockery, from inside the cave, and a lot of dust came spewing out. Scared, Birt ducked. When he looked again he saw Blackbeard still standing motionless, and at the mouth of the cave, dusty and dishevelled, stood Mr. Underhill. He looked small and pitiful, with his toes turned in as usual, and his little bowlegs in black tights, and no staff—he never had had one, Birt suddenly thought. Mr. Underhill spoke. "Who are you?" he said in his husky little voice.

"I am the Sealord of Pendor, thief, come to claim my treasure!"

At that, Mr. Underhill slowly turned pink, as he always did when people were rude to him. But he then turned something else. He turned yellow. His hair bristled out, he gave a coughing roar—and was a yellow lion leaping down the hill at Blackbeard, white fangs gleaming.

But Blackbeard no longer stood there. A gigantic tiger, color of night and lightning, bounded to meet the lion. . . .

The lion was gone. Below the cave all of a sudden stood a high grove of trees, black in the winter sunshine. The tiger, checking himself in mid-leap just before he entered the shadow of the trees, caught fire in the air, became a tongue of flame lashing out at the dry black branches. . . .

But where the trees had stood a sudden cataract leaped from the hillside, an arch of silvery crashing water, thundering down upon the fire. But the fire was gone. . . .

For just a moment before the fisherman's staring eyes two hills rose—the green one he knew, and a new one, a bare, brown hillock ready to drink up the rushing waterfall. That passed so quickly it made Birt blink, and after blinking he blinked again, and moaned, for what he saw now was a great deal worse. Where the cataract had been there hovered a dragon. Black wings darkened all the hill, steel claws reached groping, and from the dark, scaly, gaping lips fire and steam shot out.

Beneath the monstrous creature stood Blackbeard, laughing.

"Take any shape you please, little Mr. Underhill!" he taunted. "I can match you. But the game grows tiresome. I want to look upon my treasure, upon Inalkil. Now, big dragon, little wizard, take your true shape. I command you by the power of your truename—Yevaud!"

Birt could not move at all, not even to blink. He cowered, staring whether he would or not. He saw the black dragon hang there in the air above Blackbeard. He saw the fire lick like many tongues from the scaly mouth, the steam jet from the red nostrils. He saw Blackbeard's face grow white, white as chalk, and the beard-fringed lips trembling.

"Your name is Yevaud!"

"Yes," said a great, husky, hissing voice. "My truename is Yevaud, and my true shape is this shape."

"But the dragon was killed—they found dragon-bones on Udrath Island—"

"That was another dragon," said the dragon, and then stopped like a hawk, talons outstretched. And Birt shut his eyes.

When he opened them the sky was clear, the hillside empty, except for a reddish-blackish trampled spot, and a few talon-marks in the grass.

Birt the fisherman got to his feet and ran. He ran across the common, scattering sheep to right and left, and straight down the village street to Palani's father's house. Palani was out in the garden weeding the nasturtiums. "Come with me!" Birt gasped. She stared. He grabbed her wrist and dragged her with him. She screeched a little, but did not resist. He ran with her straight to the pier, pushed her into his fishing-sloop the *Queenie,* untied the painter, took up the oars and set off rowing like a demon. The last that Sattins Island saw of him and Palani was the *Queenie's* sail vanishing in the direction of the nearest island westward.

The villagers thought they would never stop talking about it, how Goody Guld's nephew Birt had lost his mind and sailed off with the schoolmistress on the very same day that the peddlar Blackbeard disappeared without a trace, leaving all his feathers and beads behind. But they did stop talking about it, three days later. They had other things to talk about, when Mr. Underhill finally came out of his cave.

Mr. Underhill had decided that since his truename was no longer a secret, he might as well drop his disguise. Walking was a lot harder than flying, and besides, it was a long, long time since he had had a real meal.

THE UNICORN

After the dragon, the unicorn is probably the most popular and pervasive of all mythological beasts. Although we tend to think of the unicorn in a medieval European setting, it was known to the classical Greeks and Romans, and in actuality is an ancient symbol that can be found all over the world, in Jewish and Hindu mythology as well as Christian folklore. Like the dragon, the unicorn also has a Chinese counterpart, the *k'i-lin,* one of the four animals of good omen (the dragon, the phoenix, and the tortoise are the other three), and the foremost of all the creatures who live on the land. While the *k'i-lin* is depicted as having the body of a deer and the tail of an ox, the more familiar version of the unicorn is the Western Unicorn, usually described as being like a white horse with a goat's beard and a long twisted horn projecting out of its forehead.

Although originally a symbol of untamable ferocity—in Solinus's words, of all creatures "the cruelest is the Unicorne, a Monster that belloweth horrible. . . . He is never caught alive; kylled he may be, but taken he cannot bee"—by medieval times the unicorn had become a meek, gentle, and mild creature, a common symbol of Christ—a beast who would be drawn to seek out a virgin and trustingly lay his head in her lap . . . whereupon the huntsmen would leap out of concealment and fall upon him with spears and knives. The unicorn's horn, gained through such cruel deceptions as these, was probably the most valued magic object in European mysticism. In Edward Topsell's words, powdered unicorn horn "doth wonderfully help against poyson," and in addition is proof "against the pestilent feaver . . . against the bitings of ravenous Dogs, and the strokes or poysonsome stings of other creatures . . . and . . . against the belly or mawe worms." It also helped you to drink as much as you wished without becoming drunk, and even made "the teeth white or clear"—all this in addition to its well-known properties as an aphrodisiac. No *wonder* there are so few unicorns left!

Even in our busy modern world, the unicorn seems to have lost none of its power to fascinate, and is as potent an archetype today as it ever was in the Middle Ages . . . as witness the story that follows, which places a Unicorn against the tawdry neon-lit setting of—of all places—Miami Beach.

Jack Dann is the author or editor of eighteen books, including the novels *Starhiker* and *Junction,* the collection *Timetipping,* and many critically-acclaimed anthologies. His most recent book is the novel *The Man Who Melted,* a Nebula Award finalist.

A theme anthology on Unicorns is *Unicorns!,* edited by Jack Dann and Gardner Dozois.

The Black Horn

by

Jack Dann

FROM HIS OCEANFRONT room on the tenth floor of the Hotel Casablanca, Judge Stephen Steiner saw the unicorn standing in the shallow end of the swimming pool below. It was almost four in the morning, and most of the Christmas tree lights of the gambling ships three miles out on the ocean had been turned off. The expanse of beach ahead was dark and ominous, except for a single light that burned to the left on the beach that belonged to the Fontainebleau Hotel. But the Casablanca pool was illuminated by green and red underwater lights, giving the breeze-blown surface of the water an almost luminary quality, as of melted, rippling gems.

The unicorn looked grayish in the light, although surely it was white, and large, at least eighteen hands high from poll to hoof. Its mane was dark and shaggy; and at first Steiner thought it was a horse. But how strange to see a horse running loose on the beach at such an hour. There must be *laws* prohibiting animals from running loose, he thought. Miami Beach is a densely populated area . . . surely there must be a law. Perhaps this horse had run away from its owner . . . perhaps it was part of a road show . . . a circus.

My God, Steiner mused, how long has it been since *I've* been to a circus . . . ?

It was then that Steiner noticed that the horse had a

horn protruding from its wide forehead. He hadn't noticed it before because the horn was black . . . and also perhaps he didn't see it because he'd *assumed* he was looking at a horse, and horses didn't have horns. But now Steiner could see that horn. It looked like black marble. It was long and fluted and would make a vicious weapon. The horn reflected the green and red light as if the light were oil flowing along its conchlike spirals.

The unicorn dipped its horn into the pool, as if to neutralize some chlorine poison in the water, and then drank.

Steiner reached for his glasses, although he didn't really need them for distance. It couldn't be, he thought, yet there it was. Perhaps it was some advertising gimmick, but Steiner discounted that thought immediately. No one would let an animal run loose at this time of night, horned or otherwise.

Then the animal raised its head, as if sensing that it was being watched. It blew air through its muzzle and looked up at the building, slowly turning its head, scanning the windows on one story, then going on to another, until finally it seemed that the unicorn had found him. It seemed to be looking right *at* him, and Steiner felt transfixed, even through the thick, protective pane of glass. The unicorn knew he was there.

It was looking at *him*.

Steiner felt drawn to it . . . it was as beautiful as a childhood fantasy. Yet there was something dangerous and even sinister about it; its very being challenged Steiner's reason, and Steiner himself. Steiner felt an almost uncontrollable urge to smash through the window and jump . . . as if by some sort of television magic he'd be able to leap through the glass and land on the unicorn's back.

He found himself pressing dangerously hard against the plate-glass window as he stared down at the animal below that was still as stone, watching him.

Suddenly he *wanted* to jump.

"No!" he cried, feeling sudden, reeling terror, for he knew in that instant that if he could have jumped, he would have. It was as if he had glimpsed his own death deep in the eyes of that beautiful horned stallion staring up at him from the pool.

He turned away from the window and closed his eyes tightly, so tightly that everything turned purple for an instant. Then, slowly, he turned back toward the window. There was nothing there, just the metal lounge chairs situated around the illuminated pool, and the dark beach and ocean stretching into flat darkness. He looked to his left, toward the dimly lit Fontainebleau beach, but there was no sign of anything there, either.

Steiner closed the curtains and sat down on his uncomfortable double bed. His hands were shaking. He reached for a bottle of kosher brandy on the nightstand beside him and took a shot right out of the tinted green bottle. The stuff tasted like hell; it was coarse, not made as well as in the past—or perhaps he just remembered the past as being better in all respects.

He suddenly thought of his wife, Grace, who had died six months ago, God rest her sweet soul. Although he had been separated from her for over ten years, she had waited . . . waited for him to come back home. But he just couldn't have gone back. Grace would have been a constant reminder of everything Steiner feared. He needed younger women to feed his ego . . . to be in awe of him. They all probably thought he had money, but they were his only barricade against the fustiness of old age . . . against death itself. They kept him feeling young.

He felt the old guilt weighing down upon him. Grace, I'm sorry. . . .

The air-conditioner was on; it suddenly felt cold in the room. The graft on Steiner's back, where he had had a melanoma removed, hurt him tonight.

He'd inquire tomorrow at the desk whether there were any reports of a horse running loose. It *was* a horse, Steiner told himself, as he lay his head against the lumpy, overlarge pillow.

But he couldn't fall back to sleep.

After morning prayers in the makeshift synagogue on the fourth floor of the hotel, Steiner met his three sisters for breakfast. He escorted them to their table on the eastern side of the grand old dining room, which overlooked the beach and the perfectly blue ocean beyond. The table was prepared, and their waitress was waiting to attend them. Behind each setting was a glass of borsch mixed with sour cream. An unopened box of egg matzoth stood in the center of the table, as prominent as a bouquet of freshly cut flowers.

Steiner sat each of his sisters and then himself.

It was Passover, and Cele and Kate and Mollie had decided it would be better for Steiner if they all spent the holiday together at a hotel. Steiner could not disappoint them . . . somehow he would get through it. Although Cele was quite well off, she lived with her two sisters in Flatbush. Those two counted their pennies as if they were all being chased by the specter of relief. But Cele would spend her money for a good cause, especially if it involved family and religion . . . so this was a real vacation for them. And who knew how long Steiner might have them, anyway? Cele was the youngest, and she was seventy-seven.

Steiner was five years her junior. . . .

"It's another *beautiful* day," Cele said brightly, placing her green linen napkin on her lap. She wore a crisp red flowerpot hat that matched her square-shouldered jacket with patch pockets. It was as if she had never left the 1940s. Her dyed blonde hair was combed down smoothly, and tightly rolled up at the ends, and she was growing a bit thin on top. She had a long, oval face with great blue eyes, the same lively eyes that used to tease Steiner sixty years ago. Cele was going to make the best of her vacation in the sun. "Don't you think so, Stephen? Isn't it a beautiful day? Of course, you *live* here in Florida, so sunshine is probably old hat to you."

Steiner managed a smile, but he was in a disagreeable mood. Two hours of sitting and standing and praying with a congregation of evil-smelling, doddering old men had sapped him of all *joie de vivre* . . . had soured his morning. Although Steiner had always prided himself on being a religious man—he donned his prayer shawl and phylacteries every morning to pray toward the east, and it was to just that habit that he attributed what wealth and fame and good fortune he had acquired over the years—he couldn't *stand* being around old people. It was as simple as that. Steiner glanced uncomfortably around the room. Just sitting in the dining room made his flesh crawl—this entire hotel seemed to be filled with the most Orthodox and the oldest of Jews. Association could kill you

. . . *would* kill you. Make your flesh shrivel right up. That was another reason why Steiner had never gone back home; even before his beloved Grace had died, she smelled of the grave. Her skin had turned wrinkled and dry, and she exhuded an odor that could not be concealed by even the most expensive perfume.

He turned to Mariana, his waitress, who was ready to take their orders. Her very presence lightened his mood. She was Brazilian, dark, strong-featured, with full lips and tilted green eyes; her wiry black hair, though disguised in a bun, was long. She couldn't be more than twenty-one, the epitome of youth itself. Steiner flashed her a smile and ordered breakfast for his sisters and himself. He felt as if he were swelling up, regaining everything he had lost upstairs in the synagogue; and he heard a pompous affectation come into his voice, which was rather loud and bombastic, but he couldn't help himself . . . and anyway, a fine, articulated sentence had *always* impressed the young ladies.

When Mariana left and the busboy was out of earshot, Steiner's sister Kate said, "You know, Stephen, you make a fool out of yourself talking like that to the waitress." Kate was two years older than Cele, and she seemed to bear a grudge against any woman under sixty . . . or so Steiner thought. Kate had once been beautiful, high-breasted and thin-waisted, but now she had become puffy. She dyed her hair orange-red. Steiner nicknamed her "the Flying Nun" because she wrapped paper around her hair every night so it wouldn't muss.

"I'll thank you to mind your own business, ma'am," Steiner said stiffly, still using the artificial inflection he used with people he wished to impress. Cele gave Kate a nasty look and shook her head. Mollie, who was the oldest, didn't seem to be listening; instead she began talking about her children, who were supposed to visit her the week after Passover.

"Well, he *does* make a fool out of himself," Kate said to Cele.

"Stephen's right," Cele said, speaking sharply but in a low voice. "Mind your business."

"We can't even talk to each other around here," Kate said petulantly, as she smoothed out the napkin on her lap. Kate was overdressed in a silk gauze summer dress trimmed with black; she also wore a small pillbox hat with a veil.

"Why are you wearing a veil this morning?" Steiner asked. "You look like you're still in mourning."

"Well, I am . . . and you should be, too!" Then she caught herself. "I'm sorry, Stephen. I'm just not myself this morning—"

"On the contrary, you're very much yourself this morning," Mollie interrupted. Mollie wore a tan suit and blouse. Her hair was gray and frizzy, and she had a crinkly, Irish-looking face.

"Mollie, shut up," Kate said, and then continued talking to Steiner. "I didn't sleep well last night at all. I have a canker sore or something in my mouth, and my whole jaw's killing me. I don't even think I'll be able to eat."

"Oh, she'll eat," Mollie said sarcastically.

"And for your information"—Kate was still talking to Steiner—"I'm wearing a hat because this is a religious hotel, and religious women are supposed to wear hats. I can't help it if the hat has a veil."

"She's right, Stephen," Cele said. "Look around, all the women are wearing hats." She self-consciously adjusted her own hat.

"Of course I'm right," Kate said softly, indicating by her tone of voice that she was willing to drop the argument.

Mariana brought the food, purposely serving Stephen first, which stimulated a *tss*ing from Kate. Steiner teased the waitress by telling her how beautiful she looked, and she blushed and backed away.

Cele changed the subject by saying, "I think we should all sit by the pool when we're finished with breakfast. That would be nice, wouldn't it?"

"I'm going upstairs," Kate said. "I'm not feeling at all well."

"Kitty, you can take me upstairs with you," Mollie said. She was slightly infirm, and had trouble navigating stairs by herself.

"I think we should *all* spend at least a few minutes together in the sun," Cele said firmly—although she was the youngest, except for Steiner, *she* made all the decisions for her sisters.

"He shouldn't be out in the sun with his cancer," Kate said petulantly.

"You see, there she goes again," Mollie said to Cele. "Always starting *some*thing."

Cele flashed Kate a nasty look, and Mollie seemed pleased with herself. Then Cele said in a calm, quiet voice, "The morning sun is not dangerous, I'm told . . . it's the afternoon sun that has the dangerous rays."

Steiner nodded without paying much attention, but he always sided with Cele. She had enough of a cross to bear, living with and supporting her two sisters. He looked up and smiled generously at Mariana as she cleared the table. He could see the tiny dark hairs bristling on her arms, and could smell her slightly pungent, musk-like odor. She returned his smile, her cheeks dimpling, and for an instant their eyes met. Steiner felt his heart pump faster . . . felt his glands open up. He imagined making love to her . . . imagined her naked and holding him like a baby in a dimly lit bedroom. She would be beautiful naked, he thought, daydreaming about how she would look with her hair undone and hanging loose down her bare back. She would look like a wild animal. . . .

She's a perfect madonna, he thought . . . but then he had thought that about every waitress and shop clerk and hatcheck and typist he had ever dated. Perhaps later, when his sisters went upstairs for their afternoon nap, he'd work up the courage to go into the hotel kitchen and ask her out. He could buy her a tall, lemony drink by the pool, talk to her in whispers, caress her, and then take her back to her apartment. . . .

That thought alone gave him the strength to take his sisters outside to the pool, where they could gab and complain and gossip in Yiddish with their newfound octogenarian friends and neighbors.

Steiner did not go upstairs with his sisters, but made the excuse that he wished to take some more sun and maybe a walk before going inside. Cele seemed a bit agitated that he would get sick from *too* much sun, but he promised to sit in the shade near the cabanas. Steiner felt nothing but claustrophobic in the presence of his sisters.

"I wouldn't mind taking a walk myself," Cele said, standing over him and looking forlornly out to sea.

"Come, we'll take a walk now down Collins Avenue, and then you can sit in the sun if you really want to."

"Well, *I* have to go upstairs," Mollie said. "My feet are *killing* me."

Kate, who had wanted to go upstairs earlier, now said, "I wouldn't mind taking a walk and doing some window-shopping. It might be good for me, make me forget how much my jaw is aching me."

"Well, I can take Mollie upstairs and—" Cele said, but she gave up in mid-sentence, accepting her responsibility to her sisters. Steiner could see the trapped frustration in her face. "All right," she said resignedly, "I suppose we should just go upstairs. . . ."

"I'll take a walk with you, Stephen," Kate said.

"Either we'll *all* take a walk or we'll all go upstairs together," Cele said, her hands gently shaking, whether from age or anger, Steiner didn't know. But he felt guilty, for he had sacrificed Cele to them just so he could be alone . . . Cele deserved better than that. The poor old girl. . . .

But Steiner was on his feet as soon as his sisters disappeared into the side entrance of the hotel. It's too hot out here anyway, he told himself, sweating under his polyester powder-blue shirt and matching slacks. He wore a white jacket and white loafers. As he passed, the gossips and wrinkled sunbathers nodded to him and said, "Good morning, Judge."

Steiner hadn't been a judge for thirty years, and even then had served only one term. But Steiner liked the title—it opened "doors" for him. Everyone called him "Judge" at the very exclusive Boca Club, where he was a member. In fact, he had had the heraldic blue and white and gold emblem sewed on all his sports jackets. Of course, he didn't attend very many functions there, as they were very expensive. But he had been known to take his dates to the club for swanky luncheons. Perhaps Mariana would visit him at his home in Fort Lauderdale, and he could take her, too. . . .

He was immersed in that daydream as he stepped through the coffee shop beside the pool area and into the large kitchen behind. There were busboys and waiters and waitresses bustling around, carrying large aluminum trays in and out of the two wide swinging doors that led into the dining area. Cooks and helpers were working at sinks and long wooden tables. Squashed prunes and apples and matzo brie and puddles of soup and juice and coffee discolored the white tile floor.

Mariana stepped backward into the kitchen, pushing the door open. She was holding a tray filled with glasses and dishes and silverware.

"Mariana!" Steiner said, overly loud. She turned to him, looking surprised, but no one else seemed to notice his presence . . . or care.

She put the heavy tray down on one of the tables and said, "Yes, Judge? Is something wrong?" She tilted her head in a most attractive manner, Steiner thought.

"Yes . . . I just thought—" and suddenly the words left him. He felt awkward and foolish . . . and suddenly paranoid that she would think he was a "dirty old man." But that was plain stupid! he told himself. She doesn't even know why I'm here yet. "Do you have any plans for this evening?" he blurted out. But even as he spoke, he realized that he had lost the advantage entirely . . . that now *she* was in the position of power.

"I'm not sure what you mean, Judge," she said, looking uncomfortable. "I'll be taking care of your table tonight, is that—"

"No . . . I mean, would you care to have a drink with me *after* dinner, after you've finished working. Perhaps we could meet at the Fontainebleau . . . by the bar. It's very nice there."

"Well . . . I don't know." She was actually blushing. *That's* a good sign.

"I'll be waiting for you at poolside at ten o'clock," Steiner said with authority, feeling much better about the venture now.

"I'm really not supposed to be going out with the guests," she said coyly, her eyes averted from his. "I could get fired, and—"

"Well . . . *I'll* be waiting for you at"—Steiner looked at his thin gold watch for effect—"ten o'clock sharp."

"I've really got to get back to work, please. . . ."

"Ten o'clock," Steiner said smartly, using his best judicial tone. Mariana nodded once, shyly, her eyes still averted from his.

Steiner turned heel back to the pool area.

Once outside, back in the sun, he felt relieved and full of nervous energy. He felt like a schoolboy dreaming about the girl he was going to take to the senior prom. He couldn't stand the thought of going back to his room or sitting in the hotel lobby, which smelled of old age and was filled with urns of fake flowers and plants. He couldn't bear to look at another old man or woman. He couldn't sleep, and he had just eaten.

He just wanted to be alone and daydream. . . .

He found himself walking along the sand toward the ocean. Perhaps he'd walk along the beach to the Fontainebleau, have a drink, and then return down Collins Avenue, thus making a circle. But once he reached the Fontainebleau and saw the pool and bar to his left, he just didn't feel like stopping. He was too filled with energy to stop and sit, so he continued walking, enjoying the brisk breeze coming off the ocean, the healthy smell of the salt air, and the pounding of the surf just inches away from his sand-encrusted white loafers. He dreamed about Mariana . . . and imagined himself as a young man courting her, a young man with thick black hair and a strong, handsome face. A strong man eyed by every bikini-clad woman he passed. . . .

But Steiner was beginning to swelter in the afternoon heat. The sun was unbearable, and Steiner had misjudged how much of it he could take. The ocean breeze, which was at first cool and refreshing, now felt hot and muggy. He turned around and started back to his hotel.

Thank goodness he didn't have far to go.

Steiner wouldn't have seen the unicorn if it hadn't made a snorting noise as he passed. It stood behind a dozen one-man red and white sailboats leaning against an old pier that was in disrepair. It stood in the shadows, as if to cool off.

The unicorn carefully stepped out from the boats and gazed at Steiner with its ocean-blue eyes. It pawed the sand with its heel, sending ribbons of sand into the air to be carried away on the wind.

Steiner stopped, transfixed again by the unicorn. He broke out in a sweat, but it was cold sweat, and from fear rather than heat. "What do you *want?*" he asked, feeling foolish talking to an animal like this, but he had to break the spell with *something* . . . a word, the sound of his voice. Suddenly Steiner was aware of a myriad of tiny details: the soft pinkness of the unicorn's muzzle; the white whiskers growing out of its chin and nostrils; its coarse, shaggy white mane and fetlocks; its cloven hooves worn from the sand; and the strange, ridged black horn that looked as if it had somehow erupted from the animal's forehead. In fact, it looked glassy, as if it might have indeed been formed from lava. In the bright sunlight it took on a reddish sheen, which seemed to deepen at the tip. Steiner was acutely aware of the splashing and gurgling of the surf, but he couldn't make out any *human* sounds, except for his own quickened breathing. This was an empty stretch of beach. Steiner was shaking, and he felt weak. The animal was so *large*. It looked like a huge Morgan, with its muscular back, strong neck, and large head. It stood square, its legs right under its shoulders. The unicorn was overpowering . . . yet it *seemed* to be gentle. It didn't move, but seemed to be made of porcelain and coal. It just stared at Steiner; and it was as if the unicorn's eyes were blue magnets pulling him closer . . . and Steiner imagined how it would be to ride this great beast, to feel its bulk beneath him and the wind whistling in his ears and the salt spray biting his chest and face. He could ride it along the beach . . . along the ocean.

The unicorn took a cautious step toward Steiner.

Suddenly Steiner remembered last night and broke the reverie. He stepped back in terror, almost falling over his own feet. The unicorn took on an entirely different guise as Steiner remembered how he had wanted to jump from his window at the mere sight of the beast. The unicorn—as if reading Steiner's thoughts—whinnied and pawed the sand. Then, ready to charge, it lowered its head.

The sharp black horn was pointed directly at Steiner.

And Steiner saw the unicorn for what it was: death. Death in its simplest, most beautiful guise. "No," he whispered to the beast. "No!" he screamed, hating it. He turned from the unicorn and ran, his narrow-toed Italian white loafers heeling into the soft sand. His eyes burned and seemed to go out of focus as he ran. His heart felt as if it were pounding in his throat. He could *hear* the unicorn behind him. He could *feel* the unicorn's horn at his back, ready to slash him wide open.

But Steiner wasn't ready for death. He wanted to live. He *had* to live. If death was going to take him, it would have to take him on the run. Steiner wasn't going to make it easy. He wasn't going to slip into any eternal slumber with a toothless good-bye. Not Steiner.

He ran as hard as he could, the blood pulsing in his chest and head, making him dizzy, until he tripped over a tangled, polished piece of driftwood and fell headlong into the sand. He turned backward, resolved to face death with his eyes open.

But the unicorn was gone . . . disappeared. There were no tracks, except for his own, no outline of equine heel or bar or furrow in the soft white sand. Steiner tried to catch his breath. He felt at once relieved and anxious. He *had* been chased by something. His breathing began to return to normal, but he had a flash of searing pain in his abdomen, and his arms and shoulders felt heavy and began to ache. He broke out into a cold sweat. He felt clammy and chilled and nauseated. It was the fall, he told himself . . . and the exercise. He hadn't run like that in forty years.

But one thing was certain: he *had* seen a horse with a horn. It might have been some sort of publicity trick, but it was no hallucination. Steiner wasn't the type to hallucinate. He might have had some crazy thoughts when the beast was chasing him, but then, who wouldn't? He felt foolish, running as he had. The damned thing obviously hadn't been chasing him, or he would have seen it when he had turned around. Actually, if it had *really* been chasing him it would have run him through with that horn in no time flat.

Still . . . it *had* to be some sort of publicity stunt, Steiner thought.

Steiner told his sisters he wasn't feeling very well and stayed in his room. He forced himself to take a swallow of brandy and tried to sleep, but he felt feverish. Frenzied, unconnected thoughts flashed through his mind. He tucked himself under the covers. The pain seemed to lift.

I'm *not* crazy, he thought, raising himself up on his right elbow to gaze below. The ocean was turquoise green in the shallows and deep cyan blue farther out. The sun was bright and warm and reassuring. Although no one was swimming in the pool, there were over thirty people sitting in deck chairs and chatting while others walked about. Everything was perfectly all right, exactly as it should be, as ordinary as bread.

Then Steiner saw the unicorn lift its head out of the ocean.

At first, he thought he was seeing a wave, a distant whitecap, but there was no mistaking that black fluted horn. There were those blue eyes and thick white mane and muscular neck. The unicorn rose out of the water, revealing itself little by little as it moved into the shallows, until the water was only up to its knees and it walked forward, kicking, lifting its long legs out of the water, onto the beach. The unicorn was dripping wet and as big as life. It stood on the edge of the empty beach and looked up at Steiner, as foamy water purled past its hooves. It *knew* Steiner was there. It had come for him again.

"Go away!" he shouted, as he shakily got up from his bed. As the pain began to radiate into his shoulders and arms and chest, he pulled the curtains closed.

But he knew the unicorn was still out there, waiting. . . .

Steiner felt much better by dinnertime. He had rested, and the aching in his arms and chest was gone, as were the sweats and fever. Steiner was prone to night sweats, anyway. He was apprehensive about opening the heavy curtains, so he left well enough alone . . . he had had enough excitement for one day.

He dressed informally in tan shirt and slacks and went downstairs to pick up a newspaper in the lobby. He leafed through it outside the shabby hotel shop that sold magazines, newspapers, aspirin, suntan lotions, cheap trinkets, and sunglasses. He was disappointed—there wasn't even a mention of a circus, or a carnival, or a runaway horse . . . or a unicorn. Well, *someone* must have seen the damn thing, too, he thought. Surely, it will be in *tomorrow's* papers.

He put the newspaper back on the rack and met his

sisters for dinner in the dining room. He felt a bit hesitant about seeing Mariana before their forthcoming tryst at the Fontainebleau, but it couldn't be avoided. If he *didn't* show up for dinner, she might think he was ill or not interested, and she might not meet him later. Still, he felt uncomfortable. But when she took his order, and Steiner smiled at her, she returned it. She even blushed. That made Steiner feel very good indeed.

Everything else went along as it had for the past five days. Cele and Kate and Mollie discussed the menu and chose each dish with care, but when the food actually came, each one complained bitterly that she should have ordered a different entrée. Kate complained about her sore mouth. Mollie talked about her children and "the grandkids" and told Cele that the veal was the wrong color.

After dinner and a wink at Mariana, Steiner accompanied his sisters to the obligatory 7:30 show in the ballroom, where the hotel rabbi—a slick stand-up comedian, who had made records and played the Catskills every year—was performing. Steiner didn't listen to the stale jokes. He kept glancing at his watch. After the show, he kissed his sisters good night and went to his room to change into fresh, more formal clothes for his date with Mariana. He felt a bit weak and dizzy, but he was determined to go out tonight, as if he had to prove something to himself.

As he entered the room, he examined himself in the full-length mirror on the bathroom door. He had a shock of white hair, which was yellowed a bit in the back; deep brown eyes; a thin nose; and a full, sensual mouth—it was a strong, angular face that had loosened with age. Although the face-lift two years ago had helped, lines still mapped his face. But he certainly didn't look his age.

He began to feel anxious here in the room, but he made a point of not going near the closed curtains. He could hear the faint murmur of the surf; it was like gentle white noise. He wondered if the unicorn was still out there as he changed into a smart-looking chocolate brown suit with a matching tie and a white-on-white shirt. His brogues were a bit scuffed; he reminded himself to buy polish. He concentrated on small details.

But he couldn't leave the room this time without finding out if the unicorn was still out there. He pulled open the drapes and looked out the salt-stained window . . . he looked by the pool and on the beaches . . . he looked at the white-crested black waves of the ocean.

The pool area and the beach were empty.

There was not a unicorn to be seen.

Steiner took a small table in front of the enclosed driftwood bar poolside at the Fontainebleau. The pool was huge and kidney-shaped, and Steiner enjoyed a tall whiskey and soda while he watched floodlit water cascading down a stonework waterfall into the pool. Palms were spaced around the pool area, and green and blue lights gave the place a festive, romantic atmosphere. To his left were the glass doors that led into the Fontainebleau shopping center; to his right, across an expanse of lawn, was the new ten-story addition to the hotel. Cozy paths wound their way between palmettos and hibiscuses, and the ocean was a dull, dark pounding behind him. Guests in evening clothes, in jeans and tubetops, in bathing suits and clogs, in gaudy slacks and Hawaiian shirts promenaded past him. Two callow-looking, teenaged lovers walked by, hand in hand, followed by a small group of executives and their wives. The whole world seemed to be carved into *twos.* But Steiner felt strong with excitement and anticipation; he felt dashing, good-looking, if just a trifle tired.

As he sat, waiting, two women who looked to be in their late thirties sat down at the wooden table beside him. One was dumpy-looking and plump; she wore clogs, white Bermuda shorts that were too tight for her, and a very revealing pink halter top. Her hair was blonde and coarse, obviously bleached. Her companion, in contrast, looked quite demure. She was tall and skinny, with short-cropped brown hair and a long, hollow-cheeked face. She wore a blue outfit—a blue blazer and a pleated white and blue skirt—which was actually quite stylish. But she had the worst teeth that Steiner had ever seen. Her two front teeth were long and crooked and widely spaced, and one protruded beyond the other. Obviously, they should have been pulled long ago. She must be a country girl, Steiner thought. Country people don't take care of their teeth . . . they hate dentists.

Steiner ignored the women and waited for Mariana. He gazed at the path that led from the shopping center: the direction that Mariana should be coming from. He sipped his drink and eavesdropped on the conversation of the men at the bar. From what he could overhear, they were microprocessor executives from Atlanta here on a convention. They talked mostly about getting laid.

The blonde woman kept smiling at the men at the bar. To Steiner's surprise, the ploy worked, because when the waitress came to take her order, one of the men insisted on buying the blonde woman a drink. He was rather good-looking in an athletic sort of way . . . what the hell would he want with someone like *that?* Steiner mused. Steiner couldn't help but stare. The man sat down, winked at his friends at the bar, and put his arm around the back of the blonde woman's chair. She was cooing and shifting about, smiling and nuzzling closer to the man as introductions were made. The other woman craned her long neck slightly to join in the conversation, but she looked uncomfortable, although she was the type who *always* looks uncomfortable. Steiner watched the executive lean forward to get a better look at the blonde's breasts; but Steiner was caught staring by the tall woman, who was looking directly at him. She smiled at him without revealing her teeth. Steiner nodded curtly and turned away.

That's *all* I need, he told himself. But he was getting anxious. Where *was* Mariana, anyway? It's ten o'clock already. I was a fool not to have gotten her home phone number. Dammit! Perhaps I can call the hotel . . . she just might be working late. Steiner called from the bar, where the rest of the men were taking bets on whether their friend would get laid or not. Steiner watched the burly executive making his pass at the blonde. Then Mr. Lareina, the maître d', came to the phone and told Steiner that Mariana had left shortly after nine. "All right, thanks," Steiner said and hung up. He wasn't going to abase himself by asking for her home phone—Lareina wouldn't give it out, anyway.

Steiner sat back down at his table. He felt dazed. He brooded and stared out at the pastel-lit path leading to the

Fontainebleau. Perhaps Mariana went home first to change.

Then he saw her. He straightened up in his chair, and waved excitedly to the dark-haired woman approaching the pool area. She was walking quickly on high heels, as if late for an appointment. Steiner felt a warm rush of anticipation. He started to get up as she approached . . . and only then realized that she *wasn't* Mariana. Up close, she didn't look like Mariana at all. She looked quizzically at Steiner, who was half out of his chair.

Steiner was mortified. He sat down reflexively. How could I have made such a mistake? he asked himself. He thought about going home, slinking away, crawling into his cool, uncomfortable bed, but he just *couldn't* leave. Mariana *had* to show. He *wouldn't* be stood up! Pain began to radiate once again throughout his arms and shoulders, then down into his chest.

"Girl troubles?" asked the skinny woman sitting at the table beside Steiner. She had a thin, reedy voice.

Steiner turned toward her. "I *beg* your pardon," he said, annoyed.

The woman tried to smile without revealing her teeth. "Your friend . . . she might just be late, that's all," she said nervously. But she was persistent. "Why don't you have a drink with *us?* We'll cheer you up, we're good company . . . and here I am a third wheel. Help us out."

"Thank you kindly, but I don't think so," Steiner said. The skinny woman pouted, an exaggerated moue.

"Oh, c'mon, buddy *I'll* buy you a drink," the executive said as he self-consciously ran his hand through his short-cropped hair. But Steiner knew his type, all right. He had probably been a bully when he was a kid, and a ROTC lieutenant in the army, and now he's some sort of zipperhead IBM-type manager who makes life hell for everyone under him. He was obviously looking for a way to cut the blonde away from her friend, and he was trying to use Steiner as a foil. "C'mon, what the hell," the man said, flashing a boyish smile, and he jumped his chair toward Steiner and then pulled his table over until it was touching Steiner's. The blonde woman laughed when the drinks spilled, and then she and her friend moved their chairs closer, too. Steiner was too embarrassed to do anything but accept the situation. He felt even more uncomfortable with the skinny woman pressing close to his elbow.

The executive waved down the waitress, and Steiner ordered another drink, which he didn't need . . . he was achy and dizzy as it was, and his right arm felt numb. "So, friend, where do you hail from?" the man asked Steiner as he massaged the blonde's arm, purposely letting his fingers brush against her breast. The skinny woman leaned closer to Steiner, as if expecting him to answer in a whisper.

"I'm from upstate New York," Steiner said. "Binghamton." He felt his skin crawl. The woman was *too* close to him. She smelled of cheap perfume, and she had chicken skin. God . . . he could imagine what she *really* smelled like.

"Is that so," the skinny woman said. "I've been through there. I used to live in Milford, Pennsylvania. Small world, isn't it?"

Steiner didn't have anything to say to that; he just leaned away from her and nodded glumly.

"I'm from Detroit," the executive said. "I'm in systems management . . . mostly consultation work for engineering firms. What's your line?"

"I'm a judge . . . was a judge, I'm retired now," Steiner replied.

"A *judge!"* the skinny woman said, brightening. "Jeeze, we don't have *any* manners here at this table. I'm Joline, and my friend here is Sandy, and he's . . . *oops"*—she said, turning to the man from Detroit—"I've forgotten your name."

"Frank," the man said, paying the waitress for the new round of drinks.

"I'll take care of that," Steiner said stiffly, automatically, but Frank wouldn't hear of it.

"You haven't told us *your* name," Joline said.

God, she has a chalkboard voice, Steiner thought. "Stephen," he mumbled.

"That's a very nice name," Joline said, warming to her role as Steiner's new companion. "It fits you, somehow."

Stephen felt trapped at his own table. He began to perspire. Joline primly sipped her drink—something white and frothy in a tall, frosted glass—through two short narrow cocktail straws. Steiner was of the opinion that sipping a drink through those straws, which were made for decoration, was like drinking coffee out of a cup without removing the spoon. Joline wriggled toward him. Every one of her movements seemed exaggerated. "I think you take life very seriously," she said, looking at him intently, as if she were working her way into something profound.

I've *got* to get out of here! Steiner thought. He looked at his watch, making it very apparent that he had other things to do. Frank and Sandy certainly didn't take any notice; they were kissing each other right there at the table like two high school kids on a bench at a roller-skating rink. I *can't* be seen with these people, Steiner told himself. Jesus Christ. . . . He glanced at Joline, who smiled and blushed a little and then firmly pressed her leg against his. She looked somehow limp, as if waiting to be embraced. Oh, Jesus . . . Steiner thought.

Frank whispered something to Sandy and then said to Steiner: "Steve, if you've no objections, we're going to take a little walk . . . we'll be right back. Give you two a chance to talk. Nice meeting you."

"See you soon, honey," Sandy said to Joline, smiling warmly as she stood up.

"We'll hold down the fort," Joline said shyly, her knee still wedged woodenly against Steiner's.

"Would you care for another drink?" Steiner asked Joline after the others had left. He had to say *some*thing to her. Her silence was oppressive, and he was uncomfortable enough as it was.

"Yes . . . thank you." Joline didn't seem to be able to look at Steiner now that her friend had left, but she leaned against him until he said, "Excuse me," and tried to disengage himself.

"You aren't going to leave me here alone, are you?" Joline asked. There was a pleading in her voice, and suddenly Steiner felt sorry for her . . . she was lonely and ugly and past her prime. He felt both loathing and pity. "No . . . I'll be right back," he said as he stood up.

"Promise?" Joline asked coyly, trying to smile again without revealing her crooked teeth.

"I promise," Steiner said. Jesus, Mary . . . he thought

as he walked away. Is *that* the way Mariana saw *me* . . . the way I see that poor old girl at the table? Could I be *that* repulsive to her? He knew the answer . . . he was an old man wearing old man's pastel clothes. He was an old man carrying a Jewish bankroll. No! he insisted. His skin might be like old clothes, but *he* wasn't old. Suddenly he understood why his wife, Grace, may she rest in peace, had become obsessed with butterflies. She had *filled* her house with butterfly-shaped bric-a-brac before she died.

He walked to the far end of the bar, as if he were going to the men's room, then ducked under the rope that separated deck from beach. Joline would be sitting back there alone, waiting. But I *can't* go back, he thought. He shivered at the thought of kissing that mouth . . . feeling that long, protruding tooth with the tip of his tongue . . . smelling her odor.

He walked along surf's edge, shoes squishing in the wet sand, and he became lost to the sound of waves pummeling the shell-strewn beach . . . lost to the waiting darkness ahead . . . lost below the clear sky filled with clusters of silent stars.

He passed a small hotel, which had one beachlamp on overhead, and standing upon the shadow line was the unicorn. It had been waiting for Steiner. It stood tall and gazed at him, only its great horned head clearly visible. The unicorn's blue eyes seemed to glow, the same melting, beautiful color of the water in the Blue Grotto in Capri. Steiner stopped, and suddenly remembered being in Europe as a young man, suddenly felt the selfsame awe of the world he had once felt. He also felt lost and empty. He grieved for himself and for the poor woman waiting for him at the Fontainebleau. What would she tell her friends when they returned? Would she, indeed, even wait for them?

Steiner gazed back at the unicorn, trying to make certain it was real and not just the play of shadows, or his imagination. It was *not* his imagination, he told himself. Staring into the unicorn's eyes seemed to stimulate memories he had forgotten for years:

He remembered swimming in the Mediterranean. He remembered a two-week vacation in Atlantic City with Grace and his two sons. He remembered riding bicycles on the boardwalk with his family. He remembered cooking eggs at four o'clock in the morning after a party and permitting the kids to come down and eat, too. He remembered his first trial . . . as a lawyer and as a judge. He remembered uneventful days with Grace . . . beautiful, precious, never-to-be-recovered days. He remembered coming home to problems with the boys and sharing dinnertime conversation across the table with Grace.

And he suddenly, desperately missed it all. He wanted the days back!

He also remembered the nameless women, and how Grace had begged him to come back. She had waited, but couldn't wait long enough. He wanted to go home . . . to Grace. He looked into the unicorn's sad eyes and saw himself, as if in a mirror. He was an empty old man who had lost his life to foolishness. He had wasted all of Grace's love . . . and now it was too late to make reparation.

Tears trembled and worked their way down his face, and the unicorn stepped toward him. It walked slowly, as if not to frighten him. Steiner stepped to the side, but did not try to run. The beast lay down beside him and rested its head in the sand, a gesture of submission. Steiner nervously extended his hand toward the unicorn's muzzle. The unicorn didn't flinch or move, and Steiner stroked its forehead. He touched its fluted black horn and saw that its tip looked red, as if dipped in blood.

He felt a contentment radiate through him as he stroked the unicorn. He also felt the throbbing return of the pain in his chest and arms, yet as the pain became greater, so did his sense of being removed from it. As he rested against the unicorn, he felt it quiver, then begin to move. It raised its head, all the while watching Steiner, but before it stood up, Steiner pulled himself upon its back. I *can* ride the beast, Steiner thought as he held onto its coarse mane as the unicorn brought itself to full height.

"Come on, boy," Steiner whispered, feeling an almost forgotten heart-pounding joy. The unicorn sensed it, too, because it broke into a playful canter. It shook its head, as if miming laughter, and kicked its hind legs into the air. Steiner held the horse tightly with his legs. He felt his youthful strength returning. He felt at one with the unicorn. The unicorn jumped, galloped, and stopped short, only to sprint forward again. It ran full-out, edging closer to the sea, until it was splashing *in* the water. Steiner was shouting and laughing, unmindful of anything but the perfect joy of the moment. Steiner felt wonderful. For the first time in his life, everything was *right.* He felt he could do *anything.* He was at one with the world . . . and he rode and balanced on the back of the unicorn as if he had spent the past forty years of his life riding the wind.

Suddenly the unicorn turned and headed straight out into the ocean. Waves broke against its knees and chest. Steiner's legs were immersed in water. "What are you *doing?*" Steiner shouted joyfully, unafraid but holding on tightly to its neck. The unicorn walked deeper into the sea, past the breakers, until it was swimming smoothly and quickly through the warm, salty water. The sea was like a sheet of black glass, made of the same stuff as the unicorn's horn. It seemed to go on forever.

As the dark water rose over Steiner, he finally accepted the wreck of his life.

The unicorn lifted its great head as it descended into the sea. Steiner took hold of its red-tipped horn, and the unicorn carried him gently down into the ocean's cool, waiting depths.

THE GIANT

Giants seem to come in many varieties, from the big to the very big indeed. Some—the giants of Greek mythology and Norse legend, for instance, and of fairy tales like Jack-in-the-Beanstalk—are *very* big. One of the Greek giants, Tityus, covered nine acres of ground when stretched out flat, and another, Enceladus, was so big the gods had to pile Mount Aetna on top of him to keep him down. In Norse myth, the giant Skrymir was so big that Thor and Loki unwittingly slept in his glove one night, thinking it a "very large hall." Even Bran the Blessed, while not quite in that league, is still huge enough that the Welsh myth describes him as looking like an approaching mountain as he wades across the channel between Wales and Ireland—wading the sea because no boat was big enough to hold him.

Several folklorists have suggested that some of the really immense giants, particularly those in the Celtic tradition, had once been gods . . . now dwindled and diminished from gods to "mere" giants with the passage of time, and especially with the coming of Christianity to the pagan North. (Interestingly, William Butler Yeats offers the exact opposite suggestion, saying that "when the pagan gods of Ireland—the *Tuath-De-Danān*—robbed of worship and offerings, grew smaller and smaller in the popular imagination, until they turned into the fairies, the pagan heroes grew bigger and bigger, until they turned into the giants.") Some giants are reasonably human-looking, some have several heads, some are grotesque and monstrous of face, with huge fangs or tusks (although here we are beginning to approach the ambiguous dividing line between giants and trolls or ogres). Sometimes they are man-eaters, like the fearsome Jack-in-Irons who haunts Yorkshire lanes at night, or like the giants in a dozen fairy tales. Sometimes they are benevolent and good-natured, willing to be helpful to human folks—although, sadly, it seems to be true that the benign giants are *also* usually portrayed as being rather stupid, and are often taken shameful advantage of by the humans they try to assist. Sometimes humans even trade on their good nature to trick them to their doom.

Interestingly, giants seem to be slowly getting smaller as the twentieth century progresses, continuing the dwindling process begun in dim antiquity. The really huge, mountain-sized giants are somewhat out of fashion, and most of the giants who turn up these days in the pages of fantasy literature are closer to ten feet tall than a hundred. That's still pretty big, of course—although, as the giant in the story that follows discovers, there's no man so big that he can't run up against a problem that's bigger still . . .

Manly Wade Wellman is perhaps best known in the fantasy field for his series of stories detailing the supernatural adventures of "John the Minstrel" or "Silver John," of which "Walk Like a Mountain" is one. The Silver John stories were collected in *Who Fears The Devil?* and in recent years there have been Silver John novels as well, the most recent of which is *The Voice of the Mountain.* Wellman has won two World Fantasy Awards, one the prestigious Life Achievement Award.

Walk Like a Mountain

by

Manly Wade Wellman

ONCE AT SKY NOTCH, I never grudged the trouble getting there. It was so purely pretty, I was glad outlanders weren't apt to crowd in and spoil all.

The Notch cut through a tall peak that stood against a higher cliff. Steep brushy faces each side, and a falls at the back that made a trickly branch, with five pole cabins along the waterside. Corn patches, a few pigs in pens, chickens running round, a cow tied up one place. It wondered me how they ever got a cow up there. Laurels grew, and viney climbers, and mountain flowers in bunches and sprawls. The water made a happy noise. Nobody moved in the yards or at the doors, so I stopped by a tree and hollered the first house.

"Hello the house!" I called. "Hello to the man of the house and all inside!"

A plank door opened about an inch. "Hello to yourself," a gritty voice replied me. "Who's that out there with the guitar?"

I moved from under the tree. "My name's John. Does Mr. Lane Jarrett live up here? Got word for him, from his old place on Drowning Creek."

The door opened wider, and there stood a skimpy little man with gray whiskers. "That's funny," he said.

The funnyness I didn't see. I'd known Mr. Lane Jarrett

years back, before he and his daughter Page moved to Sky Notch. When his uncle Jeb died and heired him some money, I'd agreed to carry it to Sky Notch, and, gentlemen, it was a long, weary way getting there.

First a bus, up and down and through mountains, stop at every pig trough for passengers. I got off at Charlie's Jump—who Charlie was, nor why or when he jumped, nobody there can rightly say. Climbed a high ridge, got down the far side, then a twenty-devil way along a deep valley river. Up another height, another beyond that. Then it was night, and nobody would want to climb the steep face above, because it was grown up with the kind of trees that the dark melts in around you. I made a fire and took my supper rations from my pocket. Woke at dawn and climbed up and up and up, and here I was.

"Funny, about Lane Jarrett," gritted the little man out. "Sure you ain't come about that business?"

I looked up the walls of the Notch. Their tops were toothy rocks, the way you'd think those walls were two jaws, near about to close on what they'd caught inside them. Right then the Notch didn't look so pretty.

"Can't say, sir," I told him, "till I know what business you mean."

"Rafe Enoch!" he boomed out the name, like firing two barrels of a gun. "That's what I mean!" Then he appeared to remember his manners, and came out, puny in his jeans and no shoes on his feet. "I'm Oakman Dillon," he named himself. "John—that's your name, huh? Why you got that guitar?"

"I pick it some," I replied him. "I sing." Tweaking the silver strings, I sang a few lines:

By the shore of Lonesome River
Where the waters ebb and flow,
Where the wild red rose is budding
And the pleasant breezes blow,

It was there I spied the lady
That forever I adore,
As she was a-lonesome walking
By the Lonesome River shore. . . .

"Rafe Enoch!" he grit-grated out again. "Carried off Miss Page Jarrett the way you'd think she was a banty chicken!"

Slap, I quieted the strings with my palm. "Mr. Lane's little daughter Page was stolen away?"

He sat down on the door-log. "She ain't suchy little daughter. She's six foot maybe three inches—taller'n you, even. Best-looking big woman I ever see, brown hair like a wagonful of home-cured tobacco, eyes green and bright as a fresh-squoze grape pulp."

"Fact?" I said, thinking Page must have changed a right much from the long-leggy little girl I'd known, must have grown tall like her daddy and her dead mammy, only taller. "Is this Rafe Enoch so big, a girl like that is right for him?"

"She's puny for him. He's near about eight foot tall, best I judge." Oakman Dillon's gray whiskers stuck out like a mad cat's. "He just grabbed her last evening, where she walked near the fall, and up them rocks he went like a possum up a jack oak."

I sat down on a stump. "Mr. Lane's a friend of mine. How can I help?"

"Nobody can't help, John. It's right hard to think you ain't knowing all this stuff. Don't many strangers come up here. Ain't room for many to live in the Notch."

"Five homes," I counted them with my eyes.

"Six. Rafe Enoch lives up at the top." He jerked his head toward the falls. "Been there a long spell—years, I reckon, since when he run off from somewhere. Heard tell he broke a circus man's neck for offering him a job with a show. He built up top the falls, and he used to get along with us. Thanked us kindly for a mess of beans or roasting ears. Lately, he's been mean-talking."

"Nobody mean-talked him back? Five houses in the Notch mean five grown men—couldn't they handle one giant?"

"Giant size ain't all Rafe Enoch's got." Again the whiskers bristled up. "Why! He's got powers, like he can make rain fall—"

"No," I put in quick. "Can't even science men do that for sure."

"I ain't studying science men. Rafe Enoch says for rain

to fall, down it comes, any hour day or night he speaks. Could drown us out of this Notch if he had the mind."

"And he carried off Page Jarrett," I went back to what he'd said.

"That's the whole truth, John. Up he went with her in the evening, daring us to follow him."

I asked, "Where are the other Notch folks?"

"Up yonder by the falls. Since dawn we've been talking Lane Jarrett back from climbing up and getting himself neck-twisted. I came to feed my pigs, now I'm heading back."

"I'll go with you," I said, and since he didn't deny me I went.

The falls dropped down a height as straight up as a chimney, and a many times taller, and their water boiled off down the branch. Either side of the falls, the big boulder rocks piled on top of each other like stones in an almighty big wall. Looking up, I saw clouds boiling in the sky, dark and heavy and wet-looking, and I remembered what Oakman Dillon had said about big Rafe Enoch's rain-making.

A bunch of folks were there, and I made out Mr. Lane Jarrett, bald on top and bigger than the rest. I touched his arm, and he turned.

"John! Ain't seen you a way-back time. Let me make you known to these here folks."

He called them their first names—Yoot, Ollie, Bill, Duff, Miss Lulie, Miss Sara May and so on. I said I had a pocketful of money for him, but he just nodded and wanted to know did I know what was going on.

"Looky up against them clouds, John. That pointy rock. My girl Page is on it."

The rock stuck out like a spur on a rooster's leg. Somebody was scrouched down on it, with the clouds getting blacker above, and a long, long drop below.

"I see her blue dress," allowed Mr. Oakman, squinting up. "How long she been there, Lane?"

"I spotted her at sunup," said Mr. Lane. "She must have got away from Rafe Enoch and crope out there during the night. I'm going to climb."

He started to shinny up a rock, up clear of the brush

around us. And, Lord, the laugh that came down on us! Like a big splash of water, it was clear and strong, and like water it made us shiver. Mr. Oakman caught onto Mr. Lane's ankle and dragged him down.

"Ain't a God's thing ary man or woman can do, with him waiting up there," Mr. Oakman argued.

"But he's got Page," said Mr. Lane busting loose again. I grabbed his elbow.

"Let me," I said.

"You, John? You're a stranger, you ain't got no pick in this."

"This big Rafe Enoch would know if it was you or Mr. Oakman or one of these others climbing, he might fling down a rock or the like. But I'm strange to him. I might wonder him, and he might let me climb all the way up."

"Then?" Mr. Lane said, frowning.

"Once up, I might could do something."

"Leave him try it," said Mr. Oakman to that.

"Yes," said one of the lady-folks.

I slung my guitar behind my shoulder and took to the rocks. No peep of noise from anywhere for maybe a minute of climbing. I got on about the third or fourth rock from the bottom, and that clear, sky-ripping laugh came from over my head.

"Name yourself!" roared down the voice that had laughed.

I looked up. How high was the top I can't say, but I made out a head and shoulders looking down, and knew they were another sight bigger head and shoulders than ever I'd seen on ary mortal man.

"Name yourself!" he yelled again, and in the black clouds a lightning flash wiggled, like a snake caught fire.

"John!" I bawled back.

"What you aiming to do, John?"

Another crack of lightning, that for a second seemed to peel off the clouds right and left. I looked this way and that. Nowhere to get out of the way should lightning strike, or a rock or anything. On notion, I pulled by guitar to me and picked and sang:

Went to the rock to hide my face,
The rock cried out, "No hiding place!". . . .

Gentlemen, the laugh was like thunder after the lightning.

"Better climb quick, John!" he hollered me. "I'm a-waiting on you up here!"

I swarmed and swarved and scrabbled my way up, not looking down. Over my head that rock-spur got bigger, I figured it for maybe twelve-fifteen feet long, and on it I made out Page Jarrett in her blue dress. Mr. Oakman was right, she was purely big and she was purely good-looking. She hung to the pointy rock with both her long hands.

"Page," I said to her, with what breath I had left, and she stared with her green eyes and gave me an inch of smile. She looked to have a right much of her daddy's natural sand in her craw.

"John," boomed the thunder-voice, close over me now. "I asked you a while back, why you coming up?"

"Just to see how you make the rain fall," I said, under the overhang of the ledge. "Help me up."

Down came a bare brown honey-hairy arm, and a hand the size of a scoop shovel. It got my wrist and snatched me away like a turnip coming out of a patch, and I landed my feet on broad flat stones.

Below me yawned up those rock-toothed tops of the Notch's jaws. Inside them the brush and trees looked mossy and puny. The cabins were like baskets, the pigs and the cow like play-toys, and the branch looked to run so narrow you might bridge it with your shoe. Shadow fell on the Notch from the fattening dark clouds.

Then I looked at Rafe Enoch. He stood over me like a sycamore tree over a wood shed. He was the almightiest big thing I'd ever seen on two legs.

Eight foot high, Oakman Dillon had said truly, and he was thick-made in keeping. Shoulders wide enough to fill a barn door, and legs like tree trunks with fringe-sided buckskin pants on them, and his big feet wore moccasin shoes of bear's hide with the fur still on. His shirt, sewed together of pelts—fox, coon, the like of that—hadn't any sleeves, and hung open from that big chest of his that was like a cotton bale. Topping all, his face put you in mind of the full moon with a yellow beard, but healthy-looking brown, not pale like the moon. Big and dark eyes, and through the yellow beard his teeth grinned like big white sugar lumps.

"Maybe I ought to charge you to look at me," he said.

I remembered how he'd struck a man dead for wanting him in a show, and I looked elsewhere. First, naturally, at Page Jarrett on the rock spur. The wind from the clouds waved her brown hair like a flag, and fluttered her blue skirt around her drawn-up feet. Then I turned and looked at the broad space above the falls.

From there I could see there was a right much of higher country, and just where I stood with Rafe Enoch was a big shelf, like a lap, with slopes behind it. In the middle of the flat space showed a pond of water, running out past us to make the falls. On its edge stood Rafe Enoch's house, built wigwam-style of big old logs leaned together and chinked between with clay over twigs. No trees to amount to anything on the shelf—just one behind the wigwam-house, and to its branches hung joints that looked like smoke meat.

"You hadn't played that guitar so clever, maybe I mightn't have saved you," said Rafe Enoch's thunder voice.

"Saved?" I repeated him.

"Look." His big club of a finger pointed to the falls, then to those down-hugged clouds. "When they get together, what happens?"

Just at the ledge lip, where the falls went over, stones looked halfway washed out. A big shove of water would take them out the other half, and the whole thing pour down on the Notch.

"Why you doing this to the folks?" I asked.

He shook his head. "John, this is one rain I never called for." He put one big pumpkin-sized fist into the palm of his other hand. "I can call for rain, sure, but some of it comes without me. I can't start it or either stop it, I just know it's coming. I've known about this for days. It'll drown out Sky Notch like a rat nest."

"Why didn't you try to tell them?"

"I tried to tell her." His eyes cut around to where Page Jarrett hung to the pointy rock, and his stool-leg fingers raked his yellow beard. "She was walking off by herself, alone. I know how it feels to be alone. But when I told her, she called me a liar. I brought her up here to save her, and she cried and fought me." A grin. "She fought me better than any living human I know. But she can't fight me hard enough."

"Can't you do anything about the storm?" I asked him to tell.

"Can do this." He snapped his big fingers, and lightning crawled through the clouds over us. It made me turtle my neck inside my shirt collar. Rafe Enoch never twitched his eyebrow.

"Rafe," I said, "you might could persuade the folks. They're not your size, but they're human like you."

"Them?" He roared his laugh. "They're not like me, nor you aren't like me, either, though you're longer-made than common. Page yonder, she looks to have some of the old Genesis giant blood in her. That's why I saved her alive."

"Genesis giant blood," I repeated him, remembering the Book, sixth chapter of Genesis. " 'There were giants in the earth in those days.' "

"That's the whole truth," said Rafe. "When the sons of God took wives of the daughters of men—their children were the mighty men of old, the men of renown. That's not exact quote, but it's near enough."

He sat down on a rock, near about as tall sitting as I was standing. "Ary giant knows he was born from the sons of the gods," he said. "My name tells it, John."

I nodded, figuring it. "Rafe—Raphah, the giant whose son was Goliath, Enoch—"

"Or Anak," he put in. "Remember the sons of Anak, and them scared-out spies sent into Canaan? They was grasshoppers in the sight of the sons of Anak, in more ways than just size, John." He sniffed. "They got scared back into the wilderness for forty years. And Goliath!"

"David killed him," I dared remind Rafe.

"By a trick. A slingshot stone. Else he'd not lasted any longer than that."

A finger-snap, and lightning winged over us like a hawk over a chicken run. I tried not to scrouch down.

"What use to fight little old human men," he said, "when you got the sons of the gods in your blood?"

I allowed he minded me of Strap Buckner with that talk.

"Who's Strap Buckner? Why do I mind you of him?"

I picked the guitar, I sang the song:

Strap Buckner he was called, he was more than eight
foot tall,
And he walked like a mountain among men.
He was good and he was great, and the glorious Lone
Star State
Will never look upon his like again.

"Strap Buckner had the strength of ten lions," I said, "and he used it as ten lions. Scorned to fight ordinary folks, so he challenged old Satan himself, skin for skin, on the banks of the Brazos, and if Satan hadn't fought foul—"

"Another dirty fighter!" Rafe got up from where he sat, quick as quick for all his size. "Foul or not, Satan couldn't whup me!"

""Might be he couldn't," I judged, looking at Rafe. "But anyway, the Notch folks never hurt you. Used to give you stuff to eat."

"Don't need their stuff to eat," he said, the way you'd think that was the only argument. He waved his hand past his wigwam-house. "Down yonder is a bunch of hollows, where ain't no human man been, except maybe once the Indians. I hoe some corn there, some potatoes. I pick wild salad greens here and yonder. I kill me a deer, a bear, a wild hog—ain't no human man got nerve to face them big wild hogs, but I chunk them with a rock or I fling a sharp ash sapling, and what I fling at I bring down. In the pond here I spear me fish. Don't need their stuff to eat, I tell you."

"Need it or not, why let them drown out?"

His face turned dark, the way you'd think smoke drifted over it.

"I can't abide little folks' little eyes looking at me, wondering themselves about me, thinking I'm not rightly natural."

He waited for what I had to say, and it took nerve to say it.

"But you're not a natural man, Rafe. You've allowed that yourself, you say you come from different blood. Paul Bunyan thought the same thing."

He grinned his big sugar-lump teeth at me. Then: "Page Jarrett," he called, "better come off that rock before the rain makes it slippy and you fall off. I'll help you—"

"You stay where you are," she called back. "Let John help."

I went to the edge of that long drop down. The wind blew from some place—maybe below, maybe above or behind or before. I reached out my guitar, and Page Jarrett crawled to where she could lay hold, and that way I helped her to the solid standing. She stood beside me, inches taller, and she put a burning mean look on Rafe Enoch. He made out he didn't notice.

"Paul Bunyan," he said, after what I'd been saying. "I've heard tell his name—champion logger in the northern states, wasn't he?"

"Champion logger," I said. "Bigger than you, I reckon—"

"Not bigger!" thundered Rafe Enoch.

"Well, as big."

"Know ary song about him?"

"Can't say there's been one made. Rafe, you say you despise to be looked on by folks."

"Just by little folks, John. Page Jarrett can look on me if she relishes to."

Quick she looked off, and drew herself up proud. Right then she appeared to be taller than what Mr. Oakman Dillon had reckoned her, and a beauty-looking thing she was, you hear what I say, gentlemen. I cut my eyes up to the clouds; they hung down over us, loose and close, like the roof of a tent. I could feel the closeness around me, the way you feel water when you've waded up to the line of your mouth.

"How soon does the rain start falling?" I asked Rafe.

"Can fall ary time now," said Rafe, pulling a grass-stalk to bite in his big teeth. "Page's safe off that rock point, it don't differ me a shuck when that rain falls."

"But when?" I asked again. "You know."

"Sure I know." He walked toward the pond, and me with him. I felt Page Jarrett's grape-green eyes digging our backs. The pond water was shiny tarry black from reflecting the clouds. "Sure," he said, "I know a right much. You natural human folks, you know so pitiful little I'm sorry for you."

"Why not teach us?" I wondered him, and he snorted like a big mean horse.

"Ain't the way it's reckoned to be, John. Giants are figured stupid. Remember the tales? Your name's John—do you call to mind a tale about a man named Jack, long back in time?"

"Jack the Giant Killer," I nodded. "He trapped a giant in a hole—"

"Cormoran," said Rafe. "Jack dug a pit in front of his door. And Blunderbore he tricked into stabbing himself open with a knife. But how did them things happen? He blew a trumpet to tole Cormoran out, and he sat and ate at Blunderbore's table like a friend before tricking him to death." A louder snort. "More foul fighting, John. Did you come up here to be Jack the Giant Killer? Got some dirty tricks? If that's how it is, you done drove your ducks to the wrong puddle."

"More than a puddle here," I said, looking at the clouds and then across the pond. "See yonder, Rafe, where the water edge comes above that little slanty slope. If it was open, enough water could run off to keep the Notch from flooding."

"Could be done," he nodded his big head, "if you had machinery to pull the rocks out. But they're bigger than them fall rocks, they ain't half washed away to begin with. And there ain't no machinery, so just forget it. The Notch washes out, with most of the folks living in it—all of them, if the devil bids high enough. Sing me a song."

I swept the strings with my thumb. "Thinking about John Henry," I said, half to myself. "He wouldn't need a machine to open up a drain-off place yonder."

"How'd he do it?" asked Rafe.

"He had a hammer twice the size ary other man swung," I said. "He drove steel when they cut the Big Bend Tunnel through Cruze Mountain. Out-drove the steam drill they brought to compete him out of his job."

"Steam drill," Rafe repeated me, the way you'd think he was faintly recollecting the tale. "They'd do that—ordinary size folks, trying to work against a giant. How big was John Henry?"

"Heard tell he was the biggest man ever in Virginia."

"Big as me?"

"Maybe not quite. Maybe just stronger."

"Stronger!"

I had my work cut out not to run from the anger in Rafe Enoch's face.

"Well," I said, "he beat the steam drill. . . ."

John Henry said to his captain,
"A man ain't nothing but a man,
But before I let that steam drill run me down,
I'll die with this hammer in my hand. . . ."

"He'd die trying," said Rafe, and his ears were sort of cocked forward, the way you hear elephants do to listen.

"He'd die winning," I said, and sang the next verse:

John Henry drove steel that long day through,
The steam drill failed by his side.
The mountain was high, the sun was low,
John he laid down his hammer and he died. . . .

"Killed himself beating the drill!" and Rafe's pumpkin fist banged into his other palm. "Reckon I could have beat it and lived!"

I was looking at the place where the pond could have a drain-off.

"No," said Rafe. "Even if I wanted to, I don't have no hammer twice the size of other folks' hammers."

A drop of rain fell on me. I started around the pond.

"Where you going?" Rafe called, but I didn't look back. Stopped beside the wigwam-house and put my guitar inside. It was gloomy in there, but I saw his home-made stool as high as a table, his table almost chin high to a natural man, a bed woven of hickory splits and spread with bear and deer skins to be the right bed for Og, King of Bashan, in the Book of Joshua. Next to the door I grabbed up a big pole of hickory, off some stacked firewood.

"Where you going?" he called again.

I went to where the slope started. I poked my hickory between two rocks and started to pry. He laughed, and rain sprinkled down.

"Go on, John," he granted me. "Grub out a sluiceway

there. I like to watch little scrabbly men work. Come in the house, Page, we'll watch him from in there."

I couldn't budge the rocks from each other. They were big—like trunks or grain sacks, and must have weighed in the half-tons. They were set in there, one next to the other, four-five of them holding the water back from pouring down that slope. I heaved on my hickory till it bent like a bow.

"Come on," said Rafe again, and I looked around in time to see him put out his shovel hand and take her by the wrist. Gentlemen, the way she slapped him with her other hand it made me jump with the crack.

I watched, knee deep in water. He put his hand to his gold-bearded cheek and his eye-whites glittered in the rain.

"If you was a man," he boomed down at Page, "I'd slap you dead."

"Do it!" she blazed him back. "I'm a woman, and I don't fear you or ary overgrown, sorry-for-himself giant ever drew breath!"

With me standing far enough off to forget how little I was by them, they didn't seem too far apart in size. Page was like a small-made woman facing up to a sizeable man, that was all.

"If you was a man—" he began again.

"I'm no man, nor neither ain't you a man!" she cut off. "Don't know if you're an ape or a bull-brute or what, but you're no man! John's the only man here, and I'm helping him! Stop me if you dare!"

She ran to where I was. Rain battered her hair into a brown tumble and soaked her dress snug against her fine proud strong body. Into the water she splashed.

"Let me pry," and she grabbed the hickory pole. "I'll pry up and you tug up, and maybe—"

I bent to grab the rock with my hands. Together we tried. Seemed to me the rock stirred a little, like the drowsy sleeper in the old song. Dragging at it, I felt the muscles strain and crackle in my shoulders and arms.

"Look out!" squealed Page. "Here he comes!"

Up on the bank she jumped again, with the hickory ready to club at him. He paid her no mind, she stooped down toward where I was.

"Get on out of there!" he bellowed, the way I've always reckoned a buffalo bull might do. "Get out!"

"But—but—" I was wheezing. "Somebody's got to move this rock—"

"You ain't budging it ary mite!" he almost deafened me in the ear. "Get out and let somebody there can do something!"

He grabbed my arm and snatched me out of the water, so sudden I almost sprained my fingers letting go the rock. Next second he jumped in, with a splash like a jolt-wagon going off a bridge. His big shovelly hands clamped the sides of the rock, and through the falling rain I saw him heave.

He swole up like a mad toad-frog. His patchy fur shirt split down the middle of his back while those muscles humped under his skin. His teeth flashed out in his beard, set hard together.

Then, just when I thought he'd bust open, that rock came out of its bed, came up in the air, landing on the bank away from where it'd been.

"I swear, Rafe—" I began to say.

"Help him," Page put in. "Let's both help."

We scrabbled for a hold on the rock, but Rafe hollered us away, so loud and sharp we jumped back like scared dogs. I saw that rock quiver, and cracks ran through the rain-soaked dirt around it. Then it came up on end, the way you'd think it had hinges, and Rafe got both arms around it and heaved it clear. He laughed, with the rain wet in his beard.

Standing clear where he'd told her to stand, Page pointed to the falls' end.

Looked as if the rain hadn't had to put down but just a little bit. Those loose rocks trembled and shifted in their places. They were ready to go. Then Rafe saw what we saw.

"Run, you two!" he howled about that racketty storm. "Run, run—quick!"

I didn't tarry to ask the reason. I grabbed Page's arm and we ran toward the falls. Running, I looked back past my elbow.

Rafe had straightened up, straddling among the rocks by the slope. He looked into the clouds, that were almost resting on his shaggy head, and both his big arms lifted and his hands spread and then their fingers snapped. I could hear the snaps—*Whop! Whop!* like two pistol shots.

He got what he called for, a forked stroke of lightning, straight and hard down on him like a fish-gig in the hands of the Lord's top angel. It slammed down on Rafe and over and around him, and it shook itself all the way from rock to clouds. Rafe Enoch in its grip lit up and glowed, the way you'd think he'd been forge-hammered out of iron and heated red in a furnace to temper him.

I heard the almightiest tearing noise I ever could call for. I felt the rock shelf quiver all the way to where we'd stopped dead to watch. My thought was, the falls had torn open and the Notch was drowning.

But the lightning yanked back to where it had come from. It had opened the sluiceway, and water flooded through and down slope, and Rafe had fallen down while it poured and puddled over him.

"He's struck dead!" I heard Page say over the rain.

"No," I said back.

For Rafe Enoch was on his knees, on his feet, and out of that drain-off rush, somehow staggering up from the flat sprawl where the lightning had flung him. His knees wobbled and bucked, but he drew them up straight and mopped a big muddy hand across his big muddy face.

He came walking toward us, slow and dreamy-moving, and by now the rain rushed down instead of fell down. It was like what my old folks used to call raining tomcats and hoe handles. I bowed my head to it, and made to pull Page toward Rafe's wigwam; but she wouldn't pull, she held where she was, till Rafe came up with us. Then, all three, we went together and got into the tight, dark shelter of the wigwam-house, with the rain and wind battering the outside of it.

Rafe and I sat on the big bed, and Page on a stool, looking small there. She wrung the water out of her hair.

"You all right?" she inquired Rafe.

I looked at him. Between the drain-off and the wigwam, rain had washed off that mud that gaumed all over him. He was wet and clean, with his patch-pelt shirt hanging away from his big chest and shoulders in soggy rags.

The lightning had singed off part of his beard. He lifted

big fingers to wipe off the wet fluffy ash, and I saw the stripe on his naked arm, on the broad back of his hand, and I made out another stripe just like it on the other. Lightning had slammed down both hands and arms, and clear down his flanks and legs—I saw the burnt lines on his fringed leggings. It was like a double lash of God's whip.

Page got off the stool and came close to him. Just then he didn't look so out-and-out much bigger than she was. She put a long gentle finger on that lightning lash where it ran along his shoulder.

"Does it hurt?" she asked. "You got some grease I could put on it?"

He lifted his head, heavy, but didn't look at her. He looked at me. "I lied to you all," he said.

"Lied to us?" I asked him.

"I did call for the rain. Called for the biggest rain I ever thought of. Didn't pure down want to kill off the folks in the Notch, but to my reckoning, if I made it rain, and saved Page up here—"

At last he looked at her, with a shamed face.

"The others would be gone and forgotten. There'd be Page and me." His dark eyes grabbed her green ones. "But I didn't rightly know how she disgusts the sight of me." His head dropped again. "I feel the nearest to nothing I ever did."

"You opened the drain-off and saved the Notch from your rain," put in Page, her voice so gentle you'd never think it. "Called down the lightning to help you."

"Called down the lightning to kill me," said Rafe. "I never reckoned it wouldn't. I wanted to die. I want to die now."

"Live," she bade him.

He got up at that, standing tall over her.

"Don't worry when folks look on you," she said, her voice still ever so gentle. "They're just wondered at you, Rafe. Folks were wondered that same way at Saint Christopher, the giant who carried Lord Jesus across the river."

"I was too proud," he mumbled in his big bull throat. "Proud of my Genesis giant blood, of being one of the sons of God—"

"Shoo, Rafe," and her voice was gentler still, "the least man in size you'd call for, when he speaks to God, he says, 'Our Father.' "

Rafe turned from her.

"You said I could look on you if I wanted," said Page Jarrett. "And I want."

Back he turned, and bent down, and she rose on her toetips so their faces came together.

The rain stopped, the way you'd think that stopped it. But they never seemed to know it, and I picked up my guitar and went out toward the lip of the cliff.

The falls were going strong, but the drain-off handled enough water so there'd be no washout to drown the folks below. I reckoned the rocks would be the outdoingist slippery rocks ever climbed down by mortal man, and it would take me a long time. Long enough, maybe so, for me to think out the right way to tell Mr. Lane Jarrett he was just before having himself a son-in-law of the Genesis giant blood, and pretty soon after while, grandchildren of the same strain.

The sun came stabbing through the clouds and flung them away in chunks to right and left, across the bright blue sky.

THE CENTAUR

Half man and half horse, the centaur is one of the few mythical creatures usually considered to be more human than beast. It's doubtful, for instance, that anyone would ask a sphinx or a griffin to tea, but centaurs, who had their own civilization and customs, were often admitted into human society. It was this, in fact, that led to their downfall. Centaurs were invited to the wedding of Pirithous and Hippodamia, but became drunk at the wedding feast and, in the quaint phrasing of *Bulfinch's Mythology,* "attempted to offer violence to the bride." This lapse in manners led to the celebrated and bloody Battle of the Lapiths and Centaurs, and was one of the chief reasons why Hercules annihilated most of the centaur race a bit later on.

In spite of the rude and barbarous side of their natures, though, centaurs remain, in Jorge Luis Borges's words, "the most harmonious creatures of fantastic zoology," and the myths spend much time detailing their good traits as well. They are often portrayed as seers and sages, and the wisest of them, Chiron, was the teacher of Achilles, Aesculapius, and many of the other heroes of Greek mythology; so distinguished was he that, when he died, Zeus raised him to the heavens as the constellation

Sagittarius. Interestingly, that indefatigable encyclopedist of the ancient world, Pliny, says that he actually *saw* a centaur with his own eyes. It had been brought to Rome from Egypt in the reign of Claudius, embalmed in honey.

In the stories that follow, we—like Pliny—are privileged to see centaurs, too, but *these* centaurs—man-made and otherwise—are very much alive . . .

Karen Anderson is a writer and poet who has appeared frequently in *The Magazine of Fantasy and Science Fiction,* as well as in *Galaxy, Alfred Hitchcock's Mystery Magazine,* and elsewhere—sometimes with solo work, sometimes writing in collaboration with her husband, writer Poul Anderson. Her work has been collected in the book *The Unicorn Trade.*

Gene Wolfe is perceived by many critics to be one of the best—perhaps *the* best—SF and fantasy writers working today. His most acclaimed work is the tetralogy *The Book of the New Sun,* individual volumes of which have won the Nebula Award, the World Fantasy Award, and the John W. Campbell Memorial Award. His most recent books are the novel *Free Live Free* and the collection *The Wolfe Archipelago.*

Treaty in Tartessos

by

Karen Anderson

IRATZABAL'S HOOFS WERE shod with bronze, as befitted a high chief, and heavy gold pins held the coils of bright sorrel hair on top of his head. In this morning's battle, of course, he had used wooden pins which were less likely to slip out. As tonight was a ceremonial occasion, he wore a coat of aurochs hide dyed blue with woad, buttoned and cinched with hammered gold.

He waved his spear high to show the green branches bound to its head as he entered the human's camp. No one spoke, but a guard grunted around a mouthful of barley-cake and jerked his thumb toward the commander's tent.

Standing in his tent door, Kynthides eyed the centaur with disfavor, from his unbarbered hair to the particularly clumsy bandage on his off fetlock. He straightened self-consciously in his sea-purple cloak and pipeclayed linen tunic.

"Greetings, most noble Iratzabal," he said, bowing. "Will you enter my tent?"

The centaur returned the bow awkwardly. "Glad to, most noble Kynthides." he said. As he went in the man realized with a little surprise that the centaur emissary was only a couple of fingers' breadth taller than himself.

It was darker inside the tent than out, despite the luxury of three lamps burning at once. "I hope you've dined well? May I offer you anything?" Kynthides asked politely, with considerable misgivings. The centaur probably wouldn't know what to do with a barley loaf, and as for wine—well, there wasn't a drop within five miles of camp. Or there had better not be.

"That's decent of you, but I'm full up," said Iratzabal. "The boys found a couple of dead . . . uh, buffalo, after the battle, and we had a fine barbecue."

Kynthides winced. Another yoke of draft oxen gone! Well, Corn Mother willing, the war would be settled soon. It might even be tonight. "Won't you, er . . . sit? Lie down? Er, make yourself comfortable."

Iratzabal lowered himself to the ground with his feet under him, and Kynthides sank gratefully into a leather-backed chair. He had been afraid the discussion would be conducted standing up.

"I got to admit you gave us a good fight today, for all you're such lightweights," the centaur said. "You generally do. If we don't get things settled somehow, we could go on like this till we've wiped each other out."

"We realize that too," said the man. "I've been asked by the heads of every village in Tartessos, not to mention communities all the way back to Thrace, to make some reasonable settlement with you. Can you speak for centaurs in those areas?"

"More or less." He swished his tail across the bandaged fetlock, and flies scattered. "I run most of the territory from here up through Goikokoa Etchea—what men call Pyrene's Mountains—and across to the Inland Sea. Half a dozen tribes besides mine hunt through here, but they stand aside for *us*. We could lick any two of them with our eyes shut. Now, you take an outfit like the Acroceraunians—I don't run them, but they've heard of me, and I can tell them to knuckle under or face my boys *and* yours. But that shouldn't be necessary. I'm going to get them a good cut."

"Well, remember that if the communities don't like promises I make in their names, they won't honor them," said the man. He slid his fingers through the combed curls of his dark-brown beard and wished he could ignore the centaur's odor. The fellow smelled like a saddle-blanket. If he didn't want to wash, he could at least use perfume. "First, we ought to consider the reasons for this war, and after that ways to settle the dispute."

"The way I see it," the centaur began, "is, you folks

want to pin down the corners of a piece of country and sit on it. We don't understand ground belonging to somebody."

"It *began,*" Kynthides said stiffly, "with that riot at the wedding."

"That was just what set things off," said Iratzabal. "There'd been a lot of small trouble before then. I remember how I was running down a four-pointer through an oak wood one rainy day, with my nose full of the way things smell when they're wet and my mind on haunch of venison. The next thing I knew I was in a clearing planted with one of those eating grasses, twenty pounds of mud on each hoof and a pack of tame wolves worrying my hocks. I had to kill two or three of them before I got away, and by then there were men throwing spears and shouting 'Out! Out!' in what they thought was Eskuara."

"We have to keep watchdogs and arm the field hands, or we wouldn't have a stalk of grain standing at harvest time!"

"Take it easy. I was just telling you, the war isn't over a little thing like some drunks breaking up a wedding. Nor they wouldn't have, if the wine hadn't been where they could get at it. There's blame on both sides."

The man half rose at this, but caught himself. The idea was to stop the war, not set it off afresh. "At any rate, it seems we can't get along with each other. Men and centaurs don't mix well."

"We look at things different ways, said Iratzabal. "You see a piece of open country, and all you can think of is planting a crop on it. We think of deer grazing it, or rabbit and pheasant nesting. Field-planting ruins the game in a district."

"Can't you hunt away from farm districts?" asked Kynthides. "We have our families to support, little babies and old people. There are too many of us to let the crops go and live by hunting, even if there were as much game as the land could support."

"Where can we hunt?" shrugged the centaur. "Whenever we come through one of our regular districts, we find more valleys under plow than last time, more trees cut and the fields higher up the slope. Even in Goikokoa Etchea, what's as much my tribe's home as a place can be, little fields are showing up." A swirl of lamp smoke veered toward him, and he sniffed it contemptuously. "Sheep fat! The herds I find aren't deer any more, they're sheep, with a boy pi-pipping away on a whistle—and dogs again."

"If you'd pick out your territory and stay on it, then no farmers would come in," said Kynthides. "It's contrary to our nature to leave land unused because somebody plans to hunt through it next autumn."

"But, big as Goikokoa Etchea is, it won't begin to feed us year round! We've got to have ten times as much, a hundred times if you're talking of Scythia and Illyria and all."

"I live in Thessaly myself," Kynthides pointed out. "I have to think of Illyria. What we men really want is to see all you centaurs completely out of Europe, resettled in Asia or the like. Couldn't you all move out of Sarmatia and the lands to the east? Nobody lives there. It's all empty steppes."

"Sarmatia! Maybe it looks empty to a farmer, but I've heard from the boys in Scythia. The place is filling up with Achaians, six feet tall, each with twenty horses big enough to eat either one of us for breakfast, and they can ride those horses all night and fight all day. By Jainco, I'm keeping away from them."

"Well, there's hardly anybody in Africa. Why don't you go there?" the man suggested.

"If there was any way of us all getting there—"

"Certainly there is! We have ships. It would take a couple of years to send you all, but—"

"*If* we could get there, we wouldn't like it at all. That's no kind of country for a centaur. Hot, dry, game few and far between—no thanks. But you're willing to ship us all to some other place?"

"Any place! That is, within reason. Name it."

"Just before war broke out in earnest, I got chummy with a lad who'd been on one of those exploring voyages you folks go in for. He said he'd been to a place that was full of game of all kinds, and even had the right kind of toadstools."

"Toadstools? To make poison with?" cried Kynthides, his hand twitching toward the neatly bandaged spear-jab on his side.

"*Poison!*" Iratzabal ducked his head and laughed into

his heavy sorrel beard. "That's a good one, poison from toadstools! No, to eat. Get a glow on at the Moon Dances—same way you people do with wine. Though I can't see why you use stuff that leaves you so sick the next day."

"Once you've learned your capacity, you needn't have a hangover," Kynthides said with a feeling of superiority. "But this place you're talking of—"

"Well, my pal said it wasn't much use to men, but centaurs would like it. Lots of mountains, all full of litle tilted meadows, but no flat country to speak of. Not good to plow up and sow with barley or what-not. Why not turn that over to us, since you can't send any big colonies there anyway?"

"Wait a minute. Are you talking about Kypros' last expedition?"

"That's the one my pal sailed under," nodded Iratzabal.

"No, by the Corn Mother! How can I turn that place over to you? We've barely had a look at it ourselves. There may be tin and amber to rival Thule, or pearls, or sea-purple. We have simply no idea of what we'd be giving you."

"And there may be no riches at all. Did this guy Kypros say he'd seen any tin or pearls? If he did, he didn't tell a soul of his crew. And I'm telling you, if we don't go there we don't go anyplace. I can start the war again with two words."

The man sprang to his feet, white-lipped. "Then start the war again! We may not have been winning, but by the Mother, we weren't losing!"

Iratzabal heaved himself upright. "You can hold out as long as we give you pitched battles. But wait till we turn to raiding! You'll have fields trampled every night, and snipers chipping at you every day. You won't dare go within bowshot of the woods. We'll chivy your herds through your crops till they've run all their fat off and there's not a blade still standing. And you'll get no harvest in, above what you grab off the stem and eat running. How are the granaries, Kynthides? Will there be any seed corn left by spring?"

The man dropped into his chair and took his head in trembling hands. "You've got us where we hurt. We can't survive that kind of warfare. But how can I promise land that isn't mine? It belongs to Kypros' backers, if anyone."

"Pay them off in the grain that won't be spoiled. Fix up the details any way it suits you. I'm not trying to make it hard on you—we can kick through with a reasonable number of pelts and such to even the bargain."

He looked up. "All right, Iratzabal," he said wearily. "You can *have* Atlantis."

The Woman Who Loved The Centaur Pholus

by

Gene Wolfe

ANDERSON'S TELEPHONE RANG, and of course it was Janet. Anderson swung his feet over the side of the bed before he hung up, then looked at his watch. Four twenty A.M. The moonlight on the melting snow outside sent a counterfeit dawn to his windows.

He switched on the reading light and found his slippers, then kicked them off again. There would not be time for slippers. The little water-horse that Dumont—Dumont would surely be there too—had made for him lifted its head and foaming mane above the rim of its aquarium and neighed, a sound so high pitched it might have been the chirping of a bird.

So like they were, no mortal
Might one from the other know;
White as snow their armor was,
Their steeds were white as snow.
Never on earthly anvil
Did such rare armor gleam,
And never did such gallant steeds
Drink from an earthly stream.

Who had written that? Anderson couldn't remember.

Before he had gone to bed he had filled the stainless-steel thermos with scalding coffee, telling himself he would not need it, that he would drink it with breakfast so as not to waste it. Wool shirt with lumberjack checks, wool hunting pants, thick socks, rubber-bottomed hunting boots, down-filled vest, parka, Navy watch cap. Gloves and compass in the parka's pockets? Yes. His sign was already in the car, and the chains were on. It started without trouble; he roared out of the driveway and down the silent street. Coming, Janet. Coming, Pholus, or whoever you are. Damn.

When winter was beginning, he had gone out in the suit he wore on campus, with the same overcoat and hat. He had learned better, floundering through the snow long before machinegun slugs had ripped the weak and frightened siren, the bird-woman whose scattered feathers he had helped Dumont gather when the soldiers were gone. There was a mail-order company that sold all sorts of cold-weather gear. Their prices were high, but the quality was excellent. Never on earthly anvil . . . How did the rest go? Something, something, something . . .

O'er the green waves which gently bend and swell,
Fair Amphitrite steers her silver shell;
Her playful dolphins stretch the silken rein,
Hear her sweet voice, and glide along the main.

No, that wasn't it, that was Darwin, the father (or was it the grandfather?) of Dumont's Darwin, the Darwin of the *Beagle.* Anderson swung onto the Interstate. For mile after mile, the red taillights of the cars in front of him looked like the red eyes of beasts, prowling the snow by night.

At last, just to hear a voice, Anderson said aloud, "They sell everything but Odysseus's wax. But then, I don't need wax." He had been thinking of the man-headed bull, Nin, of Assyria; that too had been killed, and the memory of its wings suggested the siren again. As if the CB had heard him and knew his loneliness, it murmured, "Breaker one one. This is Sombelenë for Peirithous. Come in, Peirithous."

"I'm here, Sombelenë," Anderson answered. He did not know where Janet had discovered that name. It had not been in any of the references he had checked.

"Go past the sign for the Dells, Peirithous. After a quarter mile you'll see an unmarked road on your left. We're about three miles farther on."

"Ten-four and out," Anderson said. He hated the pseudonyms, and he was certain the Army knew who they were anyway.

As if to confirm it, the threshing sound of a helicopter came from above, louder and louder, then louder still. It passed over the car at treetop level going ninety at least and disappeared beyond the crest of a hill.

"Breaker one one for Sombelenë. Chopper on the way."

"Ten-four, Peirithous."

So Janet knew, and whoever was with her knew. And of course the soldiers knew, in their helicopter.

"All hail, beloved birds," he cried,
"My comrades on the ocean tide."

Anderson passed a billboard showing the little stern-wheeler *Apollo 2* and swerved onto the next unmarked road. There were fresh tire tracks in the snow, and he began automatically to look to left and right, though he knew how unlikely it was that he would see anything from the road. Yet he might. How did it go?

Will thou yet take all, Galilean? but these thou
shalt not take,
The laurel, the palms and the paean, the breasts
of the nymphs in the brake. . . .

The sun was peeping over the snow-clad hills now, and inexplicably Anderson felt his spirits rise. He was going to a fight, and he would be fighting for the only thing he knew that was really worth fighting for. For once he could not recall a quotation, but he remembered the sense of it, and not just with his mind but in his feet and hands, belly and heart and brain. The second best thing was to fight and win. But the first best thing was to fight the fight worth fighting. Where would he be, if not here?

He topped the hill at better than eighty and saw the cars and signs and milling people. The helicopter had set down in a field just behind a wood of birch, and there were two olive-drab Army trucks. He hit the brakes and went into a long skid, steering into it just the way that racing driver had advised on television, still utterly unafraid but feeling he must somehow be drunk. The car turned ninety degrees and skidded to a stop less than a dozen feet from the nearest truck.

Anderson jumped out and drew his sign from the back seat as some earlier Anderson might have drawn a sword. The sign read: **INTELLIGENT LIFE IS SACRED.** He flourished it overhead, though he knew the cameras had not come yet. A few of the soldiers stared at him. They were young recruits for the most part, boys under twenty.

Janet ran up to him, boots splashing slush, blond hair vivid as lightning above her red ski suit. "Andy, I'm so glad you've come! They've sent for a wrecker. They're going to pull the cars out of the way."

"Then we'll lock arms in front of the wrecker," he said. "We can't ask these people to lie down in this slop." He was looking at the other demonstrators as he spoke. There were only six, five of them middle-aged women. Good people, but without leadership they wouldn't stand up to much bullying.

Send me at least into the war,
And let me lead thy Myrmidons, that thus
The Greeks may have some gleam of hope.

Dumont emerged from his van, caught sight of Anderson and waved. His parka was much like Anderson's own, but his face was thinner and he was going bald. "We don't know what it is, yet. Some of our members are interviewing the farmer who saw it. A capripede, possibly."

"Fine," Anderson said. A satyr, by no coincidence at all, looked like the conventional representation of the Devil—not such an easy thing to defend in public as, say, a little winged Eros.

"You need me out there?" Dumont asked.

"Not yet," Janet told him. "Stay with the radio."

An officer had been trudging across the snow-covered field from the helicopter. He was close enough now for Anderson to see the silver eagles on his field jacket. Roman eagles, Anderson thought. Greek aircraft—the spiral-winged. I'll bet be doesn't know it. Or care.

A bearded man Anderson had not seen before left the cluster of demonstrators to ask, "This new creature . . . will we get to see it?"

"Him," Anderson said. "Always say *him* or *her*. It's much easier for them to shoot an it. Maybe, but more likely not."

Janet smiled at the bearded man. "You'll get to see—and even talk to—quite a few eventually, if you keep coming. We might even be lucky today."

The bearded man smiled back beneath his beard and seemed to lift himself on his toes. "There's more than one out there, isn't there? I've heard of them. It makes one feel like Adam."

Anderson said, "We're on the edge of one of the largest forested areas in Wisconsin. A lot of people bring them here, and more drift in. A friend of mine who's a statistician tells me there are gradients of diminishing population we're largely oblivious to. They sense those and follow them to places like this. There are quite a few of them in Minnesota too, and upper Michigan."

Janet added, "The Smokey Mountains are supposed to be full of them. Dr. Dumont plans to go there this summer."

"Professor Anderson?" It was the colonel.

Anderson said, "Afraid so."

"The dossier I saw is a little sketchy, but I thought I recognized you from your picture. What do you teach? Biology? Bio-physics?"

"Classical literature."

"Say, that's interesting. I like Sherlock Holmes myself, and Kipling. I suppose this biological engineering stuff is a hobby with you."

Anderson shook his head.

The colonel glanced around as though expecting to see the Minotaur step out of a cowshed. "I can see where it would be a good one in certain respects. Eventually I assume there will be a licensing procedure and some supervision. At present the thing is a mess."

"The question is which side the mess is on."

"I suppose you could say that. Did you hear what they killed yesterday on Market Street in Philadelphia? A cat with the head of a snake. It was as big as a small dog."

"A great many cats are as big as small dogs, and I'd think it would be a good deal less intelligent a hunter than most cats. No doubt it was somebody's first stab at making a chimera."

The colonel seemed not to have heard him. "They do these things, and they can't handle the results. Then instead of destroying them they turn them loose. It's funny, isn't it, how all the stuff that was originally developed by some high-powered scientists eventually turns into something the average Joe can do in his basement. Take TV—you can get a kit and build as good a television as anybody can buy. Or airplanes—a man I went to the Point with is building a plane in his garage."

Anderson said, "If the Wright brothers hadn't been able to build the first one in a bike shop, there wouldn't be any planes."

"Maybe." The colonel looked unconvinced, and Anderson decided he thought the airplane had been invented by Boeing. "Just the same, my orders are to clean this up. You and your followers are interfering with that."

"They're not my followers. They simply happen to believe as I do—or rather, I happen to believe as they do."

"Your dossier says you're one of the leaders, Professor Anderson. You're a man and most of them are women; you're well educated and you're the tallest. Who would you think the leader was if you were in my shoes?"

Anderson said, "If I were in your shoes, I'd probably be wrong about a lot of other things too," but his attention was no longer on the conversation. A truck was coming over the hill, and at first he thought it was the Army tow truck. Then the bearded man and several of the women raised a cheer, and he saw the call-letters on the side.

The colonel said something inaudible to a captain, the captain mumbled to a sergeant, and the sergeant bawled something at the troops, who fell into ranks. Janet and the bearded man hustled their charges into a straggling line, and Dumont emerged from his van to join them. Anderson suddenly understood that this was what everyone had been waiting for: the Army would prove they were acting without brutality, and let an audience of millions feel the thrill of the hunt; the demonstrators would put their case before the same audience and try to stir up sympathy for the hunted.

A man with a microphone climbed out of the truck, followed by a man with a camera. Guided by unerring instinct, both made for Janet. Anderson wanted to point it out to the colonel, but the colonel was busy looking soldierly as he inspected his troops in the background. In an undertone, the man with the microphone identified his channel and announced that any footage used would make the twelve o'clock news, then switched on his mike.

"You have to realize they will be murdering a *person* out there," Janet said without preamble. "Probably someone with the heart and mind of a child."

"Do you do this sort of life-shaping yourself?"

Dumont leaned toward the mike, his eyes on the camera. "I do. You must understand that it is completely legal as well as morally impeccable. It's not like similar research on bacteria—this can breed no plagues. It's just that the products of this work are deprived of even the protection afforded wild animals."

The interviewer asked, "What is your purpose in doing what you do?"

Janet put a hand on Dumont's shoulder, and Anderson, though he knew she was projecting for the camera, felt a tiny thrill at the beauty of her profile. "We have lost so many of our fellow citizens of this world. All the larger whales, the gorilla, two kinds of cheetah, all within the last ten years. Now humanity can make real what it has always loved. Now we can see the friends our ancestors dreamed of. The world is big enough for all of us, and some of us don't want to have to live here alone."

Patrols were leaving on foot now, apparently in the hope of drawing the television crew away. Anderson sent off two demonstrators with each, telling them to stand between the hunted and the soldiers' M16s if they could. If they dared. Behind him, the bearded man was talking now. "God gave to the first human being the authority to name the creatures, and in the language of the Bible, to name is to create. 'In the beginning was the word . . .' "

Anderson found himself trudging after a patrol too. Despite their weapons and equipment, the young soldiers moved faster than he, and though their footprints were plain enough in the snow, he lost sight of them when they entered the birches. The helicopter was beating overhead again. Anderson used his sign pole for a staff. The wind that stirred the branches smelled of spring and seemed made of something purer than air; and he felt again, as he had in his car, that he was somehow privileged. After a quarter hour or so, he caught sight of the soldiers—or perhaps of other soldiers. They appeared to have halted to examine some track their own feet soon obscured. Almost at once they were gone again. Exulting in the knowledge that he had not yet heard a shot, Anderson hurried after them. . . .

The sun climbed above the trees. Twice the helicopter had whirred overhead and vanished. The pocket compass Anderson had bought only a few months before was lost somewhere in the snow. Perhaps because Dumont moved, it was him Anderson saw first, his parka looking black against the snow. Then Janet in her red ski suit facing him.

> *O Father Jove, if ever I have aided thee,*
> *Grant but this one desire.*

He called and they answered; and something in their weary voices told him they were as lost as he was, and had been debating which way to go.

A little, ice-choked stream undulated through the snow near where they stood; and there were rocks, half masked with snow. The sun, too high now to give much direction, flashed from the few whirling flakes still in the air. "Well here we are," Janet said, and laughed. "We three ringleaders! Some leaders. I'll bet you don't know the way back either. Do you, Andy?"

Anderson shook his head. "We'll find it."

"I hope Paul did better."

Anderson decided Paul must be the bearded man.

Dumont said, "We really ought to split up," and just at that moment a little figure stepped around some snow covered bushes and came hesitantly forward. Its ears were pointed and its face was the face of a clever, sickly child; two small horns pushed through a tangle of dark curls. At first Anderson thought it was—insanely—wearing a scarlet sash. Janet moaned and dropped to her knees beside it, and it let the scarlet sash fall straight. There were fingers at the end of it; its blood dripped from them.

"Your arm!" Janet whispered. "Oh my God, your poor arm."

She and Dumont produced aid kits. Never until that moment had it occurred to Anderson that if the Army were to shoot something, it might fall to him to patch that something up. Coming on top of the lost compass it was almost too much. He experienced a self-contempt as great as the euphoria he had felt earlier, yet at the same time he was compelled to look at the faun's mangled arm as though he too had bandages and penicillin.

Janet muttered, "They shot him! Can you imagine, they shot this little body, this poor baby."

Dumont was tightening a tourniquet about the faun's upper arm. "You're coming home with us, young fellow. I have a place where you can stay until that's better."

"Those aren't gunshot wounds," Anderson said.

Janet and Dumont stared at him; the faun averted its wide, melting eyes.

"I was in the Marines; I saw films, and once one of the men in our barracks got hold of live ammunition and shot a lieutenant. I've seen bullet wounds out here too, and so have both of you. Bullets puncture the skin on entry and leave a blue corona. If they have much velocity left when they exit, they blow out a cone of flesh. They shatter bone, if they hit it. These bones aren't broken. There are puncture wounds, but mostly the flesh is torn. Whatever attacked that arm did it with its teeth—my guess would be a dog."

Then slowly, between minutes of sobbing and despite naïve evasions, it all came out: the dead twin; the footprints like, but not quite like, a bear's; the terror in the winter-wrapped woods. The goat-tongue had difficulty in forming words (Anderson recalled a lisping boy who had lived across the street when he was a child), but they soon grew accustomed to its faults, and the protection its distractions had afforded them vanished. After a time they found it hard to meet one another's eyes.

"Somebody's finally done it," Dumont said at last. "Once at least—probably more. It wasn't me."

"We never thought it was," Anderson told him. He wanted to swear.

"Those tracks couldn't be a centaur's. . . ." Dumont hesitated, looking from Anderson to Janet and back. A centaur could kill with his hooves, I suppose, or his hands. But his teeth would be no more dangerous than yours or mine. Werewolves?"

"Maybe," Anderson said. "There are other possibilities—Anubis and Set, perhaps even Narashimha, the lion-man of the Vedas. Whatever they are, we're going to have to use our connections with the others to lead the soldiers to them before they kill a human being."

Dumont nodded, but Janet's blue eyes were blazing. "You would, wouldn't you! You'd see them shot down—shot down with guns!"

Suddenly she was gone. Anderson sprinted after her, with Dumont close behind him. They had not run twenty yards through the snow when Anderson heard the thunder of hooves.

Only once before had Anderson seen him. Then he had thought him roan, the human torso, arms, and face, Caucasian. Now Pholus looked black, bigger than any horse, immensely bigger than any man, muscled like a giant. Janet, clinging to his back, harnessing those mighty arms with her slender hands, might have been a child, a little girl dreaming.

He could have trampled them, but at the last moment he turned aside, sending up a spume of mud and melting snow, smiting them instead with his wild glance. Anderson caught a flash of red. Perhaps Janet had waved. Perhaps she had not. Panting, he halted.

Dumont ran on, less swiftly even than Anderson had run. Blindly. Stupidly.

Anderson did not care. In the clearing he found the faun and took him by the hand. The road and the cars, all the relics of the dying twentieth century except himself, would be in the direction opposite the one Pholus had taken. Anderson trudged toward them.

Midst others of less note came one frail form,
A phantom among men; companionless
As the last cloud of an expiring storm,
Whose thunder is its knell; he, as I guess,
Had gazed on Nature's naked loveliness,
Actaeon-like, and now he fled astray
With feeble steps o'er the world's wilderness;
And his own thoughts, along that rugged way,
Pursued like raging hounds their father and their prey.

THE DRYAD

Dryads are tree-spirits, cousins to the brook-dwelling naiads, the oreads of the mountains and grottos, and the sea-dwelling nereids. Although often described as devotees of the virgin goddess Artemis, dryads (and indeed, all the other kinds of nymphs) seem to have spent a good deal of time being chased across the landscape by an assortment of amorous gods, demi-gods, fauns, satyrs, and even the occasional love-struck human; the consequences that arose from their being *caught* were often far from happy, both for pursuer and pursued. Dryads were also known for their ecstatic dancing, sometimes dancing by themselves in their isolated forest groves, sometimes dancing in partner with the god Pan, or with other deities.

In the arts, dryads are usually portrayed as beautiful young women in diaphanous gowns, and in such guise were the subject of much pastel and sentimental nineteenth century poetry. But there is a darker side to their legend. While the other kinds of nymphs were immortal, the dryad's life was irrevocably linked to the life of her tree—to destroy the tree was to destroy the dryad who dwelt within it, and many, many dryads must have perished miserably as humankind moved inexorably through the woodlands of the world with fire and ax and plow.

A dryad is a homebody by necessity, almost by definition—she really has nowhere else to *go.* As the stories that follow demonstrate, the consequences of that limitation can be funny or tragic—or sometimes, curiously, both . . .

Jane Yolen is one of the most distinguished of modern fantasists, and has been called "the Hans Christian Andersen of the twentieth century." She is the author of more than seventy books, primarily books for children, and has been a finalist for both the National Book Award and the World Fantasy Award. Her most recent books are the novel *Cards of Grief* and the collection *Tales of Wonder.*

L. Sprague de Camp is a seminal figure, one whose career spans almost the entire development of modern fantasy and SF. For the fantasy magazine *Unknown* in the late 1930s he helped create a whole new modern style of fantasy writing—funny, whimsical, and irreverent—of which he is still the most prominent practitioner. His most famous books include *Lest Darkness Fall, The Incomplete Enchanter* (with Fletcher Pratt), and *Rogue Queen.* His most recent book is *The Bones of Zora,* a novel written in collaboration with wife Catherine Crook de Camp.

The Sleep of Trees

by

Jane Yolen

> "Never invoke the gods unless you really want them to appear. It annoys them very much."
>
> —Chesterton

IT HAD BEEN a long winter. Arrhiza had counted every line and blister on the inside of the bark. Even the terrible binding power of the heartwood rings could not contain her longings. She desperately wanted spring to come so she could dance free, once again, of her tree. At night she looked up and through the spiky winter branches counted the shadows of early birds crossing the moon. She listened to the mewling of buds making their slow, painful passage to the light. She felt the sap veins pulse sluggishly around her. All the signs were there, spring was coming, spring was near, yet still there was no spring.

She knew that one morning, without warning, the rings would loosen and she would burst through the bark into her glade. It had happened every year of her life. But the painful wait, as winter slouched towards its dismal close, was becoming harder and harder to bear.

When Arrhiza had been younger, she had always slept the peaceful, uncaring sleep of trees. She would tumble, half-awake, through the bark and onto the soft, fuzzy green earth with the other young dryads, their arms and legs tangling in that first sleepy release. She had wondered then that the older trees released their burdens with such stately grace, the dryads and the meliade sending slow green praises into the air before the real Dance began. But she wondered no longer. Younglings simply slept the whole winter dreaming of what they knew best: roots and bark and the untroubling dark. But aging conferred knowledge, dreams change. Arrhiza now slept little and her waking, as her sleep, was filled with sky.

She even found herself dreaming of birds. Knowing trees were the honored daughters of the All Mother, allowed to root themselves deep into her flesh, knowing trees were the treasured sisters of the Huntress, allowed to unburden themselves into her sacred groves, Arrhiza envied birds. She wondered what it would be like to live apart from the land, to travel at will beyond the confines of the glade. Silly creatures though birds were, going from egg to earth without a thought, singing the same messages to one another throughout their short lives, Arrhiza longed to fly with one, passengered within its breast. A bird lived but a moment, but what a moment that must be.

Suddenly realizing her heresy, Arrhiza closed down her mind lest she share thoughts with her tree. She concentrated on the blessings to the All Mother and Huntress, turning her mind from sky to soil, from flight to the solidity of roots.

And in the middle of her prayer, Arrhiza fell out into spring, as surprised as if she were still young. She tumbled against one of the birch, her nearest neighbor, Phyla of the white face. Their legs touched, their hands brushing one another's thighs.

Arrhiza turned toward Phyla. "Spring comes late," she sighed, her breath caressing Phyla's budlike ear.

Phyla rolled away from her, pouting. "You make Spring Greeting sound like a complaint. It is the same every year." She sat up with her back to Arrhiza and stretched her arms. Her hands were outlined against the evening sky, the second and third fingers slotted together like a leaf. Then she turned slowly towards Arrhiza, her woods-green eyes unfocused. In the soft, filtered light her body gleamed whitely and the darker patches were mottled beauty marks on her breasts and sides. She was up to her feet in a single fluid movement and into the Dance.

Arrhiza watched, still full length on the ground, as one after another the dryads and meliades rose and stepped into position, circling, touching, embracing, moving apart. The cleft of their legs flashed pale signals around the glade.

Rooted to their trees, the hamadryads could only lean out into the Dance. They swayed to the lascivious pipings of spring. Their silver-green hair, thick as vines, eddied around their bodies like water.

Arrhiza watched it all but still did not move. How long she had waited for this moment, the whole of the deep winter, and yet she did not move. What she wanted was more than this, this entering into the Dance on command. She wanted to touch, to walk, to run, even to dance when she alone desired it. But then her blood was singing, her body pulsating; her limbs stretched upward answering the call. She was drawn towards the others and, even without willing it, Arrhiza was into the Dance.

Silver and green, green and gold, the grove was a smear of color and wind as she whirled around and around with her sisters. Who was touched and who the toucher; whose arm, whose thigh was pressed in the Dance, it did not matter. The Dance was all. Drops of perspiration, sticky as sap, bedewed their backs and ran slow rivulets to the ground. The Dance *was* the glade, *was* the grove. There was no stopping, no starting, for a circle has no beginning or end.

Then suddenly a hunter's horn knifed across the meadow. It was both discordant and sweet, sharp and caressing at once. The Dance did not stop but it dissolved. The Huntress was coming, the Huntress was here.

And then She was in the middle of them all, straddling a moon-beam, the red hem of Her saffron hunting tunic pulled up to expose muscled thighs. Seven hounds lay growling at Her feet. She reached up to Her hair and in one swift, savage movement, pulled at the golden cords that bound it up. Her hair cascaded like silver and gold leaves onto Her shoulders and crept in tendrils across Her small, perfect breasts. Her heart-shaped face, with its crescent smile, was both innocent and corrupt; Her eyes as dark blue as a storm-coming sky. She dismounted the moon shaft and turned around slowly, as if displaying Herself to them all, but She was the Huntress, and She was doing the hunting. She looked into their faces one at a time, and the younger ones looked back, both eager and afraid.

Arrhiza was neither eager nor afraid. Twice already she had been the chosen one, torn laughing and screaming from the glade, brought for a night to the moon's dark side. The pattern of the Huntress' mouth was burned into her throat's hollow, Her mark, just as Her words were still in Arrhiza's ears. "You are mine. Forever. If you leave me, I will kill you, so fierce is my love." It had been spoken each time with a kind of passion, in between kisses, but the words, like the kisses, were as cold and distant and pitiless as the moon.

The Huntress walked around the circle once again, pausing longest before a young meliade, Pyrena of the appleblossoms. Under that gaze Pyrena seemed both to wither and to bloom. But the Huntress shook Her head and Her mouth formed the slightest moue of disdain. Her tongue flicked out and was caught momentarily between flawless teeth. Then She clicked to the hounds who sprang up. Mounting the moonbeam again, She squeezed it with Her thighs and was gone, riding to another grove.

The moment She disappeared, the glade was filled with breathy gossip.

"Did you see . . ." began Dryope. Trembling with projected pleasure, she turned to Pyrena. "The Huntress looked at you. Truly looked. Next time it *will* be you. I *know* it will."

Pyrena wound her fingers through her hair, letting fall a cascade of blossoms that perfumed the air. She shrugged but smiled a secret, satisfied smile.

Arrhiza turned abruptly and left the circle. She went back to her tree. Sluggishly the softened heartwood rings admitted her and she leaned into them, closed her eyes, and tried to sleep though she knew that in spring no true sleep would come.

She half-dreamed of clouds and birds, forcing them into her mind, but really she was hearing a buzzing. Sky, she murmured to herself, remember sky.

* * *

"Oh trees, fair and flourishing, on the high hills They stand, lofty. The Deathless sacred grove . . ."

Jeansen practiced his Homeric supplication, intoning carefully through his nose. The words as they buzzed through his nasal passages tickled. He sneezed several times rapidly, a light punctuation to the verses. Then he continued:

". . . The Deathless sacred grove Men call them, and with iron never cut."

He could say the words perfectly now, his sounds rounded and full. The newly learned Greek rolled off his tongue. He had always been a fast study. Greek was his fifth language, if he counted Esperanto. He could even, on occasion, feel the meanings that hid behind the ancient poetry, but as often the meanings slid away, slippery little fish and he the incompetent angler.

He had come to Greece because he wanted to be known as the American Olivier, the greatest classical actor the States had ever produced. He told interviewers he planned to learn Greek—classic Greek, not the Greek of the streets—to show them Oedipus from the amphitheaters where it had first been played. He would stand in the groves of Artemis, he had said, and call the Goddess to him in her own tongue. One columnist even suggested that with his looks and voice and reputation she would be crazy not to come. If she did, Jeansen thought to himself, smiling, I wouldn't treat her with any great distance. The goddesses like to play at shopgirls; the shopgirls, goddesses. And they all, he knew only too well, liked grand gestures.

And so he had traveled to Greece, not the storied isles of Homer but the fume-clogged port of Pyreus, where a teacher with a mouthful of broken teeth and a breath only a harpy could love had taught him. But mouth and breath aside, he was a fine teacher and Jeansen a fine learner. Now he was ready. Artemis first, a special for PBS, and then the big movie. Oedipus starring *the* Jeansen Forbes.

Only right now all he could feel was the buzz of air, diaphragm against lungs, lungs to larynx, larynx to vocal chords, a mechanical vibration. Buzz, buzz, buzz.

He shook his head as if to clear it, and the well-cut blonde hair fell perfectly back in place. He reached a hand up to check it, then looked around the grove slowly, admiringly. The grass was long, uncut, but trampled down. The trees—he had not noticed it at first—were a strange mixture: birch and poplar, apple and oak. He was not a botanist, but it seemed highly unlikely that such a mix would have simply sprung up. Perhaps they had been planted years and years ago. *Note to himself, check on that.*

This particular grove was far up on Mount Cynthus, away from any roads and paths. He had stumbled on it by accident. Happy accident. But it was perfect, open enough for re-enacting some of the supplicatory dances and songs, but the trees thick enough to add mystery. The guide book said that Cynthus had once been sacred to the Huntress, virgin Artemis, Diana of the moon. He liked that touch of authenticity. Perhaps her ancient worshippers had first seeded the glade. Even if he could not find the documentation, he could suggest it in such a way as to make it sound true enough.

Jeansen walked over to one birch, a young tree, slim and gracefully bending. He ran his hands down its white trunk. He rubbed a leaf between his fingers and considered the camera focusing on the action. He slowed the movement to a sensuous stroking. *Close up of hand and leaf, full frame.*

Next to the birch was an apple, so full of blossoms there was a small fall of petals puddling the ground. He pushed them about tentatively with his boot. Even without wind, more petals drifted from the tree to the ground. *Long tracking shot as narrator kicks through the pile of white flowers, lap dissolve to a single blossom.*

Standing back from the birch and the apple tree, tall and unbending, was a mature oak. It looked as if it were trying to keep the others from getting close. Its reluctance to enter the circle of trees made Jeansen move over to it. Then he smiled at his own fancies. He was often, he knew, too fanciful, yet such invention was also one of his great strengths as an actor. He took off his knapsack and set it down at the foot of the oak like an offering. Then he turned and leaned against the tree, scratching between his shoulder blades with the rough bark. *Long shot of man in grove, move in slowly for tight close-up. Voice over.*

> But when the fate of death is drawing near, First wither on the earth the beauteous trees, The bark around them wastes, the branches fall, And the Nymph's soul, at the same moment, leaves The sun's fair light."

He let two tears funnel down his cheeks. Crying was easy. He could call upon tears whenever he wanted to, even before a word was spoken in a scene. They meant nothing anymore. *Extremely tight shot on tear, then slow dissolve to . . .*

A hand touched his face, reaching around him from behind. Startled, Jeansen grabbed at the arm, held, and turned.

"Why do you water your face?"

He stared. It was a girl, scarcely in her teens, with the clearest complexion he had ever seen and flawless features, except for a crescent scar at her throat which somehow made the rest more perfect. His experienced eyes traveled quickly down her body. She was naked under a light green chiffon shift. He wondered where they had gotten her, what she wanted. A part in the special?

"Why do you water your face?" she asked again. Then this time she added, "You are a man." It was almost a question. She moved around before him and knelt unselfconsciously.

Jeansen suddenly realized she was speaking ancient Greek. He had thought her English with that skin. But the hair was black with blue-green highlights. Perhaps she *was* Greek.

He held her face in his hands and tilted it up so that she met him eye to eye. The green of her eyes was unbelievable. He thought they might be lenses, but saw no telltale double impression in the eye.

Jeansen chose his words with care, but first he smiled, the famous slow smile printed on posters and magazine covers. "You," he said, pronouncing the Greek with gentle precision, his voice carefully low and tremulous, "you are a goddess."

She leaped up and drew back, holding her hands before her. "No, no," she cried, her voice and body registering such fear that Jeansen rejected it at once. This was to be a classic play, not a horror flick.

But even if she couldn't act, she was damned beautiful. He closed his eyes for a moment, imprinting her face on his memory. And he thought for a moment of her pose, the hands held up. There had been something strange about them. She had too many—or too few—fingers. He opened his eyes to check them, and she was gone.

"Damned bit players," he muttered at last, angry to have wasted so much time on her. He took the light tent from his pack and set it up. Then he went to gather sticks for a fire. It could get pretty cold in the mountains in early spring, or so he had been warned.

From the shelter of the tree, Arrhiza watched the man. He moved gracefully, turning, gesturing, stooping. His voice was low and full of music and he spoke the prayers with great force. Why had she been warned that men were coarse, unfeeling creatures? He was far more beautiful then any of the worshippers who came cautiously at dawn in their black-beetle dresses, creeping down the paths like great nicophorus from the hidden chambers of earth, to lift their year-scarred faces to the sky. They brought only jars of milk, honey, and oil, but he came bringing a kind of springy joy. And had he not wept when speaking of the death of trees, the streams from his eyes as crystal as any that ran near the grove? Clearly this man was neither coarse nor unfeeling.

A small breeze stirred the top branches, and Arrhiza glanced up for a moment, but even the sky could not hold her interest today. She looked back at the stranger, who was pulling oddments from his pack. He pounded small nails into the earth, wounding it with every blow, yet did not fear its cries.

Arrhiza was shocked. What could he be doing? Then she realized he was erecting a dwelling of some kind. It was unthinkable—yet this stranger had thought it. No votary would dare stay in a sacred grove past sunfall, dare carve up the soil on which the trees of the Huntress grew. To even think of being near when the Dance began was a desecration. And to see the Huntress, should She visit this glade at moonrise, was to invite death. Arrhiza shivered. She was well-schooled in the history of Acteon, torn by his own dogs for the crime of spying upon Her.

Yet this man was unafraid. As he worked, he raised his voice—speaking, laughing, weeping, singing. He touched the trees with bold, unshaking hands. It was the trees, not the man, who trembled at his touch. Arrhiza shivered again, remembering the feel of him against the bark, the muscles hard under the fabric of his shirt. Not even the Huntress had such a back.

Then perhaps, she considered, this fearless votary was not a man at all. Perhaps he was a god come down to tease her, test her, take her by guile or by force. Suddenly, she longed to be wooed.

"You are a goddess," he had said. And it had frightened her. Yet only a god would dare such a statement. Only a god, such as Eros, might take time to woo. She would wait and let the night reveal him. If he remained untouched by the Huntress and unafraid, she would know.

Jeansen stood in front of the tent and watched the sun go down. It seemed to drown itself in blood, the sky bathed in an elemental red that was only slowly leeched out. Evening, however, was an uninteresting entre-act. He stirred the coals on his campfire and climbed into the tent. *Lap dissolve . . .*

Lying in the dark, an hour later, still sleepless, he thought about the night. He often went camping by himself in the California mountains, away from the telephone and his fans. *Intercut other campsites.* He knew enough to carry a weapon against marauding mountain lions or curious bears. But the silence of this Greek night was more disturbing than all the snufflings and howlings in the American dark. He had never heard anything so complete before—no crickets, no wind, no creaking of trees.

He turned restlessly and was surprised to see that the tent side facing the grove was backlit by some kind of diffused lighting. Perhaps it was the moon. It had become a screen, and shadow women seemed to dance across it in patterned friezes. It had to be a trick of his imagination, trees casting silhouettes. Yet without wind, how did they move?

As he watched, the figures came more and more into focus, clearly women. This was no trick of imagination, but of human proposing. If it was one of the columnists or some of his erstwhile friends . . . Try to frighten him, would they? He would give them a good scare instead.

He slipped into his khaki shorts and found the pistol in his pack. Moving stealthily, he stuck his head out of the tent. And froze.

Instead of the expected projector, he saw real women dancing, silently beating out a strange exotic rhythm. They touched, stepped, circled. There was no music that he could hear, yet not one of them misstepped. And each was as lovely as the girl he had met in the grove.

Jeansen wondered briefly if they were local girls hired for an evening's work. But they were each so incredibly beautiful, it seemed unlikely they could all be from any one area. Then suddenly realizing it didn't matter, that he could simply watch and enjoy it, Jeansen chuckled to himself. It was the only sound in the clearing. He settled back on his haunches and smiled.

The moon rose slowly as if reluctant to gain the sky. Arrhiza watched it silver the landscape. Tied to its rising, she was pulled into the Dance.

Yet as she danced a part of her rested still within the tree, watching. And she wondered. Always before, without willing it, she was wholly a part of the Dance. Whirling, stepping along with the other dryads, their arms, her arms; their legs, her legs. But now she felt as cleft as a tree struck by a bolt. The watching part of her trembled in anticipation.

Would the man emerge from his hasty dwelling? Would he prove himself a god? She watched and yet she dared not watch, each turn begun and ended with the thought, the fear.

And then his head appeared between the two curtains of his house, his bare shoulders, his bronzed and muscled chest. His face registered first a kind of surprise, then a kind of wonder, and at last delight. There was no fear. He laughed and his laugh was more powerful than the moon. It drew her to him and she danced slowly before her god.

Setting: moon-lit glade. 30–35 girls dancing. No Busby Berkley kicklines, please. Try for a frenzied yet sensuous native dance. Robbins? Sharp? Ailey? Absolutely no dirndls. Light make-up. No spots. Diffused light. Music: an insistent pounding, feet on grass. Maybe a wild piping. Wide shot of entire dance then lap dissolve to single dancer. She begins to slow down, dizzy with anticipation, dread. Her god has chosen her . . .

Jeansen stood up as one girl turned slowly around in front of him and held out her arms. He leaned forward and caught her up, drew her to him.

A god is different, thought Arrhiza, as she fell into his arms. They tumbled onto the fragrant grass.

He was soft where the Huntress was hard, hard where She was soft. His smell was sharp, of earth and mold; Hers was musk and air.

"Don't leave," he whispered, though Arrhiza had made no movement to go. "I swear I'll kill myself if you leave." He pulled her gently into the canvas dwelling.

She went willingly though she knew that a god would say no such thing. Yet knowing he was but a man, she stayed and opened herself under him, drew him in, felt him shudder above her, then heavily fall. There was thunder outside the dwelling and the sound of dogs growling. Arrhiza heard it all and, hearing, did not care. The Dance outside had ended abruptly. She breathed gently in his ear, "It is done."

He grunted his acceptance and rolled over onto his side, staring at nothing, but a hero's smile playing across his face. Arrhiza put her hand over his mouth to silence him and he brought up his hand to hers. He counted the fingers with his own and sighed. It was then that the lightning struck, breaking her tree, her home, her heart, her life.

She was easy, Jeansen thought. Beautiful and silent and easy, the best sort of woman. He smiled into the dark. He was still smiling when the tree fell across the tent, bringing the canvas down around them and crushing three of his ribs. A spiky branch pierced his neck, ripping the larynx. He pulled it out frantically and tried to scream, tried to breath. A ragged hissing of air through the hole was all that came out. He reached for the girl and fainted.

Three old women in black dresses found him in the morning. They pushed the tree off the tent, off Jeansen, and half carried, half dragged him down the mountainside. They found no girl.

He would live, the doctor said through gold and plaster teeth, smiling proudly.

Live. Jeansen turned the word over in his mind, bitterer than any tears. In Greek or in English, the word meant little to him now. *Live.* His handsome face unmarred by the fallen tree seemed to crack apart with the effort to keep from crying. He shaped the word with his lips but no sound passed them. Those beautiful, melodious words would never come again. His voice had leaked out of his neck with his blood.

Camera moves in silently for a tight close-up. Only sounds are routine hospital noises; and mounting over them to an overpowering cacophony is a steady, harsh, rasping breathing, as credits roll.

The Hardwood Pile

by

L. Sprague de Camp

THIS IS A WORLD wherein virtue often goes unrewarded. If R. B. Wilcox had not been such a moral man, he might have gotten the true story of the haunted woodpile for his book on the lore and legends of upstate New York. Mr. Wilcox's morals, alone, were not responsible for his failure to get the inside dope. There was also the fact that carroty-red hair did not appeal to him.

The hair belonged to Miss Aceria Jones, the hostess at The Pines. This was a self-styled tea room in the village of Gahato, county of Herkimer, State of New York. The Pines, despite the misleading sobriquet of "tea room," served liquor of all degrees of hardness and had a passable dance orchestra. Not the least of its attractions was Miss Aceria Jones. She was an uncommonly pretty girl, looking rather like a plane hostess.

R. B. Wilcox had landed at The Pines in the course of his prowl around the country after lore and legends. After dinner he tried to collect some material. The restaurateur, a Mr. Earl Delacroix, was out; so the writer tackled Miss Jones. She gave him a little lore on the theory and practice of hostessing in an Adirondack sawmill town, but nothing that could be called a legend. To his questions about the haunted woodpile, she replied that she paid no attention to such silly stories.

In the hope of squeezing a little usable copy out of his

charming questionee, Wilcox tried praise: "I'm surprised that you live up here in the sticks. I should think with your looks you could get a job in the city."

"You mean Utica?"

"New York."

"No, I would not like that. No trees."

"You're crazy about trees?"

"Well, some trees. If there was a job in a place with a Norway maple in front of it, I would take it at once."

"A what in front of the place?"

"A Norway maple—*Acer platanoides*. Do you know of a place that has one such?"

"Why . . . uh . . . no. But I don't know much about trees. Is that a native species?"

"No, a European."

"Wouldn't another species do?"

"No; it must be that. I cannot explain. But, Mr. Wilcox, it would mean much to me." She rolled her large eyes meltingly at him.

Wilcox's morals began to assert themselves. He said stiffly: "I'm afraid I don't know what *I* could do for you."

"You could find a nice, clean place that has a job open, and a Norway maple growing in front of it. If you did, I would like you very, *very* much." Another roll of the optics.

At the second "very," Wilcox could fairly feel his morals tugging him toward the door. He, or rather his morals, may have been doing Miss Jones an injustice. But he did not stay to investigate this melancholy redhead's passion for Norway maples, or her definition of "very." He paused only long enough to assure Miss Jones that he would let her know if he heard of anything. Then he passed out of the restaurant and out of this tale.

To get a proper perspective, we must go back to 1824. In that year there landed in New York a dark, paunchy, dignified man who said he was August Rudli of Zurich, Switzerland. He was, he said, a member of an old Swiss banking family, and also related to the Wittelsbachs, so that he was about forty-third in line for the Bavarian throne. He had been a colonel under Napoleon—he had a medal to prove it—and, finding the banking business too stuffy, had taken his share of the family fortune and come to America.

But it must be recorded that Herr Rudli's story contained one or two inexactitudes. He was related neither to the Wittelsbachs nor to any family of bankers. He had seen no military service; the medal was a phony. He had been in the banking business, but not in the way he had said. He had risen by sheer merit to the post of cashier. Thereupon, on a dark and stormy night, he had walked off with all the assets not securely nailed down.

As people were seldom if ever extradited across the Atlantic in those days, at least for embezzlement, Herr Rudli might have enjoyed the fruits of his enterprise for years, if he had not fallen in with an even slicker article. This article, one John A. Spooner, separated Rudli from most of his cash for a "country estate" consisting of several thousand acres of granite ridges, bog holes, and black flies in the Adirondacks. Rudli spent most of the rest in having a road run in, a biggish house built, and gewgaws imported from Europe to furnish the house. Among the more puzzling importations were two young Norway maples, which were planted in front of the house. Rudli's tract was already covered by a dense mixed forest consisting partly of sugar maple, red maple and silver maple, the first of which grow at least as large and as fast as any European maple. But Rudli had his own ideas about being a country gentleman, and the planting of imported trees evidently formed part of them.

Rudli never learned how thoroughly he had been roodled. He died of pneumonia in the middle of the first winter he attempted to spend in his new house.

After Rudli's death, the tract went through various hands. Some of it ended up as the property of the International Paper Co.; some went to the State of New York; the piece on which Rudli's house had stood went to a man named Delahanty. After a century of neglect, all that could be seen of the house was a broad, low mound covered with leaf mold, from which one stone chimney stuck up. The clearing in which the house had stood and most of the road leading to it were completely grown up. Of the two Norway maples, one had died in infancy. The other was now a fine, big tree.

Delahanty the elder sold his pulpwood stumpage in 1903. Thirty-five years later, Delahanty the younger sold the hardwood on the tract. In went the lumberjacks through the snow, and down came the beeches, birches, and hard maples. Down, too, came Rudli's surviving Norway maple, mistaken for a sugar maple, the "hard" maple of the lumberman.

In due course, the two logs that had been cut from this tree arrived in the hot pond of Dan Pringle's sawmill at Gahato. The name of the village is Mohawk for "log-in-the-water"; very appropriate for a sawmill town. In the spring, they were hauled up the jacker chain and sawn into about nine hundred feet of one-inch boards. These were put in Pile No. 1027, which consisted of one-inch FAS hard maple, FAS—Firsts and Seconds—is the highest hardwood classification.

The following summer, Pringle got a hardwood order from Hoyt, his wholesaler, that included twenty thousand feet of one-inch FAS hard maple. The yard crew loaded the top halves of Piles No. 1027 and 1040 into a box car. The foreman, Joe Larochelle, ordered them to transfer the remaining half of Pile 1027 to Pile 1040. So Henri Michod lowered himself from the hardwood tramway to the top of Pile No. 1027. He picked up a board and handed it to Olaf Bergen, who turned and plunked it on a lumber truck, which stood on the tramway with its wheels chocked. Bergen took his pipe out long enough to spit—aiming between the tramway and the pile—steered the pipe back through the mossy curtain of yellow hair that hung from his upper lip, grabbed the next board, and so forth. When Michod had finished the topmost course of boards, he gathered up the stickers—the one-by-two's that keep the courses apart—piled them on the tramway, and went on to the next course.

That was all very well. But when Michod started on the fourth course, the pile began to sway. First it swayed east and west, then north and south, then with a circular motion. It also set up a dismal moaning and squeaking as board and stickers rubbed together.

Olaf Bergen stared in childish wonder at the phenomenon. "Hey, Henri, what the Holy Jumping Judas you doing with that pile?"

"Me?" cried the harassed Michod. "I don't do nothing. It does it. Earthquake, maybe. I think I get the hell off." He jumped off the pile onto a lower one with a clatter.

"Can't be no earthquake," Bergen called down to him. "You don't see the other piles actin' up, do you?"

"No."

"Well, if it was an earthquake, the other piles would have swayed, too, wouldn't they? So there wasn't no earthquake. Stands to reason, don't it?"

"Yeah? Then what makes the pile sway?"

"Nothin'. An earthquake's the only thing that could, and there wasn't no earthquake. So the pile didn't sway. Now get back up and gimme some more boards."

"So the pile didn't sway, huh? *Les nuts,* Mr. Bergen. I know better. And, by damn, I don't get back up there."

"Aw, come on, Henri. Stands to reason it must have been your imagination."

"All right, you stand on the pile then. I take the tramway." Michod swarmed up onto the trestle. Bergen, looking confident, jumped down onto No. 1027.

But No. 1027 had its own ideas, if lumber piles can be said to have ideas. The pile began to sway again. Bergen, staggering to keep his balance, perforce had to sway, too. And with each sway his china-blue eyes got bigger.

The motion was not a very unpleasant or difficult one; in fact, it was rather like that of the deck of a ship in a stiff breeze. But that did not calm Olaf Bergen. The trouble was that this lumber pile was not the deck of a ship. Lumber piles do not, normally, act that way. A pile that does so is unnatural, perhaps unholy. Olaf Bergen wanted no part of such a pile; not even a splinter.

So he shrieked: "The damn thing's haunted!" and tumbled off even more quickly than Michod had done. There was a brief swishing of his work shoes through the weeds, and the lumber yard knew him no more, at least not that day.

Henri Michod sat down on the tramway and took out a pack of cigarettes. He would have to report this singular occurrence to Joe Larochelle, but that was no reason for not relaxing a little first.

Then he heard Larochelle's quick footsteps coming

down the tramway and put away his cigarettes. Nobody walked quite so fast as Larochelle. He always arrived places slightly out of breath, and when he talked his sentences fell over one another. By these means he created an illusion of being an intensely busy man, passionately devoted to his employer's interests. Medium-sized, baldish, and snaggle-toothed, he trotted up and gasped: "Wh-where . . . where's Ole?"

"Ole?" replied Michod. "He's gone home."

"You mean to say that lousy guy went home without saying anything to me and here I've got three cars of grain-door board to get loaded in time for the noon freight?"

"That's it, Joe."

"Was he sick?"

"Maybe. He got kind of upset when this pile began to sway under him."

"Well, of all the lousy tricks! You wait here; I'll send Jean Camaret over from the pine tram. What the hell kind of a place does he think this is, anyhow?"—and Larochelle was off again.

Presently Jean Camaret appeared. He was older and even beefier than Henri Michod, who was pretty beefy himself. Between themselves they spoke Canuck French, which is not quite the same as French French. More than one Frenchman has indignantly denied that it is French at all.

Camaret got on Pile No. 1027. Before he had time to do more, the pile began to sway again. Camaret looked up. "Is it that I am dizzy, or is it that this sacred pile shakes herself?"

"The pile shakes herself, I think. It is a thing most extraordinary. It is not the wind, and it is not the earthquake. But it makes nothing. Give me a board just the same."

Camaret was, through no desire of his own, giving a first-rate imitation of a reed in a gale, but anyone could see that his heart was not in the part. He was not suited to it. There was nothing reedlike about him. He spread his feet to brace himself, made a fumbling effort to pick up a board, then turned a large, red, joyless face up to Michod.

"I cannot move," he said. "This unhappy pile gives me the sickness of the sea. Aid me to mount, my old."

His old helped him on the tramway. He sat down, put his head in his hands, and groaned like a soul in purgatory.

Michod grinned unsympathetically. At this rate, he would get a day's pay for doing no work at all. He started to take out his cigarettes again, but Joe Larochelle bustled down the tramway. "Wh-what . . . what's the matter with Jean? Is he sick or something?"

Camaret groaned again, more horribly. "I have the sick to the stomach. The pile goes *comme ci—comme ça.*"

"Whaddya mean the pile goes this way and that way? What the hell's the matter with you? Scared because a pile sways a little?"

"This pile is different. You get on and see."

"Huh! Never thought I'd see a grown man like you scared of a little pile. What the hell, I'm not scared—" And Larochelle hopped off the tramway. The pile began its rocking-chair act. Larochelle yelped and scrambled back on the trestle.

"Anybody can see that pile ain't safe!" he bawled. "Must be the foundation beams are gone all to hell. Why the hell didn't you tell me sooner, Henri? Want us to break our necks?"

Henri Michod knew better than to argue. He grinned cynically and shrugged.

Larochelle concluded: "Well, anyway, you guys go over and help on the pine tram. Come back here at one."

When Camaret and Michod returned to Pile No. 1027 after the noon hour, they saw that Larochelle had tied it to the neighboring piles with a half-inch rope. He explained: "The foundation beams are okay; I don't see what the hell's wrong unless the supports are high in the middle so she's—whatcha call it?—unstable. But she ought to hold still with all this guying."

Neither yard worker showed any enthusiasm for getting back on the pile. Finally Larochelle shouted: "Damn it, Henri, you get on that pile or I'll put you on the soda tank!"

So Michod got, albeit sullenly. Larochelle referred to the tank of preserving solution in which freshly sawn pine planks were dunked. In pulling boards out of this tank, one had to move quickly to keep the next board from hitting one, and the solution made one's hands crack after a day. Larochelle's favorite method of settling arguments was to threaten to put a man on the disagreeable tank job out of his regular turn.

They loaded the truck, pushed it down to Pile No. 1040, and unloaded it. When this had been done twice, Larochelle put another man on the job, to stand on the edge of the pile and pass boards up. No. 1027 groaned and creaked a good deal, but the guying kept it from doing its hula.

The new man, Edward Gallivan, picked up a board and handed it to Michod, who passed it up to Camaret. Gallivan had picked up another board, when the first board twisted itself out of Camaret's hands. It flew back down, landing on Gallivan's board. Thus Camaret found himself boardless, while Gallivan had two boards.

Now Edward Gallivan liked mill-yard work well enough, but not to the point of collecting hard-maple planks for the fun of it. He cried:

"Hey, Frenchy, watch what you're doin'! You damn near took the head off me with that thing."

Camaret muttered something apologetic and looked puzzled. Michod passed the errant board up again. Again it twisted itself away from Camaret and returned to the pile with a clatter.

Camaret looked down with an expression of perplexity, suspicion, reproach, and growing alarm. That is, he would have looked that way if the human face were capable of expressing so many emotions at once. "Henri," he said, "did you grab that board away from me?"

"Why would I go grabbing boards away from you? I got enough boards already."

"I don't ask that. Did you snatch her?"

"No, by damn, I didn't. I ain't no board-snatcher."

"Now, boys," said Gallivan, "we ain't getting nowheres arguin' like this. You do it over and I'll watch."

So Michod passed the board up a third time. When Camaret took it, it swung wildly and twisted like a live thing. Camaret released it to keep from being pulled off the tramway, and it floated gently back to the place from which Gallivan had picked it. "Saints preserve us!" cried Gallivan. "I don't like that."

Michod folded his arms triumphantly. "You satisfied, Jean? I didn't have nothing to do with that."

Camaret replied hollowly: "Me, I am satisfied. I am satisfied too much. I get the sick to the stomach when I think of that. You tell Joe I go. I go home, get drunk, beat my wife, forget all about these damn boards."

Joe Larochelle blew up when the state of affairs was explained to him. Ned Gallivan smiled paternally, and Henri Michod shrugged. Larochelle had recently turned in a certain credit slip for eight hundred feet of No. 1 Common Birch, of which the local customer had not returned all the allegedly unused lumber. Maybe it was a bona fide mistake; maybe Larochelle had not split the proceeds of the discrepancy with the customer. But Gallivan and Michod knew about the slip and were pretty sure of their own positions in consequence.

Finally Larochelle yelled: "All right, all right! I'll show you how to handle these jumping boards. You wait here—" When he returned he carried a double-bitted ax. "Now," he said, "Henri, you hand a board to Ned."

When Gallivan took the board, it apparently tried to pull him off the trestle. Larochelle, standing beside him, smacked the board with the flat of the ax. It quivered a bit and subsided.

"Ouch!" said Gallivan. "You're making my hands sting."

"Never mind that, it's the way to handle 'em. I'm the guy who has to figure everything out—" Larochelle's expedient seemed to have cowed the boards, temporarily at least. They went up without protest.

Michod thought, that was just like the stupid, pretending that nothing was wrong. Anybody could see that here was something of the most extraordinary. That was the way of the world. The stupids like Larochelle had the authority, while the intelligents like himself—

This reverie was interrupted by another singular occurrence. Michod carelessly shot a board up to Gallivan when the latter was busy fishing his eating-tobacco out of his pants pocket. Gallivan made a one-handed grab and missed. It did not much matter, for the board kept right on going. It described a graceful arc and settled cozily into its appointed place on the truck.

"Hey!" yelled Larochelle. "Don't go throwing those boards; you're liable to hit somebody."

Michod kept silent, not wanting to disillusion the others about his strength and adroitness. Gallivan caught the next board; it hoisted him a foot into the air before he stopped it.

"What the hell are you trying to do, Henri?" cried the surprised Gallivan.

It was all very well to get credit for the mill-yard equivalent of tossing the caber, but to be blamed for all the vagaries of these athletic boards was something else. So Michod spoke up:

"I'm not trying to do nothing, by damn. I—" He was interrupted by finding his hands unexpectedly full of board. But the board did not stay there. It ripped his mittens in its eagerness to get up into Gallivan's hands, and thence on the truck.

Larochelle shrieked: "Stop it! Stop them!" As well try to stop a nestful of hornets by reading Jean Jacques Rousseau to them. All over the pile, boards were bouncing into Michod's uneager grasp, then flinging themselves up to Gallivan and on the truck. The load grew by leaps and even a bound or two. When they stopped, the truck was piled dangerously high. The last board took time out to thwack Joe Larochelle in passing. The foreman toppled from the tramway. As he did so he grabbed Gallivan for support. Both landed on the unfortunate Michod with a great clatter.

They picked themselves up to see the truck moving down the track of its own accord. Larochelle, who among his very modest list of virtues certainly counted energy, scrambled back onto the tramway in pursuit. The truck stopped in front of No. 1040, and its load cascaded crashingly off.

"Hey, look down!" said Michod.

The three men got down on their knees and peered over the edge of the trestle. A board had fallen off the truck during its trip and gone down between the tramway and the piles. It was now crawling after the fashion of an inchworm through the weeds. Arriving at No. 1040, it began to hump itself up the pile's side. Now and then it would be jerked upward without visible effort on its part. Its motions were like those of a rather obtuse puppy whose owner is trying to teach it tricks and putting it through them by *force majeure* when it fails to get the idea. Finally, it left the step-boards on the side of the pile and swooped up on the disorderly tangle on top of No. 1040.

Joe Larochelle did not acknowledge defeat easily. No matter how red-handed one caught him in a bit of grafting, he was as firm as an early Christian martyr and as plausible as a street map in his denials. But now he said:

"It's too much for me. You boys can go home; I gotta see the boss."

Joe Larochelle repaired to Pringle's office, which was downstairs in his home. He told his story.

Dan Pringle was a small, plump man with a large watch chain decorated with an incisor tooth of *Cervus canadensis* —the wapiti. He asked: "You been drinking lately, Joe?"

"No, Mr. Pringle. I ain't touched a thing."

Pringle got up and sniffed. "Well, I guess maybe not. Do you suppose a union organizer was back of this?"

"No, there ain't been any around. I been watching for them."

"Did you look between the piles and under the tramways?"

"Sure, I looked everywhere."

"Well, maybe. They're apt to sneak in no matter how careful you are, you know. Suppose you come back after supper and we'll take a look at these fancy boards. And bring a flashlight. We'll look around for union organizers, just in case."

Pringle and Larochelle arrived at the lumber yard as the sun was sliding down behind Gahato Mountain. Pringle insisted on creeping around the piles with his flashlight as if he were playing gangsters and G-men. He was, he explained, hoping to surprise a lurking union organizer. At Pile No. 1040 Larochelle said:

"That's her. See them boards lying in a heap on top?"

Pringle saw the boards. He also saw a young woman sitting on the edge of the pile, swinging her sandaled feet. Her green dress had obviously seen better days. About her hair, the kindest comment would be that it looked "nonchalant" or "carefree." It had apparently been red, but it had been singed off. It had grown out again but was still black at the ends and presented a distressing aspect.

"Good evening," said the young woman."You are Mr. Pringle, the owner of the sawmill, are you not?"

"Why—uh—maybe," said Pringle suspiciously. "Who—I mean what can I do for you?"

"Huh?" said a puzzled voice at his side. "What do you mean, Mr. Pringle?" Joe Larochelle was looking at him, ignoring the girl, whose feet were a few feet away on a level with his face.

"Why—I was talking—"

"You *are* the owner, Mr. Pringle? I have heard the men talking about you," said the girl.

"Just thinking out loud?" said Larochelle.

"Yes—I mean maybe," said the confused Pringle. "She just asked me—"

"Who's 'she'?" asked Larochelle.

"That young lady."

"What young lady?"

Pringle decided that his foreman was simply dithering and asked the girl: "You're not a union organizer, are you?"

The girl and Larochelle answered simultaneously: "I don't know what that is. I don't think so." "Who, *me?* Aw, come on, Mr. Pringle, you oughta know I hate 'em as much as you—"

"Not you, Joe!" cried Pringle. "Not you! I was just asking her—"

Larochelle's patience began to wear thin. "And I been asking you who 'her' is?"

"How should I know? I've been trying to find out myself."

"I think we're kinda mixed up. Here you talk about some skirt and I ask who and you say you don't know. That don't make sense, does it?"

Pringle wiped his forehead.

The girl said: "I would like to see you, Mr. Pringle, only without this M'sieu Larochelle."

"We'll see, miss," said Pringle.

Larochelle spoke: "Say, Mr. Pringle, are you feeling well? Damned if you don't sound like you was talking to somebody who ain't there."

Pringle began to feel like a rat in the hands of an experimental psychologist who is, with the best of motives, trying to drive it crazy. "Don't be ridiculous, Joe. I sound as though I were talking to somebody who *is* there."

"I know; that's just the trouble."

"What's the trouble?"

"There *ain't* anybody there, of course!"

This statement, despite its alarming implications, gave Pringle a feeling of relief. Theretofore, this maddening dispute had been like fighting blindfolded with broadswords at sixty paces. Now he had a solid point of disagreement. He said sharply: "Are you sure *you're* feeling well, Joe?"

"Sure, of course, I'm well."

"Do you, or don't you, see a girl in a green dress sitting on the edge of the pile?"

"No. I just said there ain't anybody there."

"Didn't ask you whether anybody *was* there, but whether you *saw* anybody there."

"Well, if there was anybody there I'd see 'em, wouldn't I? Makes sense, don't it?"

"We'll waive that."

"Wave what? This green dress I'm supposed to see that ain't there?"

Pringle danced distractedly on his short legs. "Never mind, never mind! Have you heard a woman's voice coming from that pile?"

"No, of course not. What gives you the idea—"

"All right, all right, that's what I wanted to know. You can run along home now. I'll do the rest of the investigating myself. No"—as Larochelle started to protest—"I mean that."

"Oh, all right. But look out the union organizers don't get you."

Larochelle grinned maliciously and trotted off. Pringle winced visibly at the last words but bravely faced the pile.

"Now, young lady," he said grimly, "are you *sure* you're not a union organizer?"

"Would I know if I was, Mr. Pringle?"

"You bet you would. I guess you aren't one, maybe. More likely an hallucination."

"Mr. Pringle! I did not ask to see you so you could call me bad names."

"No offense meant. But something's very funny around here. Either Joe or I are seeing things."

"If you have good eyes, you always see things. What is wrong with that?"

"'Nothing, when the things are there. What I'm trying to find out is, are you real or am I imagining you?"

"You see me, no?"

"Sure. But that doesn't prove you're real."

"What do I do to prove I am real?"

"I'm not just sure myself. You could put out your hand," he said doubtfully. The girl reached down, and Pringle touched her hand. "Feels real enough. But maybe I'm imagining the feel. How come Joe didn't see you?"

"I did not want him to."

"Oh, just like that, eh? You don't want him to, so he looks right through you."

"Naturally."

"It may be natural to you. But when I look at somebody I generally see him. Let's forget that question for a while. Let's not even think about it. If I'm not nuts already, I will be soon at this rate. Just what is all this funny business?"

"I don't think it is funny to have my home broken up."

"Huh?"

"You broke up my home."

"I broke up your home. I broke up your home. Young lady—What's your name, by the way?"

"Aceria."

"Miss Aceria, or Aceria something?"

"Just Aceria."

"Oh, well, skip it. I used to consider myself a pretty intelligent man. Not any parlor-pink intellectual, you understand, but a good competent American businessman. But I'm not sure any more. Nothing seems to make sense. What in the name of the great horn spoon do you mean, I've broken up your home? Did I lead your husband astray, maybe?"

"Oh, not like that. Like *that!*" She pointed to the tangle of boards behind her. "That was my home."

"Those boards? Come on, don't try to tell me some man of mine tore your house down and sneaked the boards onto the pile."

"Well, yes and no. Those boards were my tree."

"Your *what?*"

"My tree. I lived in it."

"I suppose you'll say next you were responsible for that commotion today?"

"I am afraid yes."

"Well." Others had testified to the occurrence of the commotion. Or had Pringle imagined that Joe Lárochelle had told that story—No, no, no! He wasn't going to think about that any more. "What was the idea?"

"I wanted to keep my home together. First I tried to keep the men from moving the boards. When I could not, I hurried the last ones up to get them together again."

"What *are* you? Some kind of spook?"

"I am a sphendamniad. That is a kind of wood nymph. Some people would say dryad, but that is not just right. They are oak spirits. I am a maple spirit. A man brought my tree from Austria, more than a hundred years ago. Last winter your men cut my tree down. I could not stop them, because I was hibernating, I think you call it, and by the time I woke up it was too late. That is how my hair got burned, when the men burned the branches and tops. It has grown out, but I know it looks terrible. I cannot leave my home on weekdays to go to the hairdresser, for fear the men will move the boards."

"You mean those aren't real hard maple?" snapped Pringle with sudden alertness. He climbed the side of the pile with an agility remarkable in a man of his age and girth. He looked at the boards with his flashlight. "Yeah, the grain *isn't* quite the same. Let's see; if they fooled the grader . . . I guess maybe they can go out with the rest on Tuesday."

"You mean you are going to sell these boards?"

"Sure. Just got a big order from Hoyt."

"What will happen to them?"

"Dunno. They'll be made into desks and bureau drawers and things, maybe. Depends on who buys them from Hoyt."

"But you must not do that, Mr. Pringle! My home, it will be scattered. I will have no place to live."

"Can't you set up housekeeping in another tree?"

"I can only live in Norway maples, and there are no more around here."

"Well, do you want to buy them? I'll let you have them at eighty dollars a thousand, which is less than I could get in the open market."

"I have no money."

"Well then, they'll have to go out with the rest. Sorry if it inconveniences you, but the sawmill costs alone are over seven dollars a thousand, counting insurance and depreciation."

"I do not know about such things, Mr. Pringle. I know you will break up my home so I can never get it together again. You would not do that, yes? I would like you *so* much if you did not."

She looked appealingly at him, a tear trickling down one cheek. If she had done this earlier, while it was still light, it might have worked. But all Pringle could see of her face was a dim, pale oval in the darkness; so he snapped:

"You bet I'd do that! This is business, young lady. If I let sentiment interfere with business, I'd have gone broke long ago. Anyway, I'm not convinced that you exist. So why should I give away lumber I paid good money for to somebody who's a mere hallucination, maybe?"

"You are a bad, wicked man. I will never let you send these boards away."

"Oh," he grinned through the dark. "It's to be a fight, huh? Nobody ever accused Dan Pringle of running away from a good, honest business fight. We'll see. Good night, Miss Aceria."

Pringle was as good as his word. Monday morning, he called in Larochelle and told him to load the lumber in Pile No. 1040 that day, instead of Tuesday as planned.

Michod, Camaret, Gallivan, and Bergen all looked solemn when they saw they were to work on No. 1040. But Larochelle forestalled any objections by mention of the soda tank.

So they set up the rollers. These were objects that looked like iron ladders, except that on what would be the rungs were mounted steel sleeves rotating on ball bearings. The rollers were mounted end to end on sawhorses so that they could carry boards across the tramway and across the tops of the two low piles between the tramway and the railroad spur.

Fassler, the inspector, turned the first board over with the sharpened T-piece on the end of his flexible lumber rule and made a note on his tally sheet. Gallivan, wondering if he hadn't been several kinds of fool for taking the job on Pile No. 1040, picked up the board and gave it to Michod. Michod put it on the nearest roller and shoved. *Zing!* went the rolls and away went the board.

In the normal course of events, the board should have continued its way to the box car, where Camaret and Bergen awaited it. Their mittens were outstretched to seize it, when it slowed down, stopped, and reversed its motion. *Zing!* went the rolls, but this time in reverse. Michod stared at it dumbly as it shot past under his nose, left the end of the line of rollers, and slammed down on the top of the pile.

Aceria had not been caught napping.

But Fassler knew nothing about Aceria, except for some vague talk, which he had discounted, about jumping boards. Since the tramway was between him and the box car, he could not see what had happened and assumed that somebody had pushed the board back up the rollers. He said so, with embellishments. He was a very profane man, though a slight, stoop-shouldered, harmless-looking one. People liked to play jokes on him so that they could stand around and admire his profanity.

Gallivan grinned at him. "Hey, Archie, will you say some more? Sure, it's as good as an education for a man to listen to you."

But the others were not so amused. Camaret and Bergen came up from the car. Camaret said: "I begin to get the sick to the stomach again."

Bergen said: "I'm damned if I'll work in a yard that's full of spooks."

Michod cocked a skeptical eyebrow. "You don't believe in those things, Ole?"

"Well, not exactly. But there's a powerful lot of queer things you don't know about."

"All right. You argue. I take a rest." And Michod sat down to enjoy a smoke.

The others explained to the incredulous Fassler. Finally, not knowing what else to do, they went back to work. Michod undertook to conduct the next board personally down to the box car. It went along reluctantly; just before they arrived, it shot forward, in one door of the car and out the other into the weeds before Camaret and Bergen could stop it.

So Joe Larochelle presently found his workers sitting on the tramway and settling the affairs of the universe. He yelled:

"You get back there and load that stuff or, by jeepers, you can start looking for another job!"

Gallivan grinned. "Sure, now, wouldn't that be a terrible thing?" He lowered his voice. "And wouldn't it be terrible, Joe, if the boss found out about that credit slip you turned in for Jack Smeed?"

"I dunno what you're talking about," said Larochelle. "But, anyway, I guess there's some other stuff you can pile."

So nothing more was done to Pile No. 1040 that day. Larochelle, if he had a soul, wrestled with it mightily. He had definite orders from Pringle, but he could not adopt the usual method of enforcing them because of the delicate credit-slip situation. By Tuesday night he worked up enough courage to report to Pringle.

Pringle snapped: "Sounds like they're getting pretty damned independent. Maybe a union organizer got next to them, after all. Let's see. I'll think of something by tomorrow, maybe."

Neither was altogether candid. Larochelle obviously could not explain why he could not get tougher with the yard crew, and Pringle could not explain about Aceria for fear of having people tap their foreheads. He was not too sure about his sanity himself. He thought of going down the line to Utica to be looked over, but he was afraid to do that for fear the doctor *would* find something wrong with his clockwork.

Wednesday morning, Pringle wandered down to the sawmill. There he saw something that filled him with dismay and apprehension. It was nothing more than an elderly, dried-up man looking at a box car standing on the end of the spur. That seems like a harmless enough combination. But the elderly man was the New York Central freight agent, and the car was one that had arrived with a carload of lime some months before. Pringle had not had any place to store the lime, had not wanted to build a shed, and had not wanted to pay demurrage on the car. So he had had the car jacked down to the end of the spur and hidden with brush. There it had stood, serving as free storage space while Pringle unloaded at his leisure and the Central wondered vaguely what had become of their car. Now the camouflage had been removed.

"We been wondering where that car was," accused Adams, the agent.

"I guess maybe it just slipped my mind," replied Pringle lamely.

"Mebbe. Looks like you owe us about three months' demurrage. I'll get the bill out first thing tomorrow." And Adams walked off uncompromisingly.

Later, Pringle grated to Larochelle: "If I find who took that brush away, I'll kill the—"

When Larochelle departed, a woman's voice said: "I took the branches away from the car, Mr. Pringle." There she was, standing between a couple of piles.

"You—" sputtered Pringle. He got a grip on himself. "I suppose maybe you think you're smart, young lady?"

"Oh, but I *know* I am smart," she replied innocently. "I thought out that you wanted the car hidden all by myself."

"Well, if you think it's going to make any difference about those boards, you can change your idea. They're going in spite of hell or high water."

"Yes? We will see, as you said that night." And she vanished.

Pringle yelled after Larochelle: "Hey, Joe! Spot a car for No. 1040 right away. If the hardwood gang don't want to work on it, get some men from the pine gang." He muttered to himself: "I'll show this wood spook! Thinks she can scare me—"

But the men from the pine gang fared no better than the hardwood gang. They fared rather worse, in fact. The boards slewed crosswise on the rollers, jumped off the pile, paddled the men, and finally hit one man, Dennis Ahearn, over the head. He required two stitches in his scalp, and there were no more attempts to load the car that day.

As Ahearn himself explained: "It may be the spooks, or it may be the wood, or it may be the sap runnin', but the devil himself won't get me to touch another of them damn live boards. What you need, Mr. Pringle, is a crew of lion tamers."

Pringle was angry enough over his failure to get the car

loaded. But he was a shrewd man; he would not have lasted so long as he had in the precarious Adirondack lumber business otherwise. He suspected that Aceria would try some devilment or other in retaliation for his latest attempt to load the car. Maybe there would be an accident in the mill—so he ordered extra guard rails installed around the saws. Or, he thought, he might find some morning that all the lumber trucks were at the bottom of the Moose River. True, they weighed over three hundred pounds apiece, but he was not taking any chances with Aceria's supernatural powers, whatever they were. So he hired some of the workers overtime as night watchmen.

But Aceria was not exactly stupid either. Uninformed, perhaps, as a result of living in the woods for so many centuries, but she learned quickly. So her next attack was in a quarter that Pringle had not thought of.

Mrs. Pringle, a waspish woman, was due back at Pringle's home from a visit to some relatives. There was not much pleasurable anticipation of the reunion on either side. The corrosive effect of Helen Pringle's disposition, applied over a period of thirty years, had seen to that. But whatever Helen Pringle expected, she did not expect to find a comely young woman sitting at *her* dressing table, in *her* bedroom, calmly drying a head of freshly shampooed carroty-red hair.

Aceria looked up with a quick smile at Mrs. Pringle's gasp. "Yes?" she said politely.

Mrs. Pringle's mouth moved soundlessly. Then she said: "Gug."

"I'm sorry."

"You . . . you . . . what . . . what are you doing in my room?"

It was the first time since she had been five years old that words had failed—or almost failed—Mrs. Pringle. But then, the fact that Aceria was not wearing her green dress might have had something to do with it.

Aceria, still polite, remarked: "Your room? Oh, *I see*, you are Mrs. Pringle! This is embarrassing. It was stupid of Danny not to send me away before you came back, no? But if you will leave me for a minute, I will be gone like a flash."

Thus it came to pass that Pringle found the reunion

more exciting, if no more pleasant, than he had expected. Helen descended on him and demanded to know, in a voice like a band saw going through a twenty-four-inch pine log—with knots in it—who that creature was, and didn't he have sense enough to know that nobody would want an old fool like him for anything but his money, and if he had to make a fool of himself couldn't he have the decency to keep his follies out of his wife's sight, and it was a good thing she hadn't unpacked because she was leaving forthwith. Which she did.

Through this tirade, Pringle was merely bewildered until the end. As Helen slammed the door behind her he saw the light and dashed upstairs. There was nobody there, of course.

Dan Pringle started for the mill, intending to denounce Aceria up one side and down the other. But he cooled off on the way. He began to grin and arrived feeling like a triumphal procession.

He looked around to see that nobody was within hearing, and called softly: "Aceria!"

There she was, between two piles. Pringle accused: "I suppose it was you who appeared to my wife just now?"

"I am afraid yes. I do not like to interfere in the affairs of mortals. But I had to teach you not to try to move my boards."

Pringle grinned. "That's okay, little lady. Don't give it a thought. You did me a favor. If I can count on my wife staying away awhile, maybe I can really enjoy life. So better not try any more stunts, or they're liable to backfire."

"You are still determined to break up my home?"

"Yep. Might have gotten soft-hearted if you hadn't pulled all these stunts. But now that lumber's going out if it's the last thing I do."

"I warn you, Mr. Pringle. I have some more stunts, as you call them."

"Such as?"

"You will see."

Pringle's pride—at least, the quality that his competitors called his orneriness—prevented him from giving in. He could not let things go on as they were; the turmoil at the mill was costing him money every day, and he operated on a slim margin of profit. So next day he called all his mill workers together. They assembled in a silence made obtrusive by the lack of the band saw's shriek. Pringle called for volunteers for a risky job.

Those who had not experienced the athletic boards had heard about them and were not too anxious to learn more firsthand. But Pringle offered time and a half, and they had to eat. Twenty-one responded. Pringle had decided against the use of rollers. Most of the gang would simply sit on Pile No. 1040 to hold the boards down, and four men would carry each board across the intervening piles to the box car.

The boards tugged and wiggled a bit first, but Larochelle hit them with his ax and they went along. All went well until the car had been partly filled. Then there was an outbreak of yells from the car. Seconds later Michod and a man named Chisholm popped out of it, scrambled up the nearest pile to the tramway, and raced along the trestle. After them flew a short length of board. It swung this way and that, exactly as if somebody were chasing the two men and trying to hit them with it.

Pringle knew very well who was on the rear end of that piece of board, but he could not think of anything to do. While he watched, the board dropped lifeless to the tramway. Then there was a mighty clatter from the car, and most of the load of one-inch FAS maple spilled out the open car door on the side away from the piles. The boards, instead of being nice and rigid, like respectable maple planks, were writhing like a nestful of loathsome larvae. As they flopped out onto the cinders, they bent into semi-circles like bows, then straightened out with a snap and soared off toward the woods.

"After 'em!" yelled Pringle. "You, Joe! Two bits a board for every one that's brought back!"

He scrambled down and set out after his lumber as fast as his short legs would carry him. Larochelle followed. The crew's nerves, already shaken by the sight of the unnatural pursuit of Michod and Chisholm were now completely demoralized. But a few men followed Pringle and Larochelle.

They ran and they ran, tripping over logs and falling into brooks. Eventually Aceria ran out of ectoplasm, or something, and the boards ceased their bounding flight. They were gathered up in armfuls and brought back. They were piled on No. 1040 again. The men flatly refused to enter the box car with them, where there would be no room to dodge. It took all Pringle's authority and gifts of leadership to get them to go back to work at all; the scream of the saw did not ring out over hill and pond again until after the noon hour.

After lunch, Pringle hopped about the mill yard nervously, awaiting the counterattack, which he was sure was coming. It came soon enough. A mill like Pringle's, which is not equipped for turning out little things like chessmen, accumulates a vast amount of waste. Some of the slabs and edgings can be used as boiler fuel; some can be sold locally as firewood. But there is a surplus, and also a lot of useless sawdust. On the edge of the mill yard stood a pile of sawdust twenty feet high, waiting to be fed into the waste burner, a huge sheet-iron incinerator.

Presently this pile of sawdust did a curious thing. It swirled up into a whirling, top-shaped cloud, as if a whirlwind had settled on its apex. The cloud grew until there was no more sawdust on the ground, and the cloud was as big as a house. Then it swooped hither and thither about the yard. It hid the workers from each other and stung their faces. They were not encouraged when one of them pointed out that, while the cloud itself seemed to be borne on a miniature tornado, the far-off trees stood stiff in still air. They stampeded, yelling, into the sawmill. The engineer, hearing the tumult, prudently shut down the engine, and again the band saw and the edging, trimming, and slashing saws fell silent. Nobody else was silent. Pringle, rubbing sawdust out of his bloodshot eyes, could not make himself heard at all.

The cloud made a couple of tentative rushes at the mill. But Aceria's powers were apparently not equal to getting it in a lot of separate doors and windows and reforming it inside. It hovered, teetering and swooshing menacingly, about the yard.

Many people did not love Dan Pringle, but they admitted that he had what it takes. He got the sneezing and blaspheming Larochelle and Fassler aside and sent them on an errand. They went out and ran to Fassler's car. The cloud swooped after them, but they jumped in and cranked up the windows, and off they went.

When they came back, they had two boxes full of colored sunglasses with little metal shields that made passable goggles out of them. Fassler said: "That's all there are of these things around here. We went clear up to Old Forge and cleaned out the stores. And my car stopped just before we got back. Sawdust in the carburetor."

Pringle yelled for attention. He put on a pair of the goggles, tied a handkerchief over the lower part of his face, turned up his shirt collar, pulled his hat down over his ears, and said:

"Now, if you guys have got any guts, you'll do like me and go out there and get back to work. The sawdust can't hurt you. I'm going out if I have to load the damn cars myself. Who's with me? Time and a half as long as that cloud's around."

Nobody said anything for a minute. Then Edward Gallivan mumbled something and put on a pair of goggles. Most of the others did likewise. They were, after all, a strong, tough lot, and the sight of their fat and aging boss preparing to face the cloud alone may have shamed them.

So, masked and goggled, they went back down the tramways, clutching at the piles for support as the whirlwind buffeted them and the sawdust stung every exposed inch of skin. Pringle grinned behind his handkerchief as he watched them get slowly on with their work, while Aceria's top shrieked about their ears. So, the wood spook still thought she could lick him? If this was her last stunt, he'd won, by jeepers. Or at least it was still a draw.

But it was not Aceria's last stunt. The cloud rose up and up until it looked no bigger than a marble. Everybody thought it was leaving for good, although they continued to glance up nervously at it.

Then it started down again. As it came near, they saw that it was a lot smaller and more opaque than when it had gone up. As it approached, it resolved itself into something that might be imagined by a paleontologist with the D.T.'s. It looked somewhat like a pterodactyl, somewhat like an octopus, and somewhat like Fafner in "Siegfried." It had huge batlike wings and six long tentacular limbs with hands on their ends.

The shouts that had sounded on previous occasions about the yard were but as the chirp of canaries compared with the yells that now arose. As the thing glided over the yard, workers, foreman, inspectors, everybody went away. They went in straight radial lines, like droplets of mercury when a gob falls on a table top, only much faster. They jumped fences and waded neck-deep across the Moose River. Those inside the mill looked out to see what was up. They saw, and they went, too.

Pringle danced on the tramway. "Come back!" he screamed. "It can't hurt you. It's only sawdust! Look!" The monster was bobbing up and down in front of him, moving its horrid yellow jaws. He strode up to it and punched it. His fist went right through the sawdust, which swirled out in little puffs around his wrist. The hole made by his fist closed up as soon as he drew his arm back. For it was, as he surmised, merely the same cloud of animated sawdust, somewhat condensed and molded into this horrifying form.

"Look here! It's not a real thing at all! Come on back!" He passed his hand right through one of its groping limbs, which joined together again immediately.

But there was nobody to appreciate this display of nerve. Across the river, Pringle could see the rear elevation of a couple of small figures in drab work clothes, getting smaller every minute. As he watched, they disappeared into the forest. The form floated low over the site of the sawdust pile and collapsed. The pile was back where it had been, and Pringle was alone.

The thing that perhaps annoyed Pringle the most was that this time the engineer had run off without shutting down the engines, so that all the saws were whirling merrily in the empty mill. Pringle had to go down and turn the valve himself.

It was almost dark when Pringle and Larochelle appeared at the sawmill. They looked odd. Pringle was wearing, among other things, a catcher's mask and chest protector. Larochelle wore an old football helmet, several sweaters, and a lumber-yard worker's heavy leather apron. Pringle carried a flashlight; Larochelle, a five-gallon can of kerosene and a gasoline blowtorch.

"What are you going to do, Mr. Pringle?" asked Aceria.

She was sitting on No. 1040. Larochelle had gone off to start the water pump and uncoil the fire hose.

"Going to have a little fire."

"You are going to burn my home?"

"Maybe."

"Won't you burn up the whole yard?"

"Not if we can help it. We're going to wet down the neighboring piles first. It's taking a chance, but what the hell?"

"Why are you so determined to destroy my home?"

"Because, damn it," Pringle's voice rose, "I've had all I can stand of this business! It's cost me a hundred times the value of those boards. But I won't give in to you, see? You won't let me load the boards. Okay, they're no good to me. So I might as well burn 'em up and end this nonsense for good. And you can't stop me. Your boards are tied down so you can't crawl inside 'em and animate 'em. Joe and I are protected, so it won't do you any good to get rough with us. And your sawdust monsters won't have a chance against this blowtorch."

Aceria was silent for a while. The only sounds were the hum of insects, the slap of Pringle's hand as he hit a punkie on his cheek, the whir of an automobile on the state highway, and Joe Larochelle's distant footsteps.

Then she said: "I do not think you will burn my home, Mr. Pringle."

"Who's going to stop me?"

"I am. You were very clever and very brave about facing my magics, no? And now you say, 'Ho-ho, I have beaten all Aceria's tricks.'"

"Yep." Pringle had been making a heap of edgings and bark, well away from the pile. A loud swish in the dark showed that Joe had begun his wetting down. "Now, Joe," Pringle called, "you catch the other end of this rope. We want to tighten up on the pile as soon as we pull a couple of boards out, so the rest can't get loose."

"Okay, Mr. Pringle. Here goes." There were sounds in the semidark as the two men moved around the pile, making sure that their enterprise would suffer neither from spreading of the flames nor unwonted activity on the part of the boards.

"Very clever," continued Aceria, "but I should have

remembered sooner that it is not always the most complicated magic that is most effective."

"Uh," said Pringle. He splashed kerosene over his pile of kindling and lighted it. It flared up at once into a big, cheerful flame. "No wind," said Pringle, "so I guess she's safe enough. All right, Joe, let's haul the first board out."

Aceria seemed not to mind being ignored so pointedly. As Pringle and Larochelle laid hands on the board, she said:

"You were only so-so afraid of the boards when I went into them and made them alive, no? And you stood up to my monster. But there is something you are more afraid of than the boards or the monsters."

Pringle just grinned. "Is there? All right, Joe, heave! Don't pay any attention if I seem to be talking to myself."

"Yes. Union organizers," said Aceria.

"Huh?" Pringle stopped pulling on the board.

"Yes. You would like it, no, if *I* organized your men."

Pringle's mouth dropped open.

"I could do it. I have been listening to them talk, and I know something about unions. And you know me. I appear, I disappear. You could not keep me away, like you do those men from the A.F.L. and the C.I.O. Oh, I would have a nice revenge for the burning of my home."

For the space of thirty seconds there was no sound but the breathing of the two men and the crackle of the flames. When Pringle made a noise, it was a ghastly strangling sound, like the death rattle of a man dying of thirst in the desert.

"You—" he said. And again, "You—"

"You sick, Mr. Pringle?" asked Larochelle.

"No," said Pringle, "I'm dying."

"Well?" spoke Aceria.

Pringle sat down heavily in the muck, took off his wire mask, and buried his face in his hands. "Go away, Joe," he said, and would listen to no remonstrances from the alarmed Larochelle.

Pringle said: "You win. What do you want me to do with the damn boards? We can't just leave 'em sit here until they rot."

"I would like them put in some nice dry place. I do not

mind having them sold, if they are kept together until I can find another tree of the right kind."

"Let's see," said Pringle. "Earl Delacroix needs a new dance floor in his joint. But Earl's so tight he'll wait till somebody falls through the old one. Maybe if I offered him the boards at half price—or even a quarter—"

So it came to pass that, three weeks later, Earl Delacroix surprised those who knew his penurious habits by installing a new dance floor in The Pines. He surprised them somewhat less by hiring a luscious, red-haired girl as hostess. He himself was not too pleased over that innovation. But Pringle had brought the girl in personally and given her the strongest recommendation. Delacroix's mental eyebrows had gone up a bit. Hadn't Pringle's wife left him a while before? Oh, well, it was none of his business. If Pringle, who owned most of the town, wanted a—friend—employed, it was a good idea to employ the friend, without asking too many questions.

Delacroix had been particularly intrigued when the girl gave her name as Aceria; then, when he asked her full name, a whispered consultation between the girl and Pringle produced the surname of Jones. Jones, eh! Heh, heh.

Since then, Aceria has worked at The Pines. For appearance's sake, she has a room in the boarding house next door. But its bed is never slept in. Her landlady does not know that, every night, Aceria returns to the restaurant. It is dark then, and nobody is there to see her do whatever she does to merge herself with the floor boards. Probably she just fades out of sight. On these nocturnal trips, she always wears her old green dress. Or rather, it was green, but with the coming of fall it gradually turned a rich orange-yellow.

She dances divinely, and the local boys like her but find her a little odd. For instance, sooner or later she asks every acquaintance whether he knows of a place where a Norway maple grows. She is still asking, and if you know of one I am sure she would be grateful if you would inform her . . .

THE MINOTAUR

The Greek myth of the Minotaur centers around the mysterious island of Crete, where, indeed, enough bull-related imagery has been discovered in the Minoan ruins of the Great Palace at Knossos to suggest that there just may be a core of historical truth to this particular bit of mythology . . . and that perhaps the myth itself is a distillation of even darker, more ancient legends. In the classical version, the Minotaur was a ferocious monster with the body of a man and the head of a bull (although it is occasionally described, as by Dante, as having a man's head and a bull's body), born of the unnatural coupling of Pasiphae, Queen of Crete, with a white bull that Poseidon brought out of the sea. The Minotaur was imprisoned in the famous Labyrinth—built by Daedalus, master craftsman of Greek mythology, who had also built the apparatus used to enable the Queen to satisfy her passion for the white bull—and fed a steady diet of hapless human victims, including a levy of seven youths and seven maidens extorted annually from the Athenians. At last, Theseus, son of the King of Athens, who had volunteered to be part of the yearly levy, found his way to the heart of the Labyrinth, guided by a trail of thread left behind by his lover Ariadne, daughter of the Cretan King. Theseus is said to have killed the Minotaur with a sword also supplied by the helpful Ariadne . . . but this supposed demise has not kept the Minotaur from popping up from time to time, shaggy and menacing as ever, in the pages of subsequent fantasy literature.

In the following story, a flesh-and-blood Minotaur steps from the past into the bizarre world of the far future . . . a genetically-created archetype, blinded and in pain, but with a mission he is programmed to fulfill . . .

Michael Swanwick is a Nebula and World Fantasy Award finalist, and one of the most respected new talents to emerge in the 1980s. His stories have appeared in *Omni, Penthouse, Universe, Isaac Asimov's Science Fiction Magazine,* and elsewhere, and his first novel, *In the Drift,* was published as an Ace Special earlier this year.

The Blind Minotaur

by

Michael Swanwick

It was late afternoon when the blinded Minotaur was led through the waterfront. He cried openly, without shame, lost in his helplessness.

The sun cast shadows as crisp and black as an obsidian knife. Fisherfolk looked up from their nets or down from the masts of their boats, mild sympathy in their eyes. But not pity; memory of the Wars was too fresh for that. They were mortals and not subject to his tragedy.

Longshoremen stepped aside, fell silent at the passing of this shaggy, bull-headed man. Offworld tourists stared down from their restaurant balconies at the serenely grave little girl who led him by the hand.

His sight stolen away, a new universe of sound, scent and touch crashed about the Minotaur. It threatened to swallow him up, to drown him in its complexity.

There was the sea, always the sea, its endless crash and whisper on the beach, and quicker irregular slap at the docks. The sting of salt on his tongue. His calloused feet fell clumsily on slick cobblestones, and one staggered briefly into a shallow puddle, muddy at its bottom, heated piss-warm by the sun.

He smelled creosoted pilings, exhaust fumes from the great shuttles bellowing skyward from the Starport, a horse sweating as it clipclopped by, pulling a groaning cart that reeked of the day's catch. From a nearby garage, there was the *snap* and ozone crackle of an arc-welding rig. Fishmongers' cries and the creaking of pitchstained tackle overlaid rattling silverware from the terrace cafés, and fan-vented air rich with stews and squid and grease. And, of course, the flowers the little girl—was she really his daughter?—held crushed to her body with one arm. And the feel of her small hand in his, now going slightly slippery with sweat, but still cool, yes, and innocent.

This was not the replacement world spoken of and promised to the blind. It was chaotic and bewildering, rich and contradictory in detail. The universe had grown huge and infinitely complex with the dying of the light, and had made him small and helpless in the process.

The girl led him away from the sea, to the shabby buildings near the city's hot center. They passed through an alleyway between crumbling sheetbrick walls—he felt their roughness graze lightly against his flanks—and through a small yard ripe with fermenting garbage. The Minotaur stumbled down three wooden steps and into a room that smelled of sad, ancient paint. The floor was slightly gritty underfoot.

She walked him around the room. "This was built by expatriate Centaurimen," she explained. "So it's laid out around the kitchen in the center, *my* space to this side—" She let go of him briefly, rattled a vase, adding her flowers to those he could smell as already present, took his hand again. "—and yours to this side."

He let himself be sat down on a pile of blankets, buried his head in his arms while she puttered about, raising a wall, laying out a mat for him under the window. "We'll get you some cleaner bedding in the morning, okay?" she said. He did not answer. She touched a cheek with her tiny hand, moved away.

"Wait," he said. She turned, he could hear her. "What —what is your name?"

"Yarrow," she said.

He nodded, curled about himself.

By the time evening had taken the edge off the day, the Minotaur was cried out. He stirred himself enough to strip off his loincloth and pull a sheet over himself, and tried to sleep.

Through the open window the night city was coming to life. The Minotaur shifted as his sharp ears picked up drunken laughter, the calls of streetwalkers, the wail of jazz saxophone from a folk club, and music of a more contemporary nature, hot and sinful.

His cock moved softly against one thigh, and he tossed and turned, kicking off the crisp sheet (it was linen, and it had to be white), agonized, remembering similar nights when he was whole.

The city called to him to come out and prowl, to seek out women who were heavy and slatternly in the *tavernas,* cool and crisp in white, gazing out from the balconies of their husbands' *casavillas*. But the power was gone from him. He was no longer that creature that, strong and confident, had quested into the night. He twisted and turned in the warm summer air.

One hand moved down his body, closed about his cock. The other joined it. Squeezing tight his useless eyes, he conjured up women who had opened to him, coral-pink and warm, as beautiful as orchids. Tears rolled down his shaggy cheeks.

He came with great snorts and grunts.

Later he dreamed of being in a cool white *casavilla* by the sea, salt breeze wafting in through open window-spaces. He knelt at the edge of a bed and wonderingly lifted the sheet—it billowed slightly as he did—from his sleeping lover. Crouching before her naked body, his face was gentle as he marveled at her beauty.

It was strange to wake to darkness. For a time he was not even certain he *was* awake. And this was a problem, this unsureness, that would haunt him for all his life. Today, though, it was comforting to think it all a dream, and he wrapped the uncertainty around himself like a cloak.

The Minotaur found a crank recessed into the floor, and lowered the wall. He groped his way to the kitchen, and sat by the cookfire.

"You jerked off three times last night," Yarrrow said. "I could hear you." He imagined that her small eyes were staring at him accusingly. But apparently not, for she took something from the fire, set it before him, and innocently asked, "When are you going to get your eyes replaced?"

The Minotaur felt around for the platedough, and broke

off a bit from the edge. "Immortals don't heal," he mumbled. He dipped the fragment into the paste she ladled onto the dough's center, stirred it about, let the bread drop. "New eyes would be rejected, didn't your mother tell you that?"

She chose not to answer. "While you were asleep, a newshawk came snooping around with that damned machine grafted to his shoulder. I told him he had the wrong place." Then, harshly, urgently, "Why won't they just leave you *alone?*"

"I'm an immortal," he said. "I'm not supposed to be left alone." Her mother really *should* have explained all this, if she was really what she claimed to be. Perhaps she wasn't; he would have sworn he had never bedded another of his kind, had in fact scrupulously avoided doing so. It was part of the plan of evasion that had served him well for so many years, and yet ended with his best friend dying in the sand at his feet.

Yarrow put some fragment of foodstuff in his hand, and he automatically placed it in his mouth. It was gummy and tasteless, and took forever to disappear. She was silent until he swallowed, and then asked, "Am I going to die?"

"What kind of question is that?" he asked angrily.

"Well, I just thought—my mother said that I was an immortal like her, and I thought . . . Isn't an immortal supposed to be someone who never dies?"

He opened his mouth to tell her that her mother should be hung up by her hair—and in that instant the day became inarguably, inalterably *real.* He wanted to cling to the possibility that it was all a dream for just a while longer, but it was gone. Wearily he said, "Yarrow, I want you to go get me a robe. And a stick—" he raised a hand above his head—"so high. Got that?"

"Yes, but—"

"Go!"

A glimmering of his old presence must have still clung to him, for the child obeyed. The Minotaur leaned back, and—involuntarily—was flooded with memories.

He was young, less than a year released from the creche by gracious permission of the ministries of the Lords. Filled with controlling hormones and bioprogramming, he was sent out to stir up myth. The Wars were less than a year away, but the Lords had no way of knowing that—the cabarets were full, and the starlanes swollen with the fruits of a thousand remarkable harvests. There had never been such a rich or peaceful time.

The Minotaur was drunk, and at the end of his nightly round of bars. He had wound up in a *taverna* where the patrons removed their shirts to dance and sweet-smelling sweat glistened on their chests. The music was fast and heavy and sensual. Women eyed him as he entered, but could not politely approach him, for he still wore his blouse.

He bellied up to the bar, and ordered a jarful of the local beer. The barkeep frowned when he did not volunteer money, but that was his right as an immortal.

Crouched on their ledge above the bar, the musicians were playing hot and furious. The Minotaur paid them no attention. Nor did he notice the Harlequin, limbs long and impossibly thin, among them, nor how the Harlequin's eyes followed his every move.

The Minotaur was entranced by the variety of women in the crowd, the differences in their movements. He had been told that one could judge how well a woman made love by how well she danced, but it seemed to him, watching, that there must be a thousand styles of making love, and he would be hard put to choose among them, were the choice his.

One woman with flashing brown feet, stared at him, ignoring her partner. She wore a bright red skirt that flew up to her knee when she whirled around, and her nipples were hard and black. He smiled in friendly cognizance of her glance, and her answering grin was a razor-crisp flash of teeth that took his breath away, a predatory look that said: *You're* mine *tonight.*

Laughing, the Minotaur flung his shirt into the air. He plunged into the dancers and stooped at the woman's feet. In a rush he lifted her into the air, away from her partner, one hand closing about her ankles, the other supporting her by the small of her back. She gasped, and laughed, and balanced herself, so that he could remove one hand and lift her still higher, poised with one foot on the palm of his great hairy hand.

"I am strong!" he shouted. The crowd—even the woman's abandoned partner—cheered and stamped their feet. The Harlequin stepped up the band. The woman lifted her skirts and kicked her free leg high, so that one toe grazed the ceiling beams. She threw her head back and laughed.

The dancers swirled about them. For a single pure moment, life was bright and full and good. And then . . .

A touch of cool air passed through the crowd. A chance movement, a subtle shifting of colors brought the Minotaur's eyes around to the door. A flash of artificial streetlight dazzled and was gone as the door swung shut.

The Woman entered.

She was masked in silver filigree, and her breasts were covered. Red silk washed from shoulder to ankle, now caressing a thigh, now releasing it. Her eyes were a drenched, saturated green. She walked with a sure and sensual authority, knowing the dancers would part for her. No one could mistake her for a mortal.

The Minotaur was stunned. Chemical and hormonal balances shifted in preparation for the bonding to come. Nevertheless, his arms fell to his sides. With an angry squawk, the woman he had hoisted into the air leapt, arms waving, to avoid falling. The Minotaur did not notice. He stepped forward, eyes wide and helpless, toward the immortal.

The silver mask headed straight for him. Green eyes mocked, challenged, promised.

Behind him, unnoticed, the Harlequin slipped to the floor. He wrapped long fingers lovingly around a length of granite pipe, and brought it down, fast and surprisingly forcefully, into the back of the Minotaur's neck.

Bright shards of light flashed before the Minotaur's eyes. The dance floor washed out and faded to white. He fell.

At the Minotaur's direction, Yarrow led him out to the bluffs on the outskirts of the city. There was a plaza there, overlooking the ocean. He sent the child away.

Though his every bone protested, he slowly crouched, and then carefully spread out a small white cloth before him. He was a beggar now.

Salt breezes gusted up from the ocean, and he could feel the cobalt sky above, and the cool cumulus clouds that raced across the sun. There were few passersby, mostly dirt farmers who were not likely to be generous. Perhaps once an hour a small ceramic coin fell on his cloth.

But that was how he preferred it. He had no interest in money, was a beggar only because his being demanded a role to play. He had come to remember, and to prepare himself for death by saying farewell to the things of life.

Times had changed. There was a stone altar set in the center of this very plaza where children had been sacrificed. He had seen it himself, the young ones taken from their homes or schooling-places by random selection of the cruel Lords. They had shrieked like stuck pigs when the gold-masked priests raised their bronze knives to the noonday sun. The crowds were always large at these events. The Minotaur was never able to determine whether the parents were present or not.

This was only one of the means the Lords had of reminding their subjects that to be human was often painful or tragic.

"Let's not sleep the day away, eh? Time to start rehearsing."

The Minotaur awoke to find himself sprawled on the wooden floor of a small caravan. The Harlequin, sitting cross-legged beside him, thrust a jar of wine into his hand.

Groggily, the Minotaur focused his eyes on the Harlequin. He reached for the man's neck. Only to find one hand taken up by the winejar. He squinted at it. The day was already hot, and his throat as dry as the Severna. His body trembled from the aftereffects of its raging hormonal storm. He lifted the wine to his lips.

Chemical imbalances shifted, found a new equilibrium.

"Bravo!" The Harlequin hauled the Minotaur to his feet, clapped him on the back. "We'll be famous friends, you and I. With luck, we may even keep each other alive, eh?"

It was a new idea to the Minotaur, and a disquieting, perhaps even blasphemous one. But he grinned shyly, and dipped his head. He *liked* the little fellow. "Sure," he said.

The sun was setting. The Minotaur felt the coolness coming off of the sea, heard the people scurrying to their homes. He carefully tied the ceramics into his cloth, and knotted it onto his belt. He stood, leaning wearily on his staff. Yarrow had not yet come for him, and he was glad; he hoped she had gone off on her own, forgotten him, left him behind forever. But the city's rhythms demanded that he leave, though he had nowhere to go, and he obeyed.

He went down into the city, taking the turns by random whim. He could not be said to be lost, for one place was as good as another to him.

It was by mistake, though, that he found himself in a building whose doors were never shut, whose windows were not shuttered. He had entered, thinking the way yet another alley. No doors barred progress down halls or into rooms. Still, he felt closed in. The corridors smelled—there was the male stench and the female, and intermingled with them, almost overpowering, an insect smell, the odor of something large and larval.

He stopped. Things stirred about him. There was the pat of bare feet on stone, the slow breathing of many people and—again—a sluggish movement of creatures larger than anything smelling thus should be. People were gathering; twelve, eighteen, more. They surrounded him. He could tell they were all naked, for there was not the whisper of cloth on cloth. Some walked as if they had almost forgotten how. In the distance, he thought he could hear someone *crawling*.

"Who are you?" Panic touched him lightly; sourceless, pure.

"Whrrarrwr," began one of the people. He stopped, swallowed, tried again. "Why are you in the Hive?" His voice sounded forced, as if he were unused to speech. "Why are you here? You are a creature of the old days, of the Lords. This is no place for you."

"I took a wrong turn," the Minotaur said simply. Then, when there was no reply. "Who *are* you people? Why do you cohabit with insects?"

Someone coughed and sputtered and made hacking noises. A second joined her, making the same sounds, and then others, and yet more. With a start, the Minotaur realized they were laughing at him. "Is it religious or political?" he demanded. "Are you seeking transcendence?"

"We are trying to become victims," the speaker said.

"Does *that* help you understand?" He was growing angry. "How can we explain ourselves to you, Old Fossil? You never performed a free act in your life."

Some whim, then, of internal chemistry made him want these strangers, these creatures, to understand him. It was the same compulsion that had forced him to empty himself to the newshawks before Yarrow appeared to lead him out of the arena.

"I had a friend, another immortal," the Minotaur said. "Together, we cheated the patterning instinct by making our own pattern, a safe, strong one, we were like—" his short, powerful fingers joined, closing around the staff, intermeshing—"like *this,* you see. And it worked, it worked for years. It was only when our predators worked *within* the patterns we formed that we were destroyed." The words gushed out, and he trembled as the hormones that might give him the power to explain *almost* keyed in.

But the communards did not want to understand. They closed in on him, their laughter growing sharper, with more of a bark, more of a bite to it. Their feeble footsteps paltered closer, and behind them the chitinous whine grew louder, was joined by that of more insects, and more, until all the world seemed to buzz. The Minotaur flinched back.

And then they seemd to hesitate in confusion. They milled about uncertainly for a moment, then parted, and quick, small footsteps passed through them, ran to his side. A cool, smooth hand took his.

"Come home with me," Yarrow said. And he followed.

He dreamed of the arena that night, of the hot white sands underfoot that drank up his friend's blood. The Harlequin's body lay limp at his feet, and the bronze knife was as heavy as guilt in his hands.

He trembled in aftershock as the programming chemicals cut off. The world blazed up around him, as if his eyes had just opened and he were seeing clearly for the first time. He stared at the encircling bleachers, and every detail burned into his brain.

The people were graceful and well-dressed; they might almost have been the old Lords, deposed these many years ago in violent public revulsion. The Woman sat ringside.

Her silver mask rested lightly on the lip of the white limestone wall, beside a small bowl of orange ices. She held a spoon in her hand, cocked lightly upward.

The Minotaur stared into her blazing green eyes, and read in them a fierce triumph, an obscene gloating, a very specific and direct lust. She had hunted him out of hiding, stripped him of his protection, and chivvied him into the open. She had forced him to rise to his destiny. To enter the arena.

Try though he might, the Minotaur could not awaken. If he had not known all this to be a dream, he would have gone mad.

Waking, he found himself already dressed, the last bit of breakfast in his hand. He dropped it, unnerved by this transition. Yarrow was cleaning the kitchen walls, singing an almost tuneless, made-up song under her breath.

"Why aren't you out being taught?" he demanded, trying to cover over his unease with words. She stopped singing. "Well? Answer me!"

"I'm learning from you," she said quietly.

"Learning what?" She did not answer. "Learning how to tend to a cripple? Or maybe how a beggar lives? Hey? What could you possibly learn from me?"

She flung a wet cloth to the floor. "You won't *tell* me anything," she cried. "I ask you and you won't tell me."

"Go home to your mother," he said.

"I can't." She was crying now. "She told me to take care of you. She said not to come back until my task was done."

The Minotaur bowed his head. Whatever else she might or might not be, the mother had the casual arrogance of an immortal. Even he could be surprised by it.

"*Why* won't you tell me anything?"

"Go and fetch me my stick."

Bleak plains dominated the southern continent, and the Minotaur came to know them well. The carnival worked the long route, the four-year circuit of small towns running up the coast and then inland to the fringes of the Severna Desert.

Creeping across the plains, the carnival was small, never

more than eight hands of wagons and often fewer. But when the paper lanterns had been lit, the fairway laid out, the holographic woven canvases blazing neon-bright, they created a fantasy city that stretched to the edge of forever.

The Minotaur grunted. Muscles glistening, he bent the metal bar across his chest. Portions of the audience were breathing heavily.

It was the last performance of the evening. Outside the hot, crowded tent, the fairgoers were thinning, growing quieter. The Minotaur was clad only in a stained white loincloth. He liked to have room to sweat.

Applause. He threw the bar to the stage and shouted: "My last stunt! I'll need five volunteers!" He chose the four heaviest, and the one who blushed most prettily. Her he helped up on the stage, and set in the middle of the lifting bench, a pair of hefty *bouergers* to either side.

The Minotaur slid his head under the bench. His face emerged between the young woman's legs, and she shrieked and drew them up on the bench. The audience howled. He rolled his eyes, flared his nostrils. And indeed, she *did* have a pleasant scent.

He dug into the stage with naked toes, placed his hands carefully. With a grunt, the Minotaur lifted the bench a handsbreadth off the floor. It wobbled slightly, and he shifted his weight in compensation. A surge—he was crouching.

Sweat poured down the Minotaur's face, and ran in rivulets from his armpits. The tent was saturated with the sweet smell, redolent with his pheromones. He felt a light touch on his muzzle. The woman on the bench had reached down to caress his nose with quick, shy fingertips. The Minotaur quirked a half-grin on one side of his mouth.

By the tent flap, the Harlequin lounged on a wooden crate, cleaning his toenails with a knife. They had a date with a sculptor after the show.

The Minotaur awoke suddenly, reached out and touched the cloth laid out before him. There was nothing on it, though he distinctly remembered having heard ceramics fall earlier. He swept his hands in great arcs in the dust, finding nothing.

Snickers and derisive jeers sounded from the stone in the plaza's center. Small feet scurried away—children running to deliver the swag to their masters. "Little snots," the Minotaur grumbled. They were an ever-present nuisance, like sparrows. He fell back into his daydreaming.

The sculptor had had stone jugs of wine sent up. By orgy's end they were empty, and the women lay languid on the sheets of their couches. They all stared upwards, watching the bright explosion in space, like slow-blossoming flowers. "What do they hope to accomplish, these rebels?" the Minotaur asked wonderingly. "I can see no pattern to their destruction."

"Why should a man like you—a *real* man—look any higher than his waist?" the sculptor asked coarsely. He laid a hand on the Minotaur's knee. His lady of the moment laughed throatily, reached back over her head to caress his beard.

"I'd just like to know."

The Harlequin had been perched on the wall. He leapt down now, and tossed the Minotaur his clothes. "Time we went home," he said.

The streets were dark and still, but there were people in the shadows, silently watching the skies. The sidestreet cabarets were uncharacteristically crowded. They stopped in several on their way back to the carnival.

The Minotaur was never sure at exactly what point they picked up the woman with skin the color of orange brick. She was from offworld, she said, and needed a place to hide. Her hands were calloused and beautiful from work. The Minotaur liked her strong, simple dignity.

Back at the carnival, the Harlequin offered their wagon, and the woman refused. The Minotaur said that he would sleep on the ground, it didn't bother him, and she changed her mind.

Still, he was not surprised when, some time later, she joined him under the wagon.

The sun hot on his forehead, the Minotaur again dreamed of the arena. He did not relive the murder—that memory had been driven from his mind, irretrievably burned away, even in dream. But he remembered the killing rage that drove the knife upward, the insane fury that propelled his hand. And afterwards he stood staring into the Woman's eyes.

Her eyes were as green as oceans, and as complex, but easy to read for all that. The lusts and rages, the fears and evil, grasping desire that had brought them all to this point—they were all there, and they were . . . insignificant. For the true, poisoned knowledge was that she was lost in her own chemical-hormonal storm, her body trembling almost imperceptibly, all-but-invisible flecks of foam on her lips. She had run not only him but herself as well, to the blind end of a tangled and malignant fate. She was as much a puppet to her programming as he or the Harlequin. All this he saw in a single lucid instant of revulsion.

There, on the burning sands, he tore out his eyes.

The newshawks vaulted the fence to get at him. His drama completed, he was fair game—for it *might* be he had fulfilled his true purpose and become that one out of a thousand immortals whose patterning instinct formed a new, a true and real myth.

They probed, scanned, recorded—*prodded* to find the least significant detail of a story that *might* be told over campfires a thousand years hence, in theatrical productions on worlds not yet discovered, in uninvented media, or simply be remembered in times of stress. Trying to get in on a story that might have meaning to the human race as it grew away from its homeworld, forgot its origins, expanded and evolved and changed in ways that could not be predicted.

They questioned the Minotaur for hot, grueling hours. The corpse of his friend began to rot, or perhaps that was only olfactory hallucination, a side effect of his mind telling his body that it had no further purpose. He felt dizzy and without hope, and he *could not* express his grief, *could not* cry, *could not* scream or rage or refuse their questions or even move away until they were done with him.

And then a cool hand slipped into his, and tugged him

away. A small voice said, "Come home, Papa," and he went.

Yarrow was screaming. The Minotaur awoke suddenly, on his feet and slashing his stick before him, back and forth in pure undirected reaction. "Yarrow!" he cried.

"No!" the child shrieked in anger and panic. Someone slapped her face so hard she fell. The sound echoed from the building walls. "Fuckpigs!" she swore from the ground.

The Minotaur lurched toward her, and someone tripped him up, so that he crashed onto the road. He heard a rib crack. He felt a trickle of blood from one nostril. And he heard laughter, the laughter of madwomen. And under that he heard the creaking of leather harness, the whirring of tiny pumps, the metal snicks of complex machinery.

There was no name for them, these madwomen, though their vice was not rare. They pumped themselves full of the hormone drugs that had once been the exclusive tools of the Lords, but they used them randomly, to no purpose. Perhaps—the Minotaur could not imagine, but did not care—they enjoyed the jolts of power and importance, of sheer godlike *caprice*.

He was on his feet. The insane ones—there were three, he could tell by their sick laughter—ignored him. "What are you doing?" he cried. "Why are you doing it?" They were dancing, arms linked, about the huddled child. She was breathing shallowly like a hypnotized animal.

"Why?" asked the one. "Why do you ask why?" and convulsed in giggles.

"We are all frogs!" laughed the second.

Yarrow lay quietly now, intimidated not so much by the women's hyperadrenal strength as by the pattern of victim laid out for her. There were microtraces of hormones in the air, leaks from the chemical pumps.

"She has interesting glands," said the third. "We can put their secretions to good use."

The Minotaur roared and rushed forward. They yanked the stick from his hand and broke it over his head. He fell against the altar stone, hard, nearly stunning himself.

"We need to use that stone," said a madwoman. And when he did not move away, said, "Well, we'll wait."

But again the Minotaur forced himself to stand. He stepped atop the stone. Something profound was happening deep within him, something beyond his understanding. Chemical keys were locking into place, hormones shifting into balance. Out of nowhere his head was filled with eloquence.

"Citizens!" he cried. He could hear the people at their windows, in their doorways, watching and listening, though with no great interest. They had not interfered to save Yarrow. The Lords would have interfered, and human society was still in reaction to the rule of the Lords. "Awake! Your freedom is being stolen from you!"

A lizard, startled, ran over the Minotaur's foot, as quick and soft as a shiver. The words poured from him in a cold fever, and he could hear the householders straighten, lean forward, step hesitantly out onto the cobblestones. "No one is above you now," he shouted. "But I still see the dead hands of the Lords on your shoulders."

That got to them—he could smell their anger. His throat was dry, but he dared not spare the time to cough. His head was light, and a cool breeze stirred his curls. He spoke, but did not listen to the words.

Yarrow was lost, somewhere on the plaza. As he spoke, the Minotaur listened for her, sniffed the air, felt for vibrations through the stone—and could not find her. "Inaction is a greater tyrant than error ever was!" he cried, listening to heads nodding agreement with the old, familiar homily. He could hear the frantic, hopping motions the madwomen made, forward and back again, baffled and half-fascinated by the hormones he was generating, by the cadences and odd rhythms of his words.

The speech was a compulsion, and the Minotaur paid it no more mind than he did to the sliding of muscles under skin that went into his gestures, some wide and sweeping, others short and blunt. A whiff of girlish scent finally located Yarrow, not two armslengths away, but he could not go to her. The words would not release him, not until he had spoken them all.

And when, finally, he lowered his arms, the plaza was filled with people, and the madwomen's harnesses had been ripped from them, the drug pumps smashed underfoot, their necks snapped quickly and without malice.

He turned to Yarrow, offered his hand. "Come," he said. "It's time to go home."

The Minotaur lay belly-down on the earth under the wagon. He stared down his muzzle at a slice of early-morning sky framed by two wheel spokes. The clouds of energy were still slowly dissipating. "I'd love to go out there," he said. "To see other worlds."

The orange-skinned woman scratched him above the ears, at the base of his small, ivory horns. Her hands were strong and sure. "They couldn't refuse you passage. What's stopping you?"

He nodded upward. "He gets sick—I'd have to go alone."

A triceratops beetle crept laboriously past his nose. He exhaled sharply, trying to turn it over, failed. "You two are inseparable, aren't you?" the woman asked.

The beetle was getting away. He snorted sharply again, twice. "I guess."

"Won't he be upset that I chose you over him?"

It took the Minotaur a moment to puzzle out her meaning. "Ah! You mean—I see. Good joke, very good joke!" He laughed without taking his eyes away from the beetle, watched it escape into the grass. "No, the Harlequin doesn't know that women are important."

It did not take long to gather belongings: The Minotaur had none and Yarrow few. "You can find your mother?" he asked her. They left the door open behind them, an old Centaurimen custom at final partings.

"I can always find my mother," Yarrow said.

"Good." Still, he did not let her go. He led her by the hand back along the waterfront. There, among the sounds and smells, the subliminal tastes and touches that had grown familiar to him, he leaned forward to kiss her tenderly on the cheeks and forehead.

"Good-bye," he said. "I am proud that you are my daughter."

Yarrow did not move away. There was a slight tremble in her voice when she spoke. "You still haven't *told* me anything."

"Ah," the Minotaur said. For a moment he was silent,

mentally cataloging what she would need to know. The history of the Lords, to begin with. Their rise to power, how they had shaped and orchestrated the human psyche, and why they thought the human race had to be held back. She needed to know of the creches, of their bioprogramming chemicals, and of those immortals released from them who had gone on to become legend. She needed to know everything about the immortals, in fact, for the race had been all but exterminated in the Wars. And how the Lords had endured as long as they had. How their enemies had turned their toys against them. All the history of the Wars. It would not be a short telling.

"Sit down," he commanded. There, in the center of the thoroughfare, he sat, and Yarrow followed.

The Minotaur opened his mouth to speak. At the sound of his words, resonant and deep, people would stop to listen for the briefest second . . . for just a moment longer . . . they would sit down in the road. The hormonal combinations that enforced strictest truth before the newshawks were to be in his voice, but combined with the strong eloquence of earlier in the day. He would speak plainly, with a fine parsimony of syllables. He would speak in strict accord with the ancient oratorical traditions. He would speak with tongues of fire.

The waterfront would fill and then overflow as people entered and did not leave, as they joined the widening circle of hushed listeners, as the fisherfolk came up from their boats and down from their masts, the boy prostitutes came out from the brothels, the offworld *tourista* joined with the kitchen help to lean over the edges of their terraces.

In future years this same telling, fined down and refined, elaborated and simplified, would become the epic that was to mark this age—*his* age—as great for its genesis. But what was to come in just a moment was only a first draft. A prototype. A seed. But it was to be beautiful and moving beyond all possible imagining of its listeners, for it was new, an absolutely new word, a clear new understanding. It was to sum up an age that most people did not realize was over.

"Listen," said the Minotaur.

He spoke.

THE SPHINX

What most people think of as a Sphinx has the head and breasts of a woman, a bird's wings, and the feet and body of a lion. This is the Greek Sphinx, probably the most familiar sort—it is not to be confused with the Egyptian Sphinx, which has the head of a man and the body of a lion, or the Assyrian Sphinx, which has the body of a winged bull and the crowned, bearded head of a man. The Egyptian and Assyrian versions feature mostly in statuary and monuments, as symbols of royal authority, but the Greek Sphinx plays a more active role in mythology. In Greek myth, the Sphinx roams the countryside, asking her famous riddle ("What goes on four legs in the morning, two legs at noon, and three in the evening?"), and devouring the hapless travellers who can't come up with the correct answer. (The answer, for those of you who slept through your Comparative Literature classes, is "man"—he crawls on all fours as an infant, walks upright on two legs as an adult, and in old age walks with the aid of a staff, "three legs." Now You Know. What a relief, right?)

In the stories that follow, we observe a pride of Sphinxes at play in their natural habitat, the golden pre-Dawn world of Myth, before the coming of man

. . . and then travel to the modern world to see how a Sphinx that cannot seem to break the ancient racial habit of asking riddles fares as a mascot at an exclusive country-club . . .

Karen Anderson's story "Treaty in Tartessos" appeared earlier in this anthology. See that story for author information.

Esther M. Friesner is a new writer whose work has appeared in *Isaac Asimov's Science Fiction Magazine, Elsewhere III, Fantasy Book,* and *Amazing,* among other places. Her first novel, *Mustapha and His Wise Dog,* appeared earlier in the year, from Avon.

Landscape with Sphinxes

by

Karen Anderson

THE PRIDE WAS a small one, even as sphinxes go. An arrogant black mane blew back over Arctanax's shoulders and his beard fluttered against his chest. Ahead and a little below soared Murrhona and Selissa, carrying the remnants of the morning's kill. It was time the cubs were weaned.

The valley lifted smooth and broad from the river, then leaped suddenly in sandstone cliffs where the shadows seemed more solid then the thorny, gray-green scrub. A shimmer of heat ran along wind-scoured edges.

In the tawny rocks about the eyrie, the cubs played at stalk-the-unicorn. They were big-eyed, dappled, and only half fledged. Taph, the boy, crept stealthily up a sun-hot slab, peeking around it from time to time to be sure that the moly blossom still nodded on the other side. He reached the top and shifted his feet excitedly. That moly was about to be a dead unicorn. The tip of his tail twitched at the thought.

His sister Fiantha forgot the blossom at once. Pounce! and his tail was caught between her paws; he rolled back down on top of her, all claws out. They scuffled across baked clay to the edge of a thornbush and backed apart.

Taph was about to attack again when he saw the grownups dip down from above. He leaped across Fiantha and bounded toward the cave mouth. She came a jump and a half behind. They couldn't kiss Murrhona and Selissa because of the meat in their jaws, so they kissed Father twice instead.

"Easy, there! Easy!" Arctanax coughed, but he was grinning. "Get back into the cave, the two of you. How often do I have to tell you to stay in the cave?" The cubs laughed and bounced inside.

Selissa dropped the meat she had been carrying and settled down to wash her face, but Murrhona called her cubs over to eat. She watched critically as they experimented with their milk-teeth on this unfamiliar substance.

"Hold it down with your paw, Fiantha," she directed. "If you just tug at it, it'll follow you all over the floor. Like Taph—No, Taph, use your side teeth. They're the biggest and sharpest." And so the lesson went. After a while both cubs got tired of the game and nuzzled for milk.

Selissa licked her right paw carefully and polished the bridge of her broad nose. There was still a trace of blood smell; she licked and polished again.

"You can't rush them," she said rather smugly. "I remember *my* first litter. Time and again I thought they'd learned a taste for meat, but even when they could kill for themselves—only conies and such, but their own kill—they still came back to suck."

"Oh, I remember how put out you were when you realized you still had to hold quiet for nursing," Murrhona smiled lazily. She licked down a tuft behind Fiantha's ear and resettled her wings. "But I really hate to see them grow up. They're so cute with their little spots."

Selissa shrugged and polished the bridge of her nose again for good measure. If you wanted to call them *cute,* with their wings all pinfeathers and down shedding everywhere—! Well, yes, she had to admit they were, in a way. She licked her paw once more, meditatively, put her chin down on it and dozed off.

An hour later Fiantha woke up. Everybody was asleep. She stretched her wings, rolled onto her back, and reached her paws as far as she could. The sun outside was dazzling. She rubbed the back of her head against the cool sandstone floor and closed her eyes, intending to go back to sleep, but her left wing itched. When she licked at it, the itch kept moving around, and bits of down came loose on her tongue.

She rolled over on her stomach, spat out the fluff, and licked again. There—*that* did it!

Fully awake now, she noticed the tip of Arctanax's tail and pounced.

"Scram," he muttered without really waking. She pounced again just as the tail-tip flicked out of reach. Once more and she had it, chewing joyously.

"Scram, I said!" he repeated with a cuff in her general direction. She went on chewing, and added a few kicks. Arctanax rolled over and bumped into Selissa, who jumped and gave Fiantha a swat in case she needed it. Fiantha mewed with surprise. Murrhona sprang up, brushing Taph aside; he woke too and made a dash for Selissa's twitching tail.

"Can't a person get *any* rest around here?" grumbled Arctanax. He heaved himself up and walked a few feet away from his by now well-tangled family.

"They're just playful," Murrhona murmured.

"If this is play, I'd hate to see a fight," said Selissa under her breath. She patted Taph away and he tumbled enthusiastically into a chewing match with Fiantha.

"Go to sleep, children," Murrhona suggested, stretching out again. "It's much too hot for games."

Fiantha rolled obediently away from Taph, and found a good place to curl up, but she wasn't the least bit sleepy. She leaned her chin on a stone and looked out over the valley. Down there, in the brown-roasted grass, something moved toward a low stony ridge.

There were several of them, and they didn't walk like waterbuck or unicorn; it was a queer, bobbing gait. They came slowly up the ridge and out of the grass. Now she could see them better. They had heads like sphinxes, but with skimpy little manes, and no wings at all; and—and—

"Father, *look!*" she squeaked in amazement. "What kind of animal is that?"

He got up to see. "I don't know," he replied. "Never saw anything like it in all my born days. But then, we've had a lot of queer creatures wandering in since the glaciers melted."

"Is it game?" asked Taph.

"Might be," Arctanax said. "But I don't know any game that moves around in the middle of the day like that. It isn't natural."

"And the funny way they walk, too," added Fiantha.

"If they're silly enough to walk around like that at mid-day," Arctanax said as he padded back to an extra-cool corner of the cave, "I'm not surprised they go on two legs."

Simpson's Lesser Sphynx

by

Esther M. Friesner

LATER WE ALL agreed to share the blame. We should have known Simpson was just not our kind. On the basis of blood alone we admitted him to the Club. His father was good stock: Boston, Choate, and Yale; his mother similarly Philadelphia, Miss Devon's, and Skidmore. But nature delights in sports. Who can depend on biology? We are still writing notes to next of kin, and the Club Secretary claims he will resign if those *Enquirer* reporters don't cease hanging around the Pro Shop, putting him off his game.

It was August and we were bored. The market had been sluggish, and so were we. Sterling went so far as to suggest a trip to the local massage parlor to take our minds off our portfolios before he was hissed down and sent to the bar for another round of G&Ts. As he shuffled from the room, he bumped into Simpson.

That is, he afterwards learned it was Simpson he'd encountered. The man's face was hidden behind the bulky wooden crate he bore before him. He heaved it onto the sideboard, scraping the mahogany ruinously, and blew like a draft horse.

"There!" He wiped his brow. "That's done."

We stared at the crate. It was riddled with air holes, and through these a pungent, unpleasant reek began to fill the room. Something inside hissed.

"Simpson," said Dixwell severely, "no pets."

Simpson's eyes crinkled. "Pets?" he echoed, laughing. The thing in the crate hissed again, and we heard a scrabbling sound. The smell was stronger, overwhelming the room's comfortable aura of oiled leather and good burley.

"Here I am, back from Greece with something a sight more interesting to show than slides, and what happens?" Simpson went on. "Dixie quotes Club scripture at me. Well, it's not a pet I've got in here. It's a present, a present to the dear old Club. Now, I'll need a hammer."

Wilkes was at his elbow on the moment, hammer graciously proffered. Wilkes is—or was—such an integral part of the Club that old members have long forgotten whether he was hired as butler, waiter, confessor, or handyman. New members were wisely too overawed to ask.

Simpson pried the lid off the crate. Hard pine splinters flew everywhere, and the feral stench intensified. When the lid lay grinding sawdust into the Aubusson, Simpson stood back; made a dramatic flourish, and was actually heard to remark, "Ta-*daah!*"

She did not respond to vulgar fanfare. Simpson had to rap sharply on the side of the crate before the tiny, exquisitely modelled head peeped over the wooden rim. It was no bigger than a man's hand, a head with the face of a Tanagra figurine framed by clusters of dark curls such as old Cretan priestesses wore. She opened her delicate lips and a third, more tentative hiss escaped.

"Come on, Bessie," cried Simpson, seizing the crate and dropping it to the floor with a jarring thud. "Don't make me look bad. Come out and show yourself." He tipped it over and the sphynx spilled out in a tumble of feline body, bare breasts, and goshawk's wings.

"Isn't she a beauty?" Simpson demanded. The sphynx looked at each of us in turn as he spoke, her bosom heaving and her eyes wild. You could trace the ripples of fear on her tawny flanks. Her eyes were blue. "Don't ask me how I got her through customs. Trade secret. The things I do for the Club! Wilkes, bring me a Scotch. I want to toast our new mascot."

"Simpson, you're mad," objected Haskins. "This . . . this creature is a miracle! A myth come to life! It can't—it *shouldn't* exist, and yet . . ." He stretched out a hesitant hand. The sphynx sniffed it warily, cat-fashion, then allowed him to stroke her fur. Slowly an enchanting smile spread across her face; she closed her eyes and thrummed.

"Where did you find it? How? . . ." demanded Dixwell.

Simpson shrugged. "That's a story I'm saving to dine out on."

It was Chapin, as usual, who cast a sopping-wet blanket over the whole affair. "We cannnot keep it . . . her . . . here," he decreed from the height of three hundred years of Puritan ancestry. "Quite aside from an obvious violation of U.S. Customs law, we cannot. This is a dangerous animal, Simpson. A monster!"

"Don't you know what sphynxes eat?" put in Hobbs.

Well, of course we'd all suffered through the Oedipus tale in the original Greek at prep school. However, none of us really liked Chapin, and it was hard to ignore how prettily the little sphynx purred and snuggled when Haskins scratched between her wings.

"Oh, for God's sake!" Simpson spat in exasperation. "She's never taken a bite out of me, if that's what you mean. Besides, this one's purebred; can't eat manflesh unless it's gotten according to the code. I watched them for at least a week before I nabbed Bessie, and the only time I saw one of them chow down on a local boy was when he got stupid and arrogant enough to try his hand at the Riddle." You could tell Simpson meant the Riddle to be capitalized by the way he said it.

"What riddle?" Chapin asked in minuscule. We had long suspected his education lacking. Who has not heard of the immortal riddle the sphynx propounds? What is it that goes on four legs at morning, two at noon, three at night? We also had to supply Chapin with the answer: man.

"So you see," Simpson went on, "she's harmless. A, she can only ask the Riddle in Greek—doesn't speak a word of English, besides making cat sounds. B, she can't hurt a fly with it since every schoolchild knows the answer to that old chestnut. And C, unless the victim's willing to be questioned, she can't touch him. *Now* have we got a mascot?"

We did. We all grew rather fond of Oenone, as she was

renamed. Only Simpson would call a sphynx "Bessie." She lived in a kennel in the woodsy clump off the eleventh tee and never needed leashing. It was great fun to do a round of golf and stop by to visit our unique Club pet. She bounded from the kennel or the woods when called and perched on a large boulder, like her famous man-eating ancestress. There she would jabber at us in flawless Greek, cocking her head expectantly, her rose-petal tongue darting out to lick needle-sharp fangs.

"Sorry, Oenone"—we all chuckled—"no riddles today; and the answer is man." This sent her slinking back to the kennel where Wilkes fed her 9-Lives mackerel and changed the newspapers lining the floor.

When winter came, it was Wilkes who offered to take Oenone to live with him in the groundsman's cottage. We saw little of her until spring, although I once surprised the two of them in the Club library. Wilkes was reading, and Oenone, perched on the wing chair's back, almost appeared to be following the text. When he turned a page too quickly, she hissed. He became aware of me and hastily stood up.

"Just relaxing a bit. I do enjoy a good book," he said. I glanced at the book, a paperback mystery. Despite his polished facade, Wilkes was hopelessly addicted to tales of ruthless women, spies, and blackmailers.

Oenone leaped from the chairback and rubbed against his legs. "She looks well. You're taking good care of her, Wilkes," I remarked.

"Oh, she's no trouble. Very affectionate, she is. And smart? Personally"—he lowered his voice—"I've never cared much for cats. But she's different."

I looked at Oenone's human face and pert breasts. Wilkes was innocent to the obvious. So were we all.

That spring the disappearances began.

The first to go were Reynolds and Kramer, a pair of busboys, to be followed in rapid succession by Thomson, Jones, and Green, caddies. At first no one missed them; a certain turnover in personnel is expected at any club.

Then it was Wilkes.

The police were little help. Theories flew, but the Club remained beyond implication. Or so it did until the bright May morning when Dixwell announced he was going out to cure his slice and did not return.

"This is atrocious," fumed Chapin, consulting his watch every five minutes as we sat in the bar. "Dixie swore he'd give me advice on my IBM holdings; said he had private news. Must be keeping it to himself, make a killing and leave his friends out in the cold."

Wearily I stepped down from the stool. "If it's so important to you, we can seek him out on the greens."

Chapin took a cart; I opted to walk. It was better for my health, especially in view of Chapin's driving. So it was natural that he got to the eleventh tee ahead of me by nearly ten minutes. When I came trudging over the bank shielding the sand trap I heard the whine of Chapin's voice from the woods and assumed he'd found Dixwell. Only when I came nearer did I realize that the second voice was female.

"I'll tell you honestly, Chapin," she said, "I don't like you; never have. Don't think I don't know who proposed feeding me generic tuna at the last Club board meeting. Why should I tell you if Dixie's come this way?"

"You're doing just fine on 9-Lives, from the look of you." Chapin's voice was harsh. "Mackerel's brain food; how long have you known English?"

Oenone's reply—who else could it be but Oenone?—came calm and measured. "I don't owe you answers. You have it all wrong. It's you who must play with me; by the old rules."

Chapin's barking laugh was so loud I thought I'd come upon them soon, but I only found the golf cart. They were deeper in the woods, and as I pressed on I heard him say, "And if I don't, you won't help me find Dixie before the market closes, is that it? Dying to ask that stupid riddle after all these years, aren't you?"

"Call it an ethnic whim."

"I call it blackmail; but okay." I could imagine Chapin's fatuous grin. "Ask. What have I got to lose? But the answer is man."

"Is it?" Oenone purred. The rumbling shook the blackberry bushes. I was at the edge of her kennel-clearing, about to announce myself, when I tripped over something and sprawled out of sight just as the sphynx propounded her riddle. "Who was that lady I saw you with last night?"

"Man!" snapped Chapin automatically, then goggled. "*What* did you say?"

I raised myself on my elbows and saw her. She had grown, our sweet Oenone. She was as big as a Siberian tiger, and her steel grey wings fanned out suddenly with a clap of thunder. There were blots of dried blood on her breasts.

"I said," she replied sweetly, "you lose." She pounced before he could utter another word.

I lunged away, sickened by the scream that ended in gurgles and then silence. Something snagged my feet a second time, and I went down in a deafening dry clatter, falling among Oenone's well-gnawed leftovers. I spied Dixwell's nine iron among them. Gorging, she ignored me as I tottered off.

We mounted an armed hunt, but in vain. Sphynxes are smart, as witness Oenone's quiet scholarship, learning English and—no doubt—a more suitable set of riddles. She knew she'd never make her full growth on 9-Lives mackerel. She was gone; literally flown the coop. Where she went is anyone's guess. America is larger than Greece, and there is wilderness still.

Perhaps there will come reports of backpackers unaccounted for, campers gone too long in the high country, mysterious vanishments of hunters and fishermen. Will they chuckle, as we did, and dare her to ask her silly riddle? Arrogance is never the answer to the sphynx's question. Oedipus himself was never educated at Yale.

Of course, look where it got him.

Simpson has been blackballed from the Club. Under the circumstances it was the least we could do.

THE SEA SERPENT

Of all the creatures portrayed in this anthology, the sea serpent is the only one who may actually *exist* in the corporeal world as well as in the world of the imagination. At the very least, it is the one fabulous beast whose existence is still widely *believed* in by a significant percentage of the contemporary population. For instance, there are probably very few (if any) citizens of the modern world who still believe in the actual physical existence of, say, griffins or sphinxes or centaurs—but every year there are dozens of eyewitness reports of sea serpents (or USOs, as they are sometimes called: Unidentified Swimming Objects), as there have been year after year for centuries. There are literally thousands of reports of sea serpents, many of them by trained observers: naturalists, oceanographers, experienced seamen, naval officers, submarine crews. Sometimes they have been seen by hundreds of witnesses at once, as in the famous nineteenth century sighting by the crew of HMS *Daedalus*. Nor are sea serpents restricted to the open ocean. Similar creatures known as "lake monsters" have been reported from lakes all over the world. The Loch Ness Monster—familiarly known as "Nessie"—is the most famous of these elusive creatures, but there is also "Issie," the monster of Japan's Lake Ikeda, "Champ," the monster of Lake Champlain, "Ogopogo," the monster of Western Canada's Lake Okanagan, "Manipogo," the monster of Manitoba's Lake Winnipegosis, the Black Beast of Quebec's Lake Ponenegamook, and Iceland's Lágarfljótsormur, among many others.

Whether sea serpents exist in fact or not, they have been alive and swimming in the imagination of various writers for hundreds of years. In the funny and richly-detailed story that follows, the famous fisherman Izaak Walton sets out in search of the biggest sea serpent of them all . . .

Howard Waldrop is one of the best short-story writers in the business, known for his strong shaggy humor, offbeat erudition, and bizarre fictional juxtapositions. He has won both the Nebula and the World Fantasy Awards for short fiction, and his stories have appeared in *Omni, Universe, Playboy, Shayol,* and elsewhere. His first solo novel, *Them Bones,* was published last year as an Ace Special.

God's Hooks

by

Howard Waldrop

THEY WERE IN the End of the World Tavern at the bottom of Great Auk Street.

The place was crowded, noisy. As patrons came in, they paused to kick their boots on the floor and shake the cinders from their rough clothes.

The air smelled of wood smoke, singed hair, heated and melted glass.

"Ho!" yelled a man at one of the noisiest tables to his companions, who were dressed more finely than the workmen around them. "Here's old Izaak now, come up from Staffordshire."

A man in his seventies, dressed in brown with a wide white collar, bagged pants, and cavalier boots, stood in the doorway. He took off his high-brimmed hat and shook it against his pantsleg.

"Good evening, Charles, Percy, Mr. Marburton," he said, his gray eyes showing merry above his full white mustache and Vandyke beard.

"Father Izaak," said Charles Cotton, rising and embracing the older man. Cotton was wearing a new-style wig, whose curls and ringlets flowed onto his shoulders.

"Mr. Peale, if you please, sherry all round," yelled Cotton to the innkeeper. The older man seated himself.

"Sherry's dear," said the innkeep, "though our enemy,

the King of France, is sending two ships' consignments this fortnight. The Great Fire has worked wonders."

"What matters the price when there's good fellowship?" asked Cotton.

"Price is All," said Marburton, a melancholy round man.

"Well, Father Izaak," said Charles, turning to his friend, "how looks the house on Chancery Lane?"

"Praise to God, Charles, the Fire burnt but the top floor. Enough remains to rebuild, if decent timbers can be found. Why, the lumbermen are selling green wood most expensive, and finding ready buyers."

"Their woodchoppers are working day and night in the north, since good King Charles gave them leave to cut his woods down," said Percy, and drained his glass.

"They'll not stop till all England's flat and level as Dutchman's land," said Marburton.

"If they're not careful, they'll play hob with the rivers," said Cotton.

"And the streams," said Izaak.

"And the ponds," said Percy.

"Oh, the fish!" said Marburton.

All four sighed.

"Ah, but come!" said Izaak. "No joylessness here! I'm the only one to suffer from the Fire at this table. We'll have no long faces till April! Why, there's tench and dace to be had, and pickerel! What matters the salmon's in his Neptunian rookery? Who cares that trout burrow in the mud, and bite not from coat of soot and cinders? We've the roach and the gudgeon!"

"I suffered from the Fire," said Percy.

"What? Your house lies to east," said Izaak.

"My book was at bindery at the Office of Stationers. A neighbor brought me a scorched and singed bundle of title pages. They fell sixteen miles west o' town, like snow, I suppose."

Izaak winked at Cotton. "Well, Percy, that can be set aright soon as the Stationers reopen. What you need is something right good to eat." He waved to the barkeep, who nodded and went outside to the kitchen. "I was in early and prevailed on Mr. Peale to fix a supper to cheer the dourest disposition. What with shortages, it might not pass for kings, but we are not so high. Ah, here it comes!"

Mr. Peale returned with a huge, round platter. High and thick, it smelled of fresh-baked dough, meat, and savories. It looked like a crooked pond. In a line around the outside, halves of whole pilchards stuck out, looking up at them with wide eyes, as if they had been struggling to escape being cooked.

"Oh, Izaak!" said Percy, tears of joy springing to his eyes. "A star-gazey pie!"

Peale beamed with pleasure. "It may not be the best," he said, "but it's the End o' the World!" He put a finger alongside his nose and laughed. He took great pleasure in puns.

The four men at the table fell to, elbows and pewter forks flying.

They sat back from the table, full. They said nothing for a few minutes, and stared out the great bow window of the tavern. The shop across the way blocked the view. They could not see the ruins of London which stretched—charred, black, and still smoking—from the Tower to the Temple. Only the waterfront in that great length had been spared.

On the fourth day of that Great Fire, the King had given orders to blast with gunpowder all houses in the way of the flames. It had been done, creating the breaks that, with a dying wind, had brought it under control and saved the city.

"What the city has gone through this past year!" said Percy. "It's lucky, Izaak, that you live down country, and have not suffered till now."

"They say the Fire didn't touch the worst of the Plague districts," said Marburton. "I would imagine that such large crowds milling and looking for shelter will cause another one this winter. Best we should all leave the city before we drop dead in our steps."

"Since the comet of December, year before last, there's been nothing but talk of doom on everyone's lips," said Cotton.

"Apocalypse talk," said Percy.

"Like as not it's right," said Marburton.

They heard the clanging bell of a crier at the next cross street.

The tavern was filling in the late-afternoon light. Carpenters, tradesmen covered with soot, a few soldiers all soiled came in.

"Why, the whole city seems full of chimneysweeps," said Percy.

The crier's clanging bell sounded, and he stopped before the window of the tavern.

"New edict from His Majesty Charles II to be posted concerning rebuilding of the city. New edict from Council of Aldermen on rents and leases, to be posted. An Act concerning movements of trade and shipping to new quays to become law. Assize Courts sessions to begin September 27, please God. Foreign nations to send all manner of aid to the City. Murder on New Ogden Street, felon apprehended in the act. Portent of Doom, monster fish seen in Bedford."

As one, the four men leaped from the table, causing a great stir, and ran outside to the crier.

"See to the bill, Charles," said Izaak, handing him some coins. "We'll meet at nine o' the clock at the Ironmongers' Company yard. I must go see to my tackle."

"If the man the crier sent us to spoke right, there'll be no other fish like it in England," said Percy.

"Or the world," said Marburton, whose spirits had lightened considerably.

"I imagine the length of the fish has doubled with each county the tale passed through," said Izaak.

"It'll take stout tackle," said Percy. "Me for my strongest salmon rod."

"I for my twelve-hair lines," said Marburton.

"And me," said Izaak, "to new and better angles."

The Ironmongers' Hall had escaped the Fire with only the loss of its roof. There were a few workmen about, and the Company secretary greeted Izaak cordially.

"Brother Walton," he said, "what brings you to town?" They gave each other the secret handshake and made The Sign.

"To look to my property on Chancery Lane, and the Row," he said. "But now, is there a fire in the forge downstairs?"

Below the Company Hall was a large workroom, where

the more adventurous of the ironmongers experimented with new processes and materials.

"Certain there is," said the secretary. "We've been making new nails for the roof timbers."

"I'll need the forge for an hour or so. Send me down the small black case from my lockerbox, will you?"

"Oh, Brother Walton," asked the secretary. "Off again to some pellucid stream?"

"I doubt," said Walton. "But to fish, nonetheless."

Walton was in his shirt, sleeves rolled up, standing in the glow of the forge. A boy brought down the case from the upper floor, and now Izaak opened it, and took out three long gray-black bars.

"Pump away, boy," he said to the young man near the bellows, "and there's a copper in it for you."

Walton lovingly placed the metal bars, roughened by pounding years before, into the coals. Soon they began to glow redly as the teenaged boy worked furiously on the bellows-sack. He and Walton were covered with sweat.

"Lovely color, now," said the boy.

"To whom are you prenticed?" asked Walton.

"To the Company, sir."

"Ah," said Walton. "Ever seen angles forged?"

"No, sir, mostly hinges and buckles, nails like. Sir Abram Jones sometimes puddles his metal here. I have to work most furious when he's here. I sometimes don't like to see him coming."

Walton winked conspiratorially. "You're right, the metal reaches a likeable ruddy hue. Do you know what this metal is?"

"Cold iron, wasn't it? Ore beaten out?"

"No iron like you've seen, or me much either. I've saved it for nineteen years. It came from the sky, and was given to me by a great scientific man at whose feet it nearly fell."

"No!" said the boy. "I heard tell of stones falling from the sky."

"I assure you, he assured me it did. And now," said Izaak, gripping the smallest metal bar with great tongs and taking it to the anvil, "we shall tease out the

fishhook that is hidden away inside."
Sparks and clanging filled the basement.

They were eight miles out of northern London before the air began to smell more of September than of Hell. Two wagons jounced along the road toward Bedford, one containing the four men, the other laden with tackle, baggage, and canvas.

"This is rough enough," said Cotton. "We could have sent for my coach!"

"And lost four hours," said Marburton. "These fellows were idle enough, and Izaak wanted an especially heavy cart for some reason. Izaak, you've been most mysterious. We saw neither your tackles nor your baits."

"Suffice to say, they are none too strong nor none too delicate for the work at hand."

Away from the town, there was a touch of coming autumn in the air.

"We might find nothing there," said Marburton, whose spirits had sunk again. "Or some damnably small salmon."

"Why then," said Izaak, "we'll have Bedfordshire to our own, and all of September, and perhaps an inn where the smell of lavender is in the sheets and there are twenty printed ballads on the wall!"

"Hmmph!" said Marburton.

At noon of the next day, they stopped to water the horses and eat.

"I venture to try the trout in this stream," said Percy.

"Come, come," said Cotton. "Our goal is Bedford, and we seek Leviathan himself! Would you tempt sport by angling here?"

"But a brace of trouts would be fine now."

"Have some more cold mutton," said Marburton. He passed out bread and cheese and meat all around. The drivers tugged their forelocks to him and put away their rougher fare.

"How far to Bedford?" asked Cotton of the driver called Humphrey.

"Ten miles, sir, more or less. We should have come farther but, what with the Plague, the roads haven't been worked in above a year."

"I'm bruised through and through," said Marburton.

Izaak was at the stream, relieving himself against a tree.

"Damn me!" said Percy. "Did anyone leave word where I was bound?"

Marburton laughed. "Izaak sent word to all our families. Always considerate."

"Well, he's become secretive enough. All those people following him a-angling since his book went back to the presses the third time. Ah, books!" Percy grew silent.

"What, still lamenting your loss?" asked Izaak, returning. "What you need is singing, the air, sunshine. Are we not Brothers of the Angle, out a-fishing? Come, back into the carts! Charles, start us off on 'Tom o' the Town.'"

Cotton began to sing, in a clear sweet voice, the first stanza. One by one the others joined, their voices echoing under the bridge. The carts pulled back on the roads. The driver of the baggage cart sang with them. They went down the rutted Bedford road, September all about them, the long summer after the Plague over, their losses, heartaches all gone, all deep thoughts put away. The horses clopped time to their singing.

Bedford was a town surrounded by villages, where they were stared at when they went through. The town was divided neatly in two by the double-gated bridge over the River Ouse.

After the carts crossed the bridge, they alighted at the doorway of a place called the Topsy-Turvy Inn, whose sign above the door was a world globe turned arse-over-teakettle.

The people who stood by the inn were all looking up the road, where a small crowd had gathered around a man who was preaching from a stump.

"I think," said Cotton, as they pulled their baggage from the cart, "that we're in Dissenter country."

"Of that I'm sure," said Walton. "But once we Anglicans were on the outs and they'd say the same of us."

One of the drivers was listening to the man preach. So was Marburton.

The preacher was dressed in somber clothes. He stood on a stump at two cross streets. He was stout and had brown-red hair that glistened in the sun. His mustache was an unruly wild thing on his lip, but his beard was a neat red spike on his chin. He stood with his head uncovered, a great worn clasp Bible under his arm.

"London burned clean through," he was saying. "Forty-three parish churches razed. Plagues! Fires! Signs in the skies of the sure and certain return of Christ. The Earth swept clean by God's loving mercy. I ask you sinners to repent for the sake of your souls."

A man walking by on the other side of the street slowed, listened, stopped.

"Oh, this is Tuesday!" he yelled to the preacher. "Save your rantings for the Sabbath, you old jailbird!"

A few people in the crowd laughed, but others shushed him.

"In my heart," said the man on the stump, "it is always the Sabbath as long as there are sinners among you."

"Ah, a fig to your damned sneaking disloyal Non-Conformist drivel!" said the heckler, holding his thumb up between his fingers.

"Wasn't I once as you are now?" asked the preacher. "Didn't I curse and swear, play at tipcat, ring bells, cause commotion wherever I went? Didn't God's forgiving Grace . . . ?"

A constable hurried up.

"Here, John," he said to the stout preacher. "There's to be no sermons, you know that!" He waved his staff of office. "And I charge you all under the Act of 13 Elizabeth 53 to go about your several businesses."

"Let him go on, Harry," yelled a woman. "He's got words for sinners."

"I can't argue that. I can only tell you the law. The sheriff's about on dire business, and he'd have John back in jail and the jailer turned out in a trice. Come down off the stump, man."

The stout man waved his arms. "We must disperse, friends. The Sabbath meeting will be at . . ."

The constable clapped his hands over his ears and turned his back until the preacher finished giving directions to some obscure clearing in a woods. The red-haired man stepped down.

Walton had been listening and staring at him, as had the others. Izaak saw that the man had a bag of his tools of the trade with him. He was obviously a coppersmith or brazier, his small anvils, tongs, and taphammers identifying him as such. But he was no ironmonger, so Walton was not duty-bound to be courteous to him.

"Damnable Dissenters indeed," said Cotton. "Come, Father Izaak, let's to this hospitable inn."

A crier appeared at the end of the street. "Town meeting. Town meeting. All free men of the Town of Bedford and its villages to be in attendance. Levies for the taking of the Great Fish. Four of the clock in the town hall."

"Well," said Marburton, "that's where we shall be."

They returned to the inn at dusk.

"They're certainly going at this thing full-tilt," said Percy. "Nets, pikes, muskets."

"If those children had not been new to the shire, they wouldn't have tried to angle there."

"And wouldn't have been eaten and mangled," said Marburton.

"A good thing the judge is both angler and reader," said Cotton. "Else Father Walton wouldn't have been given all the morrow to prove our mettle against this great scaly beast."

"If it have scales," said Marburton.

"I fear our tackle is not up to it," said Percy.

"Didn't Father Walton always say that an angler stores up his tackle against the day he needs it? I'll wager we get good sport out of this before it's over."

"And the description of the place! In such a narrow defile, the sunlight touches it but a few hours a day. For what possible reason would children fish there?"

"You're losing your faith, Marburton. I've seen you up to your whiskers in the River Lea, snaggling for salmon under a cutbank."

"But I, praise God, know what I'm about."

"I suppose," said Izaak, seating himself, "that the children thought so too."

They noticed the stout Dissenter preacher had come in and was talking jovially with his cronies. He lowered his voice and looked toward their table.

Most of the talk around Walton was of the receding Plague, the consequences of the Great Fire on the region's timber industry, and other matters of report.

"I expected more talk of the fish," said Percy.

"To them," said Cotton, "it's all the same. Just another odious county task, like digging a new canal or hunting down a heretic. They'll be in holiday mood day after tomorrow."

"They strike me as a cheerless lot," said Percy.

"Cheerless, but efficient. I'd hate to be the fish."

"You think we won't have it to gaff long before the workmen arrive?"

"I have my doubts," said Marburton.

"But you always do."

Next morning, the woods became thick and rank on the road they took out of town. The carts bounced in the ruts. The early sun was lost in the mists and the trees. The road rose and fell again into narrow valleys.

"Someone is following us," said Percy, getting out his spyglass.

"Probably a pedlar out this way," said Cotton, straining his eyes at the pack on the man's back.

"I've seen no cottages," said Marburton. He was taking kinks out of his fishing line.

Percy looked around him. "What a Godless-looking place."

The trees were more stunted, thicker. Quick shapes, which may have been grouse, moved among their twisted boles. An occasional cry, unknown to the four anglers, came from the depths of the woods. A dull boom, as of a great door closing, sounded from far away. The horses halted, whinnying, their nostrils flared.

"In truth," said Walton from where he rested against a cushion, "I feel myself some leagues beyond Christendom."

The gloom deepened. Green was gone now, nothing but grays and browns met the eye. The road was a rocky rut. The carts rose, wheels teetering on stone, and agonizingly fell. Humphrey and the other driver swore great blazing oaths.

"Be so abusive as you will," said Cotton to them, "but take not the Lord's name in vain, for we are Christian men."

"As you say." Humphrey tugged his forelock.

The trees reached overhead, the sky was obscured. An owl swept over, startling them. Something large bolted away, feet drumming on the high bank over the road.

Percy and Cotton grew quiet. Walton talked, of lakes, streams, of summer. Seeing the others grow moody, he sang a quiet song. A driver would sometimes curse.

A droning, flapping sound grew louder, passed to their right, veered away. The horses shied then, trying to turn around in the road, almost upsetting the carts. They refused to go on.

"We'll have to tether them here," said Humphrey. "Besides, Your Lordship, I think I see water at the end of the road."

It was true. In what dim light there was, they saw a darker sheen down below.

"We must take the second cart down there, Charles," said Walton, "even if we must push it ourselves."

"We'll never make it," said Percy.

"Whatever for?" asked Cotton. "We can take our tackle and viands down there."

"Not my tackle," said Walton.

Marburton just sighed.

They pushed and pulled the second cart down the hill; from the front they kept it from running away on the incline, from the back to get it over stones the size of barrels. It was stuck.

"I can't go on," said Marburton.

"Surely you can," said Walton.

"Your cheerfulness is depressing," said Percy.

"Be that as it may. Think trout, Marburton. Think salmon!"

Marburton strained against the recalcitrant wheel. The cart moved forward a few inches.

"See, see!" said Walton. "A foot's good as a mile!"

They grunted and groaned.

They stood panting at the edge of the mere. The black sides of the valley lifted to right and left like walls. The water itself was weed-choken, scummy, and smelled of the sewer ditch. Trees came down to its very edges. Broken and rotted stumps dotted the shore. Mist rose from the water in fetid curls.

Sunlight had not yet come to the bottom of the defile. To left and right, behind, all lay in twisted woody darkness. The valley rose like a hand around them.

Except ahead. There was a break, with no trees at the center of the cleft. Through it they saw, shining and blue-purple against the cerulean of the sky, the far-off Chiltern Hills.

"Those," said a voice behind them, and they jumped and turned and saw the man with the pack. It was the stout red-haired preacher of the day before. "Those are the Delectable Mountains," he said.

"And this is the Slough of Despond."

He built a small lean-to some hundred feet from them.

The other three anglers unloaded their gear and began to set it up.

"What, Father Walton? Not setting up your poles?" asked Charles Cotton.

"No, no," said Izaak, studying the weed-clotted swamp with a sure eye. "I'll let you young ones try your luck first."

Percy looked at the waters. "The fish is most likely a carp or other rough type," he said. "No respectable fish could live in this mire. I hardly see room for anything that could swallow a child."

"It is Leviathan," said the preacher from his shelter. "It is the Beast of Babylon, which shall rise in the days before Antichrist. These woods are beneath his sway."

"What do you want?" asked Cotton.

"To dissuade you, and the others who will come, from doing this. It is God's will these things come to pass."

"Oh, Hell and damn!" said Percy.

"Exactly," said the preacher.

Percy shuddered involuntarily. Daylight began to creep down to the mere's edge. With the light, the stench from the water became worse.

"You're not doing very much to stop us," said Cotton. He was fitting together an eighteen-foot rod of yew, fir, and hazelwood.

"When you raise Leviathan," said the preacher, "then

will I begin to preach." He took a small cracked pot from his large bag, and began to set up his anvil.

Percy's rod had a butt as thick as a man's arm. It tapered throughout its length to a slender reed. The line was made of plaited, dyed horsehair, twelve strands at the pole end, tapering to nine. The line was forty feet long. Onto the end of this, he fastened a sinker and a hook as long as a crooked little finger.

"Where's my baits? Oh, here they are." He reached into a bag filled with wet moss, pulled out a gob of worms, and threaded seven or eight, their ends wriggling, onto the hook.

The preacher had started a small fire. He was filling an earthen pot with solder. He paid very little attention to the anglers.

Percy and Marburton, who was fishing with a shorter but thicker rod, were ready before Cotton.

"I'll take this fishy spot here," said Percy, "and you can have that grown-over place there." He pointed beyond the preacher.

"We won't catch anything," said Marburton suddenly and pulled the bait from his hook and threw it into the water. Then he walked back to the cart and sat down, and shook.

"Come, come," said Izaak. "I've never seen you so discouraged, even after fishless days on the Thames."

"Never mind me," said Marburton. Then he looked down at the ground. "I shouldn't have come all this way. I have business in the city. There are no fish here."

Cajoling could not get him up again. Izaak's face became troubled. Marburton stayed put.

"Well, I'll take the fishy spot then," said Cotton, tying onto his line an artificial fly of green with hackles the size of porcupine quills.

He moved past the preacher.

"I'm certain to wager you'll get no strikes on that gaudy bird's wing," said Percy.

"There is no better fishing than angling fine and far off," answered Cotton. "Heavens, what a stink!"

"This is the place," said the preacher without looking up, "where all the sins of mankind have been flowing for sixteen hundred years. Not twenty thousand cartloads of earth could fill it up."

"Prattle," said Cotton.

"Prattle it may be," said the preacher. He puddled solder in a sandy ring. Then he dipped the pot in it. "It stinks from mankind's sins, nonetheless."

"It stinks from mankind's bowels," said Cotton.

He made two backcasts with his long rod, letting more line out the wire guide at the tip each time. He placed the huge fly gently on the water sixty feet away.

"There are no fish about," said Percy, down the mire's edge. "Not even gudgeon."

"Nor snakes," said Cotton. "What does this monster eat?"

"Miscreant children," said the preacher. "Sin feeds on the young."

Percy made a clumsy cast into some slime-choked weeds.

His rod was pulled from his hands and flew across the water. A large dark shape blotted the pond's edge and was gone.

The rod floated to the surface and lay still. Percy stared down at his hands in disbelief. The pole came slowly in toward shore, pushed by the stinking breeze.

Cotton pulled his fly off the water, shook his line, and walked back toward the cart.

"That's all for me, too," he said. They turned to Izaak. He rubbed his hands together gleefully, making a show he did not feel.

The preacher was grinning.

"Call the carters down," said Walton. "Move the cart to the very edge of the mere."

While they were moving the wagon with its rear facing the water, Walton went over to the preacher.

"My name is Izaak Walton," he said, holding out his hand. The preacher took it formally.

"John Bunyan, mechanic-preacher," said the other.

"I hold no man's religious beliefs against him, if he be an honest man, or an angler. My friends are not of like mind, though they be both fishermen and honest."

"Would that Parliament were full of such as yourself," said Bunyan. "I took your hand, but I am dead set against what you do."

"If not us," said Walton, "then the sheriff with his powder and pikes."

"I shall prevail against them, too. This is God's warning to mankind. You're a London man. You've seen the Fire, the Plague?"

"London is no place for honest men. I'm of Stafford."

"Even you see London as a place of sin," said Bunyan. "You have children?"

"I have two, by second wife," said Walton. "Seven others died in infancy."

"I have four," Bunyan said. "One born blind." His eyes took on a faraway look. "I want them to fear God, in hope of eternal salvation."

"As do we all," said Walton.

"And this monster is warning to mankind of the coming rains of blood and fire and the fall of stars."

"Either we shall take it, or the townsmen will come tomorrow."

"I know them all," said Bunyan. "Mr. Nurse-nickel, Mr. By-your-Leave, Mr. Cravenly-Crafty. Do ye not feel your spirits lag, your backbone fail? They'll not last long as you have."

Walton had noticed his own lassitude, even with the stink of the slough goading him. Cotton, Percy and Marburton, finished with the cart, were sitting disconsolately on the ground. The swamp had brightened some; the blazing blue mountain ahead seemed inches away. But the woods were dark, the defile precipitous, the noises loud as before.

"It gets worse after dark," said the preacher. "I beg you, take not the fish."

"If you stop the sheriff, he'll have you in prison."

"It's prison from which I come," said Bunyan. "To jail I shall go back, for I know I'm right."

"Do your conscience," said Walton, "for that way lies salvation."

"Amen!" said Bunyan, and went back to his pots.

Percy, Marburton, and Charles Cotton watched as Walton set up his tackle. Even with flagging spirits, they were intrigued. He'd had the carters peg down the trace poles of the wagon. Then he sectioned together a rod like none they had seen before. It was barely nine feet long, starting big as a smith's biceps, ending in a fine end. It was made of many split laths glued seamlessly together. On each foot of its length past the handle were iron guides bound with wire. There was a hole in the handle of the rod, and now Walton reached in the wagon and took out a shining metal wheel.

"What's that, a squirrel cage?" asked Percy.

They saw him pull line out from it. It clicked with each turn. There was a handle on the wheel, and a peg at the bottom. He put the peg through the hole in the handle and fastened it down with an iron screw.

He threaded the line, which was thick as a pen quill, through the guides, opened the black case, and took out the largest of the hooks he'd fashioned.

On the line he tied a strong wire chain, and affixed a sinker to one end and the hook on the other.

He put the rod in the wagon seat and climbed down to the back and opened his bait box and reached in.

"Come, my pretty," he said, reaching. He took something out, white, segmented, moving. It filled his hand.

It was a maggot that weighed half a pound.

"I had them kept down a cistern behind a shambles," said Walton. He lifted the bait to show them. "Charles, take my line after I bait the angle; make a handcast into the edge of those stumps yonder. As I was saying, take your gentles, put them in a cool well, feed them on liver or pork for the summer. They'll eat and grow and not change to flies, for the changing of one so large kills it. Keep them well fed; put them into wet moss before using them. I feared the commotion and flames had collapsed the well. Though the butcher shop was gone, the baits were still fat and lively."

As he said the last word, he plunged the hook through the white flesh of the maggot.

It twisted and oozed onto his hand. He opened a small bottle. "And dowse it with camphire oil just before the cast." They smelled the pungent liquid as he poured it. The bait went into a frenzy.

"Now, Charles," he said, pulling off fifty feet of line from the reel. Cotton whirled the weighted hook around and around his head. "Be so kind as to tie this rope to my belt and the cart, Percy," said Walton.

Percy did so. Cotton made the hand-cast, the pale globule hitting the water and sinking.

"Do as I have told you," said Walton, "and you shall not fail to catch the biggest fish."

Something large between the eyes swallowed the hook and five feet of line.

"And set the hook sharply, and you shall have great sport." Walton, seventy years old, thin of build, stood in the seat, jerked far back over his head, curving the rod in a loop.

The waters of the slough exploded, they saw the shallow bottom and a long dark shape, and the fight was on.

The preacher stood up from his pots, opened his clasp Bible, and began to preach in a loud strong voice.

"Render to Caesar," he said: Walton flinched and put his back into turning the fish, which was heading toward the stumps. The reel's clicks were a buzz. Bunyan raised his voice: "Those things which are Caesar's, and to God those things which are God's."

"Oh, shut up!" said Cotton. "The man's got trouble enough!"

The wagon creaked and began to lift off the ground. The rope and belt cut into Walton's flesh. His arms were nearly pulled from their sockets. Sweat sprang to his forehead like curds through a cheesecloth. He gritted his teeth and pulled.

The pegs lifted from the ground.

Bunyan preached on.

The sunlight faded, though it was late afternoon. The noise from the woods grew louder. The blue hills in the distance became flat, gray. The whole valley leaned over them, threatening to fall over and kill them. Eyes shined in the deeper woods.

Walton had regained some line in the last few hours. Bunyan preached on, pausing long enough to light a horn lantern from his fire.

After encouraging Walton at first, Percy, Marburton and Cotton had become quiet. The sounds were those of Bunyan's droning voice, screams from the woods, small pops from the fire, and the ratcheting of the reel.

The fish was fighting him on the bottom. He'd had no

sight of it yet since the strike. Now the water was becoming a flat black sheet in the failing light. It was no salmon or trout or carp. It must be a pike or eel or some other toothed fish. Or a serpent. Or cuttlefish, with squiddy arms to tear the skin from a man.

Walton shivered. His arms were numb, his shoulders a tight aching band. His legs where he braced against the footrest quivered with fatigue. Still he held, even when the fish ran to the far end of the swamp. If he could keep it away from the snags, he could wear it down. The fish turned, the line slackened, Walton pumped the rod up and down. He regained the lost line. The water hissed as the cording cut through it. The fish headed for the bottom.

Tiredly, Walton heaved, turned the fish. The wagon creaked.

"Blessed are they that walk in the path of righteousness," said Bunyan.

The ghosts came in over the slough straight at them. Monkey-demons began to chatter in the woods. Eyes peered from the bole of every tree. Bunyan's candle was the only light. Something walked heavily on a limb at the woods' edge, bending it. Marburton screamed and ran up the road.

Percy was on his feet. Ghosts and banshees flew at him, veering away at the last instant.

"You have doubts," said Bunyan to him. "You are assailed. You think yourself unworthy."

Percy trotted up the stony road, ragged shapes fluttering in the air behind him, trying to tug his hair. Skeletons began to dance across the slough, acting out pantomimes of life, death, and love. The Seven Deadly Sins manifested themselves.

Hell yawned opened to receive them all.

Then the sun went down.

"Before you join the others, Charles," said Walton, pumping the rod, "cut away my coat and collar."

"You'll freeze," said Cotton, but climbed into the wagon and cut the coat up the back and down the sleeves. It and the collar fell away.

"Good luck, Father Walton," he said. Something plucked at his eyes. "We go to town for help."

"Be honest and trustworthy all the rest of your days," said Izaak Walton. Cotton looked stunned. Something large ran down from the woods, through the wagon, and up into the trees. Cotton ran up the hill. The thing loped after him.

Walton managed to gain six inches on the fish.

Grinning things sat on the taut line. The air was filled with meteors: burning, red, thick as snow. Huge worms pushed themselves out of the ground, caught and ate demons, then turned inside out. The demons flew away.

Everything in the darkness had claws and horns.

"And lo! the seventh seal was broken, and there was quietness on the earth for the space of half an hour," read Bunyan.

He had lit his third candle.

Walton could see the water again. A little light came from somewhere behind him. The noises of the woods diminished. A desultory ghost or skeleton flitted grayly by. There was a calm in the air.

The fish was tiring. Walton did not know how long he had fought on, or with what power. He was a human ache, and he wanted to sleep. He was nodding.

"The townsmen come," said Bunyan. Walton stole a fleeting glance behind him. Hundreds of people came quietly and cautiously through the woods, some extinguishing torches as he watched.

Walton cranked in another ten feet of line. The fish ran, but only a short way, slowly, and Walton reeled him back. It was still a long way out, still another hour before he could bring it to gaff. Walton heard low talk, recognized Percy's voice. He looked back again. The people had pikes, nets, a small cannon. He turned, reeled the fish, fighting it all the way.

"You do not love God!" said Bunyan suddenly, shutting his Bible.

"Yes I do!" said Walton, pulling as hard as he could. He gained another foot. "I love God as much as you."

"You do not!" said Bunyan. "I see it now."

"I love God!" yelled Walton and heaved the rod.

A fin broke the frothing water.

"In your heart, where God can see from his high throne, you lie!" said Bunyan.

Walton reeled and pulled. More fin showed. He quit cranking.

"God forgive me!" said Walton. "It's fishing I love."

"I thought so," said Bunyan. Reaching in his pack, he took out a pair of tin snips and cut Walton's line.

Izaak fell back in the wagon.

"John Bunyan, you son of a bitch!" said the sheriff. "You're under arrest for hampering the King's business. I'll see you rot."

Walton watched the coils of line on the surface slowly sink into the brown depths of the Slough of Despond.

He began to cry, fatigue and numbness taking over his body.

"I denied God," he said to Cotton. "I committed the worst sin." Cotton covered him with a blanket.

"Oh, Charles, I denied God."

"What's worse," said Cotton, "you lost the fish."

Percy and Marburton helped him up. The carters hitched the wagons, the horses now docile. Bunyan was being ridden back to jail by constables, his tinker's bag clanging against the horse's side.

They put the crying Walton into the cart, covered him more, climbed in. Some farmers helped them get the carts over the rocks.

Walton's last view of the slough was of resolute and grim-faced men staring at the water and readying their huge grapples, their guns, their cruel hooked nets.

They were on the road back to town. Walton looked up into the trees, devoid of ghosts and demons. He caught a glimpse of the blue Chiltern Hills.

"Father Izaak," said Cotton. "Rest now. Think of spring. Think of clear water, of leaping trout."

"My dreams will be haunted by God the rest of my days," he said tiredly. Walton fell asleep.

He dreamed of clear water, leaping trouts.

This story is for Chad Oliver, Punisher of Trouts.

THE PHOENIX

Unlike the other creatures in this anthology, the phoenix is a singular marvel. By definition, there can only be *one* phoenix at a time, in all the world. Usually pictured as being about as big as an eagle, with scarlet plumage, a purple tail, iridescent wings, and a plumed golden head, the phoenix is obviously a handsome bird, but its fame depends not so much on its beauty as on the strange cycle of death-and-resurrection it periodically undergoes. As Pliny puts it: "Hee liveth 660 yeares: and when hee groweth old, and begins to decay, he builds himselfe a nest . . . and when he hath filled it with all sort of sweet aromaticall spices, yeeldeth up his life thereupon . . . of his bones and marrow there breedeth at first as it were a little worme: which afterwards proveth to bee a pretie bird." By the early Middle Ages, the nest of fine woods and "aromaticall spices" has become a self-made funeral pyre upon which the phoenix is totally consumed by fire, only to rise again reborn from the ashes to live for another thousand years, a cycle that repeats endlessly forever. This image has proved so powerful and enduring that the phoenix has become a worldwide symbol of resurrection and rebirth, and the phrase "a phoenix from the ashes" is still part of popular parlance.

But as the story that follows demonstrates, even a symbol of rebirth can be quite a limiting thing to own, if you have to take *care* of it every day . . .

Joan Aiken is an internationally-known writer, especially acclaimed for her children's books, and for her work in the mystery, suspense, and romance fields. Her books include *Not What You Expected, The Far Forests, Night Fall* and *A Touch of Chill.* Her latest book is the collection *A Whisper in the Night.*

A Leg Full of Rubies

by

Joan Aiken

NIGHT, NOW. AND a young man, Theseus O'Brien, coming down the main street of Killinch with an owl seated upon his shoulder—perhaps the strangest sight that small town ever witnessed. The high moors brooded around the town, all up the wide street came the sighing of the river, and the August night was as gentle and full as a bucket of new milk.

Theseus turned into Tom Mahone's snug, where the men of the town were gathered peaceably together, breathing smoke and drinking mountain dew. Wild, he seemed, coming into the lamplit circle, with a look of the night on him, and a smell of loneliness about him, and his eyes had an inward glimmer from looking into the dark. The owl on his shoulder sat quiet as a coffeepot.

"Well, now, God be good to ye," said Tom Mahone. "What can we do for ye at all?"

And he poured a strong drop, to warm the four bones of him.

"Is there a veterinary surgeon in this town?" Theseus inquired.

Then they saw that the owl had a hurt wing, the ruffled feathers all at odds with one another. "Is there a man in this town can mend him?" he said.

"Ah, sure Dr. Kilvaney's the man for ye," said they all. "No less than a magician with the sick beasts, he is." "And can throw a boulder farther than any man in the land." "'Tis the same one has a wooden leg stuffed full of rubies." "And keeps a phoenix in a cage." "And has all the minutes of his life numbered to the final grain of sand—ah, he's the man to aid ye."

And all the while the owl staring at them from great round eyes.

No more than a step it was to the doctor's surgery, with half Tom Mahone's customers pointing the way. The doctor, sitting late to his supper by a small black fire, heard the knock and opened the door, candle in hand.

"Hoo?" said the owl at the sight of him, "who, whoo?" And, *who* indeed may this strange man be, thought Theseus, following him down the stone passageway, with his long white hair and his burning eyes of grief?

Not a word was said between them till the owl's wing was set, and then the doctor, seeing O'Brien was weary, made him sit and drink a glass of wine.

"Sit," said he, "there's words to be spoken between us. How long has the owl belonged to you?"

"To me?" said Theseus. "He's no owl of mine. I found him up on the high moor. Can you mend him?"

"He'll be well in three days," said Kilvaney. "I see you are a man after my heart, with a love of wild creatures. Are you not a doctor, too?"

"I am," answered Theseus. "Or I was," he added sadly, "until the troubles of my patients became too great a grief for me to bear, and I took to walking the roads to rid me of it."

"Come into my surgery," said the doctor, "for I've things to show you. You're the man I've been looking for."

They passed through the kitchen, where a girl was washing the dishes. Lake-blue eyes, she had, and black hair; she was small, and fierce, and beautiful, like a falcon.

"My daughter," the doctor said absently. "Go to bed, Maggie."

"When the birds are fed, not before," she snapped.

Cage after cage of birds, Theseus saw, all down one wall of the room, finches and thrushes, starlings and blackbirds, with a sleep stirring and twittering coming from them.

In the surgery there was only one cage, but that one big enough to house a man. And inside it was such a bird as

Theseus had never seen before—every feather on it pure gold, and eyes like candle-flames.

"My phoenix," the doctor said, "but don't go too near him, for he's vicious."

The phoenix sidled near the end of his cage, with his eyes full of malice and his wicked beak sideways, ready to strike. Theseus stepped away from the cage and saw, at the other end of the room, a mighty hour-glass that held in its twin globes enough sand to boil all the eggs in Leghorn. But most of the sand had run through, and only a thin stream remained, silting down so swiftly on the pyramid below that every minute Theseus expected to see the last grain whirl through and vanish.

"You are only just in time," Dr. Kilvaney said. "My hour has come. I hereby appoint you my heir and successor. To you I bequeath my birds. Feed them well, treat them kindly, and they will sing to you. But never, never let the phoenix out of his cage, for his nature is evil."

"No, no! Dr. Kilvaney!" Theseus cried. "You are in the wrong of it! You are putting a terrible thing on me! I don't want your birds, not a feather of them. I can't abide creatures in cages!"

"You must have them," said the doctor coldly. "Who else can I trust? And to you I leave also my wooden leg full of rubies—look, I will show you how it unscrews."

"No!" cried Theseus. "I don't want to see!"

He shut his eyes, but he heard a creaking, like a wooden pump-handle.

"And I will give you, too," said the doctor presently, "this hour-glass. See, my last grain of sand has run through. Now it will be *your* turn." Calmly he reversed the hour-glass, and started the sand once more on its silent, hurrying journey. Then he said,

"Surgery hours are on the board outside. The medicines are in the cupboard yonder. Bridget Hanlon is the midwife. My daughter feeds the birds and attends to the cooking. You can sleep tonight on the bed in there. Never let the phoenix out of its cage. You must promise that."

"I promise," said Theseus, like a dazed man.

"Now I will say goodbye to you." The doctor took out his false teeth, put them on the table, glanced around the room to see that nothing was overlooked, and then went up the stairs as if he were late for an appointment.

All night Theseus, uneasy on the surgery couch, could hear the whisper of the sand running, and the phoenix rustling, and the whet of his beak on the bars; with the first light he could see its mad eye glaring at him.

In the morning, Dr. Kilvaney was dead.

It was a grand funeral. All the town gathered to pay him respect, for he had dosed and drenched and bandaged them all, and brought most of them into the world, too.

"'Tis a sad loss," said Tom Mahone, "and he with the grandest collection of cage-birds this side of Dublin city. 'Twas in a happy hour for us the young doctor turned up to take his place."

But there was no happiness in the heart of Theseus O'Brien. Like a wild thing caged himself he felt, among the rustling birds, and with the hating eye of the phoenix fixing him from its corner, and, worst of all, the steady fall of sand from the hour-glass to drive him half mad with its whispering threat.

And, to add to his troubles, no sooner were they home from the funeral than Maggie packed up her clothes in a carpet-bag and moved to the other end of the town to live with her aunt Rose, who owned the hay and feed store.

"It wouldn't be decent," said she, "to keep house for you, and you a single man." And the more Theseus pleaded, the firmer and fiercer she grew. "Besides," she said, "I wouldn't live another day among all those poor birds behind bars. I can't stand the sight nor sound of them."

"I'll let them go, Maggie! I'll let every one of them go."

But then he remembered, with a failing heart, the doctor's last command. "That is, all except the phoenix."

Maggie turned away. All down the village street he watched her small, proud back, until she crossed the bridge and was out of sight. And it seemed as if his heart went with her.

The very next day he let loose all the doctor's birds—the finches and thrushes, the starlings and blackbirds, the woodpecker and the wild heron. He thought Maggie looked at him with a kinder eye when he walked up to the hay and feed store to tell her what he had done.

The people of the town grew fond of their new doctor, but they lamented his sad and downcast look. "What ails him at all?" they asked one another, and Tom Mahone said, "He's as mournful as old Dr. Kilvaney was before him. Sure there's something insalubrious about carrying on the profession of medicine in this town."

But indeed, it was not his calling that troubled the poor young man, for here his patients were as carefree a set of citizens as he could wish. It was the ceaseless running of the sand.

Although there was a whole roomful of sand to run through the glass, he couldn't stop thinking of the day when that roomful would be dwindled to a mere basketful, and then to nothing but a bowlful. And the thought dwelt on his mind like a blight, since it is not wholesome for a man to be advised when his latter end will come, no matter what the burial service may say.

Not only the sand haunted him, but also the phoenix, with its unrelenting stare of hate. No matter what delicacies he brought it, in the way of birdseed and kibbled corn, dry mash and the very best granite grit (for his visits to the hay and feed store were the high spots of his days) the phoenix was always waiting with its razor-sharp beak ready to lay him open to the bone should he venture too near. None of the food would it more than nibble at. And a thing he began to notice, as the days went past, was that its savage brooding eye was always focused on one part of his anatomy—on his left leg. It sometimes seemed to him as if the bird had a particular stake or claim to that leg, and meant to keep watch and see that its property was maintained in good condition.

One night Theseus had need of a splint for a patient. He reached up to a high shelf, where he kept the mastoid mallets, and the crutches, and surgical chisels. He was standing on a chair to do it, and suddenly his foot slipped and he fell, bringing down with him a mighty bone-saw that came to the ground beside him with a clang and a twang, missing his left knee-cap by something less than a feather's breadth. Pale and shaken, he got up, and turning, saw the phoenix watching him as usual, but with such an intent and disappointed look, like the housewife who sees the butcher's boy approaching with the wrong joint!

A cold fit of shivering came over Theseus, and he went hurriedly out of the room.

Next day when he was returning home over the bridge, carrying a bag full of bird-mash, with dried milk and antibiotics added, and his mind full of the blue eyes and black hair of Maggie, a runaway tractor hurtled past him and crashed into the parapet, only one centimetre beyond his left foot.

And again Theseus shuddered, and walked home white and silent, with the cold thought on him. He found the phoenix hunched on its perch, feathers up and head sunk.

"Ah, Phoenix, Phoenix," he cried to it, "why will you be persecuting me so? Do you want to destroy me entirely?" The phoenix made no reply, but stared balefully at his left leg. Then he remembered the old doctor's wooden leg full of rubies. "But I'll not wear it," he cried to the bird, "not if it was stuffed with rubies and diamonds too!"

Just the same, in his heart he believed that the phoenix would not rest satisfied while he had the use of both his legs. He took to walking softly, like a cat, looking this way and that for all possible hazards, watching for falling tiles, and boiling saucepans, and galloping cattle; and the people of the town began to shake their heads over him.

His only happy hours were with Maggie, when he could persuade her to leave the store and come out walking with him. Far from the town they'd go, forgetting the troubles that lay at home. For Maggie had found her aunt was a small, mean-minded woman who put sand in with the hens' meal and shingle among the maize, and Maggie couldn't abide such dealings.

"As soon as I've a little saved," said she, "I'll be away from this town, and off into the world."

"Maggie!" cried Theseus, and it was the first time he'd plucked up courage to do so. "Marry me and I'll make you happier than any girl in the length and breadth of this land."

"I can't marry you," she said. "I could never marry a man who kept a phoenix in a cage."

"We'll give it away," he said, "give it away and forget about it." But even as he spoke he knew they could not. They kissed despairingly, up on the moors in the twilight, and turned homewards.

"I always knew that phoenix was a trouble-bringer," said Maggie, "from the day when Father bought it off a traveling tinker to add to his collection. He said at the time it was a bargain, for the tinker threw in the wooden leg and the great hour-glass as well, but ever after that day Father was a changed man."

"What did he give for it?" Theseus asked.

"His peace of mind. That was all the tinker asked, but it was a deal too much, I'm thinking, for that hateful bird with his wicked look and his revengeful ways."

When he had seen Maggie home, Theseus went to the Public Library, for he couldn't abide the thought of the doctor's house, dark and cold and silent with only the noise of the phoenix shifting on its perch. He took down the volume OWL to POL of the encyclopedia and sat studying it until closing time.

Next day he was along to see Maggie.

"Sweetheart," he said, and his eyes were alive with hope, "I believe I've found the answer. Let me have a half-hundred-weight sack of layers' pellets."

"Fourteen shillings," snapped Aunt Rose, who happened to be in the shop just then. Her hair was pinned up in a skinny bun and her little green eyes were like brad-awls.

"Discount for cash payment," snapped back Theseus, and he planted down thirteen shillings and ninepence, kissed Maggie, picked up the sack, and hurried away home. Just as he got there a flying slate from the church roof struck him; if he'd not been wearing heavy boots it would have sliced his foot off. He ran indoors and shook his fist at the phoenix.

"There!" he yelled at it, pouring a troughful of layers' pellets. "Now get that in your gizzard, you misbegotten fowl!"

The phoenix cocked its head. Then it pecked a pellet, neck feathers puffed in scorn, and one satiric eye fixed all the while on Theseus, who stood eagerly watching. Then it pecked another pellet, hanging by one claw from its perch. Then it came down on to the floor entirely and bowed its golden head over the trough. Theseus tiptoed out of the room. He went outside and chopped up a few sticks of kindling—not many, but just a handful of nice, dry, thin twigs. He came back indoors—the phoenix had its head down, gobbling—and laid the sticks alongside the cage, not too close, an artful width away.

Next evening, surgery done, he fairly ran up to the hay

and feed store. "Come with me," he said joyfully to Maggie, "come and see what it's doing."

Maggie came, her eyes blazing with curiosity. When they reached the surgery she could hear a crackling and a cracking: the phoenix was breaking up twigs into suitable lengths, and laying them side by side. Every now and then it would try them out in a heap; it had a great bundle in the bottom of its cage but it seemed dissatisfied, and every now and then pulled it all to pieces and began again. It had eaten the whole sackful of pellets and looked plump and sleek.

"Theseus," said Maggie, looking at it, "we must let it out. No bird can build inside of a cage. It's not dignified."

"But my promise?"

"*I* never promised," said Maggie, and she stepped up to the cage door.

Theseus lifted a hand, opened his mouth in warning. But then he stopped. For the phoenix, when it saw what Maggie was at, inclined its head to her in gracious acknowledgment, and then took no further notice of her, but as soon as the door was opened, began shifting its heap of sticks out into the room. If ever a bird was busy and preoccupied and in a hurry, that phoenix was the one.

"But we can't let it build in the middle of the floor," said Theseus.

"Ah, sure, what harm?" said Maggie. "Look, the poor fowl is running short of sticks."

As soon as Theseus had gone for more, she stepped over to the hour-glass, for her quick eye had noticed what he, in his excitement, had failed to see—the sand was nearly all run through. Quietly, Maggie reversed the glass and started the sand on its journey again, a thing she had often done for her father, unbeknownst, until the day when it was plain he would rather die than stay alive.

When Theseus came back the phoenix was sitting proudly on the top of a breast-high heap of sticks.

"We mustn't watch it now," said Maggie, "it wouldn't be courteous." And she led Theseus outside. He, however, could not resist a slant-eyed glance through the window as they passed. It yielded him a flash of gold—the phoenix had laid an egg in a kidney-basin. Moreover, plumes of smoke were beginning to flow out through he window.

"Goodbye, Phoenix," Maggie called. But the phoenix, at the heart of a golden blaze, was much too busy to reply.

"Thank heaven!" exclaimed Theseus. "Now I shall never know when the last of my sand was due to run through." Maggie smiled, but made no comment, and he asked her, "Is it right, do you think, to let the house burn down?"

"What harm?" said Maggie again. "It belongs to us, doesn't it?"

"What will the people of the town do, if I'm not here to doctor them?"

"Go to Dr. Conlan of Drumanough."

"And what about your father's leg full of rubies?" he said, looking at the phoenix's roaring pyre.

"We'd never get it out now," said she. "Let it go on holding up the kitchen table till they both burn. We've better things to think of."

And hand in hand the happy pair of them ran out of the town, up along the road to the high moors and the world, leaving behind a pocketful of rubies to glitter in the ashes, and a golden egg for anyone who was fool enough to pick it up.

THE TROLL

Trolls have much in common in their nature and habits with the more ferocious of the man-eating giants—although they are generally portrayed as being smaller, closer to human-size—and it is quite possible that just as giants may be the diminished and dwindled remnants of gods, so trolls may be the dwindled and diminished remnants of giants. Like some giants, most trolls cannot tolerate sunlight, many of them being turned to stone by its touch. Humanoid in form but less human-*looking* than most giants, trolls are usually green or gray in color, sometimes scaly, and often have preternaturally-long arms that hang down past their knees. They are almost universally described as being monstrously ugly of face, sometimes having huge tusks, often having enormous, grotesquely-malshaped noses. They are usually man-eaters, sometimes being said to prefer human flesh to all other meat. By most accounts, they are tremendously powerful and very hard to kill, sometimes continuing to struggle ferociously even after they have literally been hacked to pieces. All in all, they are as dire as any creatures to be found in the pages of fantasy literature, and few if any writers have anything good to say about them.

In the stories that follow, we find a troll inhospitably at

home in the traditional dank and gloomy cave, but also see another troll acting with equal incivility in the carpeted halls of a modern hotel, in spite of a considerable upgrading of luxury and comfort. Perhaps in some cases Heredity *is* more important than Environment, at that . . .

Poul Anderson is one of the best-known and most prolific writers in SF and fantasy. In the course of his 38-year career, he has published more than 80 books, sold hundreds of short pieces to every conceivable market, and won seven Hugo Awards, three Nebula Awards, and the Tolkien Memorial Award for lifetime achievement in fantasy. His latest books are the novel *Orion Shall Rise* and the collection *Time Patrolman*.

The late T. H. White was perhaps the most talented and widely-acclaimed creator of whimsical fantasy since Lewis Carroll. Although he did publish other novels, White's major work—and the work on which almost all of his present-day reputation rests—was the massive Arthurian tetralogy, *The Once and Future King*, one of the landmark volumes of modern fantasy. It was later the inspiration for the Broadway musical *Camelot*. His short fiction has been collected in *The Maharajah and Other Stories*. White died in 1964.

The Valor of Cappen Varra

by

Poul Anderson

THE WIND CAME from the north with sleet on its back. Raw shuddering gusts whipped the sea till the ship lurched and men felt driven spindrift stinging their faces. Beyond the rail there was winter night, a moving blackness where the waves rushed and clamored; straining into the great dark, men sensed only the bitter salt of sea-scud, the nettle of sleet and the lash of wind.

Cappen lost his footing as the ship heaved beneath him, his hands were yanked from the icy rail and he went stumbling to the deck. The bilge water was new coldness on his drenched clothes. He struggled back to his feet, leaning on a rower's bench and wishing miserably that his quaking stomach had more to lose. But he had already chucked his share of stockfish and hardtack, to the laughter of Svearek's men, when the gale started.

Numb fingers groped anxiously for the harp on his back. It still seemed intact in its leather case. He didn't care about the sodden wadmal breeks and tunic that hung around his skin. The sooner they rotted off him, the better. The thought of the silks and linens of Croy was a sigh in him.

Why had he come to Norren?

A gigantic form, vague in the whistling dark, loomed

beside him and gave him a steadying hand. He could barely hear the blond giant's bull tones: "Ha, easy there, lad. Methinks the sea horse road is overly rough for yer feet."

"Ulp," said Cappen. His slim body huddled on the bench, too miserable to care. The sleet pattered against his shoulders and the spray congealed in his red hair.

Torbek of Norren squinted into the night. It made his leathery face a mesh of wrinkles. "A bitter feast of Yolner we hold," he said. "'Twas a madness of the king's, that he would guest with his brother across the water. Now the other ships are blown from us and the fire is drenched out and we lie alone in the Wolf's Throat."

Wind piped shrill in the rigging. Cappen could just see the longboat's single mast reeling against the sky. The ice on the shrouds made it a pale pyramid. Ice everywhere, thick on the rails and benches, sheathing the dragon head and the carved stern-post, the ship rolling and staggering under the great march of waves, men bailing and bailing in the half-frozen bilge to keep her afloat, and too much wind for sail or oars. Yes—a cold feast!

"But then, Svearek has been strange since the troll took his daughter, three years ago," went on Torbek. He shivered in a way the winter had not caused. "Never does he smile, and his once open hand grasps tight about the silver and his men have poor reward and no thanks. Yes, strange—" His small frost-blue eyes shifted to Cappen Varra; and the unspoken thought ran on beneath them: Strange, even that he likes you, the wandering bard from the south. Strange, that he will have you in his hall when you cannot sing as his men would like.

Cappen did not care to defend himself. He had drifted up toward the northern barbarians with the idea that they would well reward a minstrel who could offer them something more than their own crude chants. It had been a mistake; they didn't care for roundels or sestinas, they yawned at the thought of roses white and red under the moon of Caronne, a moon less fair than my lady's eyes. Nor did a man of Croy have the size and strength to compel their respect; Cappen's light blade flickered swiftly enough so that no one cared to fight him, but he lacked the power of sheer bulk. Svearek alone had enjoyed hearing him sing, but he was niggardly and his brawling thorp was an endless boredom to a man used to the courts of southern princes.

If he had but had the manhood to leave—But he had delayed, because of a hope that Svearek's coffers would open wider; and now he was dragged along over the Wolf's Throat to a midwinter feast which would have to be celebrated on the sea.

"Had we but fire—" Torbek thrust his hands inside his cloak, trying to warm them a little. The ship rolled till she was almost on her beam ends; Torbek braced himself with practiced feet, but Cappen went into the bilge again.

He sprawled there for a while, his bruised body refusing movement. A weary sailor with a bucket glared at him through dripping hair. His shout was dim under the hoot and skirl of wind: "If ye like it so well down here, then help us bail!"

"'Tis not yet my turn," groaned Cappen, and got slowly up.

The wave which had nearly swamped them had put out the ship's fire and drenched the wood beyond hope of lighting a new one. It was cold fish and sea-sodden hardtack till they saw land again—if they ever did.

As Cappen raised himself on the leeward side, he thought he saw something gleam, far out across the wrathful night. A wavering red spark—He brushed a stiffened hand across his eyes, wondering if the madness of wind and water had struck through into his own skull. A gust of sleet hid it again. But—

He fumbled his way aft between the benches. Huddled figures cursed him wearily as he stepped on them. The ship shook herself, rolled along the edge of a boiling black trough, and slid down into it; for an instant, the white teeth of combers grinned above her rail, and Cappen waited for an end to all things. Then she mounted them again, somehow, and wallowed toward another valley.

King Svearek had the steering oar and was trying to hold the longboat into the wind. He had stood there since sundown, huge and untiring, legs braced and the bucking wood cradled in his arms. More than human he seemed, there under the icicle loom of the stern-post, his gray hair and beard rigid with ice. Beneath the horned helmet, the strong moody face turned right and left, peering into the darkness. Cappen felt smaller than usual when he approached the steersman.

He leaned closer to the king, shouting against the blast of winter: "My lord, did I not see firelight?"

"Aye. I spied it an hour ago," grunted the king. "Been trying to steer us a little closer to it."

Cappen nodded, too sick and weary to feel reproved. "What is it?"

"Some island—there are many in this stretch of water—now shut up!"

Cappen crouched under the rail and waited.

The lonely red gleam seemed nearer when he looked again. Svearek's tones were lifting in a roar that hammered through the gale from end to end of the ship: "Hither! Come hither to me, all men not working!"

Slowly, they groped to him, great shadowy forms in wool and leather, bulking over Cappen like storm-gods. Svearek nodded toward the flickering glow. "One of the islands, somebody must be living there. I cannot bring the ship closer for fear of surf, but one of ye should be able to take the boat thither and fetch us fire and dry wood. Who will go?"

They peered overside, and the uneasy movement that ran among them came from more than the roll and pitch of the deck underfoot.

Beorna the Bold spoke at last, it was hardly to be heard in the noisy dark: "I never knew of men living hereabouts. It must be a lair of trolls."

"Aye, so . . . aye, they'd but eat the man we sent . . . out oars, let's away from here though it cost our lives . . ." The frightened mumble was low under the jeering wind.

Svearek's face drew into a snarl. "Are ye men or puling babes? Hack yer way through them, if they be trolls, but bring me fire!"

"Even a she-troll is stronger than fifty men, my king," cried Torbek. "Well ye know that, when the monster woman broke through our guards three years ago and bore off Hildigund."

"Enough!" It was a scream in Svearek's throat. "I'll have yer craven heads for this, all of ye, if ye gang not to the isle!"

They looked at each other, the big men of Norren, and

their shoulders hunched bearlike. It was Beorna who spoke it for them: "No, that ye will not. We are free housecarls, who will fight for a leader—but not for a madman."

Cappen drew himself against the rail, trying to make himself small.

"All gods turn their faces from ye!" It was more than weariness and despair which glared in Svearek's eyes, there was something of death in them. "I'll go myself, then!"

"No, my king. That we will not find ourselves in."

"I am the king."

"And we are yer housecarls, sworn to defend ye—even from yourself. Ye shall not go."

The ship rolled again, so violently that they were all thrown to starboard. Cappen landed on Torbek, who reached up to shove him aside and then closed one huge fist on his tunic.

"Here's our man!"

"Hi!" yelled Cappen.

Torbek hauled him roughly back to his feet. "Ye cannot row or bail yer fair share," he growled, "nor do ye know the rigging or any skill of a sailor—'tis time ye made yerself useful!"

"Aye, aye—let little Cappen go—mayhap he can sing the trolls to sleep—" The laughter was hard and barking, edged with fear, and they all hemmed him in.

"My lord!" bleated the minstrel. "I am your guest—"

Svearek laughed unpleasantly, half crazily. "Sing them a song," he howled. "Make a fine roun—whatever ye call it—to the troll-wife's beauty. And bring us some fire, little man, bring us a flame less hot than the love in yer breast for yer lady!"

Teeth grinned through matted beards. Someone hauled on the rope from which the ship's small boat trailed, dragging it close. "Go, ye scut!" A horny hand sent Cappen stumbling to the rail.

He cried out once again. An ax lifted above his head. Someone handed him his own slim sword, and for a wild moment he thought of fighting. Useless—too many of them. He buckled on the sword and spat at the men. The wind tossed it back in his face, and they raved with laughter.

Over the side! The boat rose to meet him, he landed in a heap on drenched planks and looked up into the shadowy faces of the northmen. There was a sob in his throat as he found the seat and took out the oars.

An awkward pull sent him spinning from the ship, and then the night had swallowed it and he was alone. Numbly, he bent to the task. Unless he wanted to drown, there was no place to go but the island.

He was too weary and ill to be much afraid, and such fear as he had was all of the sea. It could rise over him, gulp him down, the gray horses would gallop over him and the long weeds would wrap him when he rolled dead against some skerry. The soft vales of Caronne and the roses in Croy's gardens seemed like a dream. There was only the roar and boom of the northern sea, hiss of sleet and spindrift, crazed scream of wind, he was alone as man had ever been and he would go down to the sharks alone.

The boat wallowed, but rode the waves better than the longship. He grew dully aware that the storm was pushing him toward the island. It was becoming visible, a deeper blackness harsh against the night.

He could not row much in the restless water; he shipped the oars and waited for the gale to capsize him and fill his mouth with the sea. And when it gurgled in his throat, what would his last thought be? Should he dwell on the lovely image of Ydris in Seilles, she of the long bright hair and the singing voice? But then there had been the tomboy laughter of dark Falkny, he could not neglect her. And there were memories of Elvanna in her castle by the lake, and Sirann of the Hundred Rings, and beauteous Vardry, and hawk-proud Lona, and—No; he could not do justice to any of them in the little time that remained. What a pity it was!

No, wait, that unforgettable night in Nienne, the beauty which had whispered in his ear and drawn him close, the hair which had fallen like a silken tent about his cheeks . . . ah, that had been the summit of his life, he would go down into darkness with her name on his lips . . . But hell! What *had* her name been, now?

Cappen Varra, minstrel of Croy, clung to the bench and sighed.

The great hollow voice of surf lifted about him, waves

sheeted across the gunwale and the boat danced in madness. Cappen groaned, huddling into the circle of his own arms and shaking with cold. Swiftly, now, the end of all sunlight and laughter, the dark and lonely road which all men must tread. *O Ilwarra of Syr, Aedra in Tholis, could I but kiss you once more—*

Stones grated under the keel. It was a shock like a sword going through him. Cappen looked unbelievingly up. The boat had drifted to land—he was alive!

It kindled the sun in his breast. Weariness fell from him, and he leaped overside, not feeling the chill of the shallows. With a grunt, he heaved the boat up on the narrow strand and knotted the painter to a fang-like jut of reef.

Then he looked about him. The island was small, utterly bare, a savage loom of rock rising out of the sea that growled at its feet and streamed off its shoulders. He had come into a little cliff-walled bay, somewhat sheltered from the wind. He was here!

For a moment he stood, running through all he had learned about trolls which infested these northlands. Hideous and soulless dwellers underground, they knew not old age; a sword could hew them asunder, but before it reached their deep-seated life, their unhuman strength had plucked a man apart. Then they ate him—

Small wonder the northmen feared them. Cappen threw back his head and laughed. He had once done a service for a mighty wizard in the south, and his reward hung about his neck, a small silver amulet. The wizard had told him that no supernatural being could harm anyone who carried a piece of silver.

The Northmen said that a troll was powerless against a man who was not afraid; but, of course, only to see one was to feel the heart turn to ice. They did not know the value of silver, it seemed—odd that they shouldn't, but they did not. Because Cappen Varra did, he had no reason to be afraid; therefore he was doubly safe, and it was but a matter of talking the troll into giving him some fire. If indeed there was a troll here, and not some harmless fisherman.

He whistled gaily, wrung part of the water from his cloak and ruddy hair, and started along the beach. In the sleety gloom, he could just see a hewn-out path winding up one of the cliffs and he set his feet on it.

At the top of the path, the wind ripped his whistling from his lips. He hunched his back against it and walked faster, swearing as he stumbled on hidden rocks. The ice-sheathed ground was slippery underfoot, and the cold bit like a knife.

Rounding a crag, he saw redness glow in the face of a steep bluff. A cave mouth, a fire within—he hastened his steps, hungering for warmth, until he stood in the entrance.

"Who comes?"

It was a hoarse bass cry that rang and boomed between walls of rock; ice and horror were in it, and for a moment Cappen's heart stumbled. Then he remembered the amulet and strode boldly inside.

"Good evening, mother," he said cheerily.

The cave widened out into a stony hugeness that gaped with tunnels leading further underground. The rough, soot-blackened walls were hung with plundered silks and cloth-of-gold, gone ragged through age and damp; the floor was strewn with stinking rushes, and gnawed bones were heaped in disorder. Cappen saw the skulls of men among them. In the center of the room, a great fire leaped and blazed, throwing billows of heat against him; some of its smoke went up a hole in the roof, the rest stung his eyes to watering and he sneezed.

The troll-wife crouched on the floor, snarling at him. She was quite the most hideous thing Cappen had ever seen: nearly as tall as he, she was twice as broad and thick, and the knotted arms hung down past bowed knees till their clawed fingers brushed the ground. Her head was beast-like, almost split in half by the tusked mouth, the eyes wells of darkness, the nose an ell long; her hairless skin was green and cold, moving on her bones. A tattered shift covered some of her monstrousness, but she was still a nightmare.

"Ho-ho, ho-ho!" Her laughter roared out, hungry and hollow as the surf around the island. Slowly, she shuffled closer. "So my dinner comes walking in to greet me, ho, ho, ho! Welcome, sweet flesh, welcome, good marrow-filled bones, come in and be warmed."

"Why, thank you, good mother." Cappen shucked his cloak and grinned at her through the smoke. He felt his clothes steaming already. "I love you too."

Over her shoulder, he suddenly saw the girl. She was huddled in a corner, wrapped in fear, but the eyes that watched him were as blue as the skies over Caronne. The ragged dress did not hide the gentle curves of her body, nor did the tear-streaked grime spoil the lilt of her face. "Why, 'tis springtime in here," cried Cappen, "and Primavera herself is strewing flowers of love."

"What are you talking about, crazy man?" rumbled the troll-wife. She turned to the girl. "Heap the fire, Hildigund, and set up the roasting spit. Tonight I feast!"

"Truly I see heaven in female form before me," said Cappen.

The troll scratched her misshapen head.

"You must surely be from far away, moonstruck man," she said.

"Aye, from golden Croy am I wandered, drawn over dolorous seas and empty wild lands by the fame of loveliness waiting here; and now that I have seen you, my life is full." Cappen was looking at the girl as he spoke, but he hoped the troll might take it as aimed her way.

"It will be fuller," grinned the monster. "Stuffed with hot coals while yet you live." She glanced back at the girl. "What, are you not working yet, you lazy tub of lard? Set up the spit, I said!"

The girl shuddered back against a heap of wood. "No," she whispered. "I cannot—not . . . not for a man."

"Can and will, my girl," said the troll, picking up a bone to throw at her. The girl shrieked a little.

"No, no, sweet mother. I would not be so ungallant as to have beauty toil for me." Cappen plucked at the troll's filthy dress. "It is not meet—in two senses. I only come to beg a little fire; yet will I bear away a greater fire within my heart."

"Fire in your guts, you mean! No man ever left me save as picked bones."

Cappen thought he heard a worried note in the animal growl. "Shall we have music for the feast?" he asked mildly. He unslung the case of his harp and took it out.

The troll-wife waved her fists in the air and danced with

rage. "Are you mad? I tell you, you are going to be eaten!"

The minstrel plucked a string on his harp. "This wet air has played the devil with her tone," he murmured sadly.

The troll-wife roared wordlessly and lunged at him. Hildigund covered her eyes. Cappen tuned his harp. A foot from his throat, the claws stopped.

"Pray do not excite yourself, mother," said the bard. "I carry silver, you know."

"What is that to me? If you think you have a charm which will turn me, know that there is none. I've no fear of your metal!"

Cappen threw back his head and sang:

"A lovely lady full oft lies.
The light that lies within her eyes
and lies and lies, is no surprise.
All her unkindness can devise
to trouble hearts that seek the prize
which is herself, are angel lies—"

"Aaaarrgh!" It was like thunder drowning him out. The troll-wife turned and went on all fours and poked up the fire with her nose.

Cappen stepped softly around her and touched the girl. She looked up with a little whimper.

"You are Svearek's only daughter, are you not?" he whispered.

"Aye—" She bowed her head, a strengthless despair weighing it down. "The troll stole me away three winters agone. It has tickled her to have a princess for slave—but soon I shall roast on her spit, even as ye, brave man—"

"Ridiculous. So fair a lady is meant for another kind of, um, never mind! Has she treated you very ill?"

"She beats me now and again—and I have been so lonely, naught here at all save the troll-wife and I—" The small work-roughened hands clutched desperately at his waist, and she buried her face against his breast.

"Can ye save us?" she gasped. "I fear 'tis for naught ye ventured yer life, bravest of men. I fear we'll soon both sputter on the coals."

Cappen said nothing. If she wanted to think he had

come especially to rescue her, he would not be so ungallant to tell her otherwise.

The troll-wife's mouth gashed in a grin as she walked through the fire to him. "There is a price," she said. "If you cannot tell me three things about myself which are true beyond disproving, not courage nor amulet nor the gods themselves may avail to keep that head on your shoulders."

Cappen clapped a hand to his sword. "Why, gladly," he said; this was a rule of magic he had learned long ago, that three truths were the needful armor to make any guardian charm work. "Imprimis, yours is the ugliest nose I ever saw poking up a fire. Secundus, I was never in a house I cared less to guest at. Tertius, even among trolls you are little liked, being one of the worst."

Hildigund moaned with terror as the monster swelled in rage. But there was no movement. Only the leaping flames and the eddying smoke stirred.

Cappen's voice rang out, coldly: "Now the king lies on the sea, frozen and wet, and I am come to fetch a brand for his fire. And I had best also see his daughter home."

The troll shook her head, suddenly chuckling. "No. The brand you may have, just to get you out of this cave, foulness; but the woman is in my thrall until a man sleeps with her—here—for a night. And if he does, I may have him to break my fast in the morning!"

Cappen yawned mightily. "Thank you, mother. Your offer of a bed is most welcome to these tired bones, and I accept gratefully."

"You will die tomorrow!" she raved. The ground shook under the huge weight of her as she stamped. "Because of the three truths, I must let you go tonight; but tomorrow I may do what I will!"

"Forget not my little friend, mother," said Cappen, and touched the cord of the amulet.

"I tell you, silver has no use against me—"

Cappen sprawled on the floor and rippled fingers across his harp. *"A lovely lady full oft lies—"*

The troll-wife turned from him in a rage. Hildigund ladled up some broth, saying nothing, and Cappen ate it with pleasure, though it could have used more seasoning.

After that he indited a sonnet to the princess, who

regarded him wide-eyed. The troll came back from a tunnel after he finished, and said curtly: "This way." Cappen took the girl's hand and followed her into a pitchy, reeking dark.

She plucked an arras aside to show a room which surprised him by being hung with tapestries, lit with candles, and furnished with a fine broad featherbed. "Sleep here tonight, if you dare," she growled. "And tomorrow I shall eat you—and you, worthless lazy she-trash, will have the hide flayed off your back!" She barked a laugh and left them.

Hildigund fell weeping on the mattress. Cappen let her cry herself out while he undressed and got between the blankets. Drawing his sword, he laid it carefully in the middle of the bed.

The girl looked at him through jumbled fair locks. "How can ye dare?" she whispered. "One breath of fear, one moment's doubt, and the troll is free to rend ye."

"Exactly." Cappen yawned. "Doubtless she hopes that will come to me lying wakeful in the night. Wherefore 'tis but a question of going gently to sleep. O Svearek, Torbek, and Beorna, could you but see how I am resting now!"

"But . . . the three truths, ye gave her . . . how knew ye . . . ?"

"Oh, those. Well, see you, sweet lady, Primus and Secundus were my own thoughts, and who is to disprove them? Tertius was also clear, since you said there had been no company here in three years—yet are there many trolls in these lands, ergo even they cannot stomach our gentle hostess." Cappen watched her through heavy-lidded eyes.

She flushed deeply, blew out the candles, and he heard her slip off her garment and get in with him. There was a long silence.

Then: "Are ye not—"

"Yes, fair one?" he muttered through his drowsiness.

"Are ye not . . . well, I am here and ye are here and—"

"Fear not," he said. "I laid my sword between us. Sleep in peace."

"I . . . would be glad—ye have come to deliver—"

"No, fair lady. No man of gentle breeding could so

abuse his power. Goodnight." He leaned over, brushing his lips gently across hers, and lay down again.

"Ye are . . . I never thought man could be so noble," she whispered.

Cappen mumbled something. As his soul spun into sleep, he chuckled. Those unresting days and nights on the sea had not left him fit for that kind of exercise. But, of course, if she wanted to think he was being magnanimous, it could be useful later—

He woke with a start and looked into the sputtering glare of a torch. Its light wove across the crags and gullies of the troll-wife's face and shimmered wetly off the great tusks in her mouth.

"Good morning, mother," said Cappen politely.

Hildigund thrust back a scream.

"Come and be eaten," said the troll-wife.

"No, thank you," said Cappen, regretfully but firmly. "'Twould be ill for my health. No, I will but trouble you for a firebrand and then the princess and I will be off."

"If you think that stupid bit of silver will protect you, think again," she snapped. "Your three sentences were all that saved you last night. Now I hunger."

"Silver," said Cappen didactically, "is a certain shield against all black magics. So the wizard told me, and he was such a nice white-bearded old man I am sure even his attendant devils never lied. Now please depart, mother, for modesty forbids me to dress before your eyes."

The hideous face thrust close to his. He smiled dreamily and tweaked her nose—hard.

She howled and flung the torch at him. Cappen caught it and stuffed it into her mouth. She choked and ran from the room.

"A new sport—trollbaiting," said the bard gaily into the sudden darkness. "Come, shall we not venture out?"

The girl trembled too much to move. He comforted her, absentmindedly, and dressed in the dark, swearing at the clumsy leggings. When he left, Hildigund put on her clothes and hurried after him.

The troll-wife squatted by the fire and glared at them as they went by. Cappen hefted his sword and looked at her. "I do not love you," he said mildly, and hewed out.

She backed away, shrieking as he slashed at her. In the end, she crouched at the mouth of the tunnel, raging futilely. Cappen pricked her with his blade.

"It is not worth my time to follow you down underground," he said, "but if ever you trouble men again, I will hear of it and come and feed you to my dogs. A piece at a time—a very small piece—do you understand?"

She snarled at him.

"An *extremely* small piece," said Cappen amiably. "Have you heard me?"

Something broke in her. "Yes," she whimpered. He let her go, and she scuttled from him like a rat.

He remembered the firewood and took an armful; on the way, he thoughtfully picked up a few jeweled rings which he didn't think she would be needing and stuck them in his pouch. Then he led the girl outside.

The wind had laid itself, a clear frosty morning glittered on the sea and the longship was a distant silver against white-capped blueness. The minstrel groaned. "What a distance to row! Oh, well—"

They were at sea before Hildigund spoke. Awe was in the eyes that watched him. "No man could be so brave," she murmured. "Are ye a god?"

"Not quite," said Cappen. "No, most beautiful one, modesty grips my tongue. 'Twas but that I had the silver and was therefore proof against her sorcery."

"But the silver was no help!" she cried.

Cappen's oar caught a crab. "What?" he yelled.

"No—no—why, she told ye so her own self—"

"I thought she lied. I *know* the silver guards against—"

"But she used no magic! Trolls have but their own strength!"

Cappen sagged in his seat. For a moment he thought he was going to faint. Then only his lack of fear had armored him; and if he had known the truth, that would not have lasted a minute.

He laughed shakily. Another score for his doubts about the overall value of truth!

The longship's oars bit water and approached him. Indignant voices asking why he had been so long on his errand faded when his passenger was seen. And Svearek the king wept as he took his daughter back into his arms.

The hard brown face was still blurred with tears when he looked at the minstrel, but the return of his old self was there too. "What ye have done, Cappen Varra of Croy, is what no other man in the world could have done."

"Aye—aye—" The rough northern voices held adoration as the warriors crowded around the slim red-haired figure.

"Ye shall have her whom ye saved to wife," said Svearek, "and when I die ye shall rule all Norren."

Cappen swayed and clutched the rail.

Three nights later he slipped away from their shore camp and turned his face southward.

The Troll

by

T. H. White

"MY FATHER," SAID Mr. Marx, "used to say that an experience like the one I am about to relate was apt to shake one's interest in mundane matters. Naturally he did not expect to be believed, and he did not mind whether he was or not. He did not himself believe in the supernatural, but the thing happened, and he proposed to tell it as simply as possible. It was stupid of him to say that it shook his faith in mundane matters, for it was just as mundane as anything else. Indeed, the really frightening part about it was the horribly tangible atmosphere in which it took place. None of the outlines wavered in the least. The creature would have been less remarkable if it had been less natural. It seemed to overcome the usual laws without being immune to them.

"My father was a keen fisherman, and used to go to all sorts of places for his fish. On one occasion he made Abisko his Lapland base, a comfortable railway hotel, one hundred and fifty miles within the Arctic Circle. He traveled the prodigious length of Sweden (I believe it is as far from the south of Sweden to the north, as it is from the south of Sweden to the south of Italy) in the electric railway, and arrived tired out. He went to bed early, sleeping almost immediately, although it was bright daylight outside, as it is in those parts throughout the night at that time of the year. Not the least shaking part of his experience was that it should all have happened under the sun.

"He went to bed early, and slept, and dreamed. I may as well make it clear at once, as clear as the outlines of that creature in the northern sun, that his story did not turn out to be a dream in the last paragraph. The division between sleeping and waking was abrupt, although the feeling of both was the same. They were both in the same sphere of horrible absurdity, though in the former he was asleep and in the latter almost terribly awake. He tried to be asleep several times.

"My father always used to tell one of his dreams, because it somehow seemed of a piece with what was to follow. He believed that it was a consequence of the thing's presence in the next room. My father dreamed of blood.

"It was the vividness of the dreams that was impressive, their minute detail and horrible reality. The blood came through the keyhole of a locked door which communicated with the next room. I suppose the two rooms had originally been designed en suite. It ran down the door panel with a viscous ripple, like the artificial one created in the conduit of Trumpington Street. But it was heavy, and smelled. The slow welling of it sopped the carpet and reached the bed. It was warm and sticky. My father woke up with the impression that it was all over his hands. He was rubbing his first two fingers together, trying to rid them of the greasy adhesion where the fingers joined.

"My father knew what he had got to do. Let me make it clear that he was now perfectly wide awake, but he knew what he had got to do. He got out of bed, under this irresistible knowledge, and looked through the keyhole into the next room.

"I suppose the best way to tell the story is simply to narrate it, without an effort to carry belief. The thing did not require belief. It was not a feeling of horror in one's bones, or a misty outline, or anything that needed to be given actuality by an act of faith. It was as solid as a wardrobe. You don't have to believe in wardrobes. They are there, with corners.

"What my father saw through the keyhole in the next room was a Troll. It was eminently solid, about eight feet high, and dressed in brightly ornamented skins. It had a blue face, with yellow eyes, and on its head there was a woolly sort of nightcap with a red bobble on top. The features were Mongolian. Its body was long and sturdy, like the trunk of a tree. Its legs were short and thick, like the elephant's feet that used to be cut off for umbrella stands, and its arms were wasted: little rudimentary members like the forelegs of a kangaroo. Its head and neck were very thick and massive. On the whole, it looked like a grotesque doll.

"That was the horror of it. Imagine a perfectly normal golliwog (but without the association of a Christie minstrel) standing in the corner of a room, eight feet high. The creature was as ordinary as that, as tangible, as stuffed, and as ungainly at the joints: but it could move itself about.

"The Troll was eating a lady. Poor girl, she was tightly clutched to its breast by those rudimentary arms, with her head on a level with its mouth. She was dressed in a nightdress which had crumpled up under her armpits, so that she was a pitiful naked offering, like a classical picture of Andromeda. Mercifully, she appeared to have fainted.

"Just as my father applied his eye to the keyhole, the Troll opened its mouth and bit off her head. Then, holding the neck between the bright blue lips, he sucked the bare meat dry. She shriveled, like a squeezed orange, and her heels kicked. The creature had a look of thoughtful ecstasy. When the girl seemed to have lost succulence as an orange she was lifted into the air. She vanished in two bites. The Troll remained leaning against the wall, munching patiently and casting its eyes about it with a vague benevolence. Then it leaned forward from the low hips, like a jackknife folding in half, and opened its mouth to lick the blood up from the carpet. The mouth was incandescent inside, like a gas fire, and the blood evaporated before its tongue, like dust before a vacuum cleaner. It straightened itself, the arms dangling before it in patient uselessness, and fixed its eyes upon the keyhole.

"My father crawled back to bed, like a hunted fox after fifteen miles. At first it was because he was afraid that the creature had seen him through the hole, but afterward it was because of his reason. A man can attribute many nighttime appearances to the imagination, and can ultimately persuade himself that creatures of the dark did not exist. But this was an appearance in a sunlit room, with all the solidity of a wardrobe and unfortunately almost none of its possibility. He spent the first ten minutes making sure that he was awake, and the rest of the night trying to hope that he was asleep. It was either that, or else he was mad.

"It is not pleasant to doubt one's sanity. There are no satisfactory tests. One can pinch oneself to see if one is asleep, but there are no means of determining the other problem. He spent some time opening and shutting his eyes, but the room seemed normal and remained unaltered. He also soused his head in a basin of cold water, without result. Then he lay on his back, for hours, watching the mosquitoes on the ceiling.

"He was tired when he was called. A bright Scandinavian maid admitted the full sunlight for him and told him that it was a fine day. He spoke to her several times, and watched her carefully, but she seemed to have no doubts about his behavior. Evidently, then, he was not badly mad: and by now he had been thinking about the matter for so many hours that it had begun to get obscure. The outlines were blurring again, and he determined that the whole thing must have been a dream or a temporary delusion, something temporary, anyway, and finished with; so that there was no good in thinking about it longer. He got up, dressed himself fairly cheerfully, and went down to breakfast.

"These hotels used to be run extraordinarily well. There was a hostess always handy in a little office off the hall, who was delighted to answer any questions, spoke every conceivable language, and generally made it her business to make the guests feel at home. The particular hostess at Abisko was a lovely creature into the bargain. My father used to speak to her a good deal. He had an idea that when you had a bath in Sweden one of the maids was sent to wash you. As a matter of fact this sometimes used to be the case, but it was always an old maid and highly trusted. You had to keep yourself underwater and this was supposed to confer a cloak of invisibility. If you popped your knee out she was shocked. My father had a dim sort of hope that the hostess would be sent to bathe him one day: and I dare say he would have shocked her a good deal.

However, this is beside the point. As he passed through the hall something prompted him to ask about the room next to his. Had anybody, he inquired, taken number 23?

"'But, yes,' said the lady manager with a bright smile, twenty-three is taken by a doctor professor from Uppsala and his wife, such a charming couple!"

"My father wondered what the charming couple had been doing, whilst the Troll was eating the lady in the nightdress. However, he decided to think no more about it. He pulled himself together, and went in to breakfast. The professor was sitting in an opposite corner (the manageress had kindly pointed him out), looking mild and shortsighted, by himself. My father thought he would go out for a long climb on the mountains, since exercise was evidently what his constitution needed.

"He had a lovely day. Lake Torne blazed a deep blue below him, for all its thirty miles, and the melting snow made a lacework of filigree around the tops of the surrounding mountain basin. He got away from the stunted birch trees, and the mossy bogs with the reindeer in them, and the mosquitoes, too. He forded something that might have been a temporary tributary of the Abisko-jokk, having to take off his trousers to do so and tucking his shirt up around his neck. He wanted to shout, bracing himself against the glorious tug of the snow water, with his legs crossing each other involuntarily as they passed, and the boulders turning under his feet. His body made a bow wave in the water, which climbed and feathered on his stomach, on the upstream side. When he was under the opposite bank a stone turned in earnest, and he went in. He came up, shouting with laughter, and made out loud a remark which has since become a classic in my family. 'Thank God,' he said, 'I rolled up my sleeves.' He wrung out everything as best he could, and dressed again in the wet clothes, and set off up the shoulder of Niakatjavelk. He was dry and warm again in half a mile. Less than a thousand feet took him over the snow line, and there, crawling on hands and knees, he came face to face with what seemed to be the summit of ambition. He met an ermine. They were both on all fours, so that there was a sort of equality about the encounter, especially as the ermine was higher up than he was. They looked at each other for a fifth of a second, without saying anything, and then the ermine vanished. He searched for it everywhere in vain, for the snow was only patchy. My father sat down on a dry rock, to eat his well-soaked luncheon of chocolate and rye bread.

"Life is such unutterable hell, solely because it is sometimes beautiful. If we could only be miserable all the time, if there could be no such things as love or beauty or faith or hope, if I could be absolutely certain that my love would never be returned: how much more simple life would be. One could plod through the Siberian salt-mines of existence without being bothered about happiness. Unfortunately the happiness is there. There is always the chance (about eight hundred and fifty to one) that another heart will come to mine. I can't help hoping, and keeping faith, and loving beauty. Quite frequently I am not so miserable as it would be wise to be. And there, for my poor father sitting on his boulder above the snow, was stark happiness beating at the gates.

"The boulder on which he was sitting had probably never been sat upon before. It was a hundred and fifty miles within the Arctic Circle, on a mountain five thousand feet high, looking down on a blue lake. The lake was so long that he could have sworn it sloped away at the ends, proving to the naked eye that the sweet earth was round. The railway line and the half-dozen houses of Abisko were hidden in the trees. The sun was warm on the boulder, blue on the snow, and his body tingled smooth from the spate water. His mouth watered for the chocolate, just behind the tip of his tongue.

"And yet, when he had eaten the chocolate—perhaps it was heavy on his stomach—there was the memory of the Troll. My father fell suddenly into a black mood, and began to think about the supernatural. Lapland was beautiful in the summer, with the sun sweeping around the horizon day and night, and the small tree leaves twinkling. It was not the sort of place for wicked things. But what about the winter? A picture of the Arctic night came before him, with the silence and the snow. Then the legendary wolves and bears snuffled at the far encampments, and the nameless winter spirits moved on their darkling courses. Lapland had always been associated with sorcery, even by Shakespeare. It was at the outskirts of the world that the Old Things accumulated, like driftwood around the edges of the sea. If one wanted to find a wise woman, one went to the rims of the Hebrides; on the coast of Brittany one sought the mass of St. Secaire. And what an outskirt Lapland was! It was an outskirt not only of Europe, but of civilization. It had no boundaries. The Lapps went with the reindeer, and where the reindeer were, was Lapland. Curiously indefinite region, suitable to the indefinite things. The Lapps were not Christians. What a fund of power they must have had behind them, to resist the march of mind. All through the missionary centuries they had held to something: something had stood behind them, a power against Christ. My father realized with a shock that he was living in the age of the reindeer, a period contiguous to the mammoth and the fossil.

"Well, this was not what he had come out to do. He dismissed the nightmares with an effort, got up from his boulder, and began to scramble back to his hotel. It was impossible that a professor from Abisko could become a troll.

"As my father was going in to dinner that evening the manageress stopped him in the hall.

" 'We have had a day so sad,' she said. 'The poor Dr. Professor has disappeared his wife. She has been missing since last night. The Dr. Professor is inconsolable.'

"My father then knew for certain that he had lost his reason.

"He went blindly to dinner, without making any answer, and began to eat a thick sour-cream soup that was taken cold with pepper and sugar. The professor was still sitting in his corner, a sandy-headed man with thick spectacles and a desolate expression. He was looking at my father, and my father, with a soup spoon halfway to his mouth, looked at him. You know that eye-to-eye recognition, when two people look deeply into each other's pupils, and burrow to the soul? It usually comes before love. I mean the clear, deep, milk-eyed recognition expressed by the poet Donne. Their eyebeams twisted and did thread their eyes upon a double string. My father recognized that the professor was a troll, and the professor recognized my father's recognition. Both of them knew that the professor had eaten his wife.

"My father put down his soup spoon, and the professor began to grow. The top of his head lifted and expanded, like a great loaf rising in an oven; his face went red and purple, and finally blue, the whole ungainly upperworks began to sway and topple toward the ceiling. My father looked about him. The other diners were eating unconcernedly. Nobody else could see it, and he was definitely mad at last. When he looked at the Troll again, the creature bowed. The enormous superstructure inclined itself toward him from the hips, and grinned seductively.

"My father got up from his table experimentally, and advanced toward the Troll, arranging his feet on the carpet with excessive care. He did not find it easy to walk, or to approach the monster, but it was a question of his reason. If he was mad, he was mad; and it was essential that he should come to grips with the thing, in order to make certain.

"He stood before it like a small boy, and held out his hand, saying, 'Good evening.'

" 'Ho! Ho!' said the Troll, 'little mannikin. And what shall I have for my supper tonight?'

"Then it held out its wizened furry paw and took my father by the hand.

"My father went straight out of the dining-room, walking on air. He found the manageress in the passage and held out his hand to her.

" 'I am afraid I have burned my hand,' he said. 'Do you think you could tie it up?'

"The manageress said, 'But it is a very bad burn. There are blisters all over the back. Of course, I will bind it up at once.

"He explained that he had burned it on one of the spirit lamps at the sideboard. He could scarcely conceal his delight. One cannot burn oneself by being insane.

" 'I saw you talking to the Dr. Professor,' said the manageress, as she was putting on the bandage. 'He is a sympathetic gentleman, is he not?'

"The relief about his sanity soon gave place to other troubles. The Troll had eaten its wife and given him a blister, but it had also made an unpleasant remark about its supper that evening. It proposed to eat my father. Now very few people can have been in a position to decide what to do when a troll earmarks them for its next meal. To begin with, although it was a tangible troll in two ways, it had been invisible to the other diners. This put my father in a difficult position. He could not, for instance, ask for protection. He could scarcely go to the manageress and say, 'Professor Skal is an odd kind of werewolf, ate his wife last night, and proposes to eat me this evening.' He would have found himself in a loony-bin at once. Besides, he was too proud to do this, and still too confused. Whatever the proofs and blisters, he did not find it easy to believe in professors that turned into trolls. He had lived in the normal world all his life, and, at his age, it was difficult to start learning afresh. It would have been quite easy for a baby, who was still coordinating the world, to cope with the troll situation: for my father, not. He kept trying to fit it in somewhere, without disturbing the universe. He kept telling himself that it was nonsense: one did not get eaten by professors. It was like having a fever, and telling oneself that it was all right, really, only a delirium, only something that would pass.

"There was that feeling on the one side, the desperate assertion of all the truths that he had learned so far, the tussle to keep the world from drifting, the brave but intimidated refusal to give in or to make a fool of himself.

"On the other side there was stark terror. However much one struggled to be merely deluded, or hitched up momentarily in an odd packet of space-time, there was panic. There was the urge to go away as quickly as possible, to flee the dreadful Troll. Unfortunately the last train had left Abisko, and there was nowhere else to go.

"My father was not able to distinguish these trends of thought. For him they were at the time intricately muddled together. He was in a whirl. A proud man, and an agnostic, he stuck to his muddled guns alone. He was terribly afraid of the Troll, but he could not afford to admit its existence. All his mental processes remained hung up, whilst he talked on the terrace, in a state of suspended animation, with an American tourist who had come to Abisko to photograph the Midnight Sun.

"The American told my father that the Abisko railway was the northernmost electric railway in the world, that twelve trains passed through it every day traveling between Uppsala and Narvik, that the population of Abo was 12,000 in 1862, and that Gustavus Adolphus ascended the throne of Sweden in 1611. He also gave some facts about Greta Garbo.

"My father told the American that a dead baby was required for the mass of St. Secaire, that an elemental was a kind of mouth in space that sucked at you and tried to gulp you down, that homeopathic magic was practiced by the aborigines of Australia, and that a Lapland woman was careful at her confinement to have no knots or loops about her person, lest these should make the delivery difficult.

"The American, who had been looking at my father in a strange way for some time, took offense at this and walked away; so that there was nothing for it but to go to bed.

"My father walked upstairs on will-power alone. His faculties seemed to have shrunk and confused themselves. He had to help himself with the banister. He seemed to be navigating himself by wireless, from a spot about a foot above his forehead. The issues that were involved had ceased to have any meaning, but he went on doggedly up the stairs, moved forward by pride and contrariety. It was physical fear that alienated him from his body, the same fear that he had felt as a boy, walking down long corridors to be beaten. He walked firmly up the stairs.

"Oddly enough, he went to sleep at once. He had climbed all day and been awake all night and suffered emotional extremes. Like a condemned man, who was to be hanged in the morning, my father gave the whole business up and went to sleep.

"He was woken at midnight exactly. He heard the American on the terrace below his window, explaining excitedly that there had been a cloud on the last two nights at 11:58, thus making it impossible to photograph the Midnight Sun. He heard the camera click.

"There seemed to be a sudden storm of hail and wind. It roared at his windowsill, and the window curtains lifted themselves taut, pointing horizontally into the room. The shriek and rattle of the tempest framed the window in a crescendo of growing sound, an increasing blizzard directed toward himself. A blue paw came over the sill.

"My father turned over and hid his head in the pillow. He could feel the doomed head dawning at the window and the eyes fixing themselves upon the small of his back. He could feel the places physically, about four inches apart. They itched. Or else the rest of his body itched, except those places. He could feel the creature growing into the room, glowing like ice, and giving off a storm. His mosquito curtains rose in its afflatus, uncovering him, leaving him defenseless. He was in such an ecstasy of terror that he almost enjoyed it. He was like a bather plunging for the first tine into freezing water and unable to articulate. He was trying to yell, but all he could do was to throw a series of hooting noises from his paralyzed lungs. He became a part of the blizzard. The bedclothes were gone. He felt the Troll put out its hands.

"My father was an agnostic, but, like most idle men, he was not above having a bee in his bonnet. His favorite bee was the psychology of the Catholic Church. He was ready to talk for hours about psychoanalysis and the confession. His greatest discovery had been the rosary.

"The rosary, my father used to say, was intended solely as a factual occupation which calmed the lower centers of the mind. The automatic telling of the beads liberated the higher centers to meditate upon the mysteries. They were a sedative, like knitting or counting sheep. There was no better cure for insomnia than a rosary. For several years he had given up deep breathing or regular counting. When he was sleepless he lay on his back and told his beads, and there was a small rosary in the pocket of his pyjama coat.

"The Troll put out its hands, to take him around the waist. He became completely paralyzed, as if he had been winded. The Troll put its hands upon the beads.

"They met, the occult forces, in a clash above my father's heart. There was an explosion, he said, a quick creation of power. Positive and negative. A flash, a beam. Something like the splutter with which the antenna of a tram meets its overhead wires again, when it is being changed about.

"The Troll made a high squealing noise, like a crab being boiled, and began rapidly to dwindle in size. It dropped my father and turned about, and ran wailing, as if it had been terribly burned, for one window. Its color waned as its size decreased. It was one of those air-toys now, that expire with a piercing whistle. It scrambled over the windowsill, scarcely larger than a little child, and sagging visibly.

"My father leaped out of bed and followed it to the window. He saw it drop on the terrace like a toad, gather itself together, stumble off, staggering and whistling like a bat, down the valley of the Abiskojokk.

"My father fainted.

"In the morning the manageress said, 'There has been such a terrible tragedy. The poor Dr. Professor was found this morning in the lake. The worry about his wife had certainly unhinged his mind.'

"A subscription for the wreath was started by the American, to which my father subscribed five shillings; and the body was shipped off next morning, on one of the twelve trains that travel between Uppsala and Narvik every day."

THE GRIFFIN

The griffin (or gryphon) is one of the oldest of mythological beasts, and 3000-year-old golden statues of it have been found in the royal tombs of Crete. The griffin has the body of a lion and the head and wings of an eagle; it's often described as having talons large enough to be made into drinking cups. Originally characterized as so incomparably fierce that, according to Pliny, it was the creature chosen to guard the goldmines of the gods, the griffin has, curiously, become progressively milder in temperament with the ensuing centuries. By the Middle Ages, the griffin was commonly thought of as a symbol of Christ, and had become one of the most popular beasts in heraldry. Today, this once most-ferocious of all creatures appears frequently in children's books, where it is almost always a benign, and sometimes even a comic, figure.

In the story that follows, we learn that a griffin, as well as being a symbol, can also be a Sign and a Portent . . .

A. E. Sandeling has published fiction in *Story* magazine.

Return of the Griffins

by

A. E. Sandeling

GUNAR VRIES, EMISSARY to the United Nations Conference in New York from the European Democracy of S———, sat on the edge of his bed in his hotel room, removing his shoes and socks.

He had declined to be present that evening at a party given in his honor by a wealthy expatriate, telephoning his regrets. In his stead he had sent his aide, a handsome young man who, besides being secretary and translator, was also a composer of symphonies; instructing him to confine himself to seduction and to the piano. As for Gunar Vries, he had had his supper sent up and after the tray was removed had locked his door and set himself to his writing his daily personal letter to his president, in which he imparted observations too detailed to be made over the phone, and letters to the members of his family, his wife Alice and his son Theodore at the Technological University. When he had signed his name for the third time, the night was late.

He was removing his second sock when the bed moved. He grasped the blankets to keep from being thrown, believing that an earthquake had struck. But the bottles did not slide from the dresser, no particles of ceiling fell, the chandelier did not sway. Only the bed moved. Then through his lifted knees he saw emerging from beneath the bed the head of an eagle, but three times the size of an eagle's head, and stretching out for a grip of the rug, an eagle's claw. Then followed a lion's body. So the lion had an eagle's head. Or the eagle had a lion's body.

When the creature emerged completely, Gunar saw that it had also two wings, great eagle wings, that now it stretched one at a time across the floor. The wing roots crackled, and the feathers swept across the rug with a swishing, rushing sound. The creature slouched to the center of the room, its forelegs lifting stiffly, like a bird's leg, but in coordination with its hindlegs, that moved in the indolently potent manner of a lion.

Still heavy with sleep, the monster fell over on its side and, gently lifting its wing, turned its head under and with closed beak nuzzled along the feathery pocket, in this way nudging itself to wakefulness and woe again. Then, lifting its head, swinging it around and up, the creature looked straight at Gunar Vries. The eagle part took prominence —the curved beak, hard as stone, the thick encasing of golden feathers over its head, touched with red at the breast and extending down its forelegs to the very toes. Lion ears protruded through the feathers but were laid sleekly back. Its eyes burned ruby bright in the semidarkness.

"Change of climate," it explained, "makes me sleepy."

Before he had entered politics, more than twenty years ago, Gunar Vries had been professor of ancient Greek civilization at the University of Alia, capital of S———. His past enabled him to recognize the creature. "Griffin?" he asked. "Is that your name?" He had several cats on his farm and a trained falcon, and spoke always with tenderness and respect to them, as now he spoke to this great creature.

"Yes," replied the griffin, "and of the pure strain. If you're wondering about the Sphinx and her woman's face, one of us became enamored of a virgin of your species; though I can't see what he saw in her."

The griffin spoke its own language, like no other in the world, and yet a concoction of them all, with archaic Greek like a warrior's chariot rumbling and shining through. It was like everything unspoken that a word cannot be put to and that is comprehended more readily than that spoken among men of different languages.

"You've been away several years," said Gunar, covering his bare feet again with shoes and socks. "What did you do in that time?"

"Took ourselves to the mountains of India," replied the griffin. "Sat in the sun, on the thresholds of our caves, or caught the Arimaspi, one-eyed men who seek gold in the mountains, ate them in a shrugging fashion, already gorged with our prowess. I might ask the same question of you. What didn't you do? By Apollo! Procreated not individuals but nations. Took the lid off a water kettle, and what steams out but ships and cities. Times have changed."

The creature's breath began to fill the room, an overlay warm breath, smelling of raw meat, the rich, dark, stinging smell of blood clots and liver.

Gunar Vries had his trousers on and his gray hunting shirt that he wore evenings by himself, but he was cold. He turned the radiator higher. "I presume," he said, standing with his back to the heat, "that you wandered down alone?"

"Only one of the vanguard," replied the creature, preening its breast.

Now Gunar Vries was fully aware of the monster's significance. They were in their time sacred to Apollo, whose chariot they drew, and as Apollo was the prophetical deity whose oracle when consulted delivered itself in enigmas, the word griffin, too, meant enigma. And because he was fully aware of this, he preferred not to seem aware.

The emissary rubbed his hands together briskly to make them warm. "What's the occasion?" he inquired.

The feigned innocence did not escape the griffin. The creature picked it apart like picking the tortoise from the shell. A hissing contempt came from its nostrils and partially opened beak. For a moment there seemed to be a geyser in the room.

"Emissary to the UN," it replied, "a conference called to promote the flowering of humanity, and all the time the delegates hard put to it to breathe with the possibility of atomic dust in the air no more than five years from now. And now you want to know the occasion! Can you think of a time when the world faced a greater enigma?"

Gunar Vries was indeed concerned for humanity. It was something he traveled with in addition to his aide and his portfolio. Yet now it seemed to him that it was humanity in the abstract he had been carrying around—the formalities, the rules and regulations, the paperwork of a conference, humanity carefully composed and delivered with dignity. At the griffin's words, humanity suddenly became a third party in the room, and Gunar shivered with life, he shook convulsively as children do in excitement.

The monster slunk around the room, which became small as the cage in which a circus lion is confined. When it came to the desk it turned its head with ponderous grace and ran its eyes over the letters. Gunar Vries stirred indignantly and stepped forward, but on second thought was stricken with shame for his disrespect and stopped still. The griffin turned away, but in the turning managed to drop the nictitating membrane of its eyes, and the perusal became an act of idle curiosity. It paddled away languidly, disdainfully, dragging one wing, and the emissary, hearing a strange clicking noise along the floor, looked down and saw for the first time the full length of the creature's talons. At each step they were nicking small holes in the rug.

The creature sat down by the window, and the tasseled end of its tail lifted and fell. There was a feminine restlessness in the way its feathers quivered, and at the same time a great seething of male energy that propelled it forward even as it sat still. "Lift the window for me," it said, "and let me out on the ledge. Isn't there a park across the street?"

The emissary drew up the venetian blind and opened the window. The night entered, cold and fragrant with grass. The lamps in the park were almost pure white, as if encrusted with snow, and shone up through the delicate branches of the trees. People were sitting on the benches, talking and glancing up at the lighted windows of the hotel, where many dignitaries were in residence. Newsboys had built a fire in a refuse can, and taximen and journalists, tired of the plush and statuary of the lobby, were warming their hands around it. An ornate ledge ran along beneath the windows of the top floor, and the griffin leaped onto this.

"It won't be harmed," Gunar Vries told himself. "It's too fabulous. Even an oaf can see." A look of being protected lay in its eyes, a true and natural hauteur from an ancient epoch. He closed the window, and in his mind's eye he saw the creature continuing swiftly along the ledge, tail and wings spread out a bit, a dark and slithering form against the faintly lighted sky.

He went to his desk, took up his pen, and wrote in postscript on the letter to his president, *My dear friend: This evening I saw one of the first griffins to return. Their coming, though unpredictable, was nevertheless inevitable. They will remain, I gather, until we decide our fate, one way or another.* Hearing a strange cry in the night, a mingling of lion's roar and eagle's scream and more than both, he wrote further, *The cry of the griffin in the great cities of the world will become as familiar as the cry of the cock in the country, and even as the cock's cry wakens us from sleep and is portentous of the morning when we shall not be alive to hear it, so the cry of the griffin, on the roofs above traffic, is troublous, calling us, humanity, to a cognizance of our existence and heralding our possible end.*

When Gunar awoke in the morning it was, as every day, to no other thought but the Conference. Not until he passed the desk on his return from his bath and saw that the letters had been taken up by his aide for mailing was he reminded of the griffin. He stood still, startled and amused by such a dream. Well, the times evoked it. He had never before worked under such a strain and the enigma of the times had taken form and substance, emerged in his dream a thing in itself, had become a living creature.

But as he was dressing, the laughter within ceased, and he was overcome by melancholy. It came to him that the griffin might have been other than a dream. His few hours of sleep had been shallow and hot, as if he had slept in a thunderstorm; remembering his sleep, he was almost certain he had not dreamed. If the fabulous being had appeared, it had been an actual one. *But, of course, it had not appeared.* He could negate the event, he could prove it had been a dream by seeing again his letter to his president, the signature constituting the end without post-script. He walked slowly to the door of the adjoining apartment, already tired as if at the end of the day. How old was he now? Fifty-six? And how long did men live, usually?

"Norbert, young man," he called, rapping at the half-open door, "you've not posted the letters yet? The three letters?"

His aide appeared at the door, opening it wider. "They made the plane at seven-thirty."

"The letter to the president?"

"All three were sealed," said Norbert, "and envelopes addressed. Did you wish to make changes?"

"A whim," he replied. He looked sharply at his aide. Norbert wrote symphonies, the modern kind; his disharmonies were not what they seemed but merged into a complete harmony. Was he not the one to understand the griffin? "If I tell him," thought Gunar, "if I tell him, laughing a little, with gestures, with shudders, why, two believing will make it untrue."

But Norbert seemed more erect than usual this morning, his eyes bluer, his fair hair fairer. He liked parties, and the atmosphere for him was still charged with his virtuosity. The emissary decided that to explain the griffin to him would bring the creature down to the level of a piano recital and the sensual laughter of short-armed women.

"Come" he said, signaling for Norbert to accompany him.

In the cab Gunar sat in a corner, holding his hat and gloves on his crossed knees, listening to Norbert read foreign newspapers on the UN proceedings. The cab came to a halt as traffic changed, and he gazed into the street. In a basement tailor shop, the name on the window so worn that the dim light within turned the letters translucent and coppery, a tailor sat sewing at his machine while his wife sat by the window, drinking from a cup.

As Gunar took in the shop and its occupants, he saw his second griffin. She—it was a female, as he could tell by the lack of red feathers on her breast—was sliding along the fence before the row of basement shops, the eagle head lifted and stiff with impending alarm.

He grasped Norbert's hand, and the young man laid down his paper. "You see," he said, as if he had tried before to convince his aide, "a female griffin."

Norbert bent across him to look. The griffin slipped

down the stairs into the tailor's shop, pushing the door open with a claw, and for a moment Gunar saw, simultaneously, the eagle's head through the window and the lion's tail waving on the stairs. Persons passing paid no attention, or only slight, as to a cat or a sparrow. The couple did not look up, neither the man from his sewing nor the wife from her cup. Gunar Vries was appalled. They went about their pursuits as before, while this enigma, this beast of life or death, slid along their streets, jangled their business bells.

"But are they so common a sight already?" he asked.

"What are?" Norbert had taken up his reading again, but courteously allowed himself to be engaged in conversation.

"The griffins. A female went into the tailor shop and you made no to-do about it."

"I didn't see one," said Norbert. "I didn't know what to look for. I'm sorry. What is it like?"

Gunar Vries drew into his corner again. "It's not a thing that you look for," he replied.

The delegates to the General Assembly of the United Nations assembled at their quarters at Flushing Meadow. Gunar Vries sat in his place, his aide beside him, taking no part in the conversation before the fall of the gavel. The chairman entered, and following at his heels was a male griffin, larger, older than the one that had slept in Gunar's room. The creature was hoary and unkempt. Its eyes were yellow fire. It seated itself to the right of the chairman and with archaic grace surveyed the persons assembled.

That evening after supper the president replied by telephone. "Gunar, what's this talk of a griffin?" he asked. "It's a beast of classical antiquity, is it not? Well, to what use are you putting it?"

Ernest Gorgas was a fine man, and there was no one Gunar respected more. But how impotent the president's voice, how distant not only in space but in time! Gunar had the peculiar anticipatory feeling of hearing it fade away, as if mankind were running instantly into a post-historic age.

"Gunar," the president continued, his voice grinding into the receiver, louder, adamant, yet deeply kind and respectful, "the plea that you made to the Assembly today for international unity was the most moving I have ever heard. It was more forceful, even, than the American Willkie's *One World*. And the delivery of it—the eloquence, the impassioned tone! Maneuvering it the way you did was uncalled for and yet the most called-for thing in the world. If you are in your way sidestepping praise, being modest, bringing up this tale of a griffin coming to your room with a warning, it's no use. Gunar, my friend, there is no appointment that I have made in my term of office that has given me greater satisfaction."

"Ernest," replied Gunar, "the man who feels that he is not deserving of praise makes no move to sidestep it. He has a deaf place in his ear the size of a pea, and with this he hears praise. No, my friend, a male griffin *was* in my room last evening. Since then I have seen two more. One, slipping along the street, female and playing nervous; the other, a more bestial creature and at the same time looking as if imbued with an omniscient intelligence. It was sitting to the right of the chairman today and commented often; succinctly, too. But though its voice was louder than any there it went unheard. At the conclusion of my speech it came to me and told me that it heard Demosthenes, and that my eloquence exceeded his. It had been sent alone to take in the American Revolution and had heard Patrick Henry—it said that that gentleman's vigor did not touch mine. I did not take these comparisons as praise but was convinced that the precariousness of our times has never been equalled and that orators are made by the periods in which they live."

A long pause followed. When the president spoke again the subject was changed. He inquired about the discussions underway, Gunar's criticism and forecast of results.

Within another day the rumor had been circulated among the delegates that Gunar Vries, emissary from S———, was suffering from hallucinations. The suspicion was not relayed to newsmen or to anyone outside the circle of official delegates. It was a matter of respect not only for the member, as a distinguished person, and for his family, but for the delegates combined. If one was susceptible to weakness of this kind, it might be construed that all were. The curious thing was that the emissary seemed to be in full command of his intelligence while at the conference table. No criticism could be cast upon the deft, perspicacious way in which he handled his country's interests. Not only this, he was one of the most energetic in tackling the problems of all humanity.

Gunar Vries was called home on the second day after his speech. Newsmen, inquiring of him the reason for his departure, were told that he believed that his president was in possession of information that could not be discussed by phone or letter or through a messenger. In Gunnar's place, to be guided by Norbert through the formalities, there appeared the youngest member of the supreme court of S———, a man not much older than Norbert, but with his own history up to ninety years already in his eyes.

Carrying his portfolio, Gunar Vries returned to S———. He was met at the airport by the president, and together they were driven to the palace. They dined and secluded themselves in the president's study.

"Gunar," said Ernest, as they sat facing each other, "I could not ask for a better emissary. You have used the energy of twelve men. Now, wound-up as you are, you will think I am crazy, you will think I am reckless putting your personal health before the welfare of the nation. But I want you to take a rest for awhile. Let someone else, not your caliber but competent enough, assume your duties. You go to your farm, wear an old hat, go hunting, milk your cows, sow your wheat. We need as many hands as we can get working the land, and as much space yielding. Go home for awhile, Gunar."

Gunar Vries had never been so frightened in his life. It was like the fear, only worse, that he had experienced as a boy of seventeen, when he had left his father and come to the city to study, when for the first time he had lived alone. For several days he had been almost unable to breathe. He had thought he would never again see his father or make a friend, he had thought that he was trapped in that one room forever.

"Has any action of mine," Gunar now asked slowly, "met with your disapproval? Have you found that the ability I evidenced as your minister of foreign affairs, have you found that this ability falls short of my responsibility as a delegate to the United Nations?"

Ernest gripped his forehead, half-hid his painful eyes with his hand. "They say that you see griffins."

"But I told you so myself."

"Doesn't it seem peculiar to you?"

"You prefer to quote the ones to whom it seems peculiar? No, my friend, it is the most natural thing in the world."

"But you are the only one who sees them."

"Does that fact make the griffin nonexistent?" He felt a sharp derision coming on, took out his handkerchief and blew his nose. He tried to suppress the snort, but could not. It was his opinion of organized disorganization.

"If you take such a derogatory view of the Conference," the president said, "you won't want to return."

"On the contrary," Gunar replied, leaning forward to stuff his handkerchief away in his rear pocket, "they need me. They can't do without me. The time will come, believe me, when everyone there will see that creature sitting to the right of the chairman. And what a creature!"

"Gunar." The president hesitated. "Before you go home, perhaps it would be wise for you to consult a psychiatrist. They have not all gone to greener pastures in the United States. There might be still a capable one or two practicing in France or Switzerland."

"I would have no belief in him if he did not see griffins himself," replied Gunar, laughing a little. "But for your sake, to relieve you of anxiety and shame, I shall resign from the UN and from the Ministry. Name someone else to the post."

He wanted to rise from the chair, as a gesture fitting to climax, but found that he could not. His heart was palpitating. Well, he had seen his father again, made a friend, and been in so many rooms he could not remember them all. A boy's loneliness doesn't last, nor does that of a disgraced diplomat. You reach out for people, you have no more enemies. . . .

Gunar traveled home by train that night, and a female griffin was co-occupant of his compartment. When he entered, she was already asleep on the couch, eagle head tucked under her right wing, left wing and left hind leg hanging to the floor. He sat opposite her and watched her in the dimly lit, rocking compartment.

He rode to his farm on the wagon of a neighbor. "You want to surprise Mrs. Vries?" the neighbor asked. The man had found Gunar, portfolio in hand, standing by his wagon, waiting for him to come from the assessor's office.

"No," replied Gunar. "I just came home, that's all."

"You are tired from the Conference?" the neighbor inquired, believing that it was over. He noticed the diplomat's sagging shoulders and sadness, and he halted the horses. "What's the world coming to?" he asked gently, confidentially, as if Gunar Vries was the one to know.

And Gunar Vries laid his brow in his hand and wept, while the morning sun got in under his overcoat collar and warmed the nape of his neck.

For several days he went about his farm like a man taking a rest. He milked the cows, drove the tractor. There was a deep, still pool in his forest and he went to bathe in it, likening it to his loneliness. If he were drowning in it and cried out, no man would be near enough to help him. But when he left the pool and dressed again, his body was clean and deserving of respect because of its contact with loneliness, and approaching the farm he loved instantly from afar every small figure working.

Then one morning he saw on the roof of the east barn a young male griffin, and he called to it. The creature turned its large golden head slantwise.

"Come," coaxed Gunar, "a lamb? A pan of milk?" And when the creature eyed him without replying, he added, "A calf?"

The griffin dropped its beak and picked at something between its toes. "But I ate, just a couple of centuries ago. Caught four Arimaspi in a ravine."

Alice begged Gunar to wait until she summoned Theodore, but he said no, that he would probably meet the boy in the city.

"Ah!" he exclaimed, for she had given him an idea. "I intend to speak on the steps of the Technological University anyway. When the scientific students see my griffin, it will be a triumph, believe me."

She went along the road with him, holding his elbow against her side and crying, and he bent his head away, unable to bear her grimaces. The griffin was slinking along the other side of the fence, and in a fit of energy suddenly both flew and ran, beating its wings close to earth, for a good half-mile down the fence. Why couldn't she see a thing like that?

He halted and caressed her, pushing back her short, pale hair. "Do you know that I love you?" he asked. "Yes," she wept.

"The tour is a minor thing," he said. "I make it simply to return to you. If I don't go, how much longer and of what consequence will our love be?"

When he set out again, alone, the griffin was returning to meet him, loping.

So he came to Afia, capital of S———, with the griffin at his side. He was dressed as for a session of the UN. He wore his favorite suit, tailored in London on a fine Scottish tweed, a white shirt, a dark red silk tie, and he carried a black Homburg and gray suede gloves. He took rooms in a first-rate hotel.

Entering the park around which were grouped the government buildings, he mounted the flagpole base and pleaded with refugees, messengers passing to and fro, and clerks eating their lunches, to recognize his companion. In the evening he let himself be enveloped by the crowds pouring into the operas and symphonies and cinemas. Jostled and stepped upon, he began to recount his experiences, and some persons, with mail order tickets and in no hurry, tarried around him. At midnight, when the streets were being deserted, he returned to his hotel, and the griffin spent the night in the vicinity.

By the second day word had circulated that this man in the streets was actually Gunar Vries, come to tell of the existence of a fabulous beast or bird. The citizens jammed the streets, the fire escapes, the roofs for blocks around the House of Commerce and Gunar made his speech on the steps facing the park. Overjoyed as he was with the size of his audience, he spoke with such passion that the griffin, already unnerved by the crowd, its flesh creeping with the emissary's harping upon its existence, suddenly rose straight up into the air, screaming.

"Can't you see it?" Gunar Vries cried, pointing to the griffin beating the air, its beak open and its tongue flickering, its eyes fierier than ever, absorbing the three o'clock sun. After hovering thirty feet about Gunar's head, it continued up and settled on a cornice three stories above him.

The people gazed upward, but lowered their eyes with no change in them. They did not ridicule the speaker, however. They were solemn and attentive, remembering the man he once was. While about them, more griffins, curious as to the throngs, flew in and came to rest on the roofs of distant buildings, their dark forms like statues of themselves against the sky.

Gunar Vries descended the steps, and the people made way for him. He was not disheartened. There was time for other cities and other assemblages. He wanted especially to draw a great crowd in New York, city of the Conference. The griffin flew down and followed at his heels; he heard its wings flapping in descent and then the click of its claws on the stone. A guttural warble in its throat, a sign of uneasiness.

Two members of the police force stepped through the crowd to Gunar Vries. The force had been reluctant to take action against him for disturbing the peace, considering his prestige, but during the course of his speech they had received instructions from Ernest Gorgas himself: "Quietly, with respect for his person as a private citizen and as a former diplomat, arrest and transport him to quarters in the Hall of Justice. Detain him there until further instructions.

"Gunar Vries," said one, "it's the president's wish."

"If I resist?" he asked.

The other officer touched his elbow, and Gunar told himself, "All their force will be unavailing and will seem afterward like a touch at my elbow." He reached behind him, laid his hand on the griffin, and brought it forward.

"If I mount you," he asked, "can you rise with my weight?"

The griffin nodded, but was perturbed and glazed its

eyes. "When you asked me to accompany you, did you also ask that I convey you? It's seldom we convey a mortal."

"That's what it comes to," said Gunar.

The griffin rose reluctantly in the stance of a lion rampant, but the emissary, stepping forward to place his arms around the eagle's neck, and seat himself upon the lion's rump, was detained by the officers, who came in under the wing, each taking an elbow and an armpit, and prevailing against him.

Gunar Vries was deposited in the cell reserved for politicians, bankers, celebrated attorneys, actresses, professors. Here were ash trays, a water cooler and dispenser. The furniture, though old and sagging, was still substantial, with faintly yellowed crocheted stars on the chair-backs. Waiting for him were his attorney and a psychiatrist, a jovial, plump young man.

"If they want bail," said Gunar to his attorney, "then give it to them. I'll be out of the country by morning."

"They're afraid of that," his attorney replied, a man as competent as he was handsome. "How would it look, Gunar," he chided, "for a man of your status to misrepresent the country? The other nations will say, 'What choice is this?' They'll have respect for no emissary from S———."

The doctor, with whom he had shaken hands and who had been listening, kindly, alertly, smoking a cigarette, now spoke up. "Mr. Vries, contrary to the expressed wishes of Mr. Ernest Gorgas, I am not going to ask your participation in any analysis. I want a few answers from yourself to clarify, not my point of view as a doctor, but your own, as a man of responsibility. Your claim to see griffins, beasts of ancient mythology. Is that true?"

"True," replied Gunar, "both that I claim to and that I see them." He took a cigarette from the silver case the doctor proffered him.

"And why griffins?" asked the doctor.

"Why not?" replied Gunar. "Because that's what they are. They're not snakes, they're not elephants. I'm sorry. I cannot make it as simple as that."

"No, no!" laughed the doctor, lighting Gunar's cigarette. His hand shook, and his small eyes, small mouth, and small mustache all laughed in his round face. "Why have they returned, I mean. Are they, to you, explanatory of our time?"

Well, here was a man after Gunar's own heart, and he would forget, in his appreciation, any ulterior motive the man might have of undermining that which he so eagerly explained.

And so he told of the creature's history and the meaning of its name, and the doctor was absorbed and nodded his head. "Tell me of a time," said Gunar, "when the world faced a greater enigma. We'll either make the earth fruitful as it has never been or we'll exterminate ourselves. We'll either wipe out everything we've built upon, all past epochs, or we'll go on to a greater time than man has ever known. If you look at the situation with your eyes open you'll find that it's quite a creature, a thing with eagle wings and the body of a lion and with eyes of fire."

Gunar ceased, having heard the flapping of wings outside the window as the griffin ascended to the roof. It had followed him, as he had expected.

"Well, it's a pity," sighed the doctor, "that only one man sees them."

The attorney bent forward impatiently. "The president is aware that as a private citizen you may speak as you wish. Nevertheless, he would like your promise, as the promise of a dear friend, that you will make no further speeches in public or in private assembly calling upon the people to recognize the existence of these creatures."

"You tell Ernest," replied Gunar, "that they're bigger than he is."

"Will you commit him?" the attorney asked the doctor.

The doctor had risen, as if he had no more to ask. He shook his head, pressed out his cigarette in the tray. "I prefer," he said, "to commit those persons who cannot see them."

The two men left him so they could consult by telephone with the president. When they returned they brought with them the guard, obliging to authority in release of the emissary as in confinement of him.

Gunar Vries picked up his hat and gloves. "There is one on the roof now," he said to the doctor, "if you care to see it."

This was an old prison, rigged up now with electricity and hot water. They went up the circular stone staircase, and the guard unlocked the gate. The griffin was lying on the parapet, dropping over the edge to watch the traffic three stories below, and at times lifting its head to look at the pigeons cooing and bobbing, circling and fluttering. It was large and dark against the pale yellow haze of the setting sun, and its feathers were delicately ruffled.

"Doctor," said Gunar, "do not let me lose faith in you."

"I see it," the doctor assured him.

The attorney coughed in vicarious embarrassment.

Gunar stepped to the parapet, the doctor and attorney following. "Can we try our flight again?" he asked the griffin. The doctor turned pale, and Gunar, watching for just this response, continued, "Its back is broad enough and its neck the right size for my arms. I'll hamper it a bit, perhaps, but we'll manage. You think now that it's not here at all for me to climb upon, but an idea came to me while I was trying to mount it in the park: if I am afraid, then I am not certain of the griffin myself. In this way, by trusting myself to it, I prove its existence."

The doctor was plunged into remorse and self-doubt. He stood stock-still, his arms hanging numbly at his sides.

Suddenly the attorney was cognizant of Gunar Vries' kindliness, of depths to the man he had not considered. He placed his hand on Gunar's arm. "Gunar," he implored him, "we shall provide you with first-class accommodation by whatever means you care to travel. I shall see to it myself. I shall speak to the president and to the Chamber of Representatives. You will be authorized to go—indeed, dispatched."

But Gunar Vries had hold of the griffin's rear leg and drew himself onto the parapet. The guard, having taken the respite to smoke a cigarette, was leaning against the gate, watching the men, believing that anything was sanctioned. And Gunar Vries, knowing that in a moment the three men would toss off their stupefaction and converge upon him, threw himself upon the griffin.

They flew in a westerly direction, passing over the city. The night moved up from behind and overtook them. With the earth so far below them, Gunar was not sure whether they were still over Europe or had reached the Atlantic Ocean.

"Can you drop a bit closer to earth?" Gunar called forward, and his voice was not as he expected it to be, bounced or pummeled by the wind, but went out into calm air, the atmosphere into which an oracle speaks.

"What for?" the griffin asked.

"But can you see any lights?"

The griffin glanced sideways in derision, enabling Gunar to see its eye, which was a blue distilled from the night, like a pure blue flame, and in it were reflected, nebulously, the lights of a city he believed to be New York.

THE PEGASUS

In Greek mythology, Pegasus was the winged horse of the Muses—born of the blood of the decapitated Medusa, and tamed by Bellerophon with the aid of a magic golden bridge—but winged horses are common in the mythology of many other cultures as well. Winged horses turn up again and again as images in painting, sculpture, and even advertising (note the winged horse which was the logo of a major gasoline company some years ago, for instance), and often seem to symbolize a yearned-for transcendence, the kind of transmogrifying freedom that liberates you from the common cares of the earth. Flying horses are symbols of freedom because their domain is the limitless and trackless expanse of the sky, where they can roam as they will, without concern for fences or borders or boundaries.

Here's a strange encounter between a winged horse and yet another symbol of freedom and the romance of unfenced horizons—the Cowboy.

Rob Chilson is a writer who has appeared frequently in *Analog,* as well as in *Isaac Asimov's Science Fiction Magazine, Amazing,* and in other markets. His novels include *As the Curtain Falls, The Star-Crowned Kings,* and *The Shores of Kansas.*

The Last of His Breed

by

Rob Chilson

"NO HORSE EVER born could take that slope at that speed and live," mused Ken Hastie, looking down it. Parts of Arizona are quite rugged, and this was one of them. He was looking down a mountainside. The slope was by no means a cliff, but he would have walked his horse down it even in his wildest youth. The tracks he'd been following approached it well spaced, obviously at a good fast lope if no real gallop.

Dismounting, Hastie kicked at a fairly fresh horseball. This morning, near dawn, he thought. There was no dead or wounded horse at the foot of the slope.

There were not even any tracks on the slope.

Leading his horse, he picked his way down it. The horse, a sturdy brown with plenty of sense in his think-tank, was no longer young either, and had come far since before sun-up; it gave him no trouble, allowing him to concentrate on the slope.

Near the bottom he found fragments of two more horseballs, widely spaced. Both were fragmented as if they had fallen some distance. There were no tracks, horse or animal, anywhere near either of them.

Hastie rolled himself a cigarette, musing. His eye tended to climb; he kept tracing the scarps and slopes above him, always swinging out into the pale keen blue of the stainless sky. Every wheeling bird-dot took his instant attention.

When he had smoked half his cigarette he said, "Well." Not a talkative man. Hastie had no words for the feelings he was experiencing, but that was not new to him. He blew smoke four ways, which the horse might have noted had it been as profound a student of human nature as he was of horse nature. But this time the act didn't signify the end of a train of thought.

Still, Hastie mounted as if this show was over. The brown carried him off along the slopes. Their day's work wasn't half done, and Hastie and the horse went about it with professional economy: eyeing the stock for fitness and flesh, discovering its locations, checking the pasturage, examining every spring and stream they passed. Hastie was not to be distracted, but not infrequently he looked aloft, and no bird passed but that his eye noted.

It was dusk when they came down, tired horse and tired man, onto the gentle series of terraces above the ranch. By the smell the ranch hands had been cutting hay; it grew lushly in these irrigated bottoms, and the smell of cows was thick. Hastie scorned to look at these fat, shorthorned animals, much less to drop his rope on one.

The ranch hands were congregated on the porch of the Number Two bunkhouse. They laughed and talked in an island in the darkness, slapping mosquitos. Hastie turned the brown loose, spread his saddle blanket, draped the saddle over the rail, there being no rain in prospect. He moved mechanically.

Though his hair was getting a little grizzled before the ears, he was by no means old; it wasn't physical weariness that tied him down. Nor hunger. He had arisen before dawn, before the cooks, and ridden off without breakfast. Cowboys scorned to carry food like damned picnickers, and he'd returned after the fires were out and the remainders thrown to the hogs. But that was usual, and he didn't even notice it.

Passing the ranch hands with a nod, he entered the darkened bunkhouse and sought his bunk. Stretching out on it, hands behind his head, he continued the day's musings. No one noticed anything unusual; it wasn't usual for him to join the evening talk. What could a cowboy talk about with ranch hands?

The foreman's name was Tim Conroy and he was a good man with cows and knew it and wouldn't tolerate a hand who wasn't also pretty damn good. No one on the R Bar A mishandled a cow; even profanity was frowned on unless it sounded cheerful. The steers' negligible minds mustn't be disturbed; they must concentrate on putting on weight—good, solid, marbled beef. And no prima donnas, either—among the hands. When work was to be done they all dived in and did it. Conroy pitched in right along with the hands, as he bluntly told them. And did more work than any, which he didn't need to tell them.

One of his work-hardened hands rested now on the rail of the boss's house's porch. His round red face earnest, looking not unlike one of his own short-horns, he looked up into the equally full-fed features of Carmichael, the manager. The Roy and Andy of the brand and name were gone; the R Bar A was owned by a New York bank.

"It's the cowboy, boss. This makes the second time. Now, yestiddy, he was up in the hills, tending to his stock. That's all right. But day before, now. What was he doin' then? Shoeing horses, I could understand, but all he did was mess around the smithy. And this mornin' he went there again. Now, boss, we *got* to git that hay in."

Carmichael had given up trying to keep the men from calling him boss. He looked into the distance, reckoning the R Bar A's fields and the number of hands.

"If it's that bad, I can find a couple of part-timers in the Springs till the season's over."

"I hate pick-up and drop-off labour," said Tim. "The cowboy's a good steady dependable man. No reason to my notion why he can't pitch hay."

Banging sounds came from the smithy. "Goddamn!" said Conroy.

"Well, I can tell you one thing." Carmichael idly kicked a porch post. "He didn't help you fix fence day before yesterday, not because he was so busy, but because he damn well wouldn't."

"What?"

"Fact. 'Fore you come, him and one of those pepper-eatin' cow-ponies of his busted down the corral fence, which is rails and not even wire, and he wouldn't help fix it. Left it to us."

"Goddamn! When he broke it down hisself? And you stood for that?"

Carmichael smiled, half-wry, half-admiring. "Tim, there's near three thousand head of longhorn stock up in the hills. They'll run twenty, twenty-five per cent of the ranch's income, end of the year. And there ain't but one man of us knows how to take care of 'em. Could you do it if he was to quit? Could any of the hands?"

Tim shook his head, but frowned and said, "But—" He stopped, started again. "You're sayin' that if *you* ordered him—"

"He calls me boss same as the rest of you, but I don't tell him to do nothing he don't want to do. I'm not givin' him orders to pitch hay."

Hastie crossed a distant yard between the smithy and the stable.

Tim's temper flared. "Goddamn! Look at him! Walks like he owns the earth."

"No," mused Carmichael. "That's a different kind of freedom. More like he doesn't need the earth. Think of a horse with wings."

Ken Hastie spent the entire summer preparing for winter. He checked his ropes and replaced any that wouldn't take the strain. He patched his waterproof. He made sure every strap of both saddles was tightly anchored, of the strongest leather. He soaped and rubbed endlessly. From spurs to wooden piggins to hat nothing escaped his eye, and his boots he replaced every autumn when he could afford to.

And every third or fourth day he checked on his stock.

Last year there had been a wild cat. He'd sold the hide in Excelsior Springs. This year nothing . . . nothing he could tell of. Now he overhauled his stoutest saddle and considered another visit to the range. Not to check on the stock. To look for a horse . . .

The scrunch of feet on gravel caused him to look up. Carmichael, the boss, or at least the bosses' representative, approached him, dressed in his dark coat. Beyond, the plum-coloured Packard was backed up to the porch. Going to town.

"A week ago you said the situation for horses in the hills isn't so good this year." Carmichael began without preliminary—the best way to deal with the cowboy.

"Yeah, they're gittin' wild, and besides, the cattle're eaten'em off the range."

"And you're not too well fixed for horses?"

Hastie thumbed his hat back, straightening up, automatically looked at the sky. "I was just thinkin' about that. Want to go back up and scout for horses, but I don't hold out much hope—and if I have to spend a month catchin'em, I won't have time to break'em. Course, I don't need cow-ponies for this winter, just good strong willin' horses."

"Strong, young, and willing. Care to come along to pick'em out?"

Hastie looked at the Packard. It had sixteen cylinders, they said, but he was only vaguely aware of what a cylinder was, and it looked the same as another car that only had twelve. It was fast, but not his kind of fast. Suppose it got the bit in its teeth, how could anyone ever hold it in?

"I got enough to do to keep me busy a week. Besides, you're a tolerable judge of horseflesh."

"Okay, I'll do my best. Anything else you need?"

Hastie shook his head, returning to work.

Carmichael stood watching him a moment. But this was the man who left Texas because they wanted him to fix fence. He'd sworn never to return, and Carmichael, to whom he'd told that, didn't for a moment doubt he'd keep his word.

"Okay, I'll see what they got."

Hastie tugged on a string, unaware of the crisis that had passed.

Hastie took food with him the next day and two horses, and was gone before sun-up. Nobody but Tim Conroy missed him.

"What a hell of a thing! And we got to have him," he said to his strawboss, Linwood by name. "The boss says it'd take the whole crew near a month to bring the wild stock down from the hills, but that ride-ever'where cowboy can do it in less'n a week, even in a blizzard."

"Catch me up in them hills in a blizzard," said Linwood contemplatively, shaking his head.

"We'd lose half the crew off the cliffs," Conroy said, glum. "What makes a man too good to pitch hay? Or manure? Hell, he ain't no better'n you or me!"

"Not as good, to my notion," said Linwood, and spat. "A man that won't work ain't in *my* class."

But Conroy was fair-minded. "Oh, he works, right enough. But only at what he wants to. Prima donna!"

"He's a lightweight. Mark my words, someday he's gonna fly off and leave us."

Hastie spent two days looking at horse tracks. He was mindful of the duty he owed his employer and looked at every cow and every stream and every bit of grass that he came across, and, spending hours scanning the mountainsides, took automatic note of distant pastures. But his mind was on none of this.

"A loner."

High up, higher than stock normally went, he found its tracks. By now he knew them as well as a face. A bit of meadow-land on a high shoulder, the snow-breath air cool in high summer. The strange horse had grazed here alone for parts of three days. The tracks and 'sign'—droppings—indicated it had been here on three successive days, but it hadn't eaten enough to feed that size of horse for three days.

Ergo, it came and went.

Hastie had seen no tracks coming or going. He looked at the sky, saw nothing. At other places he'd seen its tracks mingled with that of a few head of wild horses still pasturing here. They didn't seem to avoid it, but of course couldn't follow it.

The next day he saw it.

A distant dark shape on a mountainside. He brought it to middle distance with his binoculars, studied it as carefully as he could.

It looked like a normal horse at this distance, with these lenses, but very deep in the chest. Broad-shouldered, too, he thought. Sleek, its sides shining, not quite the *texture* of the back and neck. Dark brown with a hint of flame, near as he could make out through the chromatic aberration.

It had been grazing and grazing about in a desultory fashion, and aware of its habits as he was, he was not surprised when it began to run across the mountainside. Turning sharply down the slope, it spread its wings and was airborne.

Hastie watched it glide out, tilt sidewise in a falling turn, and start around the mountain it'd been on. Then the great wings came down and it surged forward and up in the air, its legs folded, its head high, nostrils expanded—he couldn't see that fine detail, and it was turning its back—but Hastie knew horses.

Did a distant, joyous neigh come back?

It was gone. Hastie lowered the glasses, still staring after it, with no words for his feelings. He could only repeat: "Always alone. Prob'ly the last of its kind."

A man doesn't have wings, and, having none, has responsibilities. They paid Hastie to do a job.

"I'm shiftin' the stock to the south, boss. There's good pasturage there."

"All right—I thought you said the present pasture would be adequate for awhile yet?"

"It's not in bad shape, but I want the stock on good ground before I leave."

Carmichael looked up, startled. "Leave!" He stood up from the rocking chair, looked down at Hastie beside the porch. "You're going to—why? Did Tim tell you to pitch hay, or something? 'Cause that isn't your job—"

"No, no. I got no complaints, boss, but I been here nigh on to three years now. Time I curled my tail and drifted."

"But. My God, Hastie, you can't just up and leave us. You know two years ago I couldn't find a cowboy to take your place—"

That was the occasion when Hastie had told him why he'd left Texas—he'd quit this job then. Carmichael had kept him on till he could find a replacement, which he never did.

"I been thinkin' about that. I'll put the stock where they'll be all right for three weeks, a month or five weeks if it rains. You can find someone."

Carmichael shook his head, flung out his hands helplessly.

"If you can't find anybody, you might try that fellow Slim works at the livery in town. He's a fair hand with horses and I seen him rope."

"You said two years ago he'd never be a cowboy."

"No, he won't, but he's the best around."

Hastie's real objection to Slim was that the young man had once taken a job on a ranch where he had milked cows.

Hastie himself had once owned a small ranch. He'd taken up land, cut logs, built a tiny cabin and a larger stable, a corral, outbuildings, and fixed his own fences and milked his own cow, as well as feeding slops to a pig he had kept one summer. But a man, even a cowboy, will do for himself what he won't for others, for pay. Slim would never be a cowboy.

Moving the stock was a tedious but not difficult operation. Hastie had brought them down from the mountains in the teeth of a blizzard once, and had fought through more ordinary snowstorms to bring out stock that had been missed in the earlier sweeps, bucking through waist-deep snow. Those terrible struggles against great odds were not to him romantic or thrilling. His was a flat, matter-of-fact outlook. Hard work and danger were a part of the way of life of a cowboy. Romance was for womenfolks, reading books.

He just called it a job. Tim Conroy would have approved.

It was that attitude that held Hastie motionless now.

He sat his horse with its feet on gravel, drinking from a clear mountain stream. The stream bank was just before him, about the height of his knees. Along it grew a screening line of willow and aspen. Beyond the screen was a rather brushy glade.

The horse with wings was there.

It had ignored his unsuspecting approach, hearing nothing unusual in a horse's advance to the stream for a drink; the breeze was up the mountain, from it to him. It spread its left wing now and licked the underside, oblivious.

Hastie's rope was just in front of his hand, and the

horse's neck was within easy reach of a throw. He'd seen it in motion once before, on the ground, and knew that it had to have considerable speed to get into the air, like one of those aeroplanes Hastie had heard of. It would be a savage battle, with the horse leaping and beating its powerful wings, but he could have had it.

But he'd made a man a promise.

Besides, he'd sort of made himself a promise.

And what's more, he owed it to the horse, didn't he?

The horse spread its wings, stretching, and flapped them silently a couple of times. Wind blew out from it. It was a fairly large horse, dark brown with a red cast to its hair, a hint of subdued fired where the sun ran along it. The wings weren't covered with feathers as he'd thought, but with what looked like shingles of horsehair. Hastie had never heard of agglutinated hair and thought a rhino's horn was made of horn, but he compared the shingles to horsehair licked into placed and sticking together wet, continuing to stick after drying. Glued together.

The horse, ignoring the restless shifting of the cow-pony's feet, made a lonely whickering sound and tossed its head, looking all about it. Then it charged across the dell, spread its wings, flapped them heavily and with some noise—but not much, for its size—and again, and was airborne, folding its legs back but low yet. Circling, its wings beating easily, it climbed until it found the uprush of air along the mountainside, and wheeled into the sky.

"It wouldn't'a'been right," said Hastie to no one, looking after it without expression.

The sorrel snorted softly and stamped to dislodge a fly.

Tim Conroy was outraged. "My God, boss, a man doesn't just up and walk off from a job because he feels like he's been there too long! Now if he had a reason, or could make more—We should'a' fired him a long time ago."

"I would have, if I could have found a replacement. I've come to appreciate cowboys some since, Tim, and I doubt if any replacement would've been any better. Cowboys were an independent bunch."

Tim shook his head, unable to picture a world in which the best men were so independent they thought nothing of throwing up a good job on a whim. If his best men were like that, the ranch would fall apart. Nothing would get done.

"They're not just working men, Tim. They're highly skilled technicians, like automobile mechanics. Automobiles are fairly new, so not many people know about them, but there's a lot of 'em, so there's a great need for mechanics. It was the same for cowboys."

"How could you run a ranch when all the hands are prima donnas?"

"I guess it cancels out. And they're good at keeping their word, taken all around."

Tim considered all that, shook his head. A prima donna was a prima donna to his mind. "What about Raynard? I already made it plain to him that he's no better than the rest of us. I'll have him pitchin' hay the day after he shows up. Think he'll quit? He didn't seem to take it hard."

"Hastie said he'd never be a cowboy. I expect he's right. But he's the best I could find. Cowboys are gone . . . If Slim will pitch hay, have him pitch. I just hope to hell he can handle stock, too."

Tim nodded soberly at that.

Carmichael shook his head. "Like I said. He's the last of his breed."

It would rain. Good. That'd stretch the pasturage a week, if it rained enough. Hastie sat down and slid his booted feet under his waterproof. Unbuckling his belt, he slid his pants down his legs to the boot-tops, then drew his feet out of his boots. In the old days, during round-ups, he undressed that way routinely. He had only to dive his feet down into his boots and pull up his pants to be ready to ride, in the event of an emergency, and the loose waterproof kept everything dry.

Sliding dexterously sideways into the bedroll, he lay musing, looking at the stars being cut off by the encroaching clouds.

Hastie had finished moving the stock, as he'd promised, but hadn't gone back to the ranch. It no longer held anything he wanted.

It had been a long life, though he wasn't forty yet. Cowboys were gone, and the future belonged to the ranch hands, fixing barbed wire and stall-feeding short-horns with grain. There just wasn't much place left for a man who hadn't been able to make a go of ranching on his own. To continue working, you had to be a ranch hand.

Not me, he thought.

Hastie wondered how it felt to pilot an aeroplane. He thought he knew the breed of men who did. Young, they were, and independent, and proud of themselves, their craft, and their skill . . .

His father'd been like that. Hastie was born on the open range, a birth that killed his mother. With that, the heart went out of his father, who was killed in a common dust-up at a corral branding when his horse went down.

After his father was killed, Hastie was taken in hand by a small rancher his father had befriended. The old man raised him on up to years of discretion. He'd been good at breaking horses and roping cattle before he was old enough to drink. He'd ranged the west from beyond the Canadian border to beyond the border of Old Mexico. For a time there in the south he'd ridden the high trails of outlawry, rustling cattle south of the border and bringing them north, to sell them again south of the border.

He'd associated with The Men Who Can't Come Back, that inglorious legion, at that time, and been offered the job of working a machine-gun with some of them, in the pay of a gang of ragged promoters of liberty, equality, fraternity. But he didn't speak the language, and those people didn't speak his language. Their promises, even the white men, were no good, and he wouldn't associate with someone he couldn't trust. So he'd come back, and had ridden down from the high trails, which he figured meant he was grown up now and not a wild young cowboy.

"I always thought growin' up and gettin' old were the same thing. Now I figure one causes the other. Wonder which . . ."

The brown came down out of the mountains alone. It wore no saddle, nor were there reins on its bridle. Yet its presence smelled of death. The ranch hands milled about, hushed and solemn.

"He had two horses, boss," said Tim Conroy, subdued. "This'n and the sorrel. One packed and the other rode."

"Likely he and the sorrel are piled up at the bottom of some slope," said Carmichael.

"What about Hastie?"

"We're bound to look for him. But, Tim, this crew can't handle that. We haven't all that many good riding horses, not suitable for mountain work—"

"Or men who can ride that well," said Conroy quietly.

"Right. I'll take Raynard; we'll ride Hastie's horses—have Slim saddle the bay and the new gelding. We'll take the brown along for Hastie, it doesn't look too tired. Evidently it never panicked."

"It was out to pasture when it happened, I reckon."

"Yes. The two of us'll have to do—you keep the hands busy."

"Right. And—good luck, boss."

For days Hastie had sought a certain place he'd never seen. A cove or valley high up on a mountain, shielded from the northwest winds. It needn't be very big, nor have much pasturage.

When he found that bedding ground, he found more: the spring where the winged horse drank. Characteristically, this was not even on the same mountain; it swooped over above a narrow valley for its morning drink. Hastie spent all night getting into position; there was time only for a couple of hours of restless sleep before the pre-dawn light woke him.

He was ready, suppressing any reaction to the chill of morning, looking down on the spring. It was like a cup hacked out of a steep house roof. The wind was favourable, behind the horse on its matutinal swoop. Hastie was calm, at peace. He'd left his camp neat, the horses unhobbled, all promises filled.

And there it came, wheeling against the blue-grey sky, great wings spread wide. It grew and grew and grew. Then the wings came together, and again, and again, and Hastie's hat vibrated on his head. He slitted his eyes and didn't move. Wheeling sharply, its wing tip seeming to brush the steep scarp, it came level and folding its wings, landed springily at a trot on the nearly level spot before the break in the slope where the spring bubbled out.

It walked coolly forward, lowered its proud head, standing almost under Hastie on the rim of the cup. He'd studied its tracks well and knew where to put himself. It drank, raised its head, looked about; lowered its head again. Hastie, who'd had no breakfast, let it drink its fill. Then he sprang on its back.

It reared with an angry neigh, wheeled in the close quarters, bucked once, kicking. Hastie's legs held its wings closed, but as it erupted out of the cup he gambled, slipping first one leg up and then the other far enough to let it unfold them. The horse sprang forward, neighing again in fury, and beat its wings. Hastie's hat flew off; the string caught it. A bucking leap took them into the air. The world swooped and spun around them. Hastie gasped for breath, fear an emptiness in his belly, a grip in his legs and hands. His fingers ached in the horse's mane.

The horse made an amazing buck in mid-air, but it was nothing to Hastie, since it lacked the spine-wracking jolt at the end. It spun about abruptly, dived, beat upward, and none of these evolutions were so severe as those a horse could make, thrusting hoofs against solid ground. Only the slippery insecurity of horsehair under his pants made them dangerous. Hastie still panted, but his stark fear had eased.

Then the horse turned upside down. He felt his legs slipping, only his hands held him on, death was near—thousands of feet down—But the horse could no more tolerate that then he, and righted itself in time.

It can't fly upside down! he thought. And he knew he'd won.

The horse levelled out, sobbing for breath and fear, and looked back at him. Its eyes were white-ringed. A surge of confidence came over Hastie and he let his eyes sweep around. Mountains before and behind and to every side, slopes here, there and everywhere, valleys and canyons below. All their snow.

The horse was over the first panicked fury, building up strength for the next bout. Hastie leaned forward, talking softly to it. Now he was confident; he knew he could not fail. For Hastie knew horses. He could foresee each successive battle, each trick and sleight and feint, and knew that he could not lose. Each battle would leave him stronger and the horse more docile.

"There now, there now, it's not so bad, is it?"

He'd made up his mind never to tie it down, he'd brought no rope with him, nothing but hobbles and bridle.

It would be the ultimate test of his skill, to tame and train this creature of the sky without breaking its spirit or letting it escape. But he felt nothing but the most unutterable confidence in his ability.

They flew easily across the sky, riding the thermals above the mountains, swooping and soaring, and his heart beat high for fear and joy. What a horse!

Abruptly it 'broke in half', kicked in mid-air, bucked, spun, flipped over on its back—that nearly caught him—and bucked again. Hastie, gasping for breath, held on with a fierce elation, knowing he could not lose, that this was his fated horse, this sky his sky.

He'd been training for this all his life . . .

Tim Conroy watched sharply to his right, and when the rake came even with the hay, he heaved down on the lever. The curved tines of the rake raised and dumped the rolling cylinder of hay they'd scraped up. The little pint pony perked steadily on at its light trot and he dropped the tines again. The pony was smart and already knew the pattern, making now for the next line of hay. Tim held himself ready at all times to kick his heels in the air and roll backwards out of the big iron seat if bumblebees should go for the horse, lest he fall off in front and be dragged to death when the horse panicked.

At the end of the field they circled and he glanced swiftly around, saw nothing amiss, and let his eyes go to the mountains beyond. Slim and the boss were still out there, but it'd been a couple of days, and Tim knew that they'd never bring the cowboy back alive. He doubted if they'd even find the body. Fell off some cliff, likely, or went off when one of those half-wild ponies started bucking for no reason at all, as they frequently did. He shook his head morbidly. Too bad.

But there were near three thousand head of stock up there, and their care now became a part of his, Tim Conroy's, responsibilities. He'd sized up young Slim Raynard and agreed with Hastie; the man'd never be a cowboy. He took orders too easily, as if he knew no better than anyone what to do.

Tim shook his head again. But for the moment it wasn't the responsibility he regretted. It was the man. *There* was a man who walked like he had wings on his back and didn't need the earth. Strange how empty that quiet man had left the ranch.

"Too bad. They don't make men like that no more."

Tim heaved the rake's teeth up, dropped them. For a moment his gaze focused on the sunset sky. A large dark object with wings wheeled across its glory and gold. But Tim was a ranch hand, whose cows never died on distant ranges. "Tracks in the sky" meant nothing to him. He couldn't even have said whether or not it was a bird, though he never realised that.

ABOUT THE EDITORS

GARDNER DOZOIS was born and raised in Salem, Massachusetts, and now lives in Philadelphia. He is the author or editor of seventeen books, including the novel *Strangers* and the collection *The Visible Man.* He is the editor of *Isaac Asimov's Science Fiction Magazine;* he also edits the annual series *The Year's Best Science Fiction.* His short fiction has appeared in *Playboy, Penthouse, Omni,* and most of the leading SF magazines and anthologies. His story "The Peacemaker" won the Nebula Award for the Best Short Story in 1984, and his short story "Morning Child" also won the Nebula Award in 1985. He has many times been a finalist for other Hugo and Nebula Awards. His critical work has appeared in *Writer's Digest, Starship, The Washington Post, Thrust, The Writer's Handbook, Science Fiction Chronicle,* and elsewhere, and he is the author of the critical chapbook *The Fiction of James Tiptree, Jr.* His most recent books are *Magicats!,* an anthology edited in collaboration with Jack Dann, and *The Year's Best Science Fiction, Second Annual Collection.* He is currently at work on another novel, tentatively entitled *Flash Point.*

JACK DANN is the author or editor of seventeen books, including the novels *Junction* and *Starhiker,* and the collection *Timetipping.* He is the editor of the anthology *Wandering Stars,* one of the most acclaimed anthologies of the 1970s, and several other well-known anthologies, including the recently published *More Wandering Stars.* His short fiction has appeared in

Playboy, Penthouse, Omni, and most of the leading SF magazines and anthologies. He has been a Nebula Award finalist ten times, as well as a finalist for the World Fantasy Award and the British Science Fiction Association Award. His critical work has appeared in *The Washington Post, Starship, Nickelodeon, The Bulletin of the Science Fiction Writers of America, Empire, Future Life,* and *The Fiction Writer's Handbook,* and he is the author of the chapbook *Christs and Other Poems*. His most recent books are *Magicats!,* an anthology edited in collaboration with Gardner Dozois, and *The Man Who Melted,* a novel. He is at work on a new novel, *Counting Coup,* and is editing a Vietnam anthology entitled *In the Fields of Fire* with his wife, Jeanne VanBuren Dann. Dann lives with his family in Binghamton, New York.